Ruqaya Izzidien is an Iraqi-
currently based between Mor
from Durham University she has lived and worked in Cairo and the
Gaza Strip.

The Watermelon Boys

Ruqaya Izzidien

hoopoe
AN IMPRINT OF AUC PRESS

First published in 2018 by
Hoopoe
113 Sharia Kasr el Aini, Cairo, Egypt
420 Fifth Avenue, New York 10018
www.hoopoefiction.com

Hoopoe is an imprint of the American University in Cairo Press
www.aucpress.com

References to speeches and announcements made by historical figures on pages
221, 228, 235, 263, 265, 266, and 276 are taken from *Enemy on the Euphrates* by Ian
Rutledge. Copyright © Ian Rutledge, 2014. Reproduced with permission of Saqi
Books Ltd.

Exclusive distribution outside Egypt and North America by I.B.Tauris & Co Ltd., 6
Salem Road, London, W2 4BU

Dar el Kutub No. 26604/17
ISBN 978 977 416 880 2

Dar el Kutub Cataloging-in-Publication Data

Izzidien, Ruqaya
        The Watermelon Boys / Ruqaya Izzidien.—Cairo: The American Uni-
    versity in Cairo Press, 2018.
        p.   cm.
        ISBN: 978 977 416 880 2
        1. English fiction
        832

1 2 3 4 5   22 21 20 19 18

Designed by Adam el-Sehemy
Printed in the United States of America

Part I

1

THE PRESENT IS AN ARROGANT time in which to live, always has been. Humans of the present look back at their people, land, and history, and whisper to themselves with glee, *We are not them.* But we were always them. We are our history; we are the crimes of our ancestors. And we wait, mouths agape, to hear tales of hope, as though good could triumph in such a world.

But every century, every desperate land, every present, has its own moment of optimism, an instant in which its people are so sure, just like their fathers before them, that something better is possible. They tell themselves that their souls are better now, more compassionate, more powerful. *This time it will be different.*

So, even when he was lost, face down in the sludge, still unconscious, the man on the banks of the River Tigris would come to believe it too. Proof that even when a person has no name, no memory, and no idea how he ended up on the shores of Baghdad, hope can prevail. Yes, humans have a long history of mistaking desperation for courage.

And when he felt a prod in his back, his body aching, his mind flooded with unanswered questions—none of it took away his unshakable belief that, eventually, all would be well.

"Told you he wasn't dead, Mariam. Told you," someone shrieked, as the man heard small feet thumping into the distance. He sat up, blinking river dirt out of his eyes.

"Wait," he said, with a grunt that shocked even himself.

The sun disappeared behind two figures standing over him. He rubbed his eyes and squinted up at them. The sky was obscured by two pairs of large beetle eyes, made wider by thick black outlines that shaped them into lemons, and by four braids, half twisted into folds of gray cloth. The smaller girl broke the silence with a squeal that wobbled her oversized cheeks.

"Are you all right?" asked Mariam, politely. "I . . . we thought maybe you needed help. Should I fetch my baba?"

"No. Where am I?" he tried to whisper, but it came out as a growl.

"Nahar Street is that way," she said, pointing.

"Baghdad?" he asked. She nodded, and he thought she spoke again—though he couldn't be sure. He stood up, swaying, his head throbbing. He rubbed at the dirt dried to his chest and slapped at his sleeves. For a second he remembered, and was sure he saw his companion and his horse on the bank across the Tigris.

"Bring my horse around, would you, Karim?" he called across the river. "And, no, we can't take turns riding him. I don't care what your story says—he'll not end up in the river if I can help it." The man threw back his head and laughed. "See how well I know you, Karim."

The girls exchanged a glance.

"Let's go, Salsabeel. He's crazy," said Mariam, walking away.

"Look!" said Salsabeel, pulling on her friend's sleeve, using the full force of her plump form to drag them both back to the man. He was standing, still swaying slightly, and examining the river. "Are you a soldier, Ammu?" she asked gently, indicating his belt's insignia. He looked down and his hands darted around his muddied uniform. "Then how did you come to be here, in the mud?"

His breathing quickened and he clasped his hands together to stop them shaking.

He turned with a slight wobble and shook his head with a gasp.

And then he ran.

2

Winter 1915
Baghdad

HE RAN. HE WASN'T SURE if his legs were heavy from the clay of the Tigris or from the ache of the cuts it surely concealed, but he ran anyway. His hair was matted with sand and dirt, and the thumping in his head made him feel like a man was running behind him, playing the tabla drum on the back of his skull.

He flicked his eyes as he ran, inspecting the alleys on either side for any trace of the familiar. He found himself in a narrow street lined with shanasheel oriel windows, their wooden panels knotted into webs of hexadecagonal stars and tesselated honeycombs. He ran past ten, eleven shanasheel, each betraying its hidden residents with the gravelly clank of a clay water flask, the tittering of gossip, or wafts of earthy tea. Something about the tea tugged in the man's stomach; it was a memory he could not quite place, but it was a comforting sensation, he thought. Why, then, did it fill his chest with such an ache? He put a hand against the street's stone wall and shut his eyes for a moment.

He caught only flashes of the scenes in front of him: reams of smoke trailing up from an open-air stone oven, the green woven belt of a passing man, but most of all it was the eyes—everywhere he looked, flashes of eyes—curious, amused, and disapproving. A huddle of women, with visors peeping out under their veils, stared at him as they hurried by, before averting their eyes from him—with some terror, he thought. Maybe this was it. Would he roam these streets forever, aching with this unshakable sense of absence? It was surprisingly painful to feel loss and not recall where to place it. He even considered for a moment if this was his journey to the afterlife. He tugged at his belt and pulled it up a little higher on his waist. Whatever had happened to him, whatever the reason he was coated in days-old dirt and reeked like a butcher's cast-offs, he was still here. And it brought him relief when he told himself he had defeated the odds, unknown as those odds were. He would remember, he had to, or what was the point of it all? And he swore then that if he had to run every inch of Baghdad, he would remember.

He wound around unfamiliar alleys and passed crooked homes. Like the flashes of a moving picture, he watched a magenta and cobalt minaret disappear over his shoulder and found himself inside the tubular hall of Baghdad's weavers' bazaar, where the horizon disappeared behind an infinite stream of stone arches. Bold rugs were suspended from iron hooks, and each merchant marked his territory with the display of his most intricate creation on the wall above his workshop, as he sweated below. Scores of weavers worked in counterbeats, deftly tossing shuttles of wool through dancing pins, and tapping their pedals in a rhythmic jig. He felt himself in a colony of praying mantises, as the workers bobbed their bent heads and spread their arms in an embrace of their looms.

Light beamed in from looming windows casting a haze on the thread cobwebs that zigzagged around the weavers, and making the floor of discarded fibers in the window's glare light up with a dusty glow. A sea of Baghdadis careened down the bazaar: men in dishdasha robes and suit jackets clenching their wares under their arms, women with bejeweled braids, and others, cloaked in warrior black from head to toe, their suspended huntress faces gleaming as they eyed the market stalls. He wound through the carpet of shredded wool, kicking up a multicolored wake. As he passed each stone arch, another appeared on the horizon. And, God, the stench. Had Baghdad always smelled so bad? He filled his lungs with the reek of sweat and piss and sourness that had fermented in the heat and sand for weeks. He pinched his eyes shut and let his legs and ears navigate. Shoppers called out angrily as he jostled them but he kept his eyes sealed, stopping only when he felt the sun warm his forehead.

"May I shave your face, sir?" a street merchant called to him as he exited the bazaar. "That beard is a veritable beehive. Let me see to it."

"Take your photo?" another yelled from across the road. A crowd of shoppers tussled past.

The man slumped to the floor and leaned against the teardrop archway of Baghdad city's North Gate.

"Some syrupy hot zalabya, sir? The best this side of Baghdad," said a man from beyond the gateway. "I can see you're in need of a—"

But the man would never know what it seemed he needed. He covered his ears and filled his lungs. "Enough!" he said. He put his head to his knees and rocked, humming his favorite Sherif Muhiddin melody. He heard laughter and mocking murmurs, which only grew louder as he tried to drown them with his humming.

"It's all right," he told himself. "I will remember and it will be all right." He heard a woman yell, but he kept rocking, thinking of the sluggish, sorrowful oud, sharing the musician's epic as his own tragedy.

"A madman!" a woman shouted. If he had opened his eyes, he would have wondered why tears had erupted onto her cheeks, but all he heard were the unrelenting accusations that he was a madman, pelting him from the gateway. He shut his eyes and hummed his melody, loudly enough to block out all else.

"Mad!" she yelled. Then, after a few moments, she took him by the shoulders and began humming the tune with him.

He opened his eyes and dropped his arms, the dried mud on his face now moist again. The woman crouched beside him, and he knew he had been mistaken: a person with a face as kind as hers could never have called him mad.

"Ahmad!" she gasped, her eyes shining. "I found you, Ahmad."

3

AHMAD COULDN'T RECALL MUCH OF what followed. Years later he would remember that evening through flashes of water that glinted moonlight into his face, through the trees filled with orange blossom, and by the steady pace of hoofs.

For all their gaps, these memories would become his most vivid. It was in the flicker of a woman touching his brow, her face as she explained what was happening to him, as she stood in the doorway while a man stared into his eyes. He would wake for a few minutes, and recall with irritation that he could not remember something before he returned to sleep. Some days he felt he had been awake for hours, alone and in the dark, digging into his brain. His boys, his baby, his wife: he was sure these were truths. Their voices swirled in his mind and sometimes he felt like they could have been in the room, sitting so close to him that he felt his lungs deflate under the weight of his heart. And then, just occasionally, he felt the flicker of a small hand in his.

Ahmad didn't know how long he spent in this bed, remembering and not remembering, waking in bursts before disappearing, as though dragged by gravity back into unconsciousness to reunite with the images of bodies, slumped, unmoving, around archeological ruins. In the moments when he felt in control of his history, he would switch his ring from his left hand to his right. It helped him to remember.

His eyes shot open and his right hand felt odd. The ring. *The list.*

He shut his eyes and strained.

1. *My wife*
2. *My sons and my baby girl*
3. *The war*
4. *I don't know what happened*
5. *But I am not dead*

He ran through the list on his fingers, then counted his prayers on them until he fell asleep.

It was early one morning that Ahmad awoke to a hoopoe's call. It sounded as if it were hooting right beside his eardrum, singing him awake from his pillow. It was that sudden rush of sound he felt after he surfaced out of the river. A haze of light was streaming horizontally onto his bed, and the air was thick, damp, and earthy. He noticed the room for the first time, the wall he was sure he'd never looked at before, though it seemed so familiar.

With a gasp he spotted a forehead poking over the end of the bed, hidden behind his left foot.

"Baba?" asked a hesitant voice.

For a long moment there was silence as Ahmad gazed at his feet, then his face contorted with a neglected smile, and he croaked, "Yusuf."

Yusuf ran to the bedside and flung his arms around his father. "They said you wouldn't remember."

Ahmad lay silently for a few minutes, staring at his son. A pool formed in the outer crease of his eye and spilled down the side of his face, disappearing into his hairline to join the hoopoe. "How could I forget you, Yusuf?" he replied softly, with a cracked smile. "Is it possible to forget a person who jumps on top of a poor sick man in bandages?"

Yusuf laughed, and poked the yellowing bruises on Ahmad's face, now clear of grime.

Ahmad shut his eyes, lifted a hand to his crown, felt a misshapen triangle fill the cup of his palm, and recalled, with a flare, gunfire, the rock, the river, Ctesiphon. Oh, God, what had become of him? He opened his eyes, saw Yusuf staring at him expectantly, and choked down the memory of the battle on the river.

"Ah, yabni . . . my son, I wish it were possible to forget such cruel people, but alas . . ."

"Then I should make sure you remember me even more strongly," replied Yusuf, hugging his father with deliberate force.

"I have missed you truly, my son," said Ahmad, shutting his eyes. "Even when I could not remember you, I missed you."

The two were silent for a moment, when Yusuf asked, "Do you remember what happened to you?"

"Perhaps it's better that I don't," replied Ahmad, quietly. It was not quite an untruth, but he still felt a pang of guilt. How do you confess fear to a child when you have sworn the world is safe? How do you explain the particular color that sand turns when doused with blood? How do you explain that the memory of a color can repulse you because you have never seen it anywhere else?

Ahmad could recall only snapshots from the battle of Ctesiphon; the iconic arch he had visited as a child, that adorned all the foreign postcards, was now a graveyard to his Ottoman comrades and English enemies. He recalled the shining face of a young Arab at his feet and his stomach lurched. He recalled their haphazard retreat from the front line, toward the Tigris, and his shock as he looked at himself in the waters—unrecognizable, ragged, his face covered with a sticky, gritty red. And he recalled jumping into the amber river, dispersing into it deep pink swirls, from the blood of God-knows-who, his arms gripping something to keep him afloat. And then nothing.

Yusuf watched his father, then said with a smile, "But what you imagine might be worse than what actually happened, you know. What if you were just bumped on the head by a goat?" Ahmad smiled.

"Now," said Yusuf, "can we say hello to Mama? She kept telling me off for sneaking into your room, but now you can tell her I cured you."

"So you disobey your mother as well as your father?"

"I treat everyone equally." Yusuf sniggered.

Ahmad hauled his aching limbs out of bed, wincing at the slightest motion. He wondered how long it had been since he had last stood. Yusuf grabbed his father's hand and asked, "Haven't I grown since you saw me last? Everyone says I'm finally starting to look twelve."

Ahmad chuckled. "How should I remember?"

Ahmad felt his son's grown hand—and he had noticed, sadly, how big he had become—leading him through a courtyard, down a corridor that felt both familiar and unsettling, and out into a garden of dazzling light and sweet scents. He rubbed his arms and felt under his palms the limbs of a stranger, lean and bony, where they should have been heavy from a lifetime of laboring. His body moved like it was borrowed from another.

But I am home, he reminded himself. Any body would do.

Ahmad rounded a corner of the house and froze when he saw her. He gasped. The hazy image of a woman mopping his brow—how could he have allowed himself to forget that face? "Dabriya," he whispered, trying to mask the quiver in his throat.

She had called in every favor to track down Ahmad after he had disappeared at Ctesiphon. There was no trace of him among the survivors and little information about those who had fallen. And when hope of ever hearing any news—even permission to grieve—had disappeared, Dabriya had found her husband caked in dirt, blood, and flies under the archway of the Old City, just a few hours' ride from his home.

Ahmad gazed at Dabriya's face and staggered into her embrace.

"Habibti," he said, his arms on the back of her veil. "I'm sorry, my love," he croaked. "I'm sorry I couldn't see you. I'm sorry it took me so long."

"Well, timekeeping isn't this family's strength," she replied, not attempting to mask her smile. She blinked, pressing her palm to Ahmad's back and stroking his ribs, whispering her thanks to God.

For days, Dabriya boiled pot after pot of ground tea on the outside fire, ready at a moment's notice for the endless stream of well-wishers who came to welcome Ahmad back to the neighborhood. She was grateful to have an outlet to distract her from the confusion of his return. She wanted to scream the words that would free all that was trapped between her ribs. But she doubted such words existed. What sound could capture her relief that he had returned? That her family was whole again, after having believed herself widowed and her children fatherless?

And, for a time, Dabriya and her children forgot about the shadows that had darkened their home in Ahmad's absence. The sullen indifference that for months had lived on their eldest son Emad's face loosened. Emad thought the constant frown of his black brows made him unreadable, but it only served to make him look pubescent, tired, and lost, and these were truths of their own, too. With the return of her father, little Luma could not stop giggling—when he hiccuped, when he dropped his fruit, especially when he sneezed—with the relief that all her fuzzy memories of Ahmad were not dreams. He was real.

Questions once so inimical to restful sleep were forgotten in the shadow of the orange harvest and dusk prayers on the river shore. Ahmad's uniform had been tossed, unwashed, to the back of a cupboard, and, as no officials came for him, there it remained.

After a while, Ahmad stopped trying to remember the journey that had landed him in Baghdad's reeds. He stopped switching his ring from one hand to the other and checking his list of truths. He stopped counting the number of sunsets he shared with his family, and the number of watermelons they cracked open at sunset. But he knew something was missing from his memories, something that, even all these weeks later, would wake him in the night, screaming a name he could never quite recall, with a face that disappeared as he crossed back into consciousness.

But the knowledge that he had the capacity to forget his wife, his home, himself—that never left. And every morning, after he had touched his forehead to the floor with gratitude, he took the small photograph that used to stand at Dabriya's bedside, and tucked it into the folds of his belt. Just in case.

4

"WELCOME, WELCOME," SAID DAWOOD, SMILING so broadly that his eyes disappeared. His tarboosh was positioned precisely in the center of his crown, his leather sandals smelled newly sewn, and a slim green and red patterned belt held his striped robes in place. Ahmad felt an itch on his head and was suddenly conscious of his fraying ghutra. He had forgotten how grand his neighbor's house was: wooden shanasheel were dotted around the exterior, and alabaster arches striped with blue led to an inner shaded courtyard, overlooked by a long oak balcony. Dawood led him to a low seating area in a corner of the courtyard. A small fountain, surrounded by colorful geometric tiles, bubbled in the middle.

A maid scurried out with a woven tray holding two glasses of tea and a fan of freshly sliced watermelon triangles. It was only after they had eaten several pieces that Dawood spoke.

"Although I am truly glad of your company again, brother, there is more than one reason I requested it today."

"Which is the chief reason I accepted your invitation, as you know," Ahmad replied, and the two chuckled.

"Has the army contacted you?" Dawood asked. Ahmad shook his head. "You must be very careful. They may send people to search for you, and the first place they'll look is here."

Ahmad shook his head again. "Maybe once the war is over. But if they haven't come yet, I think I'm safe for now."

He gave a wry smile. "And who will they send for one soldier, who is probably lying dead in Ctesiphon?"

"So you won't be returning to the army?" asked Dawood, raising his eyebrows.

"It's not like that," Ahmad said quietly.

"Well, that's how they will see it."

"No need to look so happy," said Ahmad.

"Not happy," said Dawood, "but they didn't deserve you. Our army isn't what it used to be."

"Say it enough and it will come true, brother," said Ahmad sharply.

"Then why haven't you returned?" said Dawood, a bit too quickly. Ahmad sighed heavily and Dawood looked away. "I'm sorry, it's your decision."

Ahmad examined his friend for a moment. Once he said it there was no taking it back.

"I thought of you, Dawood, when I believed my time had come." Dawood's eyes softened. "I can't tell you how terrible it was, seeing my brothers ripped apart, but I truly thought that it was a price worth paying. I thought that when it came to it I could give my life for our freedom, for Baghdad, for my family to live safely." Ahmad shut his eyes, trying to ignore the knot in his throat. "But imagine kneeling in a stream of blood and brains, like it's the third fucking river of the land, being yelled at by a Turk to fight, to vindicate my brother, whose guts are spattered across my right thigh. That's when I thought of you, Dawood. That's when it hit me that I was defending our land against colonizers so that the last invaders can keep ruling us." Ahmad looked at his friend and turned his palms to the sky. "This is our city and we are fighting for no stake in it."

Dawood leaned toward Ahmad and put a hand on his shoulder. "I'm sorry, brother," he said. "I truly wish I was wrong."

Ahmad shook his head. "I can't deny it." He sighed. "It is no longer the army of our fathers."

They sat in silence for a moment, Ahmad, eyes shut, gripping the back of his knee with one hand and Dawood staring down at the tray of watermelon.

And when Ahmad finally swallowed the knot, and released his leg, and opened his eyes, Dawood smiled at him, just enough.

"You heard about the Sharif of Mecca?" asked Dawood.

Ahmad nodded. "The *English* Arab rebellion," he said, raising his eyebrow.

"You can pull that face," said Dawood, "but the English are the only ones promising us our own country. A Baghdad ruled by Baghdadis, can you imagine?"

"Every day," said Ahmad, slowly. "I miss the days when I had no notion of a free city."

"Maybe it's too late for us," said Dawood. "Maybe we will just become another Constantinople—maybe your army will come in and slaughter all our Armenian brothers and that will be the end of our glorious city."

Ahmad blinked incredulously. "Firstly, it isn't my army any more, and secondly, don't be ridiculous. This is Baghdad—the entire city is Armenian or Jewish or Chaldean. It could never happen here."

"They always say it's impossible before it happens," said Dawood. "Who would have thought the Turkish Unionists would order the killing of all their own Armenian soldiers?"

"We might be ruled by Turks, but you're forgetting that we aren't actually Turkish, and neither are our soldiers. Why would any of us care about Unionist aims for the Ottoman Empire? Who would execute his own neighbor? There would be nobody left in our city if they ordered us to kill all the men who believe in something different to them." Ahmad stared at his friend.

"I know, brother," said Dawood, "I know, but think of the cost. What if we are wrong? We cannot risk losing those we love." He tilted his head and frowned. "What if they come to Baghdad, like they went to Van, to Constantinople? What if they come and capture or kill every Armenian on this side of the Euphrates? It will be too late."

Ahmad winced. All this time he had been talking of abstract dangers in distant lands. How could he have missed what Dawood was trying to tell him? He'd been too busy defending his city's name to think about what would actually happen if the Turkish Unionists had their way in Baghdad.

"You understand what I am saying, brother?" asked Dawood.

Ahmad nodded. "I must warn Mikhael."

When Ahmad visited Mikhael on his modest lands a few buildings upstream, he thought the old man might sob or need to lie down, but he did neither. When Ahmad told him he was worried for his safety, that he had heard how the Armenians in Anatolia were being besieged, killed, and exiled, Mikhael did not yell out or curse the perpetrators.

"You'll come and stay with us," said Ahmad, "until we know what the danger is, until it passes."

Mikhael looked at Ahmad. "I know you mean well, yabni, but none of this is news to me. I've been worried for my life for years, and I'm sure I'll be worried for many more, or until they come for me." Mikhael put a hand on a post of his goat enclosure, turning to look at his goats. His white hair feathered forward beneath his cap. "But I will happily accept your invitation if it will bring either of us a little comfort."

Mikhael didn't understand how it had come to this. Surely someone should have come to the Armenians' defense—should have protested, at least? One minute the Turkish Unionists were shouting slogans of justice and equality, and the next, Armenian lives, homes, even children, were the obstacle to Ottoman glory. And the Turks believed it. He hadn't thought he would live long enough to see the masses fall for the lies of men in power again. And he realized, then, how predictable people were.

Mikhael moved into a small ground-floor room that opened onto the stony courtyard of Ahmad's house. He probably didn't protest as much as decorum dictated he should, but he had never had much time for decorum. As the weeks passed, Mikhael tended his goats each morning before Ahmad's family rose, returning with the day's milk. He spent his afternoons sleeping and his evenings weeding Ahmad's garden or playing guessing games with Yusuf, Emad, and Luma. Outwardly, he was uncomplaining, and sprightly for his years, but sometimes, when he was at his home, there were moments when his legs gave way at his helplessness for the families that were hunted, had perished crossing deserts, or who were slaughtered, their bodies left to float down the Euphrates, not always in one piece.

Dawood's position in the Baghdadi law courts had provided him with useful, well-informed contacts within the city and in wider Ottoman lands, who were willing to pass on news for the right price. Though Dawood could never be sure that reports of Unionist attacks to the north, or British progress to the south were true, it was an alternative source of news to the local reports. Ahmad and Mikhael followed keenly both Dawood's updates and local accounts, which were filled with Ottoman heroism and news of the construction of the illustrious Baghdad Railway. Apparently it was fully operational between Constantinople and Kut, which, to Ahmad, seemed improbable and of little relevance. In the British press, too many Armenian lives were lost for them to be presented as more than a unit of mathematics, though Mikhael questioned the enthusiasm with which the grisly reports were written. Nevertheless Ahmad deciphered the British papers with Dawood's help—his friend could read at least four languages with ease—with hunger and skepticism, and with the knowledge that everything they heard or read was likely already out of date.

Though the war continued to grow bloodier across the land that the foreign papers called Mesopotamia, Ahmad and his family found a suspended solace in their reunion, and in their distance from Baghdad City. They knew they were at war—or at least that their rulers were—but when they were sitting beside the river cracking seeds, or jumping for the peaches on the highest branches, they could almost convince themselves that their isolation would last forever. Dabriya consoled herself with the knowledge that finding happiness amid brutality is not defeat: it is a victory that has always inspired peace with more focus than any weapon. Whoever could find a corner of joy in the midst of a war, she thought, surely had a duty to enjoy it for as long as they could.

Ahmad would cross the Tigris many times that spring, spending hours in Dawood's cool courtyard maneuvering pawns and knights, as they grazed on watermelon triangles, discussing politics in abstract. One evening of chess and chatter stretched well into the night and Ahmad rowed his small boat home by moonlight. He found Dabriya sitting on the riverbank, leaning against a tree. He hopped out with a smile and clasped her hand. She sighed heavily.

"What is it?" he asked.

"Just relief," she said, shaking her head.

Ahmad bit his lip. "I didn't realize how late it was. I'm sorry."

"You're here now," replied Dabriya.

"I was just across the river. What could possibly happen?" He smiled.

"If you knew how it felt to have your fears come true . . ." She trailed off. Ahmad lowered his head and held Dabriya's hand with both of his. She looked down, avoiding Ahmad's eyes as she spoke. "So many things should have been taken from us. I should be jumping for joy, shouldn't I?" Ahmad stroked her palm with his. "I'm so happy that you're back, Ahmad, but I'm always, always afraid that you'll be lost again."

"It's all right to be afraid, but just know that I'm not going anywhere. This is our home, and we will be safe and together until this war ends."

"You must want to join the English fight against the Turks," whispered Dabriya.

Ahmad looked at his wife's face. How he had longed for her eyes, their maddening saffron glow every time she watched him leave, and their palm green when she lay beside him at night. He could never deny her wishes. He didn't have it in him and they both knew it.

"But I want to be here more," replied Ahmad. He ran his hand along the hair that poked out at the peak of her veil. He had forgotten even her hair, how thick it was under his fingertips and darker than the sky on the longest night. His stomach soared. Was this what happiness felt like? It had been so long since he had felt anything beyond the eruption of adrenalin, and exhaustion as it ebbed away.

"I will tell the rivers and the earth, and all the undeserving people on it, that I do not belong to them. I belong to you," he said. "The Ottomans and the English can go kill each other in the desert and leave us savages in peace."

Dabriya turned to him. "When we heard you were missing, the world just continued, not even pausing for your absence," she said. "And I thought everything we ever did would just fade away like it never happened."

He leaned back against the tree, clasped her hand again, and whispered, "But it didn't."

Dabriya smiled beside him, leaning against the palm trunk, as two bats danced above the trees. "Ahmad," she said softly. "Who is Karim?"

The name sent a jolt through Ahmad's veins. *Karim.* He felt bile rise in his throat as he remembered the pale-cheeked boy, barely older than Emad, lying at his feet, his left knee and right hip bent at impossible angles.

"Do it, Yuzbasi Ahmad," begged Karim, grasping at his uniformed thigh, his cheeks wet. *"Please do it."*

"I can't," said Ahmad, the muzzle of his gun pointed at the boy. Karim's wispy, barely-there beard was coated with dust. "I can't."

"Do it, quickly," said Karim, as his body sank into the sand. "Don't let me die like this. Please, Abu Emad."

He knew he should shoot, should do as his protégé asked, but Ahmad also knew that he could not. He had ended many lives, but this was one he could not take responsibility for, no matter how close death already was. Karim would probably die slowly, painfully. And if, by a miracle, he lived, he would never again know what it was to walk.

Ahmad swung his gun onto his back and dropped to his knees. He scooped Karim into his arms and retreated from the British. Karim screamed curses at him.

A thud to the back of his head sent Ahmad to the ground, and Karim flying, his body limp. There were no screams this time.

Ahmad came round to a labored rocking motion under his stomach. He was face down, slung over a camel's back. The sight of its bulging feet pressing into the sand hypnotized him briefly. He grunted.

"Can you walk?" asked a Turk from below.

Ahmad recognized him as a captain from the badge on his shoulder. "I think so," he said. He slid off the camel to the ground, his knees buckling. A crowd of troops swarmed around him, enveloping him as he struggled to his feet. He couldn't recognize a single face, and it was only then that he remembered Karim. His only true friend from the crowds of men around him.

"Where's Karim? The boy who was with me, his legs were . . ." He trailed off.

"We couldn't save him."

A chill ran down the back of Ahmad's neck. "He's dead?" he asked, though it came out as a squeak.

"No idea," replied the captain. "We couldn't carry you both and you were in better shape."

Ahmad felt sick. What if the English had taken Karim? Oh, God, the things they would do to him. He pictured Karim's legs, askew and limp. The poor boy begging for release from a slow and painful death. "I should have done it," he said. "I should have done as he asked."

"Ahmad." Dabriya was shaking his shoulder. Ahmad sat up with a jolt. He couldn't remember how he had come to be on the ground. It was so easy to forget, he thought, and then he laughed— a phlegmy sound he tried to cloak with a cough. If only it were easy to forget. His cheeks felt cold and he hoped he had not been crying. She must not see him cry. She must not know what he had done. She must not know what he had not.

5

Autumn 1910
Llwynypia, Wales

THE CLOUDS THAT HUNG ABOVE the Rhondda Valleys had a way of making everything below them appear gray. Even in the summer, the skies were more ashen than blue. They blocked the sun from redbrick houses, from the freshly painted signs that hung above the butcher's and the baker's, but most of all they shrouded the hilly forests that surrounded the valleys, dulling the brightness of lush deep greens and rolling yellow meadows. And the permanence of gray in Carwyn Evans's life felt like theft. He had spent all summer waiting for a break in the clouds that might give him a glimpse of the endless shades of green he felt he deserved. These were his treetops, his horizon of dipping hills, his green, and the clouds had no right to deprive him of them.

The gray of his schoolhouse, though, he couldn't blame on the skies. It stood there, at the end of his road, taunting him every time he left his home to visit the butcher, or the baker, or the forests, reminding him of everything he had ever tried to escape. There were many things that Carwyn was good at. By the age of two he could count to ten in Welsh and English, and he could add and subtract just eighteen months later. He could clean a floor faster than his mother, Mari, and he could polish his father's boots with ease. When he was six his long legs could throw him higher into the air than those of his classmates. There were many things that Carwyn Evans was good at, but reading was definitely not among them.

When his mother tried to teach him his letters, all he saw were corners and arcs in rows on a page, and when he started going to the gray schoolhouse, he felt his palms grow sticky every time he was called on in reading class. But no matter how much his classmates snickered, he could not get the letters to stand still long enough for him to read them. When he turned eight he joined Mrs. Davies's class and the back-bent woman offered him the patience that none of his other teachers had. Every day when the bell rang at three, he pulled up a low stool and sat beside his teacher's desk, until lines became letters and letters became words. And though the ink still danced, the more he practiced, the faster he was able to place the letters in their proper order. He didn't believe he would ever read as well as his classmates, but swore he would work twice as hard, if he had to, to read at half the speed of the other boys.

When the first school term of 1910 began, he found a spot on a bench near the back of the classroom, but not so far back that he might draw attention to himself. When November came around and Mr. Williams still had not called on him to read aloud, he began to believe that his luck might have changed. And just as Carwyn began to relax, he saw Mr. Williams raise a callused forefinger and point at him, right between the eyes. "Explain to me, boy, what you know about the pit crisis."

Carwyn's stomach clenched. He told himself that at least he didn't have to read, that he was the son of a miner; he could do this. The boy beside him was breathing heavily, diffusing puffs of warm air into the room. Carwyn pulled his elbows in, away from him.

He stood up slowly.

"Well, sir," he began, and then he looked at his teacher. "Yn Saesneg?" he asked.

"Yes, boy, you know the rules, speak in English."

"They opened a new pit in Ely and sent men to mine it for thirty days to set their . . ." He stopped and looked at Mr. Williams.

"Yes? Hurry up."

". . . to set their . . . cyflogau." Carwyn scratched his ear.

"Their *wages*," said Mr. Williams.

"Yes," said Carwyn. "But after the thirty days, the company offered them a shilling less than the miners need, because they said that the miners worked slow to try to get themselves a higher wage."

"That was in July," said Mr. Williams, raising his eyebrows.

"Since then, they have locked out all our miners—including my dad—because they won't agree to the wages, and today the workers of the three big mining companies stopped working." He looked at his teacher—surely he would be allowed to sit now.

"One last thing," said Mr. Williams.

Carwyn felt all the eyes of his classmates on him and his cheeks burned. He cursed his white hair and equally pasty skin—always ready to betray his anxiety. "You didn't explain why they stopped working," said his teacher.

Carwyn racked his brains for the right word. He knew it—he was sure he knew the word in English. Mr. Williams glared at him impatiently. Was he trying to trip him up?

Carwyn shrugged, and tried to feign confidence. "Y streic."

Mr. Williams nodded. "Yes, the strike," he said. "But that is three times now you've spoken in Welsh. Please come to the front."

Muttering broke out around him. They had heard rumors that Mr. Williams still meted out this punishment, but they'd had no reason to believe it yet.

Carwyn dropped his chin. He lifted his legs from under the long table and swiveled on his buttocks, absently tapping the heavy-breathing boy with his shoes. He walked to the front of the class, sliding his feet along the floor.

"We don't have all day, boy."

Carwyn sped up, stood in front of his teacher and bent his head. Mr. Williams placed a wooden plaque looped on a small rope around his neck. Carwyn looked at his chest and read the words "WELSH NOT." He shook his head and returned to his seat.

When the day ended and a child circled the school ringing an old brass bell, Carwyn's class dispersed, but Mr. Williams beckoned him with a twitch of a finger.

"I don't enjoy this, boy, but you must learn," he said. Carwyn held out his hands and stared at the tweed on Mr. Williams's chest. He felt two cracks across his palms and a slow burn grew, like fire, but he didn't move. On the third crack he looked Mr. Williams in his miserable beady eyes. He didn't give a monkey's uncle about the scorching in his palms, but the humiliation of wearing that sign just for speaking three words of Welsh tormented him. And in that moment, Carwyn was sure of three things: that this man had enjoyed beating him very much; that he could not understand why the powerful enjoyed torturing the powerless; and that he would never let his struggle with words be the cause of such humiliation again.

He forced himself not to rub his hands as he slipped the plaque off over his head. And as he walked toward the classroom door, anger filled his chest. His fists shook as he told himself that he was not powerless. He turned his head back to that coward of a Welshman and wished him a good afternoon with a smile: "*Prynhawn da, syr.*"

6

Summer 1916
Baghdad

IT IS SAID THAT GOD allowed Hell two breaths away from its own flames each year. Humankind would feel its first on the hottest, most blistering day of the summer, and the second on winter's most bitterly cold day. For the people of Baghdad, the summer seemed so filled with disobedient breaths from Hell that they longed for the kiss of winter.

The summer months brought with them strained tempers, a shriveled garden and the unfortunate coincidence of heat with the month of Ramadan. In other lands, the sun gives life as essentially as the rains, but in Baghdad, the heat exists to suffocate the life out of every being.

Winter began as a temperate relief, both for the scorched land and its scorched residents. In that small window of Heaven, after summer had ended and before the icy nights pummeled the region, the rivers ran low and children piled into the Tigris. For a full lunar month, the air and the rivers and the sky were the temperature of happiness.

It crept up on them subtly at first, the flood of 1917. Every spring brought with it heavy rains, so with each gain the river made on the family's land, they assured themselves that it was everything they had expected. When the palm trees lost the base of their trunks to the Tigris, Yusuf felt the thrill he always did when change was in motion. When the rains first abated, he walked out to the edge of the watermelon patch and marveled at how wide the river had become. Each morning when he woke, he would grin with excitement as he remembered the novelty of their very own lake, as though it were the anticipated visit of a mischievous relative.

Yusuf happily helped his parents pick the rows of watermelons closest to the water's edge, even after pointing out that they weren't ripe. Emad shook his head but Dabriya smiled at Yusuf and told him she didn't want the water to rot them. Though it struck him as strange when he saw Mikhael herding his eight goats through the family's house and onto the roof, he assumed they were just moving in too. Mikhael spent two days fashioning a peaked roof from palm fronds and sturdy sticks and trapping his goats under it.

On the third night of rains, Dabriya shook Yusuf awake, told him to dress quickly and help them bring the watermelons indoors. He could hear the rain echoing so loudly that he thought for a moment that they had lost their roof. He ran downstairs and as soon as he stepped outside the river swallowed his ankles. The ground was sticky and sucked his feet with every step. At first he tried to keep his clothes clean with each slip, but within four circuits to and from the house he knew there was little point. Mud caked his legs and arms, and his clothes were soaked. After salvaging two rows of watermelons, around a third of their carrots and most of their onions, the family retired indoors, wet, muddy, and freezing.

Dabriya stroked Yusuf's head, and went to fetch all the blankets, animal skins, and wool that she could find. She wrapped a blanket around each son, and joined Ahmad and Mikhael in the storeroom to dry the food they had saved, and to check their winter wood store had not succumbed to any leaks. Emad boiled some water over a fire and told Yusuf to stand in a copper vat and strip. Yusuf looked at his feet as he removed his dripping robes, except a long undershirt, and Emad pretended not to notice that more than floodwater was dripping off Yusuf's face.

Emad poured a small cupful of warm water over his brother's head. He rubbed a bar of watermelon and olive oil soap between his palms, then over Yusuf's hair. Yusuf whimpered but didn't move.

"Here," said Emad, passing Yusuf the soap, "clean your arms and legs." Yusuf obeyed silently, and when he had finished, he found his brother holding out a warm woollen blanket for him.

"I won't look," he said. As Yusuf warmed himself by the fire Emad fetched a dish of water from the roof and cleaned himself without bothering to heat it, which made him angry at himself, and—if he was honest—a little angry at Yusuf too. When their mother had roused Emad, he had immediately jumped to action in panic. He knew that a flooding of their crops would mean they could all die of starvation, could drown even. He knew that there was nothing exciting about water creeping up to their home. He scooped water up with a clay cup and poured it over his head. He wished he found the sound of rain hitting the metal pans around the house thrilling rather than tormenting. He told himself it was good to be aware, to be prepared, that a fifteen-year-old should be able to look after his family. But, really, he wished he could be the boy who laughed when it rained and cried when it flooded.

By the time the family could take four steps outside their door without drowning their ankles in mud and floodwater, half of the watermelons they had salvaged had already begun to rot. Everyone was tired of eating them, but Dabriya insisted they save the carrots and onions until they absolutely had to eat them. She carefully picked out as many black melon seeds as she could find, wrapped them and stored them in a pot near the fire.

Luma barely noticed the change at first—though, of course, something felt different, even to her. Mostly, she just enjoyed the extra attention she received from her housebound family, and they, in return, enjoyed her exaggerated talking and laughter.

When all the watermelons had either swollen to putrefaction or been eaten, Dabriya tried to find ways to make carrots and onions interesting. When their first meal of soup was cooking on the fire, cheers rang throughout the house, but by the seventh day of watery mashed carrots, mealtimes were far more subdued. Yusuf could not stop itching and rubbing his waist, and the family's eyes seemed to pop as they devoured their dinner. Every few days, no matter how treacherous the rain, Mikhael would disappear to the roof and return with a bucket of milk and three pots of rainwater, which would last the family until the next milking.

Mikhael returned from the roof one day with a platter of meat, taken from the skinned body of his smallest nanny goat, whose remains, out of sight of the family and other goats, he had thrown off the roof with tears at the indignity, to be buried later, just meters from the house. The meat brought jubilation to meals, and some color back into their cheeks. During that first meal, as Yusuf and Emad were laughing between mouthfuls of stewed goat, Ahmad caught Mikhael's eye and placed a hand to his chest.

The floods brought with them the inevitable stench of rot and the inevitable flies that follow. But they also brought a silence that mercifully extended to any discussions of war or politics. For all they knew, the war had ended weeks before. Mikhael tried to give his portions of boiled carrots to Luma and Yusuf, but was scolded by Dabriya.

After months fighting for the Ottoman army, Ahmad was used to surviving on rations, but his children were still unaccustomed to the ache of hunger, and he would do all he could to keep it that way. He had not lived through the battle at Ctesiphon, surviving the icy Tigris water, only to be defeated by rain. He had not returned to his children to watch them starve. So he instructed Dabriya to divide half his plate of food every night between his three children, which she did with a sad smile. He, in turn, pretended not to notice that she split her own portion with him.

When the food became more liquid than solid, their lunch was reduced to a single carrot each. Only one of Mikhael's goats was still able to produce milk, but she barely yielded a cupful in a week. Yusuf and Luma took to eating their carrots on the front doorstep together, as though the waters might recede from embarrassment. Luma wolfed her carrot and rested her head on Yusuf's lap. He found that he felt less hungry if he chewed his slowly, dragging out the meal to a more respectable length. Luma stared at the muddy garden from his lap. He heard her stomach growl. He clenched his own and felt it knot and ache.

He snapped the chewed end off his carrot and held out the rest to Luma. "Here," he said. "Eat it slowly, though, or it will make you more hungry." Luma sat up and stared at the carrot.

"Take it," he said. "I already ate mine. This one is from the extra carrots I have in my room."

"Don't be silly," she said, with a giggle.

"It's true," said Yusuf, "I prayed and prayed for it, and one day I found a special box of carrots. But they're just for children, so we can't tell anyone."

"Why?"

"Because if we do, whoever put the box there might take it away. You don't want that, do you?"

Luma shook her head. "All right," she whispered, taking the carrot, and returning her head to Yusuf's lap.

Two days later, Ahmad deemed the ground solid enough for a damage survey, and set out into the muddy depths of the garden. The peach trees had thrown their fruit to the ground, and the watermelons that hadn't floated away were discolored, misshapen, and let off a stench. He headed for the guffa, passing a fallen palm tree; the water rose above his knees and within a few paces had reached his hips. As he neared the circular boat, he felt the ground give way under his feet, and fell backwards, the cold water hitting his back and ballooning his clothes, sucking them down with its creeping weight.

Emad helped his father carry the fallen palm tree. It had swollen, and had black spines dripping from one end, which dribbled a bitter syrup over his shoulder. He held one end on the submerged shore and the two slowly tipped the other onto the lip of the guffa. Emad was covered from head-to-toe with fermenting waters and smears of unrecognisable gunk that must once have been fruit. He spat as some made its way into his mouth. He tried to make a joke to himself that this was a metaphor for his role in life, but he had never been very good at laughing at himself.

Ahmad was crawling across the tree-trunk, his weight forcing the guffa low in the water as he neared it, when he heard a whimper. Amid the brown sludge and thinning twigs of the guffa he saw a small guest. It let out a bleat, and struggled weakly when Ahmad joined it in the boat and picked it up. He removed his belt to fashion a sling and pulled at the tree-trunk, guiding the boat toward the shore with one arm, as the other clasped the goat into his chest. "Come on, old thing," he crooned.

Emad upturned the guffa, and found it a sunny spot on which to dry, then the two of them took the kid to the house, to squealed greetings. After Mikhael had fed it their single cup of goat's milk, rinsed it with cups of warm water and wrapped it in the thickest blanket in a corner near the fire, the family heard a distant greeting.

"Ammu Dawood!" shouted Yusuf, running out to greet him. Ahmad stood up, his pulse beating in his head. He swayed. Dabriya held him by the arm and walked him to the back gate of the house.

"Salam, I've brought supplies!" said Dawood, pointing to the basket of fresh fruit and vegetables in his hands, and the bread that his daughter Amira carried. Yusuf felt suddenly hot when Amira caught him staring at the platter of bread in her arms.

"I've been trying to cross for days, but the guffa took a lifetime to repair and dry," said Dawood.

"We only recovered ours today," said Ahmad.

"Have you been cut off from the track for long?" asked Dawood.

Ahmad didn't want to tell him how little food they had left, so instead he murmured the customary thanks to God, as he often did when he was too embarrassed to answer a question.

Dawood promised to bring over more supplies from his house, and even said that they had healthy reeds and grasses that Mikhael could cut to feed the goats. When Dabriya began to pre-pare the food he had brought, Dawood and Amira went to find clean water to wash off the mud from their trip across the river.

As they passed an open doorway, Amira stopped suddenly. Yusuf was standing beside his sleeping area wearing only his under-trousers, untying a piece of rope from around his waist. Instinctively, Amira looked away, but she stole another glance, sure that she must have been mistaken: it couldn't have been so much worse on this side of the river. As the rope came away from Yusuf's skin, Amira shivered as she saw blood seep from pinched skin, old scabs, and the contour of the rope's shape etched into his withered frame. Amira turned a corner and jumped when she heard a voice.

"Amira sad?" Amira paused and squatted down to Luma's level.

"No, Luma, I'm fine," she said softly, touching Luma's cheek. "Have you been very hungry?" she asked, fiddling with the end of her black braid, which fell below the hem of her loose veil.

"Sometimes," said Luma, nodding earnestly. "But my brother gives me extra carrots from his secret box," she added, with a smile. "Then I'm not hungry."

"Yusuf?" asked Amira, knowing the answer.

Luma nodded. "But don't tell any grown-ups, or the carrots will go away."

"Where is this box?" asked Amira slowly.

"Yusuf's room."

Amira tried to smile.

"Are you sad?" asked Luma.

"No, Luma, I just missed you, that's all. Shall we go downstairs?"

"All right," said Luma.

Amira pulled herself to her feet and held Luma's hand, trying not to think of Yusuf's graying skin, gashed with red. And she knew that the rope around Yusuf's gaunt waist was not just to constrict away the pain of his hunger: it was the price he paid to keep his sister's stomach full.

7

AHMAD, YUSUF, AND LUMA HAD crossed the river with Dawood, and were awaiting the sandy tones in the sky that would tell them it was time for supper. Ahmad followed his son toward the kitchen, drawn by the scent of cinnamon and rosewater. Yusuf could smell bread being heated in the clay oven, the aroma of toasted wheat like a punch to his abdomen. He made his way to the oven, just outside the kitchen, and watched one of the maids deftly stretching, flipping, and baking the bread. His stomach grumbled.

"I caught you," chuckled Dawood, sneaking up behind them. He kissed Ahmad's cheeks, and patted Yusuf's shoulder.

"I wasn't going to take any," said Yusuf.

"I know." Dawood smiled. After a silence, he said, "I heard from some of our neighbors that your watermelon delivery was extremely professional last season. Better than your father's was when he was much older than you, I believe. He got stuck in a shallow river and came home soaked to the armpits many times, as I recall." He smiled at Ahmad, who shook his head.

"Did they really say I was good? The boat was so heavy to steer."

"I'm a court judge, remember? I'm not allowed to tell untruths." Yusuf smiled at Dawood and sighed, breathing in the wafts of fresh bread.

"Come, come," said Dawood, indicating behind his guests. His daughter appeared in a frilled dress and a loose veil with gold edging.

"Amira!" said Yusuf, a little too loudly. He blushed and Amira waved at him, pretending not to notice. Amira's mother, Naima, entered, wearing a blue and green long-sleeved dress, accompanied by her older daughter, Farah, whose green eyes were an exact copy of her mother's. Naima offered her salams to her guests and was halfway through instructing them to sit when they heard the front gate slam against stone. They ran into the courtyard and found Mikhael, panting, his face wet with sweat or tears, or perhaps both.

"They've come," he said. "The Ottoman Army has come for me."

"You saw them?" asked Ahmad.

Mikhael nodded. "They're searching door to door. They're going to take me."

Ahmad clutched Mikhael's shoulder. Now that it was actually happening, he could not believe it. His heart was hammering and he thought he would vomit. His father's oldest friend, taken by an army he had fought for. It must be a misunderstanding. The army was full of Baghdadis—they would never arrest one of their own. Impossible.

"No, they will not," said Dawood. "Get inside. Now." They walked into the corridor. Ahmad breathed deeply and removed his outer robe, passing it to Mikhael.

"Wear this. It looks more Arab," he said. Mikhael put on the robe and looked at Ahmad. "They will never guess you're Armenian from looking at you—not with the tarboosh you're wearing," he said, more confidently.

"Come, hide in the water cellar just in case," said Dawood. "The rest of you, take seats in the courtyard and act normally. I'll be back soon."

Ahmad felt his son's hand clasp his. "It's all right, Yusuf," he said. "Mikhael is safe now." Ahmad and Yusuf took seats in the corner of the courtyard, opposite Amira and her mother.

✽

Yusuf jumped at the bang from the front gate. There was a clatter of footsteps and ten soldiers in Ottoman uniform filed into the courtyard, rifles pointing at anything in their way. They ran two by two through the house, slamming doors open. Two stormed past Yusuf and he saw their guns shaking as their eyes searched.

Ahmad stood and walked toward one standing on the near side of the courtyard, and Yusuf followed him. Ahmad offered a tentative salam as a soldier yelled, "Got him," from a room across the building.

Ahmad froze. "Got who?" he asked, trying to keep his voice calm. Poor, gentle Mikhael, he thought, as he pictured his friend emaciated and starving, or cut into pieces and thrown over the riverbank, identifiable only by his feathery hair bubbling on the surface of the waters. "Please," he said. "Don't do this." The soldiers formed a wall in front of him and Yusuf. He wanted to tell them he was one of them, that Mikhael was one of them too. But he stood silent, useless.

"Baba," said Yusuf. "What's happening, Baba?"

"It's all right, I'll fix this," he replied. "I can fix this."

Yusuf stood on tiptoe to try to see past the soldiers. Through a gap between two of the soldiers' waists he spotted Amira, her sister, and her mother on the other side of the courtyard. A sergeant stood beside them with one arm flung out to stop them crossing it. Naima charged at his arm, fists raised.

"Get your filthy hands away from my daughters," she yelled, as she launched herself, her chin making contact with his elbow. Her head snapped back and she slumped to the floor. Amira screamed and tried to reach for her, restricted by the arm of the Turk in front of them.

"What are you doing?" Yusuf pleaded, pulling at the arm of the soldier in front of him, straining to see the opposite side of the house. "What have you found?" He watched Amira, with her braids and her frilly dress on the other side of the courtyard. He saw her put her hand to her mouth. "What is it?" he yelled, but Amira was silent and motionless. "Someone tell me," he said, hopping around, looking from Amira to the soldiers. "I don't understand, Baba, what's happening?" he pleaded.

Yusuf crouched down to the ground. And then he understood.

He saw four boots marching ahead of two newly-stitched leather sandals. The sandals alternated between walking and being dragged as they struggled to keep up.

He crawled between a soldier's legs and stumbled forward.

"No!" cried Yusuf. "No, he's not even Armenian!" But nobody looked at him.

He ran in front of the soldiers who were dragging behind them Dawood. "Stop!" he yelled. "He's not Armenian. I promise!" One of the soldiers hauling Dawood away looked at him, but didn't break pace.

Yusuf fell to the floor in front of the entrance to the garden. He was vaguely aware of distant crying and other people yelling. He didn't notice Dawood calling to his daughters, who were yelling back and pounding their fists on the soldiers obstructing their path to him. He didn't notice one of the soldiers shutting his eyes. He didn't notice his father trying to reason with the army.

Dawood's sleeve ripped as he was hauled past Yusuf and his father. "Ahmad," hissed Dawood. "Don't let the bastards get away with this."

Yusuf ran to the entrance of the courtyard, slipping past Dawood and the soldiers with their guns. He flung his arms out to block the doorway. "I promise he is not Armenian. I swear it." Tears started rolling down his cheeks. "I promise—I promise, with God as my witness," he cried.

The sergeant whispered to him, "Nobody is accusing him of being Armenian, boy."

"Then why? Please let him go. Please."

"It's out of my hands. I'm just following orders. Now get off the floor and let him leave with some dignity."

"What orders?" Two soldiers stepped over Yusuf without much difficulty, Dawood following with resignation.

More soldiers followed suit, clambering over Yusuf, and the last man whispered, "Don't take it personally; it will be the same for all Jewish men like him."

8

Winter 1910
Llwynypia, Wales

CARWYN'S FATHER WAS ONE OF the most experienced miners in Llwynypia; some would say he was the best in all of Glamorganshire. Iestyn Evans's friends would put it down to his strong stomach muscles and his flexible knees; his wife always teased that it was because of his short stature; but he suspected that the generations of miners before him in his family had strengthened his senses. His spine tingled when something was amiss, and he could keep track of all the men nearby without taking his eyes off his hands. He didn't need his lamp to tell him when the air had turned noxious: he just knew. And he could tell the difference between a gas that would kill them in minutes, and when fat old Oriel had released his own brand of methane. Mining was in his bones and his blood, and everyone knew it.

Carwyn had felt prickles on his neck ever since he'd seen his father leave the house at four that morning, just after a bugle had woken him. It was the first sign that something was different. A few hours later, when he left for school, the air hit him across the face, sharp and dewy, and he knew it then, too: something was happening.

And when he sat in class staring at the permanent crease between Mr. Williams's eyebrows, and heard chants in the road, just on the other side of the schoolhouse, he made up his mind.

When the bell rang that afternoon, Carwyn took the road to the colliery. He followed the clusters of men joining the miners who had already gathered there, and the claps of shoes on cobblestones—through Y Pandy Square, past the Jenkins bakery and the office of the *South Wales Echo*, until the roar of the crowd exploded as he turned the final corner before the pump-house.

He lowered his head and twisted his body, snaking between the grown men, each of them identically musta-chioed, and clad in long winter overcoats and flat caps. His heart raced as he wondered how he would ever pick his father out from among them, and it raced some more for the thrill of this moment of defiance. And when a man beside him growled out a chant for a fair wage, Carwyn felt, for the first time in his life, an undeniable power rise from the ground beneath his feet, as he yelled the words back. His spine prickled and his eyes tingled, and as he maneuvered himself through the crowd, he noticed he was beaming.

The closer Carwyn got to the pump-house towers, the denser the crowd became. He put his fingertips on the ribs of men to create gaps in the crowd to squeeze through. He was close to the front. He could see a line of policemen in capes and domed helmets, protecting the pit from the front line of protestors. It had been a while since he'd seen another boy his age, but he didn't care. Carwyn didn't know exactly what he was feeling; all he knew was that it felt good to be there, with the noise, and the boots, and the caps. Maybe it was the his-tory of the moment, or just the sense of purpose. Whatever it was, it made his whole body tremble.

And, just like that, cheers turned to panicked shouts. He heard a man's voice telling the crowd to stop. Carwyn strained to see over the sea of caps. The man in front of him pushed back and Carwyn scrambled to keep his balance. The crowd heaved, and he heard angry exchanges a few rows ahead.

"Stop throwing stones," yelled a voice. "You're making it worse." Carwyn saw a metal fence rise above the crowd, still half attached to the ground.

"Restrain yourselves, men!" shouted another voice. Carwyn felt a gust of air spin past his left ear, and saw a brick fly over the crowd in front of him and disappear into the pump-house. Within seconds he heard men yelling, cursing the mothers of the policemen, cursing the English, cursing the Cambria Combine Company. There was a surge and the crowd pushed at Carwyn from the front, but there was nowhere to move and, as if in slow motion, Carwyn felt himself rise off the ground, suspended among the men. He pointed his toes, treading in midair, and his neck grew hot with fear as he moved wherever the crowd moved, powerless to control his body. He was so focused on getting his feet onto the ground that he hadn't noticed the tips of truncheons raised above the crowd. The man in front of him was crushing Carwyn's ribs as he pushed back, away from the police. When the truncheon made contact with the man's shoulder, Carwyn's feet touched the cobblestones. He didn't even take a breath to compose himself before bending double and ramming his way through the men, using his head and fists to part them. He only knew that he had to get out of there—he had to.

He hadn't noticed that the sun had set until he made it to Y Pandy Square. He leaned an arm against the fountain and gasped for air. A portly man put a hand on his shoulder and Carwyn jumped. The man laughed and held out a paper bag to him. Relief flooded Carwyn as he took a piece of candy from the bag and popped it into his mouth.

"Ta." He thanked the man, suddenly aware of how hungry he was. He was hungry most days, though, and he could thank the Cambria Combine Company and their withholding of wages for that, too.

"Hurry on home now, bach," said the man. "It's not safe any more, no place for boys."

"Yes, it is," said Carwyn. "This is my pit too."

"They aren't our policemen. They sent them in from England, so don't expect them to treat you gently just because you're a boy. To them, you're just another uncivilized Taffy."

"I have to be here," said Carwyn. "My dad is out there somewhere." The man nodded and held out the paper bag to him again. Carwyn took another piece of candy.

"Be careful, bach," the man said gently, and then he left. Carwyn steadied himself against the fountain. He startled when he heard glass smash behind him. A cluster of men bundled through a shop window and emerged a few minutes later, dressed in at least three extra layers of clothing.

"What are you doing?" he called after them. "That's not yours!" But the men didn't even glance at him. The sound of scuffles and boots on cobblestones filled the air. The winter mountain mist descended on the valley, filling the black streets with a glowing haze, so Carwyn didn't see them coming. It began with the blast of whistles, a chorus of high-pitched shrilling descending from the hill toward the square. Carwyn climbed onto the statue in the center of the fountain, trying to see something—anything. He heard the footsteps then, and the unmistakable thud of batons hitting flesh. Roars erupted and men yelled Welsh curses at the English policemen beating them. From his vantage point, Carwyn saw lines of police arriving on the far side of the square, batons raised, hitting anyone who got in their way.

"Stop!" screamed Carwyn. "What are you doing? Stop!" He clung to the statue with one arm, waving the other at the crowd below. Nobody noticed him.

He looked back at the road that led to the pit. "No," he gasped. He looked from the road to the crowd of capped miners, evading the batons, and back again.

"Horses," yelled Carwyn, pointing at the road. "They've sent the army!" The crowd heaved below him. The arm holding onto the fountain ached.

He just had time to hear a man say, "No!" before something hit his arm, and he tumbled through the air.

"He's just a boy," screamed the voice. "Get away." More thudding, more batons. He opened his eyes, just for a moment, and smiled as he saw his father's face looking down at him. Blackened and bloody.

"Carwyn, bach," gasped Iestyn. "I found you, Carwyn."

9

Winter 1916
Baghdad

YUSUF LAID HIS HEAD ON the floor and stared at the stone archway above. His heartbeat echoed violently through his body and his fists bounced off the floor in a frenzy of shaking.

"Anyone for klecha?" he heard his mother ask from the gate, followed by a clatter as the biscuits fell to the floor.

"What happened?" asked Emad. He kneeled beside Yusuf, and his face seemed to age in an instant.

"They took him," Amira said softly, from the courtyard. "They took Baba."

Dabriya gasped and ran to her side. "Oh, my dear," she said. "I'm so sorry." She stroked Amira's head.

"They dragged him away," Amira replied. "I don't under-stand—how can they just take him? And where to?"

Emad put a hand to Yusuf's head.

"Come on, up you get," he said, taking his brother's hands. "It won't help them to see you like this."

Yusuf sat up, and his sister jumped onto his lap. "Yusuf sick?" Luma asked him.

"No, Yusuf fine," he replied, patting her palm tree of hair.

Naima and her daughters moved into Ahmad's house and in the days that followed they sprang to attention every time they heard approaching footsteps. With each false alarm, they hoped that the passerby would be Dawood, but feared that the soldiers would return for his wife and two daughters. Neither happened. Every sunrise, they awoke to find a little more hope had left them, as wretched as the orange blossoms migrating from their branches. Ahmad kept an eye on the British newspaper that somehow made its way to his watermelon patch every week—each time hidden under an oblong melon, twisted on its end. He turned the search into a game for the five children now under his roof, which worked well to begin with, but was less successful once the winds had exiled the last of the blossoms downstream, taking all their spirits with them.

Sometimes Ahmad would go to the forest of palm trees in his garden, weave his way to a place of solace and, when he was sure he was alone, grip the fuzzy bark of a palm tree, submitting to the shadows in his soul in a silent weep.

"I have to do something," he said to Dabriya one morning as she shook him to rise for morning prayer.

"That is what we do every sunrise, and four more times every day," she replied, though she knew that was not what he meant.

"But I still ache with guilt and helplessness."

"I've just got you back, Ahmad. Please."

Ahmad stood, washed, and joined his wife in prayer.

Four weeks had passed since Dawood was taken. Emad and Yusuf were by the river, repairing the guffa with handfuls of muddy pitch.

"Once it's mended the girls can have their boat back," said Yusuf, patting the side of the coracle. "So they can visit home as often as they like."

"It won't bring their father back," said Emad.

"Well, it won't keep him away either, so we can at least try to cheer them up," replied Yusuf.

"Yusuf, I've been trying to avoid this but—"

"Clearly you haven't," said Yusuf, quickly.

"Look, what happened is terrible, but this is war and war is terrible," said Emad. "And nobody said this would be easy. Just look at what happened to Baba."

"Baba came back," said Yusuf, "and do you remember how kind Ammu Dawood was to us while Baba was gone?"

"Yes," said Emad, quietly. He held out a pitcher of water. "Right, I think we're done," he said, emptying the pitcher over Yusuf's hands, then went to wash his own in the river. "Everyone has to make a sacrifice, Yusuf," he said.

"Yes, so as long as it's not you," said Yusuf.

"Once upon a time," said Ahmad with a smile, leaning back against the apricot tree, "a man called Nasreddin Hodja bought mutton weighing two okas from his local butcher." He looked down at his sons, at his daughter, and at Dawood's two girls. "He took it to his wife so that she would make him tashrib for dinner, and set off to work. Mrs. Hodja made the tashrib, but the moment she finished there was a knock at the door, which she opened to find a group of friends. What else could she do but offer them the food? And what else would they do but guzzle it all?" Dawood's daughters were staring at Ahmad, with interest or bewilderment, he was not sure which.

"When Nasreddin got home to find no tashrib stew, his wife said dramatically, 'Oh, it was a terrible tragedy! The wretched cat ate the whole thing!' Nasreddin whipped the cat up off the floor and put her on the scales. She weighed exactly two okas.

"'My dear wife,' he said, holding the cat out to her, 'if this is the two okas of meat, then where is my cat?'" Ahmad smiled at Amira and Farah. They tried politely to smile back, but an uncomfortable silence descended on the group.

After a few minutes, Amira spoke up: "He is just gone," she said, without looking up. "I don't understand it."

"And he will come back, like I did," Ahmad said.

"He helped make Baghdad's laws and built our school. How can that mean nothing to them?" asked Amira, leaning back. "How can it count for nothing?"

Ahmad followed her gaze up to the apricot tree above them. "Your father is Baghdadi, just like the rest of us. Nothing the army does can change that."

"I think . . . when they look at us, they don't see us. They see only our religion," said Amira. "They see that our clothes are a little different and hear that our Arabic is a bit thicker. They don't care about all we've contributed for hundreds of years. They don't care that we are from here too. It's not enough."

"You *are* enough," said Yusuf. "You're Baghdadi, just like us." Amira's sister scowled at him.

"If that were true they wouldn't kidnap the Jew and leave the Muslim," said Farah. "And if we're no longer Baghdadi, then who are we?"

Ahmad didn't know what to say. He wanted to tell his friend's daughters that he would do anything to help Dawood, to save him, to make Baghdad a home for all Baghdadis. But with a family of his own to protect, he said nothing, and it made him feel all the more angry at his helplessness.

"Why would they take him? My father is a good man," said Amira.

"Because . . ." said Dabriya, appearing from between the trees. She looked as if she had been there for a while. ". . . your father is a very powerful man, and that makes them feel threatened." She looked at Dawood's daughters. "Your father is coming home—he is still protected by his position and by the fact that he is Baghdadi. Don't you think that if they had harmed him, we would know?"

Amira nodded slowly.

"Now go and get yourselves something from kitchen."

Amira stood and pulled her sister to her feet. Yusuf, Emad, and Luma followed them.

"Ahmad," said Dabriya, with a hand on his shoulder.

"I know. There's nothing I can do." He furrowed his brow and shut his eyes.

"Go," whispered Dabriya.

Ahmad stared at her, frozen.

"Join the revolt. Fight to free our brother and our land from the Turks, if that's truly what you want," she said, her eyes flashing green. "Bring us independence from all invaders. And then come back. God, come back to me."

"But—"

"Do you think you can hide anything from me? If you stay in this place, those demons in the forest will destroy you. Memories of Karim will destroy you. So you destroy them first."

A ripple of shock jolted through Ahmad at the mention of Karim's name. "The things I have done," he said. "If you knew."

"You silly man," said Dabriya. "Little happened that you haven't already told me in your sleep."

Ahmad shut his eyes. Surely she could not know.

"And here I am," said Dabriya, "beside you, telling you to do what you must to forgive yourself."

Ahmad stared at his wife. There was nothing more comforting in the world than her compassion. He took Dabriya's hand in both of his. She gave a sad smile and hugged him.

"It's not that I support the English . . ." he said.

"I know," said Dabriya.

". . . but I cannot abandon Dawood. I cannot abandon another brother."

"Karim," said Dabriya, softly. Her heart grew tight every time she thought of Ahmad thrashing as he wept, or screamed, Karim's name. "You want to bring him home, Ahmad. I know."

"And that will only happen when we are free of colonizers, when we decide how Baghdad is ruled."

"Do you think the English will keep that promise?" asked Dabriya.

"What choice do I have but to believe it?" He shrugged.

Dabriya touched his cheek.

"I will come back," he said.

"And I will bear your absence, if it will lighten your load, if it will bring you back to me."

10

DABRIYA HAD ALWAYS BEEN FAMILIAR with upheaval. She was one of those sorts who had grown so accustomed to change that she grew restless when all was calm. She told herself that she wished she could be the kind of person who was content with a calm life, but she knew neither fortune nor choice would allow it, so she lived her curse as if it were a blessing.

When she was little, she and her brothers would sleep wherever their fancy took them—one night on the kitchen floor, the next on the roof. She had told herself it was an adventure, that none of her friends had any choice about where they slept. And she neglected to mention that this was because they all had bedrooms.

When her father's temper twitched at a word he didn't like, she imagined she was a wild animal tamer; she just had to learn to communicate in a way that would keep him thinking he was in control. Oh, God, she longed for him to understand her, but she knew that, for most of the day, she was forgotten amid his daily struggle for work, the state of their home, and her seven other siblings. In those days, she believed that a parent had a finite source of love that must be shared among their children. She would one day grow to hate the memory of such childish thoughts—as if anything could reduce her love for her own three children. Now she tried not to think of all the terrible things she had felt toward her parents when she was young—when her father was afraid and poor and deathly tired of the pressures of an unforgiving world.

Yes, Dabriya felt at home with upheaval, but she had never, not for a single day in her childhood, known what it was to feel secure. She used to think she was doomed to die young; she even fantasized about how poetic her death would be—lost at sea among swelling waves, or offering her life to save someone else, or so sudden and tragic that people would whisper her name in awe for centuries—but such thoughts were banished on the day she first felt a kick in her belly. Some might argue that her change of heart was just as sacrificial, but with none of the melodramatic desire for folklorehood. She grew determined to live, to raise that child, and by God's good word, she would save him from her curse and raise him to know and love stability.

And she succeeded, for a while. But how do you promise security to child who lives through war? Dabriya envied the women of the past, and of the future, who would never know what it was to have no right to raise your child as you wished.

So many things had changed since Emad was born, since Yusuf, and especially since Luma. But for the adaptable, the die-young, the unknowingly selfless Dabriya, there was comfort in the things she knew nobody could change. The sun had always cast shadows of the same color and same length every day. No matter who ruled her land, no matter the war, or the century, or how many of her people they killed, no man could ever change that. And it brought her peace to know that the sun and the shadows were constant, unchangeable, forever.

She didn't know if it was for the stability of a ritual, or just to be contrary, but whenever Ahmad was away, Dabriya would light a candle each Friday, whisper a prayer into it and set it afloat on the river at the bottom of the garden. The first Friday after Ahmad had left to join the British revolt against the Ottomans, Emad found Dabriya on the shore. She jumped as she heard his foot crack a branch.

"Sorry," he whispered. "I wanted to make sure you're all right."

Dabriya sniffed, and gripped her candle guiltily. "I'm fine—I just never expected to be back here again."

Emad nodded. "I don't like him fighting for the English—you know that," he said. "But I pray every minute that he comes home safely."

"That's all I ask, Emad."

"Not in a hundred years could I believe a word those conquerors say," said Emad, shaking his head. "Baba is fighting for our freedom, but we'll walk away with nothing when the English win."

"I hope you're wrong, but right now I don't care, so long as he comes home."

"I don't know how you do it, Mama." Emad sighed. "To allow him to leave again . . ." He paused. "You must be the bravest person I know."

Dabriya scoffed.

"I mean it."

"I am nothing special, Emad. This is what women have always done, but we don't write the history books. We rebuild countries, but the stories always end at the victory, so the men, they never talk of our fight."

"I'm not like that."

"You and Yusuf," said Dabriya, clasping her candle, "you are my hope for the world. You will be the generation that brings justice to our land."

Emad sat down beside his mother. He took the candle from her, and said, "I want that for us, for you. So tell me. Tell me the stories that are forgotten. Tell me who you were before you were Mama."

Dabriya smiled.

11

Your father and i used to live across the road from one another. It was one of those back streets in the middle of the city. There were no houses like this back then. We had no privacy. If you sneezed too loudly, your neighbor would bless you. Your grandfather wasn't an unkind man, understand, but sometimes he let his shame speak for him, and his shame was an ugly character.

One day, my father asked me to leave my game of Baat with my brothers to help him with something, and I huffed about being asked to do something when my brothers were left to play. Now, I don't know how his day had been before that, but my response was the last straw for him. He exploded and yelled so close to me that I could feel his breath on my face. "I don't need you, you need me," he said. "I have other children." Of course, he was right in a sense, but those words uttered in a flash of fury, with no thought to the weight they would carry for his daughter, probably left his mind as soon as he'd said them. But they would never leave mine.

Do not judge him too harshly, yabni. The point is that your father, and his brother—Uncle Tarek—could hear this from across the alley, and their reactions could not have been more different from one another. When I next saw Ahmad, he gave no hint that he had heard what Baba had said to me. He just asked if I wanted to sit on the pontoon bridge or toss mud into the river. . . . We would see who could throw a handful furthest, and in those days I was still the strongest. Tarek, though, said the most awful things. He told me I would never be worth anything next to seven brothers, that my father was right to say those things to me so that I learned my place early on. Then Tarek told me to kiss his boot.

Emad's hands covered his mouth and he shook his head.

Oh, don't be shocked. He was like that. And maybe I would have forgiven him if I'd known of the sickness that would take him. But all I thought of after that day was my revenge.

The next Friday, when Ahmad, Tarek, and their dad went to prayers at Abu Hanifa Mosque, Ahmad waited until Tarek had his nose to the ground and his bottom in the air, and he cut two holes in Tarek's dishdasha—one over each buttock. Oh, we were so cruel to him after that—I think that was your father's first regret, you know. I'd never seen him sob until the day Tarek's cough grew hacking and bloody. We knew it then, we knew we would have to live with how we had cast him out before he died, for one single thing he said to me, most likely out of jealousy. Dabriya sighed.

But that was much later, of course. When he was ten, Ahmad planted his first apricot tree in a patch of earth behind his father's house. In the summer he would carry water from the Tigris each day to water it. That first year he sold every single apricot on the tree. The next year he planted another, and by the fifth year he had filled every patch of that land. By the time we were old enough to marry he had saved enough money to buy this beautiful stretch. Dabriya raised her hands at the earth around her.

We lived a most basic life, Emad, but it was wonderful. Our trees gave us shade and we slept outside all summer. By winter he had built us a small room—his arms were strong even back then. To begin with I was in charge of preparing and planting seeds. We spent three years growing and selling the most delicious fruit, by the grace of this river. By the time you came along, your father had joined the army to bring us in a little more money and I was pretty much running the garden myself. I missed him, of course, but you were good company. And in his absence, I remembered how much I loved him, how lucky I was.

He was so wonderful back then, Emad. I wish you could have seen him, so determined, so sure, so unburdened.

Dabriya cleared her throat.

"It's funny," said Emad, "he doesn't sound like Baba, but I see bits of him in it."

Echoes, yes. The freedom from burdens. Before this war, before blood drenched our shores, before Baghdad was cracked in two like some foreign land, before you were even a thought in our minds, before your father carried all of Baghdad on his back, he was an ordinary kind child, remarkable only for his grace, just another boy called Ahmad.

Part II

12

Winter 1910
Llwynypia, Wales

CARWYN COULD NOT HAVE KNOWN the irreversible effects of his decision to go to the pump-house, rather than head home on the day that English soldiers attacked protestors. It seemed so small, such an insignificant choice at the time, to turn right up the street, instead of left. Maybe if his teacher hadn't been so cruel, maybe if he had forgotten his jacket, maybe if he'd known his mother was stewing cawl that night. But he was a boy of twelve and, like most boys of that age, he thought his actions were of little consequence.

So, when his father bent over him, at the foot of the fountain as the British Army attacked, it wasn't really Carwyn's fault that Iestyn received a truncheon to the back of the head. It wasn't really Carwyn's fault that when his father carried him home in his arms, reeling from a blow to the head, he tripped over debris from the ransacked shops and fell to his knees among shards of glass and wood. No, none of it was really Carwyn's fault. But for the rest of his life he would pay for that one small decision, turning right, instead of left.

In the aftermath of the clashes with the police, it was difficult for the injured to seek any treatment. If a doctor treated Iestyn for a truncheon to the head, or bits of shop-front in his knees, he knew he would be arrested for instigating the riot, no matter how he had acquired the injuries. So his wife, Mari, did some jagged sewing, the stitches turning neater after Iestyn passed out. Carwyn, still unsure what it all meant, skipped school to tend to his father while Mari was out looking for clothes to wash and floors to scrub. And—out of boredom or fervor—Iestyn would relentlessly hum the quietly hopeful Welsh hymn that begged for his pure heart. It was such a sorrowful melody that neither of them ever tired of it.

By the time they realized infection had set in, it was too late for even the neighborhood veterinarian to save much of Iestyn's leg. And so, as many had before him, Iestyn Evans was reduced to two dates carved on stone, the numbers much closer to each other than was rightly fair.

When Mari married Robert five months later, Carwyn knew she had had little choice. Robert insisted that seven years of education were more than a miner's son needed; his boys had worked the Cornish mines since the age of seven, as he never tired of saying. And with that, Carwyn left behind his numbers and letters at the schoolhouse and became another boy of the mines.

He wished he could say that his mother was happy, in the beginning at least. But in all the selfless ways that Iestyn had brought a quiet happiness to the home, Robert did the mirror opposite. His words were seldom unaccompanied by spittle. He believed it was not grace but duty that led his wife to wash his clothes, to feed his children, to clean his misfired shit off the privy. He received thanks with spite and never returned them.

Carwyn spent little time with his two new stepbrothers, except on their shared walk to and from the mine. All he observed—with gloom and relief in equal measure—was that they seemed just as unhappy with their new life as he was. For all three Englishmen, the village and its mine were full of quips that excluded them, but Carwyn, at least, had language on his side.

Apart from a handful of perfunctory mining words and its resemblance to vague memories of Robert's grandmother's language, Welsh was entirely foreign to Robert and his sons. It was no surprise, then, that he came home one day, puce in the face, and declared a ban on the language *under his roof.* It was a futile rule, with a high penalty. Carwyn grew used to the daily thrashings, while his mother took the occasional elbow to the chest whenever she got in the way, usually while insisting that Carwyn needed more time to get used to not speaking Welsh.

Twelve years of school and he can't speak English? was Robert's usual reply, the number of years he furnished for dramatic effect corresponding with the shade of purple he turned. No matter how hard Carwyn tried to please Robert, the beatings were inevitable, so he stopped trying and instead made a game of his misery. One day, when his stepfather antagonized him over supper for staring at him, Carwyn saw his chance.

"What are you looking at, boy?"

"Moron," replied Carwyn. Robert raised his fist, but Mari held his arm before he could take a swing.

"It's Welsh for carrot, Robert. He was looking at the carrots."

"Think you're so clever, boy?" said Robert, but he dropped his fist. Profuse apologies and corrections would follow and, although everyone knew it was a deliberate slip, to Carwyn it was a victory that made life bearable.

When his half-brother Adam was born three years later, everyone thought it would be the biggest surprise of 1914, but ten days later, the same government that had given the order that had caused Carwyn's father to be maimed—stealing the right to strike from every Welsh miner—declared Britain at war with Germany. Whether it was empathy with Belgian refugees, or simply that Wales desperately needed a cause, Carwyn was surprised by how quickly Welsh hearts were won over by the English war. These were the very men who had come to his Welsh valley and thrown out demands in a foreign language. Now the same valley was only too happy to support their war. It made no sense to Carwyn. Why should Llwynypia care about what went on in Westminster? Yet from sunrise to sunset, all anyone discussed was the war. Some of the miners even spoke excitedly about the day they would enlist. Maybe he was biased because of Robert's anglicization of his home, but Carwyn didn't care. And he stopped telling anyone who'd listen that the war had nothing to do with Wales. He even tried to avoid provoking Robert, though he wasn't particularly successful.

Carwyn awoke on his sixteenth birthday in the summer of 1914, and noticed all at once how his arms hung much wider than he recalled, and he had to lower his head to get through the doorways. Perhaps that was why Robert hadn't hit him for months, though Carwyn was sure that with the right motivation, Robert could be tempted into aiming a few punches his way.

It transpired, though, that Robert had been working on non-physical ways to disrupt Carwyn's life. When his stepson knocked over a pitcher, Robert pushed Carwyn against the wall and spat in his ear, "I think it's time you make yourself useful, don't you?" Carwyn turned his face away from Robert, who grabbed his jaw and pulled it around.

"What do you mean? I'm already mining twice as much as any of you," said Carwyn, breathing heavily.

"No, you imbecile. Serve your country in this war."

"That's your country, not mine," said Carwyn, peeling Robert's hand off his face.

"Same thing. You're no use to your mother and me here. You're just a sad reminder to her of your father." Carwyn shoved Robert by the shoulders, sending him four paces back.

"You think I stay here out of choice? I'm here because I know exactly how you'd treat my mother—or brother—as soon as I was out of the way."

Robert said nothing.

"Too scared to beat me, aren't you, now that you might actually get hit back?" Carwyn could have sworn he saw the man's blood boil as the color rose in his jowls.

Robert stepped toward Carwyn and whispered. "I promise you this, boy, I'll have you sent to that war if it's the last
thing I ever do." Carwyn pushed him away, laughed and whispered an insult he knew Robert wouldn't understand as he left
the room.

Robert's threats were not idle. Ten days after the war
began, he ventured out to a recruitment station with the aim
of bribing a boy to sign Carwyn up, but when confronted by
a crowd of uniforms it occurred to him that he had no idea
what personal information they required, and that perhaps he
shouldn't draw attention to himself: What if they tried to get
him to enlist? He turned on his heel and left the street, furnish-
ing his walk with an exaggerated limp.

Instead, Robert hounded Mari relentlessly to send her son
away, turning foul for hours when she refused him. For weeks
he tried to convince her, his demeanor bouncing from bully to
juvenile, until one day Mari told him to send one of his own
sons to war. That brought her a swift slap to the face, but Robert did not broach the subject again.

It occurred to Mari that Robert might have intended her
to find the blade concealed in a pocket of his mining clothes,
but it was a chance she could not afford to take. So in the end,
Robert was granted his wish when the only person in the land
with the power to convince Carwyn to go to war did just that.

Carwyn held his little brother in his hands, trying not to look
at the mossy sleeves of his uniform. They would never be his
arms while he wore that color. His head would never be his
own while it carried that cap. He kissed his mother's cheek,
and joined the other recruits of the village. And he told himself, as did every gentle man forced into service, that he would
be a kind soldier, that he would be different. He told himself
whatever lie he needed to hear, because what kind of man
joins the army that killed his father?

13

Summer 1916
Northeastern Arabian Desert

A GUST BLEW SAND ACROSS Ahmad's face. It took his eyes a few seconds to adjust to the peach haze of dawn and his skin, tight and dry, almost cracked as he squinted away from the horizon. He stood, and a shower of sand rained down from his clothes. A hundred sleeping blanketed bodies surrounded him, dotted about like fallen pupae.

It took him a moment to remember where he was. It had been much easier to find his way into the ranks of the rebellion than he had imagined. Dawood's wife, Naima, had known exactly whom to leave word with, and four days later, Ahmad was questioned by Abu Iman in an old guffa storehouse upstream. It was a rather cursory procedure. Abu Iman told him that recruits who had served in the Ottoman military were to skip the basic infantry training to hasten their arrival in the field. The following night, when the sky was at its blackest, Ahmad stepped silently from his bed, kissed the floor and the angels, held his wife, and shook each of his children gently, staying true to his promise that he would rouse them before he left.

When Luma awoke the confusion and parting brought her to tears. Yusuf held her in his bed and stroked her brow until the sun had risen and begun to cast light and long, drooping shadows, when she finally fell asleep.

By the time Ahmad arrived in the Old City, dawn prayer was being called across the minarets; he took two right turns and three left from Moshi's Café and met an unnamed man in a side street. He thought that in the entire region of the Vilayat of Baghdad there could be no street that was shadier and more suspicious-looking than this. It would be the first place he would search for any untoward dealings. But his dawn enrollment was straightforward, and that was how, just weeks later, Ahmad found himself marching through the desert every morning, with a hundred men, not one of them able to numb the absence of his sons, his daughter, his wife.

Ahmad took a gulp of the chalky air. He would see them again. He would make sure of it.

"Salim," Ahmad whispered to his neighbor, "wake up."

Salim grunted. Ahmad stood slowly, and darted between rows of sleeping comrades toward the designated latrine area. When he returned, the camp had started to stir.

"Morning," said Salim.

"Morning," Ahmad replied. "Yabaa!" he exclaimed, shaking his head. "I have sand everywhere. *Everywhere*."

Salim grinned. "Welcome to the club. Now you know why they call it the crack of dawn."

Ahmad grimaced.

"Attention!" shouted Major Downer, striding down the rows of men. Ahmad tried to keep a straight face, which he was getting better at. He couldn't deny that the major had excellent Arabic, but his accent was still one of the most amusing and strangely disarming he'd ever heard. He particularly enjoyed hearing the major roll his Rs far too long and from too deep within his mouth. "You have ten minutes to pack and collect your breakfast," his commander continued.

Ahmad rolled up his blankets and stared at Salim wrestling with his own shrub of twisted blankets. "They're never going to fit on your load if you dance with them," he teased.

A heavy-set bearded giant of a man pushed past Salim, kicking sand into his blankets and bag. "Oy!" called Salim after him, but the man was already meters away.

"Probably too scared to take me on," muttered Salim, shaking sand out of his hair.

"Aren't we all?" said Ahmad.

The major marched to the front of the encampment, facing the rows of rebels, each busying himself with blankets or wolfing down unleavened bread. "Brothers," he called out. As silence fell, he continued, "It is with great sadness that I must report that Abu Jirair, Abu Yassin, and Abu Mahmud lost their lives in yesterday's reconnaissance mission."

Ahmad noted with interest how the major used their patronyms rather than their given names. Maybe he should give him more credit. The major called for a moment's silence and removed the circular rope agal keeping his ghutra head-covering in place, holding it to his stomach as he stared at the ground. Salim and Ahmad exchanged stares. Maybe he was giving him the right amount of credit after all.

The giant gruff scoffed, which seemed reasonable to Ahmad.

"Right then," said the major. "Let's get on."

Within minutes the troops were marching north. An hour into his first morning desert marching, Ahmad was struck by the familiarity of it all. The march, the heat, the orders. He'd expected the Arab Revolt—as the Major called it—to be more collaborative, or at least to differ from his role in the Ottoman Army. They had no idea where they were headed or what their target would be. Was there a target? After four hours of stumbling through indistinctive dunes, the sun was burning his head and his uniform was soaked. "Is our trudging through the desert really the most efficient use of time and energy? I can't even tell where we're going," he puffed to Salim.

"I think we're headed south-west now." His friend was looking at the sun.

"So we have no information as to what we're doing?" he asked.

Salim shrugged. "What did you expect?"

"I don't know," said Ahmad. "Perhaps to have a say."

"I've tried talking to the major about my ideas, but he laughs them off."

"Is that so, *Captain* Salim?" Ahmad smiled.

"Laugh if you like," said Salim, and Ahmad reddened a little. "I know how young I look, and I'm terrible with a rifle. But I was raised on my father's military stories—sometimes they went on for days."

"The battles or the stories?" said Ahmad.

Salim chuckled. "Both."

"Your father can't like you joining the English, then," said Ahmad, "if he was a military man."

"Yes and no," said Salim. "He's glad I'm finally going to fight, but he's not sure it's for the right side. You have to understand, Basra has been swarming with Englishmen for a while now."

"What's that like?"

"Well, they're entitled fools, of course, but the Indians are pleasant enough—most of the English here are sepoys anyway."

"Not the ones in charge though," said Ahmad, tilting his head toward the major.

"Not the ones in charge." Salim nodded.

Both because he felt a little guilty for teasing Salim, and because his curiosity was piqued, Ahmad asked: "If you were the major, what would you have us do?"

"Stop the trains," replied Salim, gulping down water from his leather flask. "It's all about the trains."

Ahmad cocked his head expectantly. "Go on."

"Well, it's all the Ottomans talk about—their treasured railroad, spanning the length of Anatolia and Mesopotamia? If we take that, they lose all their supplies, reinforcements, and bragging rights," said Salim. He grinned. "You have to admit I make a good point."

"You do, but sadly for us, they don't seem interested in our input. I'd like a train to do all this marching for me, though," said Ahmad, between breaths. "I'm out of practice."

"Think about it," said Salim. "Imagine how soon we could all go home if someone would just take me seriously."

Once the sun had given way to a petrol-black sky, dotted with silver bullet holes, the troops set up their encampment for the night. With stomachs full of tashrib broth Ahmad, Salim, and the rest of the group readied themselves for bed.

"Just one minute," called the major, raising his voice. "Attention, please! Tomorrow will be the day of our next operation." A chorus of noise erupted, which echoed endlessly over the empty dunes.

"Silence!" commanded Major Downer. "I needed to keep the details of the attack to myself due to the recent infiltration of our missions—I want to keep you, our men, safe." More muttering broke out.

"Attention!" called Major Downer. "Tomorrow, we'll be heading east two hours just before dawn to attack and divert an Ottoman garrison that is sending troops on a trajectory toward our men south of here."

"You mean we're still near Baghdad?" said Salim, under his breath. "Have we been killing ourselves in the desert just going in circles?"

The major raised his voice above the commotion: "We will then occupy their location to prevent them resuming their trajectory. You will be glad to hear . . ." he said, and waited for quiet, ". . . that we outnumber them by two soldiers to one, and both sides are aware that our weapons are far more sophisticated."

A static buzz of whispering broke out. Ahmad heard laughter and muttered exchanges of relief. He had to admit that their numbers were a relief to him. With any luck, the Ottomans would retreat immediately. He did not know what he would do if he came face to face with his old unit, and he didn't want to find out.

"So, what made you join us?" asked Salim.

Ahmad told him about his guilt over Dawood's abduction, about the new promise of a free Baghdad. He left out the part about Karim: he could share the story of Dawood's abduction, and maintain his image as a decent man. What good would it do for him to talk about the worst thing he had ever done? "That was the moment at which I realized what I was a part of, and what it would cost me." He meant it, of course, but he had exaggerated his sincerity, his singular, moral motivation, and it helped him to face the day. With so much guilt what did a little deception matter?

"The call of a better world?" said Salim.

"I suppose," said Ahmad, thoughtfully. "But mostly now it's fear of what kind of world I helped to create, that I spent years serving." That part he meant. Because, live or die, he had to ensure that the Baghdad he left for his children would never allow them to be ripped from their homes.

"They made it easy for you to make up your mind," said Salim.

"Yes and no," said Ahmad, shrugging. "I won't lie to you—I don't care about the English and their grand schemes. I just know I have to do something, and if our aims align . . ."

Salim laughed.

"I only mean their war is nothing to me. I have my family, my friend to think about. It was my army that took Dawood away, the men I'd fought with. And if the English want to return Baghdad to us then I have no problem fighting beside them."

"No, no, I understand," said Salim.

"You do?"

"Yes, except I've not really thought about Ottomans or English, or anything except ending the war."

"Is that why you joined?" asked Ahmad. "To end the war?"

"Now you make me sound ridiculous . . . but you aren't far off," said Salim. Ahmad raised his eyebrows. "Like all stories of impulse, mine's about a woman."

"Like many of the best stories, too," added Ahmad, with a smile.

"She promised she would marry me when the war was over. So I'm . . . helping it along," said Salim. He pulled out a handkerchief and wiped his forehead. "And I suppose returning with a few stories of gallantry won't hurt."

"I'm sure there's nobility in that story too," said Ahmad, "in its own way."

Salim laughed.

"Let's make tomorrow count then," said Ahmad, shutting his eyes. "For the sake of your bride."

"For Ayesha," said Salim, his eyes glinting yellow. "Goodnight, Abu Emad," he said to Ahmad.

"Goodnight, brother."

14

ON THE MORNING OF THE battle, nerves mounted with each millimeter of light that emerged above the dunes. Anxious chatter hummed above the hundred marching men, who were buoyed by the reassurance of their imminent victory.

"Brothers," called the major, as the horizon edged from black to navy blue. "This is the last point at which we are concealed from the enemy camp." He surveyed his unit. "I'm proud to be leading you over this dune, brothers. Take a few minutes to prepare yourselves. Remember to stay alert, and to stick to your formation." Then, drawing a fist to his chest, he said forcefully, "Also remember, this battle is already ours."

Ahmad and Salim sat together silently. They emptied their water flasks, adjusted their uniforms, and then it was time to go. The hundred pupae stood to attention and followed their major up a steep dune. Salim's boots slipped clumsily as he scrambled up the loose sand and Ahmad put a hand on his shoulder.

"For Ayesha," he whispered, and Salim let out a heavy breath.

As he neared the top of the dune, Ahmad noticed the troops in front of him were slowing at the apex. He rounded to the top of the dune, pushing to keep those in front of him moving. Then he spotted what had caused them to slow as they clambered out of the pit. The horizon was eclipsed by the silhouettes of soldiers racing toward them, mounted on enormous Arabian stallions.

"Oh, my God," whispered Salim.

15
Summer 1916
Basra

"YOU'VE HEARD WHAT THE ENGLISH are calling it now?" Ayesha asked, lowering a sack of sugar onto her cart. "The Venice of the East." She sniggered. "They put a little painting of our river on a piece of paper and send it out to their relatives to show how beautifully European it looks, hoping they'll all come to visit their new conquest." She stared at Abdelmajid's blank face poking over the top of his counter. He stared back, his jowls wobbling. At first he looked shocked, then—realizing that was not the anticipated reaction—gave a loud, overzealous laugh.

"Exactly," said Ayesha, slightly puzzled. "Someone needs to tell these people that the real Venice is actually closer to them." Abdelmajid nodded.

"Now, we've got the olive oil, butters, aloe vera, and sugar," said Ayesha, counting them off on her fingers. "Did you manage to find me sandalwood and lemongrass oil?"

"Yes, my lady, only the best quality too," replied Abdelmajid, turning his portly figure around to search his shelves. "So the business is going well?" he asked.

"I'd hardly call it a business," replied Ayesha with a smile, "but I think the women of *Venice* appreciate it."

"Well," said Abdelmajid, handing her two small vials, "it is very clear that you have a brilliant mind for trade." He gave her a toady smile. A bead of sweat rolled down his temple as he watched Ayesha's pale hand withdraw into her cloak. He tried to mask his panic by pretending to adjust his tarboosh, but it fell to the floor, lifting the remaining shreds of hair atop his head. With a swift movement, he bent below the counter, patted the hairs back into place and replaced the tarboosh. When he stood, Ayesha was examining the reed basket of ginger roots beside the counter.

"With a brain like yours, you might even have a real job one day. Maybe you'll become a merchant, like me," said Abdelmajid, nodding magnanimously.

"Yes," said Ayesha slowly, counting out two silver twenty-kurus coins and placing them on the counter. She lifted the handle of her cart, then turned to face Abdelmajid and said, hiding a smirk, "But I'm happy with my woman's job, thank you. I don't think I could manage to do what you do." She pushed the door open and went out into the street.

Ayesha pulled her cart along the earthy route home, passing the endless oak and stone porticos that had charmed locals and visitors for centuries. She tugged her supplies alongside the Shatt al-Arab river and stared furiously at the water as she passed a group of British men outside Old Basra Villa, a spectacular domed building that was now adorned with tricolor flags and notices advertising a social club.

A man in sandy trousers called out jubilantly in English as he exited the villa. He turned to face the building, laughing at a friend who followed him, and walked backwards, coming to a halt in Ayesha's path. She glowered at him. Whatever he was saying, it didn't need to be shouted in the middle of the town, and he certainly should not just strut around getting in other people's way.

The British man said something and raised a hand that seemed apologetic, but it made little difference to her. She did her best impression of an English curtsy and circled her outstretched fingers in the air regally, waiting for the man to move. His cheeks turned pink and he muttered something before he walked away.

"Imbecile," said Ayesha, storming off. Her face had turned red and she was halfway between fury and embarrassment. She spun around to protest the man's behavior, but he had been joined by his friend, so instead she gritted her teeth and continued on her way, growing angrier at herself with each step for having said nothing.

The cheek of him, though. This place was loved by visitors as the City of Shanasheel long before the English had arrived and decided it had to be described in European terms of beauty. She crossed narrow arced bridges and ducked under riverside branches, and was still muttering to herself when she reached her grandmother's door.

"What is it this time, dear?" asked her grandmother, with a smile.

"Oh, just the English, acting like they discovered a new land, renaming everything dear to us."

"I should have guessed that's what was bothering you."

"I'm so predictable, aren't I?" Ayesha sighed.

"No. Never that, as you well know," her grandmother replied, tenderly cupping Ayesha's chin. "Now stop trying for compliments and tell me about your purchases. Did you find everything?"

"I have to return for the henna in two days."

"Then let us unload and begin."

For four hours, Ayesha and her grandmother boiled sugar, oil, and butter, pounded apricot seeds, and ground dried figs. They made powder from lemon skins, and crushed the pulp of watermelon. The herbal creams, fruity skin polishes, and fragrant oils filled their home with scents thickly sweet, sharp and bitter, aromatic and calming in turn.

"You know I heard from Salim's father," said Ayesha's grandmother, with a sideways glance.

"Oh?" said Ayesha, staring down at the thick gloop of sugar paste she was stirring. "What did Abu Salim want?"

"His son, the carpenter, joined the rebels, but I suppose you already know that?"

"You suppose right," laughed Ayesha, wiping her neck with a cream and lilac handkerchief. "I told him not to go, but you know how men can be."

"Well, you did say you wouldn't marry him until the war is over."

"Who wants a wedding when the city is in chaos?"

"All I'm saying is that a boy who goes to war for you is a boy worth marrying before the war is over."

Ayesha smiled at her grandmother. "Well, that is a bit of a contradiction, Bibi."

Abdelmajid always knew when Ayesha was about to enter his shop, and whenever he heard the alternating squeak and trundle of her cart rolling toward his building, he dipped his fingertips into a pot of Levantine olive oil and with almost elegant routine, slicked his mustache with a curl, and flattened the rebellious hair on either side of his head. Whatever oil that remained he would use to pat down the overgrown hairs that spread from right to left over his bare crown. Occasionally he even had time to perch himself on his stool with one hand jauntily placed on the counter, a British newspaper in the other.

Today, of all days, he made sure to have time for jaunty angles. His hair was slick before he heard the cart rattling toward his shop, and as he sat on his stool, his nose was in a newspaper, but his eyes were focused on the entrance to his shop.

"Salam, Abdelmajid," called out Ayesha, cheerfully. "Not interrupting you, am I?"

"No, no, just finishing today's paper." He smiled, folding it briskly.

"I won't take up much of your time. I just need that henna. I hope it arrived?"

"Take a seat while I fetch it." He indicated a low stool below a shelf of attar perfumes.

"I'm happy to stand," said Ayesha, and Abdelmajid disappeared behind a curtain to the back of his shop. As Ayesha browsed the attar curiously, she heard low, frantic murmuring behind the curtain, though she was soon distracted by the waves of rich scents coming from the large vials. She sniffed each in turn, lost in the realization that each smelled different yet similar to the last. She shut her eyes and wondered which scent Salim would wear on the day of their marriage.

"Here we have it," said Abdelmajid, ducking past the curtain. "The very best quality too." He patted the paper parcel and a small cloud of khaki powder puffed out, covering his fingers with dust. Ayesha fished a coin from a folded leather pouch and placed it on the counter. Abdelmajid seemed to hesitate, but Ayesha pretended she hadn't noticed.

"I'll just take that, shall I?" she said, nodding at the paper package. Abdelmajid held out the henna in his palms. Ayesha pinched it with her fingertips so that she ran no risk of accidentally touching his hand. She took the parcel, and felt a palm clutch her wrist.

"Ayesha, I have to say something," murmured Abdelmajid.

"Let go of me," said Ayesha, even quieter, glaring up at Abdelmajid from beneath thick arched eyebrows.

"I just want to—"

"Do not touch me. Let go."

Abdelmajid's eyes widened and he released her wrist.

"Marry me, Ayesha. I've never wanted to marry anyone else." Ayesha was already pulling her cart toward the door.

"Ayesha!" he called.

"This is inappropriate, Abdelmajid, you should not approach me like this. I've told you before that I'm promised to another and seek nothing else."

"But we're perfect for each other. We're both modern businesspeople. I can teach you about my business and you can help me run it."

"Perhaps you should help me run my beauty business," said Ayesha, turning back to him, her eyes flashing.

"It doesn't have the same potential—"

"You're really not as business-minded as you think. I have told you my answer, and it won't change, no matter how many times you ask. Now please never speak of this again."

"But you're always so nice to me," said Abdelmajid. "Because I am polite it means I want to marry you?" She shook her head and laughed. "Do not fool yourself, you silly man. I would never marry someone like you." Ayesha avoided looking at Abdelmajid, whose back had shot upright at the sound of her laughter. He examined her closely, his eyes scanning her body, from her flushed face to her raised hands, down to her feet as they span around and raced toward the door.

16

Summer 1916
Northeastern Arabian Desert

"Oh, God, oh, God," yelled Salim, as the sound of hoofs on sand grew louder. The bearded giant man elbowed his ear as he clambered past him toward the front of the charge. He felt a knee dig into the back of his leg and a fist pulling on his forearm.

"Get off me!" he roared, wrenching himself free.

"Salim, it's me," a voice said. Salim turned to Ahmad's face. The two were jostled forward in the charge, and the grip on Salim's arm returned, firmer.

"They'll destroy us," gasped Salim, stumbling on, his eyes set on the approaching Ottoman horses. "Oh, God."

"This isn't the time for fear, Salim," said Ahmad, swinging his rifle to his front. "We can still win this, you know we can. Let them come to us, tire out their horses, and rely on their swords."

"All that will do is delay the inevitable."

"Focus, Salim," said Ahmad. "We can do this."

The line of cavalry slowed, then came to a halt.

"Watch out, brothers. They'll charge at any moment," called out Ahmad. His head jolted with each pulse of his heart as he waited for the rush. He turned to Salim, but he was gone. He stood on tiptoe but still couldn't find his friend in the crowd.

"We still outnumber those men," yelled Ahmad, to the men at his sides, each braced to run, with their rifles drawn.

"They're only on horses because they're scared to face us down here with their puny guns."

A sea of legs and hoofs began sprinting at them.

Ahmad would have liked to say that, in that moment, he thought of Dawood's safe return, of Dabriya and her eyes, which alternated like the two seasons of Baghdad, of her hips that he had to touch once more before he died. He'd like to claim that he was inspired by thoughts of Yusuf, of Luma, of Emad, of everything they could be, if only the world would let them.

But that was never the case. Not once during a single battle of his life did he think of his family, his city, or his future. He didn't think of much at all, except of shooting, winning, surviving. He charged forward, and felt the gust of his hundred brothers running beside him. He heard the continuous release of gunshots on both sides, and saw two men fall from their horses.

"Accuracy, men!" he yelled. "Pick off as many as you can before they reach us." Ahmad fired his rifle at a mounted soldier, who flopped sideways off his horse and to the ground. He kneeled down, hit another in the neck, then ran forward to his right and knocked off another two.

And as he took aim, he looked, but he saw only targets. The pulsing squirts from his second victim's neck and the intestines that had webbed over the side of a horse as his bayonet struck another target, emptying him of his insides, these were things that no longer shocked Ahmad. Not there.

He heard a whimper from his left and saw a young man, only a few years older than Emad, his hands over his ears.

"Get your gun up!" said Ahmad, pulling on the boy's elbow. "Hey, you'll get yours—" He heard a whistle and saw the pellet slice through the boy's left temple and out of the right, a spray of scarlet shooting to the sand. Ahmad dropped to the ground. Two riderless horses galloped past him. He took the young man's gun and stood. He aimed a shot at a soldier fumbling with his rifle, who rolled off the back of his mount. Two large blasts exploded behind Ahmad, somewhere in the distance, but, looking around, he saw nothing out of the ordinary for a battle. He surveyed the scene—around forty horses remained in front of him. He rolled onto his back to look behind him and saw haphazard lines of rebels, firing, reloading, and stepping over scores of bodies, some moving and groaning, others not. Three mounted soldiers had made it to the rebels' line, their kilij swords drawn. Ahmad shot one, and saw the giant rebel fighter stick his bayonet into the other two almost routinely, tugging each man off his horse as he withdrew his weapon.

Ahmad rolled back onto his front, reloaded his rifle and emptied it of its rounds. One soldier fell off his horse, his face promptly crushed by a hoof to the nose, sending blood and brain pulp flying. Ahmad heard a whistle and felt a searing heat on the left side of his head. His vision blurred and his hearing only worked in pulses. The gunshots seemed to grow distant and then they stopped altogether.

17

Summer 1916
Near Ahmad and Dabriya's home,
the outskirts of Baghdad

YUSUF COULDN'T BELIEVE SHE HAD agreed to meet him. He had always found Amira difficult to read: she said so little, and even less since her father had been taken. But here she was.

"You don't get seasick, do you?" Yusuf asked, as she appeared between the date palms at the end of his garden. He could have kicked himself. Surely he could have come up with a better opener than that. He gritted his teeth to burn off some of his embarrassment.

"You look nice, I like your bangles," he said.

Amira smiled. "I've never really been on a guffa trip before," she said. "Well, only to cross the river, but that hardly counts."

"You'll love it," said Yusuf. "It's the best way to see Baghdad. Here," he said, beckoning her. He led her through the rows of date palms to a small patch of riverbank where the guffa was lashed. He'd arranged the watermelons in rings around the edge of the coracle, layering them on top of each other. The flood of the previous winter had guaranteed a bad summer harvest, mitigated only by the extra seeds that Dabriya had preserved from before the flood. Many of the fruits were undersized and his guffa was much emptier than it had been on previous years. He'd left an empty space in the center, and on one side he'd fashioned a seat and back rest from the largest watermelons he'd found in the garden. He stood on the edge of the riverbank, his sandals holding the lip of the boat in place, and pointed at the boat.

Amira tightened her veil over her shoulder and stepped into the guffa. It wobbled, and she grabbed Yusuf's forearm, then sat down quickly before taking a seat. His skin felt warm where she had touched it. He turned away, grabbed the long paddle from the riverbank and pushed the vessel into the river, the waters slapping against the side as the guffa forced its way into the current.

When they were children, Yusuf had done most of the talking, chattering endlessly through the games Amira had invented. She would usually stay silent for much of his narration before offering a perceptive addition or one-word quip. He didn't know when it had changed, but Yusuf—whose usual curse was to speak without thinking—now found it hard to talk in front of her without revising his thoughts, checking them for potential embarrassment.

"What did you tell your mother?" he asked.

"That I was going downstream," said Amira, "so not exactly a lie."

Yusuf laughed. "Do you think she would have forbidden you to come?" he asked.

"She keeps finding reasons to tell me that I'm a woman now," said Amira, smirking.

"What are you? Fourteen? I think you've got some life left in you," laughed Yusuf.

"Well, I don't think it's entirely unconnected to us staying in a house with two boys."

"Two *men*, you mean," said Yusuf, thumping his chest.

Amira smiled. "Don't you think your mother also would have forbidden you to take me on your delivery trip?" she asked.

"Good point," said Yusuf, "though Mama sort of lost the will to discipline us when Baba went missing." He bit his lip. "Sorry," he said, "I didn't think."

"It's all right."

"Listen, my father made it back once before and so will yours. He's much more powerful and well connected."

"That's probably why he was sent away in the first place, don't you think?"

"Your baba is the most persuasive and adaptable person I've ever met. Trust me, he knows how to handle whatever situation he's in."

Amira frowned. "Well, show me how this is done, then," she said, nodding at the guffa.

"It's pretty much as you see it. Paddle against the water or steer using the riverbed—hold that branch back, can you?" He pointed to an upcoming tree. Amira stood on tiptoe and the boat wobbled. Yusuf dug his paddle into the riverbed and spun them around the narrow corner. He tried not to watch her too closely, but when she moved, her bangles clinked and her braids swung beneath her veil, their copper clasps catching his eye. That wasn't all he saw in Amira, though. Her sadness when she gazed at the shore, he knew that look too, and something about the unmistakable abandonment she endured made him feel understood, in a way that neither innocent Luma nor withdrawn Emad ever could.

But once in a while, when the foliage fluttered in the whispers of the river, or when a bird landed on the boat, Yusuf thought he saw Amira's eyes turn a little brighter. As he navigated a bend, she stood up in wonder as they passed a prancing hoopoe couple, curtains of pink and orange petals that dipped their tassels into the river, and date palms that were so unbending they seemed to stare back sternly if either child dared look at them.

"He's here, Mama," shouted a boy from the shore—he was so small that it seemed bizarre for him to be running so surely. "Mama!" he repeated, "The watermelon boy is here." The child ran to the edge of the shore and placed two woven baskets in front of him. "Six, please," he said, as Yusuf spun the boat to shore. Amira and Yusuf lifted six bulging watermelons into the baskets gently, and the boy dropped three nickel coins into Yusuf's palm.

"See you next time," said Yusuf, with a wave, as he pushed off with his paddle. The boy waved as he pulled in vain at a basket's handle.

Yusuf and Amira continued down the Tigris, stopping at marble-statue riverbanks with intricately carved houses like the ones they had heard about in *The One Thousand and One Nights* stories, and overgrown gardens with accidental bougainvillea blooming over the riverbank.

It was when the afternoon call for prayer was rippling down the river that, having reached the wilderness that marked the end of his deliveries, Yusuf edged too close to a turn and the boat scraped to a halt. He took the hem of his thobe, twisted it, and tucked it into his belt. He jumped out of the guffa into the river on the shore-side, and—carefully avoiding the reeds—dug his bare feet into the muddy basin to push the vessel free. When the base of the boat made a wet bubbling noise, Yusuf heard Amira titter.

"That was the *boat*," he said pointedly.

"If you say so . . ."

"Hello?"

Yusuf jumped. He turned to see a man walking toward the shoreline, holding a glass of tea. He wore a thobe and a ghutra, but neither could mask his reddened cheeks or the exotically colored hair that peeked out at his temples. Yusuf's mouth fell open, and then he smiled.

"Didn't mean to make you jump," said the foreigner.

"You speak Arabic?" asked Yusuf, surprised.

"All part of the job."

"So . . . you're a soldier?" asked Amira.

"Clever girl."

"*Woman*, according to my mother." She smirked. "You don't look like a soldier. Why are you all the way up here?" The man tapped his nose.

"What does that mean?" said Yusuf, tapping his own nose.

"It means it's none of your business," laughed the soldier.

"And how come you have orange hair?" said Yusuf.

The soldier flipped two first fingers at Yusuf and muttered something under his breath.

"Excuse me!" shouted Amira. "Don't be rude." The soldier's cheeks turned even redder.

"What do you mean?" said Yusuf.

"That," said Amira, holding up her first two fingers, "is really rude. I saw some soldiers do it in Basra when I went with Baba."

"I—er, it's not *that* rude," said the soldier.

"Yes, it is," said Amira flatly.

"Well, I'm sorry about that, just don't call my hair orange." Amira pouted. "Can I help you with your boat?"

"It's not a boat, it's a guffa," said Amira. "And we've freed it from the mud anyway."

The soldier nodded. "Very well," he said. He turned to leave, but stopped and asked, "Let me give you some tea to make it up. Please, I feel badly now."

Yusuf shrugged and looked at Amira. "I'm actually quite thirsty," he whispered, "and I'm not offended, really."

"You should be. They like using that sign on us, thinking we don't know what it means."

"But I'm *really* thirsty," he said. Amira sighed.

"All right," she said, and turning to the soldier, "We accept."

Yusuf stepped back into the guffa and pushed it upstream slightly, avoiding the shallow waters by prodding the space in front of it with his paddle. The soldier stepped forward, helped to pull the boat in and lashed it to some reeds.

He introduced himself as Harry, a name at which they tried their best not to laugh.

"Wrigley's?" he asked, holding out a finger-sized box to Yusuf and Amira. Yusuf stuck out his lip but Amira took one, split it in half, and passed a piece to Yusuf.

"You'll like it," she said. Yusuf chewed on the Wrigley's with a smile, and Harry led them a few paces to a wool blanket on a green verge. He poured them two cups of tea.

"I'm always prepared for tea," he said. "It's not quite the same as the tea back home, but it's the best I've found."

Yusuf looked down at his cup. "There's something wrong with it," he said. "The water's muddy."

"No." Harry laughed. "It's got milk in it." Yusuf stared at him incredulously. "Give it a try." He winked.

"It's nice," said Yusuf, sipping. "But I'm so hot that I'd enjoy it even if it was mud."

"Try this." Harry reached into his pocket and produced two spherical red candies in clear wrappers. Amira and Yusuf each took one, and popped them into their mouths.

"Haram!" exclaimed Yusuf, shutting his eyes. "Don't let me eat such a candy when I will never be able to eat it again." Harry laughed, and Yusuf grinned, pleased with himself.

Amira and Yusuf remained on the overgrown bank with the undercover soldier, whom they taught crude curses in Baghdadi and Jewish Arabic. He told them about the parties and theaters sweeping across Basra with the arrival of the British, how local businesses were bringing in more than double the usual profit, and of all the new imports that the British had brought with them. He also told them of his journey in a ship across the ocean, which particularly impressed Yusuf. Amira hadn't revised her initial poor impression of the soldier, but she wasn't going to judge all of his compatriots by him, not with the prospect of theaters, social events, and eastern spices. Not when an English victory might bring her father home.

"So," said Yusuf, "how did you end up this far north? We've never seen any other English soldiers here."

"And you mustn't tell anyone that you met one today, either," said Harry, sternly. "You wouldn't want to get me killed, would you?" Yusuf shook his head. "You know my army is trying to fight its way up here to free you from the

Turks. With any luck you'll be seeing many more of us up here soon." Yusuf thought of his father and Amira of hers. "So let's just keep this meeting between us for now, okay?"

18

Summer 1916
Northeastern Arabian Desert

"Don't be so dramatic," a voice said.

Ahmad opened his eyes to see the gruff bearded man towering over him. "Up you get," he said. He looked down at Ahmad for a moment, then burst into a booming guffaw. "You thought you'd died, didn't you?"

Ahmad sat up as the blood rose to his face. "Did we win?" he asked, standing up. He touched his left temple. His hand came away sticky. "Feels like half my brain is hanging out."

"The bullet just skimmed you. Here," said the man, handing Ahmad a cloth. "Tie it up with this. I'm Abu Hamza, by the way," he said, putting his hand to his chest. And, for a moment, Ahmad wondered at the peculiarity of cracking jokes when they were surrounded by bloodied corpses and a desert burned red by war. He should be used to this by now.

"Abu Emad," said Ahmad. He paused. "So, did we win?"

"They retreated right after you 'died,'" said Abu Hamza with a smirk, "but we don't have enough men to pursue them. Help me with this chap." He indicated. Ahmad grabbed the ankles of a whimpering man, as Abu Hamza grabbed his underarms. They hauled him away from the front line to where the medics had congregated. They stepped over bodies that were missing entire limbs, that were bleeding so heavily that Ahmad couldn't work out where the injury began. He saw one body with no discernible face.

"What was the major thinking?" he spat. "This was nothing more than a suicide mission. And why did the Ottomans bolt so early? This makes no sense."

Abu Hamza shrugged. "You're still bleeding. The medics—"

"I'm fine," said Ahmad, walking toward a small crowd of survivors who were shifting injured men. He searched each of the injured men's faces and shook his head. What a pointless waste of life. "Where's the major?" he asked one of the group, "We cannot let them use us like this again."

The men were quiet until a sand-covered fighter with a heavy forehead replied, "Forget the major. Where's that skinny friend of yours?" The group erupted into chatter, and the rebel pointed a finger to the sky. "I swear to God I saw him flee in the other direction, cowering on the floor like a dog."

"That's a lie." Ahmad glared at him.

"We all saw it," he replied, drawing a circle around the group with his finger. "If it's a lie, then where is he?"

"How can you even think that? Nobody is forced into fighting here, we all chose to come." Ahmad pretended that the ache in his throat was just a battle trophy and had nothing to do with doubt.

"Well, somebody told the Ottomans of our plans, and the only person I saw not charging toward them was that little runt."

"Don't be ridiculous," Ahmad said. "That disaster of a battle was down to the English sacrificing us, not treachery. Did the Turks take your brain when they fled?"

"Don't expect anyone to believe you," said the man with the heavy forehead. "You two are closer than husband and wife."

"Right," said Ahmad, angrily. "Is that all you've got? I'm off to find Salim—and I'll be sure to inform him of your loyalty."

Ahmad walked away from the frontline, stepping over bodies, searching each one for Salim's elfin ears and pointed chin. Medics were bent over those who were still writhing, like larvae, groaning or clutching at the sky. When he reached the end of the battleground he found a cluster of bandaged men, some lying on stretchers, others chatting, but most were sitting and staring vaguely into the distance. Ahmad approached the chatting men. "Have you seen Salim?" he asked, miming Salim's height with his hand. He received only blank looks, so he wandered beyond the battleground into the dunes that were still untainted by the combat. He walked for several minutes before he caught his foot on something and fell onto all fours.

It was a head he identified easily from the dome-shaped kabalak cap that he used to put on every day when he fought for the Turks. "What on earth are you doing back here?" he muttered to himself, dusting sand off the soldier's uniform. He saw the same crescent belt buckle by which the chubby girl had identified him all those months ago when he had washed up on the muddy banks of Baghdad. Ottoman soldiers. On the wrong side of the battle lines.

"What the heck?" He screwed up his nose in confusion.

"Over here too," he heard a voice call. He turned to see the looming form of Abu Hamza.

"What?" said Ahmad.

"Sorry, followed you—they didn't trust you not to cover for Salim when you found him." Ahmad shook his head and Abu Hamza continued, "Anyway, there's a ditch over here. Two more dead Turks."

Ahmad shook his head, walking away from the ditch when he stumbled again. "Not another one." He dusted sand off the limb that had caused him to trip. It was a fist. Ahmad forced the hand open and found two circular pull rings that had been clamped so hard they had cut the palm. He rolled the body over and saw its impish chin. "No!" he gasped. Ahmad frantically dusted the sand off, looking for signs of an injury. "Wake up, you're fine," he cried, slapping Salim's face. He dusted the sand out of Salim's hair, turned the body over, and saw a cavernous hole in the back on his friend's head.

Ahmad came to on the ground. He didn't know how he had got there, his nose and eyes so close to the back of Salim's head that he could smell the metal in his blood. He could see bits of gray worming out of his friend's head, his hair pasted to what remained of his skull with a red gloop. And there, lodged in his petrol black hair, was the bullet, glinting like a star in its last moments of brilliance before being blasted into space.

19

Autumn 1914
Woking, England

CARWYN'S BUTTOCKS HAD TURNED NUMB from the hard wood of his seat and his head vibrated against the grotty window pane. England rushed past outside in a smear of green. He looked away sternly, determined not to admire his surroundings. It was the first time he had ever left Wales, but the gravity of the moment was dulled by the vague sensation that he wasn't really there. He felt as if he hadn't had enough sleep; he squinted, his view filtering into a colored moving picture. Surely at any moment he would wake up and find himself in his stone home, near the forest and the hills and the mines and everything that made him Carwyn, son of Iestyn.

He inspected the seats ahead of him, expecting someone to notice the strange atmosphere hanging over the carriage, but nobody did. He pulled out his Bible, and paused to trace the Welsh cover with his forefinger before opening it.

"A fellow Welshman!" said the man across from him.

"Don't say that too loudly," replied Carwyn, automatically.

"It's not like these buggers understand Welsh anyway, isn't it?" said the man. "Mind you, they'll probably think we're speaking German." He laughed. "I'm Owain." He held out a hand.

Carwyn shook it. "Carwyn."

Owain looked out of the window and then at Carwyn. "Does this mean you've enlisted?" he asked.

Carwyn nodded. "Unfortunately. You're headed for Woking too?"

"Yes. It's good to know I'll be billeted with a happy old chap," said Owain, with a smile.

Carwyn shrugged, and the train groaned. "I think we're here," he said, stuffing his Bible into his satchel.

Carwyn could feel Owain behind him, repeating, "Excuse me," as he tried to keep up. They were met on the platform by two men in khakis; a small crowd formed around them and they called out names from a list, before loading everyone into the back of a truck.

To Carwyn, the vehicle seemed to move in slow motion. All around him Welshmen were chattering and introducing themselves, and all he wanted was a moment of silence, or even a lavatory break, so that he could have just a minute to collect himself. He was billeted in the same barrack as Owain, as were about half of all the Evanses of Wales, it seemed.

The first days were hard for Carwyn. It wasn't the waking at dawn or the endless marching, but how they policed everything about him. He had thought it would be an easy transition from miner to soldier, but after his first morning he realized he would have to leave behind everything that made him Carwyn. His feet had to be angled like every other man's feet, his thumbs had to be pointed like every other man's thumbs. He marched when they marched and he talked how they talked. And he did it, for what choice did he have? He marched for hours through mud and rain; he yes-sirred and stood to attention. But inside he rebelled. He fueled his marches with anger toward his second lieutenant and he cursed his fellow Welshmen for giving up Wales so freely. And he told himself he would show them. He clenched his chin, and twisted his first two fingers just slightly out of place and he whispered, "I am not you."

Owain had grown up farming sheep in Brecon, which Carwyn thought was appropriate because he had the wiry, unkempt curly hair that he had only ever seen before on sheep. It grew as fast and as matted as a Welsh mountain ram's, despite Owain's efforts to keep it short. He had proved to be a persistent friend. He was uncouth and blunt but that suited Carwyn, who had no interest in decoding the actions of disingenuous men.

"Look, I'm sorry about your dad, but this war has nothing to do with it," said Owain, looking down the bench in the mess hall for eavesdroppers.

"Of course it does," snapped Carwyn. "The English didn't support us when we needed their help—in fact, they beat us down. Why should we help them with their fight?"

Owain shook his head.

"If an English politician was in my shoes, he'd do more than not join up, he'd go off and help the others—"

"Quiet!" said Owain. "Someone will hear you."

"Nobody can hear me."

"You still need to watch out. That kind of talk will ruin you. You took an oath and you'd better bloody stick to it."

"I'm not going to forget who I am and what these people did to my family."

"Damn it, Carwyn, don't bring your own fucking issues into every situation," Owain said. "None of us here give a jot about English politicians. I didn't join for them. I joined because it was the right thing to do. It was my decision and it has nothing to do with the English, so don't use them as an excuse for your choices."

Carwyn considered this. It was true he was prejudiced against any decision from Westminster, of course. He just didn't see why that mattered. Once a scoundrel, always a scoundrel.

If he was honest with himself, he had hoped his insubordination would be noticed. But nobody saw when he left a mess beneath the blankets on his bunk, or set the laces on his boots askew when he stored them for the night. As far as the second lieutenant knew, he was a quiet Welshmen who followed orders and caused no trouble. He rarely drank and didn't curse like rest of the beer-shifters; he marched without weakening or complaint. When they charged at sandbags he'd shout with the rest of his platoon, and kick the bag off his bayonet with a grunt. And as the weeks passed it became easier to yell for king and country, and harder to remember that he had once insisted he was not like these men at all.

By April 1915 the men of the Fourth Battalion of the Welsh Borderers were marching thirty miles in a day, carrying a full pack of equipment. They had spent six months training for deployment, marching two deep and falling into fours, rushing toward their imagined enemy, dropping to the floor to avoid detection, and emptying their lungs as they sank bayonets into sandbags. Carwyn had grown leaner, more efficient, and had the stamina of a horse.

He spent his free time practicing his reading or playing cards with Llyr and Tomos from his barrack. When they marched he would sing along with them, and they applauded his skill on the firing range. Carwyn found relief in his aptitude, allowing himself to enjoy the absence of Robert and the valley and all its ghosts. And in those moments when he was alone, Carwyn told himself that despising his father's killers did not absolve him of the responsibility to do the right thing—that good and evil were not absolutes. And was it really so terrible to be associated with miners and farmers who were brave enough to volunteer their lives? Maybe he wasn't as unique as his arrogance had sworn. Maybe these were his people, and he was exactly like them.

And so Carwyn encouraged the men when they grew tired of marching; he woke with the sound of a bugle every morning and performed each task with the objective of perfection. And with the routine, with no weight of decision each day, it became much easier for Carwyn the soldier to shake off the memory of his dead father than it had ever been for Carwyn the miner.

20

Summer 1916
Northeastern Arabian Desert

ABU HAMZA KNEELED BESIDE AHMAD, put a hand on his shoulder and slipped his hands beneath Salim's back and legs, effortlessly lifting his body to his enormous chest. The battle had left little strength in Ahmad, and it took all that remained to bring himself to his feet and to follow each step he took with another as he paced behind Abu Hamza, clutching Salim's fist and the two pins within it.

Abu Hamza returned to the battleground, making sure to leave the curved waves and small ridges as undisturbed as possible. To Ahmad, Abu Hamza seemed to glide as he stepped over four or five corpses to reach the area where the surviving rebels had congregated. Ahmad had to trot to keep up. The group of around fifty men parted and a hush fell as Salim's body was carried through them. Ahmad fell to the ground, one hand fiercely gripping Salim's fist.

He would recall this moment repeatedly over the following days, how it must already have been clear that the men's suspicions about Salim had been wrong, for there was no sound from them, apart from the flapping of ghutras in the wind.

Abu Hamza stepped forward to where the battered major stood facing his troops, and laid Salim's body down before the crowd. He removed Ahmad's hand from Salim's, extracted the two grenade pins and held them up to the crowd.

"Let there be no doubt," said Abu Hamza, barely speaking above a whisper. "We are only alive because of the man we called a traitor. He alone prevented their ambush."

"Good heavens," said the major, slipping into English. "The man's a hero." Abu Hamza scowled at him.

"How did he know?" asked the man with the heavy forehead, which seemed to sit even lower on his face.

The hush returned for several moments, before Ahmad stepped forward to face the crowd. "That's Salim for you," he said, but his eyes were met either with blank stares or not at all. "He was always thinking of the bigger picture. He always talked about the importance of planning and we never took him seriously," said Ahmad, adding, "Well, I didn't."

"Now hold on," said the major, switching back to Arabic. "We had a strategy. The problem was that they knew it."

"I don't know who your superior is and where he gets his information, but it is flawed and we pay for his shortcomings with our lives," said Ahmad to the major, pointing to the crowd. "They were waiting for us, and all we did today was lose half our men and send maybe half of theirs down with them. How is that a legitimate tactic? In that case, all it will come down to is a matter of population."

"Of course I agree, and there will naturally be an inquiry into how they knew we were coming."

"That's not even the biggest problem," said Ahmad. "You promised us we would fight for our homeland, not that we would be used as obstacles to stop the bullets hitting the English."

Angry chatter erupted from the crowd of rebels and Major Downer turned a darker shade of red that was barely noticeable under the blood from the battle and the burns from the long marches in the sun.

"Now, look here, I'm with you on this," said the major. "I want to see a free Baghdad too. Truly."

"If you are with us, then you must agree that we cannot go blindly into battle, with no say in how we shape our own country."

"Well," said the major, "that is precisely what you signed up for."

A disapproving chorus broke out, fingers shaking up at the sky and pointing at bloodied wounds. Sand and sweat were jumping from body to body.

"Quiet," whispered Ahmad, and a silence fell. "We signed up to an Arab revolt, not the English military. That's the condition on which we came here."

The major considered this, and turned to Ahmad, away from the crowd. Ahmad couldn't tell if he was angry or just uncomfortable.

"Do you have a better idea?" asked the major, quietly.

"Salim did," said Ahmad, with a sigh. "If we cut off their trains, we could end this war before it has even started."

"Then let's come up with a decent plan, and I'll make it happen," said the major, with a curt nod.

"But first," said Ahmad, "we must bury these bodies, and we must honor Salim."

21

AHMAD FACED MANY PROTESTS WHEN he insisted that the dead on both sides be buried, and more still when he insisted that any of the enemy's individual keepsakes be salvaged and returned to the Ottomans to identify their dead. He didn't know if it was the failure of the mission or the exhaustion that follows adrenalin, but their protests did not last long and the surviving soldiers were soon digging graves on two sides of a plateau. Salim's burial was markedly silent. After digging a ditch for his friend, Ahmad leaned over his body and plucked Salim's handkerchief from an inside pocket. He kneeled beside him, whispered a prayer, and, digging his fingertips under Salim's back, rolled him into the ditch.

After that first burial Ahmad and Abu Hamza took two horses to Basra to deliver the news in person. It was unfair that many families would not know for weeks that their sons and fathers had perished, but Salim's family deserved to know of his final act of heroism, and it gave the major time to obtain approval for their new operation. Ahmad tried to distract himself with the colors that lined their journey south along the river—smatterings of emerald and olive that gave way to scarlet wild tulips and periwinkles—but his mind was never far from the undignified thud that Salim had made as his body flopped into the ditch, or the surprising rigidity that had met his fingertips as he touched his friend for the last time.

Seven nights later, Ahmad and Abu Hamza reached the peaks outside of Basra, with echoes from a dozen minarets circling them, springing from hill to hill.

"Let's rest there and continue at dawn," said Ahmad, pointing to a tree sheltered by two mounds. "Very soon it'll be too dark to see anything." Abu Hamza dismounted, tied and watered the horses, before unloading dry wood from a leather bag. Ahmad laid out four blankets on the ground, and retrieved bread and onions from his horse's back.

He waited in silence for Abu Hamza to kindle a fire, then attached the three-day-old bread to branches and held them above the flames. Abu Hamza peeled and soaked the onions in some water until he'd softened their flavor. Ahmad had grown used to their muted routine, and tonight—like the past six nights—they worked, ate, and fell asleep in silence, with only whispered supplications passing from their lips.

22

Summer 1916
Basra

WITH EVERY THIRD STEP SHE took, Ayesha's heels were battered by her cart in her haste to get far away from Abdel-majid's shop. Her arms, neck, and shoulders were tingling, as though he were standing right behind her, though she knew he wasn't.

She could still feel his grip on her wrist and see the stubby hairs on his cheek quivering, when she knocked briskly on the iron gate. She heard a man's voice answer from the other side.

"I'm here for the bride," said Ayesha, pointing to her cart out of habit.

"Ah, yes, do come in," the voice replied. "I'll fetch my wife." The gate opened, and Ayesha took a step inside, and waited for the woman to come out and lead her through.

"Ah, you're here at the perfect time, dear." A long-faced woman appeared, with outstretched arms. "Can I get you some water or tea? Coffee?"

"No, thank you. I'd like to start work if she's ready for me," replied Ayesha.

"This way then," said the woman. Ayesha took out a wide reed basket with a tall handle and filled it with jars, bottles, and a number of clay slates and cloths. The woman watched her curiously, before leading her through an arch-way, up some stairs and into a shaded outdoor terrace that was open to the outskirts of Basra on one side, and blocked from prying eyes by shanasheel lattice windows on the others. The terrace was framed with two types of jasmine, an orange bougainvillea, and a banana tree.

"What a beautiful place," said Ayesha, "and perfect for us, as it will be getting dark by the time I've finished."

"Right, I'll fetch my daughter then," replied the woman with a smile.

"Could I have a large bowl of water, as hot as you can make it?" asked Ayesha. The woman left with a nod.

Ayesha arranged herself on a low stool facing away from the light, and placed a higher one perpendicular to her, when she heard soft footsteps approaching.

"You must be Marwa," said Ayesha, turning with a smile. "Yes."

"I'm Ayesha," she said, taking from Marwa the bowl of steaming water. She placed a glass jar in the bowl. "Why don't you sit here?" Ayesha indicated, and Marwa stepped forward onto the higher stool.

"Nothing to be afraid of. It's fun, actually," said Ayesha, with another smile.

"That's what I heard from my mum's friend," said Marwa. "Do I need anything before we begin?"

"Just make sure you're comfortable. Shall we start on your arms?" Marwa nodded and slipped off her abaya cloak to reveal a sleeveless white nightdress. Ayesha shifted her stool and placed Marwa's arm on her knee. She opened the jar and retrieved from it a sticky translucent orange substance, which she pinched and stretched deftly between her hands for a few minutes until it turned a glowing gold.

"This is a kind of sugar. The sensation will be uncomfortable to begin with, but you'll get used to it," Ayesha said encouragingly. She placed the lump of molten sugar at the base of Marwa's forearm, stretched it tightly along her skin, and snapped it back, pulling with it scores of tiny hairs. Marwa tensed, but Ayesha continued stretching and snapping the sticky paste, and Marwa soon stopped jolting at the pain.

For two hours, Ayesha peeled off every hair from Marwa's legs and arms, switching to a new pot of sugar when the first lost its stretch. She distracted Marwa by asking her about her wedding and the groom, a technique that had never failed her yet. She then withdrew a ball of thread from her basket, cut off a measure, twisted it around three fingers and placed the end in her mouth. Standing over Marwa, she twisted and lifted the thread across the bride's face, giving her satin-smooth skin and perfectly lined brows.

Ayesha pulled out her new packet of henna with a frown, fighting the urge to replay her conversation with Abdelmajid. She mixed it with a small amount of water on a clay slate and, working quickly against sunset, she used a thorn she had collected from an orange tree to draw an intricate pattern of lacy flowers and swirls across each of Marwa's palms. She dabbed the dried henna with cloth soaked in lemon juice.

Looking down at the henna remaining on the slate, Ayesha realized she had prepared far too much—"My mind was somewhere else," she said. She tore off a large banana leaf, split it into two, scraping the fist-sized amount that remained into one, then covering it with another, then wrapped the two together with thread.

"There, that should do. And now the fun part," smiled Ayesha, stretching out an ache in her back. She opened a jar of cream made with ground apricot seeds and olive oil, and spread it across Marwa's face with a cloth. After a few minutes, she washed it off with cooled water from the bowl.

Ayesha then removed the corks from four oils and three creams. "Smell them and tell me which you like," she said. Marwa chose a jasmine oil and a citrus-scented cream.

"After you wash tomorrow, put three drops of the oil on your hand, and rub it into your hair, then use this cream all over your body," Ayesha explained. "You're going to feel wonderful."

Squinting at the sinking sun, Ayesha clapped her hands and said, "Time for me to go home." She wrapped the unused henna-painting thorns and placed them in her basket with the empty pots and the used cloths. "You have enough cream and oil for a year, but if you want more just leave a message at my house—your mother knows where I live." She stood up with her basket hooked onto her elbow. "Any questions?"

Marwa shook her head and said, "Thank you. It feels so real now."

"You're going to have an unforgettable day. Just remember to enjoy it before the moment has passed you by," Ayesha said, adding, with one last smile, "and also remember to recommend me to your friends if you liked my work." With that she went down the stairs, into the garden, picked up her cart handle, and trundled it behind her into the budding night.

It was only once she was walking alongside the Shatt al-Arab that Ayesha remembered the incident with the Englishman. She wondered if she would ever get a chance to set him straight. She crossed an arced bridge, each plank creaking with her footsteps and with the wheels of her cart. She took the small footpath off the bridge and into the overgrowth that led to her grandmother's house. She felt better when she told herself she could pay a visit to Old Basra Villa and give them a piece of her mind . . . if she ever walked past it again—because she could not see herself returning to that dreadful shop with that intolerable man. She would have to find a new supplier, so it was fortunate that she had a fresh batch of all her products.

The sun was close to that lowest point where it would soon burst on the spikes of the minareted horizon, and in these last few moments, its light pink glow would cast long shadows, even beneath the smallest child.

Ayesha had just long enough to hear four footsteps beat on the earth behind her before she was face down in the sand, the scent of earth filling her nostrils. She was still too confused to call out when she felt two hands touch her side and flip her over to her back, and a fat, clammy fist place itself over her mouth.

"How dare you speak to a man like that," spat Abdelmajid. "You should feel honored that I would even look at your conceited face." Ayesha's eyes widened in horror, and she choked as she tried to sit up and yell from beneath his hand, but Abdelmajid placed a foot on her stomach and pushed her to the ground.

"If you were my relative I would not let you walk around with your face done up like that," he snarled. "It's disgusting. No wonder men look at you, even though you are too thin to be called a woman." He shook his head.

"Now, I'm going to release my hand. You make a noise and I will crush your stomach so hard that I'll break any chance you'll ever have of carrying your own son of a bitch. Understood?" Ayesha blinked away any sign of fear, stared at the coarse hairs on the arm above her face, and nodded.

"There. Not so hard to behave yourself, is it?" said Abdelmajid, removing his hand.

"I swear," whispered Ayesha, as Abdelmajid's eyebrows shot up, and a finger pointed at her. "I swear I didn't mean any of those things, you just shocked me."

"Oh, I'm sure you didn't, you little whore. I bet you ran on and told your little whore friends about the silly fat man who keeps asking you to marry him, didn't you?"

"You know I'm not like that," said Ayesha. "I'm just trying to run a business. I'm not interested in marriage."

"You were interested when it came to that carpenter boy. He doesn't know what real business is. Why would you consider such a child?" he sneered.

"I just did what I had to to get rid of him," said Ayesha, sadly. "I'm not ready for marriage, and if I were, I would ask my grandmother to find me a successful businessman rather than a boy who went to war."

Abdelmajid gave a maniacal smile, and tilted his head. He leaned over to grab the handle of her cart and Ayesha felt his foot loosen. She sat up and tugged on his leg and scrambled away on all fours, as Abdelmajid overbalanced.

She screamed as she felt two fists grab her around the ankles and drag her backwards, dropping her beside the cart.

"Lying bitch! Did you think I would just let you walk away? After you laughed at me like that? No. You owe me." Ayesha stopped screaming, and as she stared into Abdelmajid's yellowing eyes, something flickered in her own.

"You're wrong," she whispered slowly, pausing for added drama. "I didn't tell my my friends that you're a silly fat man." Abdelmajid froze.

"I told them about the ugly bald man who doesn't understand when a woman says no." She laughed at Abdelmajid's expression. "Do you see yourself? The only way you can get any woman to look at you is in the dark, attacking her like a coward."

"Whore!" he said, a bead of sweat escaping his hairline. He shook her by her clothes, slamming her against the ground.

Ayesha laughed. "What does that make you, old man? My carpenter boy is a thousand times the man than you could ever be. Especially with those three pathetic hairs on your head."

Abdelmajid was enraged and inadvertently lifted his chin to hide his scalp. "Shut up," he hissed. "You don't—"

"Did you think I didn't notice you flatten them every time I came into the shop?" Ayesha scoffed, her eyes flashing. "I told all my friends how ridiculous you are."

"You are going to regret that," he said quietly.

"You're forgetting that I know exactly what you're thinking. But you're probably too much of a coward to do it." Abdelmajid stamped his foot down harder on Ayesha with a sneer, and she stifled a groan. Abdelmajid bent over the cart and brandished a large bottle of lemongrass oil. He pulled out the cork and poured the oil over Ayesha's mouth and nose. She coughed and turned her head away, spitting thick streams of golden liquid.

Abdelmajid watched her, waiting for her to finish coughing. He ran a hand through the air over the cart deliberately, watching Ayesha from the corner of his eye. His frustration grew when he saw that she was looking elsewhere. With one hand, he lifted her by the back of the head. Her scarf slid back, and Abdelmajid stared at the black curls that fell onto her forehead. Ayesha's expression did not falter.

"Do you have anything to say for yourself?" he asked.

"It's funny," said Ayesha, ignoring the stinging on her scalp, "you think *I'm* the offense to God, yet you remove the hijab of a Muslim woman."

Abdelmajid brought his face close to Ayesha's and grinned. "God would thank me for what I'm doing. Whores do not deserve to wear His clothes."

"You'll burn in Hell, with all the other men who think they can speak for God."

Abdelmajid brought his face close to hers and hissed, sending bullets of spittle into Ayesha's face, "He'll be glad that I rid the world of another temptress who thinks she can disrespect men." She raised her eyebrows slowly and smiled, watching Abdelmajid's expression turn to confusion. She felt hair rip from the back of her scalp as she pounced on Abdelmajid's bulbous nose with her teeth.

"You little bitch!" said Abdelmajid, clasping his face. Ayesha spat out a walnut-sized piece of flesh into her hand, as a crimson bead trickled down her chin. Abdelmajid was hopping on the spot, crushing her stomach, but Ayesha maintained her smile and stared at the draping riverside tree above her.

"Damn you to hell, you filthy whore!" screamed Abdelmajid. He took hold of the largest jar he could find from the cart, plunged a hand into it and pulled out a lump of soft, white cream. He pinched Ayesha's jaw open with his fist and scraped the cream into her mouth. She spat and coughed it out, but her gaze remained on the tree. Abdelmajid plastered another handful of cream into her mouth and laughed as she spluttered and wheezed.

Ayesha was snorting, focusing on the curtain of green swaying slightly above her. She had tried to pull back from under Abdelmajid's foot, and tugged at his legs, but she couldn't manage to shift either of them. She clawed at his arms and face each time he came near, but she knew it was more for her own satisfaction than anything else. She knew what she was doing when she goaded him. She knew what was coming.

She had swallowed large amounts of the lavender cream in her throat, but she couldn't open the airway to her mouth. She smelled the henna even before Abdelmajid had unwrapped it from the leaves she had so carefully placed it in. As he leaned over her, she felt the stub of his nose drip blood onto her forehead and it rolled into her hair.

She probably should have been more prepared, but when the bitter, earthy henna filled Ayesha's nose, it hit her in the brain. It was wet, thick, and rolling down the back of her nostrils. She could feel herself jolting and coughing, but she would not take her eyes off the tree. For the first time she heard the lapping of the river behind her and she allowed herself to imagine crawling into the water and floating down the river, like the creature on her handkerchief. Then there was a burning knot in her chest and her whole head was searing.

Ayesha passed a silent curse on the man's soul and a prayer for her own. And when two fat fingers shot up her nose, she spluttered, gagged, and juddered, her thin limbs knocking rabidly against the ground until, just like that, they didn't.

23

Summer 1916
A hilltop outside Basra

THE BLACK OF THE PREVIOUS night was turning lilac when Abu Hamza shook Ahmad awake. He sat up with a start, shivered, and brushed a shower of earth off his head. Abu Hamza placed a piece of stale bread and a flask of water on Ahmad's lap and began loading their horses. As they had traveled south, the desert had given way to an earthy landscape dotted with shrubs, becoming marshy sludge as they edged toward Basra. Ahmad ate his bread noisily, watching the outline of the spired city emerge in the distance against a rising haze.

The two men headed toward the city and spotted a British encampment in the distance. After loading their weapons onto their horses, they dismounted and each held an open palm in the air, while leading their horse with the other.

"We are allies," called Ahmad, from a distance. "Sent by an English major," he added, ignoring the muzzles pointed at his chest. When the two drew closer, Ahmad indicated his pocket. "I have a letter." He reached for it and held it out as he approached a lieutenant at the front.

"Don't you speak English?" asked the lieutenant. Ahmad shook his head.

"Sit," the lieutenant said, taking the letter and pointing to the ground. Ahmad gave Abu Hamza a sideways glance, but lowered himself with the most gracious smile he could muster. The lieutenant scanned the letter, his eyes bouncing up to Ahmad and Abu Hamza at intervals and glancing back down to the paper. He flicked two fingers off the edge of the paper, and an officer was promptly at his side. The lieutenant muttered something to the man, who disappeared into a tent a few meters away.

"They'd better hurry up," whispered Ahmad, after Abu Hamza joined him on the ground.

"No conferring," said the lieutenant. Ahmad's eyebrows arched in confusion. He dug his hands into the ground beside him and felt the wet underbelly of the marshes. He tried to shut out the noises of the troops in the background and tuned his ear to the mutterings in the nearby tent. He heard an exasperated voice, but he wasn't sure what it said.

"*Arabs*, Major," said Matthews, entering Major Montague's tent.

"We are in Arabia, Matthews. Show me this letter." He gestured at Matthews's hand.

"So, what's the problem?" he asked, after he had read the document.

"The lieutenant thought you might want to have a conversation with them. You know, to *confirm* . . ." The officer trailed off. The major sighed and left the tent. The small crowd of officers around Ahmad and Abu Hamza stood to attention.

"Lieutenant," said Major Montague, "I understand you aren't satisfied with the letter these two men presented."

"I am satisfied, but as you're in command here, I thought you would want the opportunity to . . . verify their story."

"Story?" said the major.

"With all due respect, sir, any old Arab could write this letter and impersonate an ally."

"Yes, Lieutenant, particularly two Arabs who don't speak a word of English. Anyway, I've known Major Downer since our days at Chawker's so you can rest assured that I know his hand."

"I didn't know the two of you were acquainted, sir."

"Still, that doesn't excuse you treating two of our allies as criminals now, does it?" He smiled at Ahmad and Abu Hamza. Ahmad attempted to understand the conversation from the men's body language and tones, and tried to look as if he understood what was being said.

"I think the argument is about us," Abu Hamza said.

"Yes," said Ahmad, "and I think we're winning."

One of the armed privates looked uncomfortable and began to lower his rifle painfully slowly, as though he hoped the movement would pass as imperceptible. Ahmad watched from the corner of his eye. He fought the urges to laugh, and to slap the rifle away from the soldier.

"Now give these men and their horses some water and shade and let them be on their way," said Major Montague.

"Sir," nodded the lieutenant.

"Oh, and, Lieutenant?"

"Sir?"

"You should be careful not to make enemies of allies."

Ahmad and Abu Hamza arrived at the gates of Basra city much later than they had hoped, as the sun was well into its brutal ascent. A belted perfumer in deep red and green robes pointed them downriver in a surprisingly feminine puff of overpowering lavender and woody oud.

They rode alongside the Shatt al-Arab, which filled the city's waterways, setting the routes of the main thoroughfares and meeting places. The sandy buildings framed the river with wooden façades, shaded balconies, and walnut shanasheel. But what Ahmad noticed before any of these were the scores of British soldiers casually strolling along the streets. He gave a sideways glance to his companion.

"Another world," said Abu Hamza.

"There must be no English left in their own country," said Ahmad, with a nervous laugh.

Abu Hamza watched an officer walk past him without a moment's hesitation. "You almost have to admire their confidence," he said.

"So long as we're all agreed that we are fighting for Arab independence, I don't care how they strut about here."

The two continued riding downstream until they reached a small pillared shop front whose sign bore the image of an elephant riding a tricycle. Ahmad dismounted and asked an attendant at the door for the house of Fahad Abu Salim. They led their horses down an alleyway of two-storey buildings and they tethered them in the shadow of a small mosque with a mosaic ring of red and blue around its dome. Ahmad asked a man sitting on a chair in the shaded side of the alley for Salim's house. His face fell and he pointed to an open door on the bend in the lane.

Abu Hamza knocked and offered, "Salam," to the residents. He heard a groan from inside, and quiet sobbing.

"How?" mouthed Ahmad to Abu Hamza. "How can they possibly have heard about Salim?"

"They can't have," said Abu Hamza. "It's not possible."

Ahmad walked into a small passage that reeked of old coffee. He could hear indistinct words and more sobbing coming from further down the corridor.

"Abu Salim?" he called.

"Enter," croaked a voice. Ahmad turned into the room and saw Salim's eyes staring at him from a weathered face, and an old woman sobbing into a string rug on the floor.

He felt uncomfortable seeing her prostrate, as if he were watching a couple kiss or the birth of someone else's child—but she didn't even register his presence.

"We all come from God and to Him we return," Ahmad and Abu Hamza said in unison.

"I'm sorry," said Ahmad. "We didn't know you had heard."

The man blinked slowly and graciously. "It is a terrible loss, God rest her soul," he said, resting his forehead in his hand. Ahmad bit his lip and looked at Abu Hamza.

"God rest *his* soul," Ahmad said softly. The woman looked at Ahmad for the first time, then sat up. She had patches of dry skin on her jaw and under her nose, and the fresh tears on her temples now trickled down the sides of her face.

"Did you know my granddaughter?" she asked quietly.

"Your—who?" said Ahmad, clumsily.

"Ayesha, God rest her." The woman pursed her lips. "Isn't that why you're here?"

And then he understood.

"No," Ahmad whispered, clenching his jaw. "Not this too."

Abu Salim was the last to understand, and when he did a wail rang out over the street, its echo traveling above the small domed mosque in the alley to the pillared shop with the elephant on a tricycle, and through the portico gateway of Basra's city walls, where the richly dressed perfume seller felt an unexplained shudder pass through his bones.

There was mourning, without a doubt. The kind of unrestrained sorrow that only people of the twin-rivered land had the sincerity to reveal. The four mourners watered the ground with grief, regret, and loss. And amid it all, outbursts of halfhearted laughter as they shared stories of Ayesha's audacity and Salim's bravery, although Abu Salim's neighbors would always put the laughter down to manic grief.

"We all know who killed her," said Ayesha's grandmother after a silence.

"Who?" said Ahmad.

"Tell me his name and we'll take care of it," said Abu Hamza, without hesitation.

"Oh, I could sort him out on my own," said Ayesha's grandmother, with a smile that made Ahmad shiver. "In fact, I already tried. I went over there with a vial of acid that would burn whatever parts of him I choose. But he was gone, that spineless excuse for a man—he always was a coward."

"Who was it, though?" asked Ahmad.

"The spice-shop man, that son of a dog Abdelmajid."

"I suspected, but are you certain?" said Abu Salim.

"Quite certain. He kept asking her to marry him and she wouldn't give him the time of day. That was all it took to turn him into a woman killer."

From across the room Ahmad heard Abu Hamza grit his teeth. Apparently, so did Ayesha's grandmother, who turned to look at Abu Hamza.

"And I can prove it, just as soon as he shows his face again."

"How, if he has fled?" asked Ahmad.

"Because she bit the slimy old coward's nose right off his face!" she said, clearly pleased that he had asked. She paused for shock to show on Ahmad's face.

"Oh, yes, that was my Ayesha—proof that she was her defiant self, right until the end." She sighed. "That's the only thing that comforts me now, knowing that, although she was afraid, she must have scared the living daylights out of him too."

"Brave woman," said Abu Hamza.

"And clever," said her grandmother. "See, she hid her murderer's nose in her hand, so that I'd know. And when he returns, there will be no doubt. Then I'll get him. Mark my words, Ayesha, I'll destroy that man."

By sunrise, the grief had not left, as it seldom would, but reservation floated in the air, concealing itself in the dewy mist of Basra's canals. As Ahmad and Abu Hamza drank their second tea of the morning, Ahmad reached into his belt and pulled out a brown paper package. Sand fell to the floor in the salon as he thrust the package into Abu Salim's hands.

Abu Salim delicately lifted its folds; a handkerchief fell into his lap and he lifted it to his nose. "Thank you," he said to his guests. "I'm so grateful to have something that was his, something that gave him comfort in the end."

"I'm sorry we couldn't bring more," Ahmad said. He had failed Salim, like he had failed Karim all those months ago in the battle at Ctesiphon. Ahmad shook his head.

The room was silent for some time, though none of the four occupants seemed to notice, until Abu Salim spoke again. "I wish I hadn't lived long enough to see this day," he said, into the handkerchief. "I wish I had died in ignorance."

Ahmad bit his lip and looked at Abu Hamza, who shrugged.

"It's just not right. They could have been so happy," said Ayesha's grandmother.

The two had forgotten they were not alone in their grief, so they jumped when Ahmad spoke up. "It's a terrible time to be a kind soul," he said sadly.

"God rest them," said Abu Hamza, putting down his empty tea glass and staring pointedly at Ahmad. Everyone knew that a second drained cup of tea was the unspoken cue to leave.

That evening, Abu Salim stood over a fresh mound in the cemetery.

"Ayesha, my daughter," he said. "You were the light of my son's life. And now my son is gone and his light with him." He sobbed, and fished from his pocket Salim's handkerchief, which Ayesha had embroidered with a Euphrates turtle. He held it to his cheek for a moment, then thrust it into the fresh earth with his fingertips. He drew his hand across the ground and covered the handkerchief with dirt, blowing with it a whispered prayer, softer and more powerful than the shamal winds.

"May this bring you both the comfort you sought. Be together in death, if not in life, my gentle, gentle children."

24

Summer 1915

Aboard SS *Megantic*

THE WAR WAS A TIME of self-discovery for most of Carwyn's countrymen, and he was no different. He had learned of his surprising aptitude with the gun and his stamina for long marches. But his first days aboard SS *Megantic* opened his eyes to another previously undiscovered characteristic: his merciless seasickness.

The calm waters off the coast of Avonmouth quickly gave way to rugged waves that beat the ship, tossing it about like a tiny rowboat. Carwyn alternated between the privacy of his cabin, which was, mercifully, empty of its three other occupants, and going up on deck to feel the wind on his face. Neither did his nausea any good. The men gathered on deck as they passed the Strait of Gibraltar, and chattered even more excitedly when they first saw the African shore emerge from the starboard deck. Even Carwyn forgot about the constant nag of bile and the hooks that pulled at his tonsils when he saw the lights of Alexandria. Who would ever have thought that Carwyn Evans of Llwynypia would travel to Egypt? Perhaps this was not so terrible, he thought. Perhaps his late father would have been proud that he had journeyed so far.

When Carwyn had received his drill uniform and sola hat, he had known the battalion would be sent east. The first thing he did was go to the nearest bookshop in Woking and spend his pay on a travel guide to the Ottoman lands with basic Turkish and Arabic phrases. Owain asked why he bothered when he could manage without. Carwyn wanted to tell him that he was terrified he would forget how to keep the letters moving if he stopped reading even for a few days. He wanted to explain how powerless it felt to be unable to express yourself. But instead he just laughed and replied, "Now you're thinking like the English, Owain."

So when the *Megantic* sailed into Alexandria for coal and water supplies, and a cluster of Egyptians in bumboats threw ropes at the railings, lashing themselves to the liner and bumping along at an unstable pace, Carwyn couldn't help but try out some Arabic.

"Marhaba," he said, holding his hand in the air, and looking down at the men.

The Egyptians below laughed and replied in English. "Want to buy cigarettes?" asked the closest.

Carwyn reached into his pocket, found a coin, and, not knowing whether it would be enough, held it up questioningly.

"Yes, yes," nodded the man, who dug his hand into a bag, swung his arm back behind his head and threw the tin of Ferik toward Carwyn with a tail of string that attached it to the seller. He caught the tin at his chest, and saw a stained handkerchief tied to the string. He removed both, tied the coin inside the handkerchief and threw it back down.

Carwyn was not alone in his purchases. Men from his battalion and the Royal Welsh Fusiliers who shared the ship with them had gathered on deck, offering money and belongings in exchange for cigarettes, playing cards, and tins of biscuits. They were soon chastised by their lieutenants and sent below deck, after being told they would have to replace any military equipment they bartered.

When they arrived at the Greek port of Mudros, seventeen days after setting sail, Carwyn was glad that their journey was over. And although privates were not permitted to disembark, he enjoyed watching the port from the deck. The sight of green and brown hills and blue waters made it hard to imagine they were at war. If not for all the destroyers and other ships filling the port, he might not have believed it at all. And when his second lieutenant and even the lieutenant—Lieutenant Morgan—afforded themselves the luxury of taking a dip in the seemingly crystal blue Aegean waters, Carwyn laughed. The men had not fully considered the effect a busy port would have on the hygiene of the waters. He watched them flailing and cursing as they swam back to their small boat, spitting and slapping the water around them as it dawned on them that they were swimming in a port full of floating ships.

But Carwyn would not have laughed so much if he had known what turbulence would follow the calm of Mudros. Two weeks later and fewer than one hundred kilometers away, Carwyn, Owain, and the rest of the Fourth Battalion found themselves headed for the front-line trenches of Gallipoli in the dead of night.

Carwyn stumbled up from Anzac Cove, grabbing onto shrubs and gray dirt as he headed toward the left flank of the Allied advance. They moved low on the ground, with whispered commands. Carwyn grazed his knees and felt dirt hit his face, but not once did his platoon—led by Lieutenant Morgan—slow. He felt an eerie sense of the surreal; it was impossible to see the enemy lines, and he had to keep reminding himself that they were out there.

When the men neared the apex of the hill and began ascending through access trenches, a file of New Zealanders began to descend in the other direction. Even in the darkness, Carwyn could see—and smell—the beating that the trench had given them. Their faces were cracked with dirt and blood, and they gave off the distinctive odor that he would soon recognize as that of aged, baked flesh.

Carwyn had heard that you always remember your first shell, and as he marched through the thick network of trenches, he jumped as he heard one explode somewhere between his position and Anzac Cove. He tried to act indifferent, but his throat dried and he felt a sudden clamp on his chest that would accompany him all the way to the trench.

The closer they got to the front line, the deeper the access trenches grew. And the more they walked, the heavier the clouds of flies and the stench of rot.

"We're here, boys," said Lieutenant Morgan, as the men filed into a trench behind an officer from New Zealand, weaving around the traverses that gave it a gap-toothed shape. Carwyn walked down, keeping his head low. The stench was worse than he'd thought possible; it was sulphur and piss and rancid beef. It reminded him of the time he'd found a decomposing sheep in the River Rhondda, except the smell now was inescapable. He stumbled over a clod of earth and clutched at the side of the trench, where his touch met with a cold, hardened hand, sticking out of the wall.

Carwyn swallowed a yell. He told himself to act normally, that this was normal, but nothing about it felt normal at all.

"Oh, you found Sheikh Andy," said the New Zealander, turning back to Carwyn. Carwyn stared at the hand poking out, white against the darkness of the trench wall. He could still feel it on his palm, dry, shriveled, and bony, its skin loose and thin.

"I mean, never knew the fella, but we call him Sheikh Andy because it'd be rude to pass him and not shake his handy." He looked up at Carwyn, who could not hide his mortification.

"Don't worry, you'll take your laughs where you can get them soon enough," said the officer, turning away to lead them to the end of the trench. "And he might get offended if you don't. He's a dry old egg."

Carwyn did get used to the bodies. They all did. When he first poked his rifle over the trench, his wrist hit bone—a pelvis, he thought. It had been built with bodies, piled high on the parapet and dusted with earth—for olfactory purposes, Carwyn suspected, as much as any sense of dignity.

In daylight, it was worse. The corpses filled the access trenches as though they were a decorative addition. The flies and the stench were heightened by the summer sun. Everything required precision—even when a man wanted to take a shit, he had to go to the designated shitting trench and get his business done as quickly as possible to avoid spending too much time in the territory of flies. Carwyn determined he could do it in one breath, so he didn't risk the flies entering his mouth.

In the first day, Carwyn learned more than he had in his months at Woking. There was no marching, no bayoneting, no stationary target to shoot at. Mostly they provided constant annoyance to the Turks, shooting randomly over the trench, ensuring that they maintained the advances previous platoons had made. He sipped from his pint ration of water over the course of the day and covered the bully beef stew with a handkerchief as he swept it into his mouth, trying to minimize its contact with the swarm of flies that he was sure had been assigned to badger him. Within three days, the flies had won, and Carwyn joined the scores of men plagued by vicious dysentery that left his intestines unable to function, the endless stew only making matters worse.

When he wasn't shooting at the enemy, he would distract himself with his Bible or his travel book. At night he hunched in a corner between the third traverse and the front trench wall and slept, as British ships shelled the Turks from the cove, and platoons maneuvered below. A few times, he tried to sneak a look over the trench wall in the dark but there was nothing to see. He couldn't even tell whether Britain was winning or losing or changing matters at all.

When Lieutenant Morgan told them that the battalion would be part of an advance, coordinating with the Indians, Australians, and New Zealanders, Carwyn was grateful for the distraction from his dry throat and itching scalp. Their task, he was told, was to reclaim the ridge of Damakjelik Bair from Johnny Turk.

They set off once the sky turned black, clambering out of the far eastern side of their trench to head northward along the coast. Carwyn's knees scraped against rocks as he crawled along the ground, following Owain's feet for guidance. Thorns pierced his hands but the stinging was a welcome relief from his gurgling intestines. It took them hours to cover just a couple of miles. They ignored the thundering of distant shells—in fact, the sound brought Carwyn comfort, a reminder that Allied ships were providing them with cover.

When they swung east, Carwyn began to feel the nerves in his belly, tapping at his navel, reminding him of his mortality. It was easy to forget the cost of death when it had become so common, but that nudge sent Carwyn back to his father's bedside, and the horror that could result from one single bad decision.

"Iesu Grist," he whispered to himself. "Lord, help me."

They could see the enemy line. They could hear the popping of machine guns attacking the enemy trench, fired by allies on an opposite hillside. And when the bullets stopped, and Lieutenant Morgan whispered, "Charge," Carwyn stood up, braced his gun and followed Owain across the earth, and down into the trench.

Carwyn had spent the last day preparing himself for the blood, and he was used to the sight of death. But he had not prepared himself for the face of a young man staring down a bayonet as he realizes his time is up. He hadn't prepared himself for the slushy noise a bayonet makes as it slices into a man's abdomen, and the deflating whine he gives as life drains out of him.

The blood drained from the wound when Carwyn put his foot on the man and withdrew the bayonet. And then he stuck it into another man, who tried to beat it away with a knife, but even in his weakened state, Carwyn was too strong and too fast for him. It was much easier after that, once all the kills had melded into one. By dawn, his company emerged victorious. The ridge was theirs.

It seemed useless, then, after such a conclusive victory, to have his only companion in the platoon killed by a stray bullet that whizzed into the trench the next morning, sending his blood to join that of the Turks. It dropped from the sky, with a crack, shattering the cup of tea Owain was sipping, shattering his teeth and shattering his curly-haired crown.

Carwyn knew it was selfish to look upon Owain's death as a punishment for his own sins, but there it was. He took it as proof from God that he deserved to lose the only loved one he had within a thousand miles. Proof that he had chosen the wrong path: because if you are a man who takes life, you are a man who deserves to lose it.

It was the first of many losses for Carwyn's side. Damakje-lik Bair was high, steep and exposed, so just two days after their victory, the Ottomans led a bloody counterattack, reclaiming their losses and taking hundreds of Welsh lives.

Over the next months, Carwyn defended their retreating position with his comrades. They grew thinner; their skin cracked and bled easily. Half of them were weakened by dysentery and all were weakened by thirst.

When Britain decided to withdraw from Gallipoli in December, fewer than half of Carwyn's battalion remained to guard the rear of their evacuation from North Beach. The battle of Gallipoli was over, but the Fourth Battalion of the Welsh Borderers would not be heading west just yet.

25

Autumn 1916
Ahmad and Dabriya's home

AMIRA THOUGHT NOTHING OF THE footsteps coming up the path. She didn't even look up from *The Tale of Tom Kitten* as they neared her spot under the apricot tree. It was only when she heard a deep cough from five feet away that she gasped. Unmistakable.

"Baba," she cried, rushing to her feet. He smiled with a warmth that filled his entire face, and pulled her into his arms.

"Mama!" called Amira. "Farah! Come now!"

And the joy of a father returned to his family overshadowed the wretched months that it followed, proof to those who believe that, even in conflict, life can still triumph.

"Sit, sit," said Naima, pulling her husband to the ground. "You must be exhausted, Dabriya is bringing you tea." Dawood examined the three women circled expectantly around him, and it made him laugh to see the same expression upon each face.

"Very well." He smiled, knowing what they were waiting to hear. "After they took me they marched us out of Baghdad, toward the north, and we just walked, endlessly, it seemed. I lost count of how many nights had passed after the fifth or sixth. We walked every morning and every evening, until we thought our knees would break. They let us rest when the heat became unbearable, but that was more for our guards' comfort than our own, I think."

"Why didn't you buy a horse, Baba?" asked Farah. Dawood stroked his beard, which was grayer than it had been the last time she had seen him.

"I did, and I rode it for the first day or two, but some of the other men were too frail to make the journey on foot . . ." He trailed off. "By the time we reached Mosul, they gave us relative freedom, since we were out of the way of the battle with the English, and too far away to be useful collaborators."

Dawood tried to control a scowl as he lingered on the final word.

"We lived and ate together and life was tolerable but, Lord, I missed you all." He looked at Naima, who returned a smile. And he knew she closed her eyes to hide the sting of tears in them because he did that too. He cleared his throat.

"And then last Friday they told us we were free to return— we thought it was a joke at first. I didn't even look up from my newspaper. When I heard that the guards at the entrance to the city were allowing men to pass I left at once. I didn't even go back to the sleeping quarters, not that I had any belongings to speak of. I went straight to the city gates, bought myself a donkey to ride and here I am."

"Why would they release you now, though?" asked Naima. "Doesn't that make you suspicious?"

"Not when you hear that they've run out of gold. They're forcing us to switch to this new worthless paper money."

"What does that mean? That they're going to take all our money?" asked Farah.

"We're to hand over all our nickel, silver, and gold and we'll receive paper that has a value written on it instead."

"You must have been a *really huge* threat if that's what it took to send you home," said Amira, quietly. "It's like they don't even bother to hide what they think of us."

"They're beyond looking for our approval now, Amira."

"That's exactly the problem with them," she said, raising her voice. "They think they get to decide who deserves to belong, and they're not even from here! I welcome the English. Let them come. At least they won't cast us out just because we speak and look a little different."

"It'll all be better when the war is over," said Dawood, putting a hand on Amira's head. "It will."

"Two days' travel in that direction and we'd get to the ancient city of Babylon," said Dawood, pointing out of the carriage. "You remember our lesson on Babylonia?" Amira nodded and stared out wistfully.

"Remember the Hanging Gardens of Babylon, Yusuf?" Amira asked, gently kicking Yusuf's foot. Emad looked at them out of the corner of his eye.

"Yes," Yusuf replied, but he continued staring in the opposite direction.

"Will you take us, Baba, when the war is finished?" asked Amira.

"Of course," replied Dawood, with a smile. "We'll go everywhere when it's over."

"You do realize that the gardens aren't there any more, don't you?" said Emad to Amira.

"So? We can still see the lion and the walls and the palace ruins," replied Amira, glaring at him.

"Now, let's try to make this a happy Eid, even if we are all missing Abu Emad." Emad and Amira glowered at each other but said nothing.

The carriage slowed and jerked as it came to a halt.

"Out we get," said Dawood, clapping loudly.

The first thing Yusuf noticed when he stepped to the ground was a man in a suit playing an upbeat tinny tune on a stringed joza as a group of small boys tussled with each other, casting occasional sideways glances at the adults. Throngs of people were filing into the large meadow, carrying babies and yelling at children who had stopped in wonder. A man towered over Yusuf and waved a plate of hot, syrupy bas-bousa under his nose.

"So noisy," muttered Emad, pressing his palms to his ears, before wafting a cloud of flies away from his nose. "Is this supposed to be fun?"

"Try to enjoy it, Emad," said Dawood, "and at the very least don't ruin it for everyone else."

Emad rolled his eyes. "It's always my fault, isn't it?" He walked off toward the river.

"Yusuf, can you fetch the food from the carriage, please?" asked Dawood. Amira and her father had carefully packed a large woven palm-leaf basket with Yusuf's favorite foods. As he carried the basket over the meadow to Dawood and Amira, Yusuf breathed in wafts of tangy stuffed vine leaves, the pickled scent of cold sabich sandwiches, and a zesty margah that smelled as though it may have leaked. Yusuf tried—and failed—to recall the last time he had smelled, let alone tasted, such foods. The flood had left them with barely enough fruit to fill their stomachs and he had long forgotten about their drowned okra and vine plants. He lifted the basket to his nose and disappeared into a remembrance of the ripe riverside garden, Ramadan dinners with laughter, and of Baba.

"Hey, boy, want to have your photo taken?" A man shook his arm as he walked past, and Yusuf jumped.

"No." He scowled.

"Remember this day forever," the man replied, with what he must have thought was a cheeky smile. Yusuf scowled harder and walked off.

"Cheer up, Yusuf," said Amira, as he placed the basket beside her. "If anything, my father's return is a sign of good things to come." She handed him a sandwich.

"Or that we've used up all our luck," replied Yusuf, glumly, wolfing down a piece of fried aubergine, trying to mask his pleasure at how perfectly crisp and juicy it was.

"Come with me. We're going to cheer you up," said Amira, taking Yusuf's hand. She let go abruptly once he had stood and turned away for a little too long. Yusuf grabbed another sandwich and folded it behind his sash for safekeeping. "Come," she said, leading Yusuf to a crowd of children. They passed stalls of merchants selling wooden lions and airplanes.

"Don't you want your very own Babylon lion to take home with you?" called the merchant, raising the wooden carving to the sky, with a thespian flutter of his other hand.

Amira stared up at it with a smile, then realized Yusuf was watching her. "It's not like any of us have time for luxuries like that these days," she said, flicking a dismissive hand at the seller. "Now let's see what this lot are up to that has made them so unbearably noisy."

A man stood on an elevated rock at the edge of the meadow, near a cluster of trees, with his arms held in the air.

"Whoever swims to retrieve it first," he said, waving an inflated goat's stomach, "will win a special Eid prize." The crowd of children burst into squeals, and there was competitive shoving. Yusuf's eyes shone.

"What's happening here?" asked Emad, walking over, raising his eyebrows at the goat stomach.

"We have to get that ball," whispered Yusuf, pointing at it.

"Easy," said Emad, with a shrug. He pulled the back of his thobe between his legs and up to his stomach, strapping it in place with his sash. He turned to Yusuf. "Well, come on then." He pointed to Yusuf's thobe. Yusuf remembered the sandwich stuffed into his sash, but he couldn't back down now. He mimicked Emad's actions, and tucked the end of his dishdasha into his sash, under the sandwich. He looked from his bare knees to Amira. This was likely to end in embarrassment.

"Ready?" shouted the man with the ball. Yusuf felt an elbow in his side, and a pair of hands on his shoulders.

"Go!"

All eyes followed the path of the goat's stomach as it flew over their heads and landed in the river with a flat splash.

"We can do this!" yelled Emad, with a grin, slapping Yusuf's shoulder. The two jumped into the river with a crowd of other boys and thrashed toward the ball that was bobbing slowly away from them. Yusuf felt hands grabbing at his ankles as he swam forward, took a breath and dived under a sea of legs and ballooning thobes.

"If I get the ball, Baba will come home," he repeated to himself. He was glad he had always lived on the river: He could hold his breath longer than anyone he knew, even his own father. The longer Yusuf held his breath, the less congested with bodies the water became. And when he could hold it no longer he kicked his way to the surface behind a larger boy with thick arms and fast legs. He looked around for Emad and found him behind a few boys.

"Go!" his brother mouthed at him.

"If I get the ball, Baba will come home," he told himself again. "Please, God," he begged aloud, between strokes. But the stocky boy was pulling further ahead. Yusuf kicked himself forward with a bubbly snort, but he could not catch up.

"Crocodile!" a voice yelled, and the group of boys behind him paused, then erupted in screeches as one boy after another felt the grazing of leathery skin against his legs. In a moment the festive atmosphere disappeared amid screaming and frantic thrashing toward the shore. The race leader dashed back toward the riverbank and Yusuf had kicked ahead. He lunged for the goat's stomach to far less applause than he had anticipated. He rested his torso on it and panted, kicking himself back to shore. As he climbed out of the river, he passed Emad and the two brushed arms, exchanging a discreet slap of the palm.

*

Yusuf and Emad lay on their backs, their arms jutting, like the shimmering dragonflies above them. They were halfway through the bag of boiled candy that Emad's cunning ruse had won them.

"I can't believe they thought there were crocodiles in the Tigris!" Yusuf said, banging a palm on his forehead.

"I can," laughed Emad. "What surprises me is that we got away with it." He rolled onto his stomach to dry off the back of his clothes. The two had placed their sashes alongside their legs and had eaten the boiled eggs and fried aubergine from between the pieces of soggy bread in Yusuf's belt.

Yusuf turned his head to his brother. "I wish we could have more days like this," he said.

Emad took another candy from the bag. "I suppose it wasn't so bad," he replied, with a smile.

Yusuf shut his eyes and rolled onto his side with a sleepy grin.

He didn't know how long he had been asleep when he heard a man calling. He had been lulled by the familiar hum of children screeching new rules to old games, parents consoling wailing babies and opportunistic sellers peddling their wares. He sat up, rubbed his face and looked for the culprit who had woken him.

"Come on, children, gather around," called the voice; the goat-stomach man had returned to his stone in some attempt to organize the bedlam. Yusuf noticed that he had placed a white blazer over his dishdasha, despite the heavy heat.

"It's time to receive a very special kind of eidiya." Yusuf nudged Emad awake.

"What is it?" asked Emad, with a dry cough.

"Eid gifts," whispered Yusuf, excitedly. Emad sat up, put on his sash and they walked over to the crowd of gathering children. Yusuf recognized Amira's veil and came to a halt beside her.

"Hello," he said.

"Are you going to share those?" She smiled, pointing at the bag of candy in Yusuf's hand. He held it open for her.

"Nobody else had a chance, did they?" she said, with a trace of disapproval and admiration, looking from Yusuf to Emad and back again. She took a green candy and popped it into her mouth.

"Worth it, though," said Yusuf, trying not to dribble as the candy rolled in his mouth.

"Boys and girls," called out the man on the stone loudly, "I am very happy to tell you that I have strips of Wrigley's to give you today." He held up handfuls of rectangular packets. There was murmuring among the crowd of children as some asked what a 'Wrigley's' was.

"I've had these before," said Yusuf to Emad, as the trio neared the crowd. "They're a bit odd, actually."

"These treats come to us by way of the generosity of our honored guests, though unfortunately they cannot be here today," the man continued. "Attention, please, children. Now, a lot of effort went into bringing these Eid treats upriver, so let us have a cheer for our benefactors and guests who made today possible, the British Army and Lieutenant General Stanley Maude." The man gave an exaggerated clap that generated quizzical looks, but a quiet murmur of thanks rose from scattered corners of the meadow.

"What is this?" said Emad, stopping in his tracks. "Wrigley's isn't eidiya, Mr. Goat Belly! The English don't know anything." He stormed off toward the carriages, only stopping to call back, "Everything has to be done the English way, doesn't it? I hope they lose, if only to teach them a lesson." He glanced at Yusuf, rolled his eyes and gave a roar of frustration.

Yusuf looked uncomfortably at Amira. He was aware of people murmuring and eyes flicking from his brother to him.

"Ahem," said Mr. Goat Belly, tearing open the packets of Wrigley's. "As I was saying, this gift comes from our generous guests who are welcome visitors in our home." He raised his voice and hands as he ended the sentence.

"Sounds like he's been practicing that speech for a while," sniggered Amira. A soft applause broke out and the man held his arms in the air, smiling so widely that his eyelids met each other in mutual congratulation.

"Thank you, thank you," he said. "Now gather around, children. Ready?" He fanned some of the Wrigley's strips in a raised hand and tossed them over the heads of the children. Yusuf saw a taller boy grab two before they hit the ground, and charged forward, pulling Amira with him.

"We have to get some!" whispered Amira frantically, as another handful was pitched into the crowd.

They both jumped to try to catch some of the third handful, but most were intercepted by taller children. Amira dropped to the ground, pulled Yusuf down beside her and scanned the grass for shots of white.

And as they sat there, among the legs of clambering children, it felt to Yusuf as if a veil separated him and Amira from the rest of the world.

"What?" she said, the color rising in her cheeks. He wouldn't, he told himself. He couldn't. And before he could stop himself, he had.

"You're perfect," he said. Amira's face flickered. She reached out and touched his fingers. And, just like that, everything was forgotten: the war, his father's absence, the British and the Ottomans and the fighting all across the world.

"Yusuf," she whispered.

"What?"

"There!" she shouted, retracting her hand and pointing to a spot behind Yusuf's left foot. He turned, but someone had already picked up the strip of Wrigley's.

"Not here," said Amira, standing. "Baba might see." And with that she left, her head bent low to hide the glow in her cheeks.

And then Yusuf couldn't help himself. His father's absence had beat away throughout every thought; throbs of loss that dulled any prospect of joy. But for those few moments, Amira had soothed the ache, and he lay back on the ground, shut his eyes and laughed his heart out.

"Well, someone's having fun," said a voice above him. Yusuf's eyes shot open. His brother was staring down at him.

He sat up. "Why did you run off?"

"That man was unbearable," said Emad.

"But I needed you," he said. "We could have beaten those boys again."

"Yusuf, grow up," said Emad. "You didn't really fall for any of that, did you?"

"What's wrong with a bit of fun? It's Eid!"

"When have we ever celebrated Eid with those stupid Wrigley's? They're trying to change us."

"Ah, this again? 'The English are bad.'"

"Pretty much," snapped Emad.

"Why are you always such an old grump?"

Emad glowered at him. Grumpy, boring, stick-in-the-mud—he'd heard them all. "I'm *sorry* I don't love the men invading our country, Yusuf," said Emad. "I mean, they're buying your loyalty . . . with English sweets. . . . Surely even you aren't that blind."

Yusuf clenched his fists. "Have you ever even met an English person? Because I have and he was kind and respectful, and just . . . normal."

"When did you ever?" said Emad, scornfully.

"And he spoke Arabic," said Yusuf, ignoring the question.

"You're funny, Yusuf," said Emad, sighing. "But use your head for a minute. Would they sacrifice thousands of soldiers just to liberate some strangers from the Ottomans, and get nothing in return?"

"Who cares why, so long as we get our own Arab land?"

"Just like the Indians have their own Indian land?"

"Who?"

"See, you don't even know!" said Emad, throwing his hands in the air.

"Emad, we have to believe them. Baba is out there fighting for them . . ."

"Everyone is flawed, Yusuf, even Baba."

"Say that again!" said Yusuf, shoving his brother. "What's wrong with you?" He dropped his voice to a whisper: "Do you want the Ottomans to kill Baba?"

"Who do you think the Ottoman Army is made of? Turks? Around here they're all Arabs anyway!" Emad thought of all the times he'd been dismissed as sullen and paranoid, all the times he'd been compared to his younger, more cheerful brother or—worse—not compared at all. "That's all this is. The *Ottomans* are fighting the *English*, but all that really means is Arabs on one side are fighting Arabs on the other. Whatever happens, we lose and the foreigners win." There was a biting silence as they looked at each other, then away.

Yusuf whispered slowly, "Why did you have to do this today? I finally had the slightest bit of happiness and you took that from me." Emad looked at his brother, his hand gripped around the bag of candy in his pocket. And just like that, looking at the little boy who had cried in the floods, the only boy in the world who shared his blood, Emad's anger and jealousy disappeared, as if they had never existed.

"I know," said Emad, sadly. Yusuf blinked at the ground. "I'm sorry, Yusuf," whispered Emad. With the weight of the two rivers clinging to each shoulder, Emad leaned gingerly forward and put his arms around his brother. He turned his head away as the rift of an entire land rolled down his cheek.

26

Autumn 1916
Cairo

WHEN THE SURVIVING MEMBERS OF Carwyn's battalion arrived to recuperate in Egypt, the excitement of an exotic location provided a much-needed distraction to men who were weakened by months of thirst and whose sense of normality was completely awry. But the call of the Pyramids and the Nile could do only so much for those who were damaged to their core.

Carwyn had no grizzly fascination for sarcophagi, amulets, or canopic mummification jars. He just wished he could lean his head against the stone wall of his old room, walk down to the icy river or eat a meal at his mother's side. And while his platoon found diversion in the YMCA and the mess hall, or explored the local bazaars, spluttering on hookahs and local beer, Carwyn spent his evenings walking the Corniche of the Nile with a local porter called Boutros.

They had met when Llyr had dragged Carwyn along to barter and translate his way into the Windsor Hotel, which housed the Officers Club.

"We won't go *into* the club," said Llyr, as they headed toward the service entrance. "I just want to see if they'd let us. How many boys do you know who speak Arabic? Maybe they'll give us some leftover pigeon or unfinished champagne."

"You're in Cloud Cuckoo Land, Llyr," said Carwyn. "There's no way they'll risk their necks for you. And, anyway, you should know my Arabic is pretty bad."

"Better than mine," said Llyr, with a grin.

Carwyn laughed.

Carwyn introduced himself in Arabic to Boutros, who was smoking on a step outside the Windsor.

"Well, I've not heard that accent before," said Boutros. "What are you—Italian?"

Carwyn snorted. "Welsh. Could we have some . . . food, drink?" he asked, now twice as conscious of his accent. He tried not to think back to his schooldays, the "Welsh Not" plaque and Mr. Williams. "That the English didn't finish?"

"More than my job's worth," said Boutros. "You're not the first to try, though maybe the first to try in Arabic." He smiled.

Carwyn turned to Llyr and explained, "Like I told you."

Llyr threw his hands into the air. "Fat lot of good you are," he said. "Let's be off then. We might catch the others before they head out tonight."

Carwyn turned to thank the porter.

"You're going?" Boutros asked. "I could take you somewhere much better than this place, if you want to eat and drink. Much cheaper too."

Llyr was not interested in spending his evening away from his platoon, with *some strange Arab we just met in an alley*, which was how Boutros and Carwyn ended up spending the evening together in a poky bar that seemed to drip smoky sweat off its wood-paneled walls.

Boutros ordered them rice with a green, viscid sauce that Carwyn thought smelled a little burned, though it tasted tangy and filling.

"First Arabic lesson," said Boutros, raising a pinch of green rice in his hand "Mulukhiya."

"I like it," said Carwyn, between mouthfuls, drinking from a cup of murky beer. "What's the second lesson?" Boutros swallowed, and slammed his fist on the table energetically.

"Fuck the English!" He laughed. "No offense."

"Trust me," said Carwyn, raising his cup, "none taken."

So although Carwyn would decline to go riding in Giza with Llyr (*Who comes to Egypt and doesn't see the Pyramids?*) and never joined the battalion in their trips to the British bars and sporting clubs, he witnessed a side of Egypt that his compatriots never knew existed, and these adventures helped him to forget. Boutros took him to the Hanging Church for mass, for the closest shave of his life in Sayyida Zaynab, and to play backgammon in the dusty back streets behind the cotton market. Carwyn learned to barter and swear, to laugh at the English pronunciation of words that came much easier to his Celtic tongue. He gritted his teeth when Boutros asked him to translate an army song about a covetous Egyptian whore. Sometimes, when Boutros asked him what the point was of being in Egypt, Carwyn found himself defending the British, defending their need to recuperate at their barracks and hospitals and recreational clubs, which occupied half of the city. He didn't mean to do it, but something about Boutros's tone made Carwyn feel like he had to justify his own existence. He would not have to live with this dilemma for too long, though, because by October his battalion received word from Lieutenant Morgan that they would be leaving Egypt for Mesopotamia, marching north to capture Baghdad.

Carwyn told himself it would be better this time. The lieutenant had said that the British were a welcome sight for the Arabs in Baghdad, who had been cruelly dominated by the Turks who ruled them. He told himself that this wasn't Boutros's Egypt or Turkish sovereign shores, it was liberation. Whatever he needed to hear, Carwyn told himself because there was no Owain to do it for him, and Boutros, half laughter, half despair, sure as hell wouldn't.

When the Fourth Battalion of the South Wales Borderers disembarked on the banks of Basra, the first thing most men noticed was the stench; they filled their diaries with details of flies, sweat, and sewers. But for Carwyn, there was one detail about Mesopotamia that—in the beginning at least—overshadowed every other: the rain. It caught him by surprise when the first drop hit him squarely on the bridge of his nose as he stepped out onto the wooden docks. He thought he had imagined it in a moment of homesickness, but the downpour that followed left no space for denial. Mesopotamia's wet season had begun, and the cruel nostalgia that came with the rains would keep the Welshman company the entire season.

Each of the men in Carwyn's platoon prepared for the journey north in his own way. Carwyn read his books slowly and repeatedly. Llyr packed and repacked his belongings, and Tomos confidently announced the merits of their upcoming confrontations.

"We outnumber them three times over," he said, "so you can stop fiddling with your flask, Llyr."

"Just want to be prepared," muttered Llyr.

"We are prepared," said Tomos. "We have better weapons, better training, and our enemies have never shown themselves to be as good fighters as Europeans." Carwyn looked up from his book on phonetic Mesopotamian Arabic and tutted.

"Got something to say?" asked Tomos. Carwyn didn't answer.

"That's what I thought," Tomos muttered. "As cowardly as the natives you love so much."

"You're funny," said Carwyn, not taking his eyes off his book. He'd known men like Tomos his whole life. He knew how to get to them. "The European is a better fighter?" Carwyn laughed. "Really? More courageous? Were you there at Anzac? We lost the ridge in a matter of hours to the *natives*."

"Almost sounds like you're glad our men died," said Tomos.

Carwyn felt a throb in his chest, but swallowed it. "You know who you sound like, don't you?" he said, turning a page dramatically. "The bloody English right before they beat a Welshman up." Tomos was on his feet. Carwyn felt his hands shake, and he gripped the cover of his book tighter, but he refused to look at him, to show him the emotion Tomos was itching to incite.

"Better an Englishman than a budoo, Johnny T," hissed Tomos. "And you want to watch what you say, boyo. Someone might report you to the lieutenant."

Carwyn pretended not to hear him, and turned his head to the opposite page, trying to mask his angry breathing by biting his lips. Sure enough, Tomos shouted something unintelligible and left the room. Carwyn put his book down and shut his eyes. He was so used to being angry that it felt like a constant state. He was angry at brainless Tomos, angry at Owain—even though he knew it was selfish—and, these days, even angry at his mother who had given in so easily to Robert's threats and sent her son away. And it had cost him his soul: he would die a killer, and nothing would ever change that.

Carwyn's platoon packed their few belongings and joined their battalion on the narrow paddleboat that sailed north. They crammed themselves shoulder-to-shoulder and traveled against the flow of the Tigris. And when they disembarked, they dug trenches, they fired their weapons, shot dead their enemies. They did it with the expertise of men who were no longer fresh to war. And, slowly, the British advance edged north.

The battalion captured Turkish trenches; it bled and spilled blood; its men lost limbs and sanity and slipped in the mud as machine-gun artillery throttled them from above, and still they advanced.

And Carwyn did it all too. What alternative was there? There was no way out of the life he had chosen. So he shot men with routine and if anything moved in front of his trench, he killed it.

He lowered his chin and slipped in the mud as he marched forward. The sandy sludge caked his shins all the way up to his knees, and his elbows, too, from all the times he stretched out an arm to stumble over a mound. And soon enough, his entire platoon was so covered with mud that Tomos made the inevitable joke of comparing them to the budoos they were fighting.

Guilt would be waiting to greet Carwyn when it was all over, but until then, he avoided looking at the sky. He tried to tell himself that the enemy were occupying soldiers, that they were a fair target, that he was liberating the Arabs. It often worked, giving his actions a moral superiority. But sometimes it didn't. Sometimes he thought that this was exactly what the English soldiers would have told themselves when they descended on Llwynypia all those years ago.

And through it all, the rain never relented, like it had followed him all the way from Llwynypia, just to remind him of who he was, of what the boy in the cloudy valley would think if he could see him now. The people back home would call him brave, but the valley and the clouds and the forest, he knew they would judge him.

27

Winter 1916
Northwest of Kut

AHMAD THOUGHT HE WOULD HEAR it first but, as it happened, his bones sensed it approaching before his ears did. It was the unnerving tingling sensation he felt when he was being watched, or when it was about to rain. As it loomed nearer, he could hear the distinct hum and he could feel it underfoot: the 18.15 from Baghdad. As the engine rumbled toward him, Ahmad raised his hands to his mouth and blew a whistle to his left, a sound he heard repeated immediately as the signal was passed down a line of eight soldiers, spread out parallel to the railroad line. Ahmad crawled to join the man who received his signal, gave him a nod, and turned to face the direction of the track, just in time to see a thick blast of sand and flames punch the sky with an enormous bang, a clatter, and, finally, a strained grating sound that emerged from a cloud the color of the last seconds of dusk.

Ahmad tapped the officer on the arm, noticing for the first time a spray of scars across his face that pinched and puckered his skin. They wrapped their ghutras over their heads, covering their noses and mouths. A sharp ping hit Ahmad's shoulder, and half a bolt thudded to the ground beside him. After twenty counts, the two climbed over the dune that concealed them and ran up toward the burning tracks. Their feet kept sliding and digging into the sand as they went up the incline. With every step, a tide of sand enveloped their feet as though it had been lying in wait to grab their ankles. Spread over fifty meters to his left, a flood of rebels silently grappled up the sand as the two-hundred-strong battalion fought their way to the exploded train. Ahmad felt his calves burn with each step he took to the top of the slope, where he caught sight of the wreck.

The mine had exploded below the train's second carriage; their timing was still off. Ahmad thought that if they could hit the engine directly, it would be a lot harder for the Ottomans to recover the train. The engine and front two carriages had derailed and lay beside the track at awkward angles to one another. He stepped over a piece of twisted metal, and saw beside it what looked like a human leg. He tapped it with his foot, and thought he saw it twitch, then walked off with a shrug.

With a nudge to the fighter following him, he pointed to the engine and the two ran toward it, grateful for the cloth filtering the thick cloud of smoke from their faces. Ahmad saw a blackened figure clamber out of the side of the cab and attempt to limp away, grasping his shoulder. There was a bang and the figure was flung to the ground by the force of a bullet to his head. Ahmad squinted through the fumes at the fighter who had fired, but the night and smoke made it impossible to recognize him.

"Good shot anyway, whoever you are," muttered Ahmad, and left the shooter to search the engine. Even as he said it, he felt strange. The words tasted foreign in his mouth. Everything these days seemed foreign. All he saw, all he said, all he did, it was as though he were watching it happen to someone else. He shook the thought from his head and jogged toward the back of the train. He saw his men swarming over it, searching the ground, climbing into carriages, and Abu Hamza passing salvaged weapons down a line of officers and loading them into a coveted British-supplied truck, which Major Downer had nicknamed Polly, after a "similarly hefty Pollyanna from Dorset." His battalion of Arabs was an unfortunate audience to an otherwise tolerable gag. They referred to the truck as Burak, in an arguably sacrilegious tribute to their Prophet's heavenly steed.

Ahmad paced parallel to the train, watching as the silhouettes of men shifted artillery, loaded Burak, or chased down fleeing Ottoman forces, putting swift ends to their dashes into the desert. The backdrop of sky went from starlit to deathly black as Ahmad neared the blaze, scouring for an absence of cohesion or manpower, but for the first time in three of their rail attacks, he found no task left to fulfill. And in that moment, as the carriage blazed, surrounded by dismembered and charred limbs, Ahmad saw only victory. Surely this was the cost of freedom? Surely this was what liberation looked like? The dead men from the train had denied him his right of a better Baghdad, and he could not be blamed for challenging them, for fighting them, for winning. So, the scenes that would once have cracked his heart brought him resolve. This was how every enslaved man, since the beginning of time, had claimed his freedom.

Ahmad slapped at his throat. The coupling of fiery heat and perspiring humans had drawn mosquitoes, which gathered methodically at unguarded necks and foreheads. He checked his watch, and headed to the engine, jogging the length of the train, instructing haulers that they had four minutes to complete the unloading. Ahmad thought he heard the sound of hoofs on sand, but it was impossible to see anything, even without the light of the blaze plunging the surrounding desert into further darkness. He hoisted himself on top of the tail carriage, and joined the two watchmen.

"Is there movement?" he asked, scanning the horizon.

"Nothing, sir," replied one of the watchmen, from behind his binoculars.

"Good. Be ready for the signal." They nodded, and Ahmad slid down the side of the carriage, suspended himself and dropped to the ground.

By the time the Ottoman forces showed up, Ahmad and his comrades were already three miles away and Burak was comfortably on his way to Basra, weighed down by the spoils of the attack. The Arab rebel forces had plundered anything of use, if just to deprive some Ottoman soldier of a few luxuries; Ahmad even took the pack of cigarettes he found in the engine, though he had no interest in smoking them. What they couldn't carry, they dumped in a ditch and covered with sand, ash, and pieces of twisted iron. They piled sand into the train's engine, though they didn't have time to loosen the bolts on some of the carriage wheels.

Four hours later, when they reached their encampment, each man felt he had earned the right to feel relief and triumph, and self-congratulation, and only a fool would question the mood of spirited men at war.

But it was a spirit that fled whenever it pleased, leaving them with nothing but the stench of their sweat, an endless, parching desert, and communities of mosquitoes, surviving on the scratches and bleeding lips of haggard fighters. When this spirit left them, not even the memory of victory helped to ease the discomfort of the vast desert furnace. It scorched like famine and it could beat seasoned burly warriors into faded wrecks who could no longer mask their longing for a mother or a lover or even a good beating, if it would only take their minds off the merciless fucking heat.

And so did the first of Mesopotamia's two seasons continue, with progressively calculated railroad ambushes, fleeting euphoria, and a growing tolerance to flies, itching, and all variety of human odors. The day that the rains finally reached the desert, the battalion greeted it as if it truly were their mothers and lovers pouring down from the sky, their spirits returning to shower them with the bittersweet gifts of winter.

The first drops of water thudded against the woven camel-hair fabric of their tents on the blackest of nights. The desert grew lonelier in the bleakness of winter, robbed of the moon and stars. But that night, Ahmad awoke to a patter and to the smell of musty, prickling damp. He leaped out of his blankets, barefoot on the chilly sand, and stood under the sky. He barely noticed that half the camp had had the same notion, and while they all chattered excitedly, praised God, or tried to catch raindrops in their mouths, he stood alone with flung-out arms; he dropped to his knees and offered his face to the rain. And just the lightening of his heart—those few drops of rain—had him believing again. He laughed uncontrollably at the sky and told himself all would be well. Dear God, man's very survival is so fragile, so influenced by his heart.

The onset of rain was a celebrated but short-lived reprieve, for what force winter stole from the heat, it gave to the rain. Within a week, warmth and sunlight seemed infinitely preferable to marching in a windy downpour through a stubborn sludge of drowning sand, which crept into their boots, freezing and shredding their softened toes.

By the time the battalion had arrived at their first target of winter, Ahmad was grateful for the distraction. They had improved mines, with less gunpowder, and rather than destroying the railroad, they disfigured it into twisted tracks, which made repairing it more arduous and time-consuming for the Ottoman forces. Ahmad had commended the scar-faced soldier—who introduced himself as Abdullah from Basra—to the major, and he was now tasked with scaling and sabotaging the telegraph lines that ran alongside the track. They were careful to leave this task to the end so as not to alert anyone to the attack, and they frequently cut off the telegraph in other areas too, in the hope that the targets might appear random and disguise their operations.

Ahmad had to admit that their technique had vastly improved since their first nighttime attack eight weeks ago. After reports that three Ottoman soldiers had crept away from their first ambush, they carried out their attacks during daylight and now fired their rifles from a nearby ridge to minimize close combat. And they attacked only trains carrying military consignments—to do otherwise risked coming face to face with an entire unit of heavily armed Ottomans.

Their latest ambush began in much the same way as the others: they derailed the engine and took out any accompanying enemy soldiers, at first from a distance, and later by storming the train for survivors. It was an aid consignment headed to Amara, but they were to keep a portion and send the rest with Burak to the British forces in Basra.

Ahmad paired himself with Abu Hamza as he descended on the train; they went to the end carriage, with around ten other soldiers and the two watchmen. Ahmad was caught off-guard by the fear in the Turk's eyes as he opened the carriage door. He should have been expecting that an ambush would include actual ambushing. The Turkish soldier managed say, "I thought you—" before raising his gun up to Ahmad, who raised his own rifle and emptied a bullet into the soldier's forehead, before continuing his search of the carriage. He thought it was a stupid way to die, captured, alone, and all because he had wielded a gun. Why bother resisting?

With the search turning up nothing more of interest, the group began unloading the eight crates of medical supplies, which seemed a waste of an entire carriage. But, Ahmad thought, you can only transport as much as you have. Abu Hamza forced one open and found some bottles, bandages, and sealed bags. Ahmad scoured the crates, which were spread around the carriage, and spotted a small pile of books on the floor by the furthest crate. He looked at Abu Hamza and raised his eyebrows. Abu Hamza examined the books.

"What's odd about medical books in an aid consignment?" he said.

"Why is one open?" whispered Ahmad. He felt the swish of guns being lifted behind him. He kicked the crate. Nothing happened. He kicked again, and Ahmad was sure he heard someone exhale.

"Either you come out or we'll shoot the crate," said Ahmad. "Your choice." There was a pause. Ahmad plunged the tip of his bayonet into the crate.

"Don't shoot," yelled a voice. Ahmad raised his eyebrows knowingly at Abu Hamza. "I'm coming out, don't shoot."

"No weapons," said Ahmad.

"I'm not armed."

Ahmad tapped the crate with his bayonet. "Out you get."

The far side of a crate lifted and out of it emerged a Turkish soldier, with a bruised cheekbone, a knee that was bleeding through his uniform, and a red crescent on his left arm. "I'm just a doctor," he said, catching Ahmad looking at his shoulder.

"Then why hide?" The doctor stared at him in a way that made Ahmad feel foolish. Ahmad turned to the fighters with their rifles loaded behind him. "Boys, what do you think the Turks would do if they caught an Arab rebel fighter?" he asked. Chatter broke out recalling limbs in sacks floating down to Basra. Ahmad smirked at the doctor. "Did you ever apply your surgical skills to those who . . . let's say, no longer needed it?"

"I've heard the rumors, of course, but I'm in the business of saving lives," replied the doctor, calmly, "not dismembering them."

Ahmad paused.

"What are you doing here?" said the doctor. "Look at yourselves. Before all of this I might have saved your life."

Even as he shook his head, the image of Karim popped into his mind, begging Ahmad to put him out of his misery. He ignored the echo of his friend, ignored the doctor's reason, ignored his own history in the Ottoman Army.

"Don't pretend your lot have done anything for us except oppress us," said Ahmad.

"Trust me, life was better under Turkish rule than it ever will be if you win this wa—" The doctor gasped as he felt the threat of Ahmad's rifle against his chest.

Ahmad glared at him dangerously, "You can't treat men like dogs and expect them not to bite."

"Abu Emad," said Abu Hamza, softly.

Ahmad smiled. "Don't worry, brother. I am not the dog in this scenario." He pulled the gun away from the doctor, and shoved him into the crowd of soldiers behind him.

"Bring him with us," said Ahmad, with a laugh. "Let's see how long he can take being treated like a dog before he starts to bite."

28

Winter 1916
Near Ahmad and Dabriya's home,
the outskirts of Baghdad

"JUST GIVE ME TWO MINUTES," said Yusuf, raising a finger sheepishly.

"Wonder where you're off to," said Emad, sarcastically. "If you want me to keep quiet about it you're going to have to do two-thirds of the steering," he said, with a smile.

"I gathered that," said Yusuf with a shrug.

Emad lashed the boat to reeds on the banks of Dawood's garden, and lay back inside the guffa.

Yusuf leaped ashore and headed upstream, weaving between palm trees, ducking under low branches and reclining trunks until he came upon what he had seen from the guffa: Amira. She was splashing her toes in the water, fiddling with a gray shawl draped over her head.

"Hello," he said, with a wave.

She turned to him with a smile. "Hello," she replied.

For an instant he thought perhaps she was avoiding eye contact, staring at his chest rather than his face. It was hard to tell. It was often hard to tell with Amira. "Jemima-duck not attacked you today, then?" he asked, pointing to the duck.

"We had a stare-off, but I think I won." She patted the ground beside her and Yusuf removed his sandals and sat.

They were silent, swishing their toes through the water, interrupted only by Jemima's distant crooned warnings. Over the weeks Yusuf had learned not to feel pressured by Amira's long silences, almost like when they were children. He had grown comfortable with games that required few words, in stark contrast to the long, rowdy debates of their fathers. Like aged accomplices, they only talked when they had something to say.

Yusuf asked once how it felt to have her father home with her, and she told him earnestly that after the elation had worn off, it had filled her with more worry than his absence—he was a constant reminder of what the war could still take from her.

Yusuf dropped his head slowly and Amira nodded, and that was all it took. They heard a rustle behind them and Amira looked out at the river.

"Having a nice romantic time, are you?" Farah chanted with glee. Amira scowled at her sister. "Careful, Amira, or I'll tell Baba on you two," Farah said. "So, Yusuf, do you like Amira's hair?" She was flicking the ends of her own braids, which hung a foot below her veil. "Such a beautiful black, like dirty coal. Don't you wish you had beautiful yellow hair like mine, Amira? Just like an English lady." Farah stroked her braids deliberately, eyeing Amira. "Or green eyes like a foreigner?" she said, cocking her head to one side.

"Green eyes like snot, maybe," said Yusuf.

Farah, undeterred, looked at Amira. "Poor thing, the only one in the family to inherit all Baba's features," she said. "You'll probably get his mustache too, soon enough." Farah let out a false, high-pitched laugh and skipped off.

"Are you speaking from experience?" Amira called after her sister. She stared at her feet, muttering to herself.

"Don't listen to Camel-face," said Yusuf.

Amira giggled. "I never think of anything clever to say until it's too late."

"Well, camels are notoriously quick thinkers," replied Yusuf. "I keep thinking you must have left your door unlocked and a camel wandered in."

Amira laughed loudly. "She's really self-conscious of her big teeth, so I should remember that for next time." She looked at Yusuf, noticing his jaw had grown sharper than the last time she'd dared to stare at him. "Thank you, Yusuf," she said.

Yusuf mimicked a camel munching grass, chewing loudly and exaggerating his lips.

"It's like she's standing right here eating maqluba," laughed Amira.

"All right, I really should go—I have all these watermelons to deliver," he said, standing up and walking back toward Emad. He smiled, and she waved, and that was all, but it was enough.

"About time," said Emad, from the center of the guffa. Yusuf climbed into the large space beside him. They had also packed a small quantity of soap and oil that Dabriya and Ahmad had heated, squeezed, and pummeled out of watermelon pulp.

"See you soon!" Yusuf yelled, as he passed Amira, pushing off with the paddle.

Yusuf took first shift. He paddled and steered more expertly than he ever had before, pushing the boat downstream. Emad sat in the basin of the boat, leaning his head against the tightly packed watermelons.

And Amira, despite herself, couldn't take her eyes off Yusuf as he guided the boat away from the shore, pushing off the paddle as if the guffa were weightless. His shoulders were already wider than they had been in the summer, his waist disappearing under his dishdasha. He ducked below low-hanging vines and young palm trees. He pushed with such force that the boat jumped a little. She shut her eyes. This was a bad idea.

29

Winter 1916
Northwest of Kut

AHMAD LARGELY IGNORED THEIR TURKISH guest, but his name, Mustafa, frequently cropped up in conversations with the scarfaced Abdullah. Since their earlier desert crouches, Ahmad had recognized a dependency in Abdullah: he frequently sought Ahmad's confidence and it was often overwhelming. But with an enemy prisoner to crack, Ahmad was prepared to offer the occasional back-slap and forced laugh in exchange for the interrogation power of a man rendered both vulnerable and intimidating by the gashes across his face.

One late evening in midwinter Ahmad joined Abdullah, as he sipped tea with sage and read from a highly embellished Qur'an.

"Sorry to disturb, I won't be long," said Ahmad, raising a hand apologetically.

"Not at all. Breaks keep my mind fresh," said Abdullah. "What is it?"

"Any luck with the prisoner?"

"Mustafa? Nothing, I'm afraid."

"But you two are always talking," said Ahmad.

"He keeps trying to flip my questions on me. I think he's going a little mad."

"About?"

"For one, he has this paranoid theory that the major is laughing at him."

"Probably not paranoia," said Ahmad.

"No, I mean beyond the ordinary. He says that whenever the major talks to him, he pauses and smiles."

"He is probably bored. He's had the misfortune to be the captive of one hundred fifty men, none of whom need his medical expertise."

Abdullah laughed a little too loudly. "His latest hobby is guessing how I got my scars."

"How did you?" said Ahmad, raising his eyebrows.

"It's one of those stories where the illusion is better than the truth," said Abdullah.

"I'm sure there has to be at least some thrill in it."

"Imagine if you found out that it was my pet kitten. You'd wish you had never asked."

"Those gashes were not made by any cat," said Ahmad, staring at Abdullah's nose and recalling the midnight thrashing he'd heard coming from Abdullah's corner of the tent.

"Well, it's a story of similar disappointment, I'm afraid," said Abdullah. "And I have become far too comfortable with my fierce reputation to let my secret out just yet." He was clearly enjoying the attention, and Ahmad didn't like being toyed with. He forced a smile to his lips.

When the new year came to the encampment, it brought with it some much-needed distraction. Abdullah had forged a connection with some traders, who had transported an unimaginable array of luxury food to a desert meeting point. Abdullah was almost blasted off his camel when he returned from his nighttime escapade to retrieve the goods, having shocked one of the watchmen out of his open-eyed doze.

On the night of January 6, 1917, Abdullah shook Ahmad awake.

"Look what I brought us," said Abdullah. "For Christmas." He had brought traditional gemar cream, date molasses and tahini, nut-stuffed pastries, and semolina basbousa dripping with syrup. There were meat-filled kubbas and vine leaves bursting with fragrant rice, and six watermelons. Ahmad felt a chill of pleasure run down his spine as the sticky scent of syrup filled his nostrils.

"We could have just a bite now?" said Abdullah, shivering slightly.

"No, let's wait, it is not our celebration," replied Ahmad. "I'll meet you here an hour before dawn prayer, and we will prepare the Christmas feast." Abdullah nodded and they left for the warmth of their blankets.

When the major woke that morning, his first thought was of his wife and two daughters—most likely still asleep, another Christmas come and gone without him. He felt a tremendous ache in his throat, but dispelled it with an assurance that this time next year he would surely be asleep in his own bed, just like them. He sighed, forced his body off his cot, and dressed before stepping through the flaps of his tent.

"Have a blessed Christmas, Major Downer," sang a chorus of grinning faces. There were whistles and cheers, and the major stood, staring awkwardly at the spread of food. Abdullah handed him a small bottle that brought with it a cloud of a sickly-sweet woody scent.

"It's not quite what you would have had back home," said Abdullah, "but what do you think?"

"Christmas in January?" stammered the major. "How did you—"

"A third of us are Christian so it's only right that we should do something for them," said Ahmad. "But, really, it would have been just a lamb on a fire without all of Abdullah's work." It was a commendation he truly meant. Abdullah smiled a wide, toad-like smile, and Ahmad thought that perhaps he had been too quick to disregard him. Surely a man who went to such effort to spread happiness was a man of worth.

"Thank you," said the major, struggling to form the words. "My dear brothers, of all the days I have lived, I have never needed this delight more than I have today." He smiled painfully, then turned hurriedly and ducked into his tent.

30

Spring 1917
Kut

AFTER INCURRING HEAVY AND HUMILIATING losses against the Turks early in 1916, the British finally began to make ground against their enemy during the winter, conquering towns as they traveled north up the two rivers of Mesopotamia, nearing their final target of Baghdad. They had reached as far north as the town of Kut, where—the previous year—thirty thousand besieged British and Indian forces had perished.

"This time," Tomos pointed out, "it's personal." He wasn't wrong. As Carwyn's battalion marched into the town—now abandoned by Turkish forces—the residents spilled into the streets to watch the British forces march along the main thoroughfare, staring with unreadable gaunt faces, beneath ghutras and fezzes. Carwyn watched his feet march, listening to the sludge under his boots, from mud picked up miles away, and realized for the first time something that had never occurred to him before. Last year the world had been so absorbed in the siege of Kut and the thousands of British men trapped in the town by the Turks, forced to eat their horses and then the dogs, that he had not thought about the residents who were caught up in it too.

Carwyn shook his head and felt his arm brush past a small cluster of men.

"Look at them, sons of bitches," whispered one, "marching through here like kings."

Carwyn's head shot up and he stared at the man. It would be hard to say which of them was more alarmed: Carwyn, shocked at what he had heard, or the man, shocked that he had been understood. They watched each other for a moment, each fearful of what they saw staring back at them. The man broke their stand-off and spat on the ground. "You thieving conqueror," he said.

Carwyn lowered his face. He thought he might feel shocked at the accusation—after all, the lieutenant had sworn repeatedly how grateful the Arabs were for being liberated, but in truth, he was just tired of arguing with his heart about the merits of this war.

That night, when the men retired to an abandoned Ottoman building, Tomos smiled at Carwyn. "Did you see their faces? They should have been bowing down to us," he said. "We freed them, we did."

"Tomos," said Carwyn, sharply, "stop trying to start something."

"I really wasn't," said Tomos, rolling his eyes. "We've been fighting for weeks, and we finally reach Kut and all we get are vicious stares."

"What did you expect? We brought our fight to them. They had nothing to do with our siege but they starved just like everyone else."

"Yes, and when we win, we'll give them this country Turk-free. Any Arab with a brain should support us."

"Give them?" Carwyn laughed. "Since when was it ours to give?"

"When we conquer Baghdad it will be."

Carwyn put his head into his hands. "No," he said sadly.

"No?" asked Tomos.

"Don't you see?" said Carwyn, dropping his hands. "We're not liberating anyone. We're conquering them—you said it yourself."

"I mean just for now. They will be free eventually. Anyway, what do you care?"

"Iesu Grist, Tomos," said Carwyn, getting to his feet, "do you ever think about anyone but yourself?" He left the room and walked down a corridor, his throat tightening. If he was honest with himself, Carwyn wasn't even angry at Tomos, who behaved as predictably as he always had. He was angry that Tomos had broken his illusion that maybe, deep down, there was something virtuous about this war. It was a singular hope and the only thing that let him believe he had not completely forsaken himself.

"I can't do this. I can't do this," he whispered as he turned a corner.

He felt a hand tug on his arm.

"This way," whispered Llyr, pulling him into an empty room. There were remnants of burned papers in one corner. "Pull yourself together Carwyn," he said. "If anyone sees you like this—"

"Llyr, don't you see? Don't you see what we're doing?"

"Carwyn, bach, I always knew what we were, and the sooner you accept it, the better."

"I can't," said Carwyn, gasping for breath. His whole body burned with the surge of blood and adrenalin. "I can't. I'm not a conqueror. I'm not a man who can take the land of ordinary men. I'm just not."

"Then you'd better learn bloody quickly to pretend you are or they'll take you out back, put a bullet in your head and you'll never see your mam or fucking Llwynypia again. Is that what you want?"

Carwyn shook his head.

"Deep breath, now," said Llyr.

Carwyn breathed. He felt calmer at least. He knew what he had to do.

"Just act normal," said Llyr, "and everything will be okay."

*

And, on the surface, all was well with Carwyn. He shot alongside his men and he ate with them at night. Nobody saw him firing at the ground instead of at their enemies, or disappearing at night to raid the building they were camped in for newspapers, or anything to feed his obsession with the British war. Nobody saw the journals he'd spent all his pay on in a Basra bookshop that detailed the wealth of oil in Mesopotamia and the history of the British Empire. Nobody saw him rush to hide in a corner when he discovered the same minister behind the Gallipoli failure was the one behind the English attack on the Rhondda. Nobody saw him vomit at the name of Winston Churchill.

He became an expert at hiding his true thoughts. And eventually he allowed himself small victories, innocently inquiring what their aim was with each battle, as though there were any logical, moral aim of war in Mesopotamia. But he knew what this was. A conquered man always knows conquest when he sees it.

31

Spring 1917
Samarra

MAJOR DOWNER'S BATTALION SPENT THE first weeks of the year sabotaging Ottoman infrastructure to assist Lieutenant General Maude's push to conquer Lower Mesopotamia. Ahmad and his comrades were posted to Ottoman lands just north of the front line and they were tasked with attacking stations, bridges, and telegraph lines, as well as artillery and medical shipments. Within two months, they had derailed and ransacked twelve trains, destroyed three flood bridges, and ambushed Kut and Qurna stations.

"It's almost been too easy," said Abdullah, as the battalion marched north one night, just as the days were becoming warm once more. They had been doing all their marching at night recently: It was too dangerous to venture anywhere near the railroad during daylight. With all the precautions that the major had implemented, Ahmad sensed that their attacks had become notorious and that there could not be a worse time for any of them to be captured.

When the battalion reached their target of Samarra station, just over one hundred kilometers north of Baghdad, Ahmad barely noticed the methodical familiarity of the mission. Watchmen were sent out to scout the surrounding area, just as they always did; they fired on the building from a distance, just as they always had; and Abdullah was rattling on to Ahmad about missing his "modern, intelligent wife," just as he always did.

The station was the kind of building that aimed for grandeur but settled for handsome windows, due to financial constraints. Months wandering the desert had made Ahmad faster and stronger than he had ever been. His gun felt weightless in his hands and he could carry two men's equipment with ease. He stared through the station's arched windows, his eyes darting expertly in search of movement. But his mind wandered to the softness of Dabriya's braids, how they framed her strong jaw; the flare of her eyelashes when she shut her eyes. He was a few meters from the window when he saw a uniformed back scuttle across the floor, just as he was lost in memories of the dark amber shine of the skin on Dabriya's spine. When the barrel of a gun emerged, he shot the uniform and heard a thud. Half a second later there was a stifled yelp and the unmistakable sound of a weapon clattering to the floor. Ahmad saw his comrades knock down the station door and enter. He checked his surroundings, and followed them in. They had spread out through the building, searching for any survivors, and three men had gathered around an Ottoman soldier who was on his knees, his palms open to the air. The guard that Ahmad had shot dead through the window was on the floor in front of the kneeling soldier, who hung his head and sobbed quietly. As Ahmad joined the guard, the soldier looked up at him.

"You," he spat at Ahmad. Ahmad stared at him. Something about his beard reminded him of—

"Oh, God," whispered Ahmad.

"You filthy traitor, Abu Emad."

Ahmad froze. "Karim?" he gasped. "How did you . . . I thought you died—"

"Don't look at me like that," said Karim, scowling.

"Oh, Karim, all this time . . ."

"A lot has changed, it seems." He nodded at Ahmad's uniform. "Your entire company mourned you, thinking you'd died out there, and you've been here all along, playing colonizer with the English." Ahmad wanted to explain that he had no interest in the English, that he wanted a free land for his old comrades as much as for himself, that Baghdad was no longer safe for all of its people. He was about to open his mouth to say that Arabs shouldn't be the ones to lose their lives for the battles of foreign leaders, but caught sight of the lifeless brown eyes of the poor pubescent Arab soldier, his blood spilling out across the floor, and he retched acid and bile, and seven months of unbearable, foolish, deathly irony.

32

Spring 1917
Baghdad

EVEN AS OTTOMAN BAGHDAD FELL to the British on March 11, 1917, war continued to rage on for Britain, and for Europe. But for the two Baghdadi boys, there was little distinction between the fall of Baghdad and absolute conquest. There are really only two reactions to the outcome of a war, and in this case, Yusuf and his brother Emad acutely depicted these extremes. Emad withdrew to his room and occasionally to the mosque, with anger that was, predictably, targeted at Yusuf. For Yusuf, a British victory meant the return of his father, so there was unrestrained glee in everything he did, even his attempts to cheer his morose brother, but this served no purpose other than to sharpen the punches and insults that Emad threw at him. And so they were; equally pleased and displeased that the British had conquered Baghdad.

Just six days later, Dawood took Amira and Yusuf to explore the changing city under its new rule. Yusuf came to a halt in the middle of Jadda Street, a huge grin on his face as he saw a British officer reach into a pocket and pass candy to three children playing in the sand-dirt that coated every surface in the city. He ignored a distant yell, and stared up at the endless grand columns and the dizzying metal balcony rails above him, which seemed to beckon him across the road with the curl of their iron fingers.

A man was yelling at Yusuf from inside a fancy car. He called him an ignorant country boy and colorfully educated him on proper road usage. But Yusuf smiled, pinched his five right fingers together as though grasping a handful of boiled rice, and twisted his wrist to offer his fingertips to the brilliant blue of the promising Baghdad sky. The fancy car man did not heed Yusuf's gesture for patience, and drove toward the boy, narrowly missing his sandaled feet. Yusuf wasn't certain he'd have noticed even if his toes had been sacrificed.

"Come on," called Amira, from up the road, and Yusuf hurried to catch up, only half listening to her descriptions of all the places her father would take them to. They stepped through an unassuming wooden entrance and Yusuf was immediately hit by a sharp acidic scent, and an overbearing chorus of clanging, which went rapidly from irritating to hypnotic. Endless arcades lined the two sides of a stone alley, each arch housing craftsmen furiously sweating as they hammered away at misshapen trays or meticulously melting metals into glossy fountains of youth for war-weary cooking pots. Majestic skylights kept watch over the market, as they had done for seven centuries. It certainly knew how to build a reputation, the Coppersmiths' Market.

"Come," whispered Yusuf, clutching Amira's hand and breaking into a run. A man looked up from polishing a coffee-pot and Yusuf withdrew his hand. Long planks of wood had been secured across the top of the alleyway, joining to form a tip, which was effective in protecting shoppers from the sun, but Yusuf made a mental note never to visit during the winter rains. Generations of dust and copper powder floated in the air and seemed to slide down the shafts of light. It was how Yusuf imagined snow would look: Millions of tiny flecks parachuting into rivers of light from the windows. In a moment of morbidity, he thought the windows looked as if they were in tears, mourning the market's final decades of life, but he caught himself and laughed at the notion of the world-famous Abbasid market ever seeing decline.

Dawood took Amira and Yusuf to the Scribes' Market, where he allowed each of them to pick a book. Amira rifled among a pile of English books and shrieked when she saw the unmistakable spine of a Beatrix Potter story. Yusuf saw her face drop a little when she realized it wasn't *Jemima Puddle Duck*, but she passed her father *The Tale of Squirrel Nutkin* with a smile.

"Aren't you a bit old for these now, Amira?" asked Dawood. "Why don't you choose something more suitable for your age?"

"I haven't got this one, though," she said, "and the pictures are so adorable."

Yusuf, feeling pressured to choose an English book too, surprised them both by picking up a book by a man called David Fraser. He told them he wanted to improve his English, but he just picked up the most serious-looking English book he could find. He was proudly flipping through it when he noticed Dawood chatting with the bookseller, who handed him a sheet of paper.

"What's that, Ammu?" asked Yusuf.

"It's from the English—some kind of statement to Baghdadis," replied Dawood, furrowing his brow. "The scribes have been working all night to produce copies for them."

"What does it say?" gasped Yusuf. Dawood was silent for a minute. Yusuf watched a smile slowly appear on his face.

"Tell us!" said Amira

"It's about their plans for Baghdadis and our independence," said Dawood. He pointed to the paper. "Here it says:

'. . . *our armies do not come into your cities and lands as conquerors or enemies, but as liberators. Since the days of Halaka your city and your lands have been subject to the tyranny of strangers, your palaces have fallen into ruins, your gardens have sunk in desolation, and your forefathers and yourselves have groaned in bondage. Your sons have been carried off to wars not of your seeking, your wealth has been stripped from you by unjust men and squandered in distant places.'*

"And then they talk about how Baghdad will be allowed to flourish," continued Dawood.

"'But you people of Baghdad, whose commercial prosperity and whose safety from oppression and invasion must ever be a matter of the closest concern to the British Government, are not to understand that it is the wish of the British Government to impose upon you alien institutions.'"

"I told Emad he was being paranoid," cheered Yusuf. "Nobody clever enough to win this war would be foolish enough to put foreign rule where it doesn't belong."

"Indeed," said Dawood. "There's lots in it about helping art, philosophy, and literature to flourish once again."

Amira let out a sigh of happiness, and put an arm around her father's waist. Dawood patted her shoulder. "Things will be so much better for us now, my love," he said.

Yusuf smiled and looked over Dawood's arm at the letter. It was long and he recognized only about a quarter of the English words. "What else?" he asked, looking up at Dawood, who pointed to the bottom of the text and read:

"'Many noble Arabs have perished in the cause of Arab freedom, at the hands of those alien rulers, the Turks, who oppressed them. It is the determination of the Government of Great Britain and the great Powers allied to Great Britain that these noble Arabs shall not have suffered in vain. . . . Therefore I am commanded to invite you, through your nobles and elders and representatives, to participate in the management of your civil affairs in collaboration with the political representatives of Great Britain who accompany the British Army, so that you may be united with your kinsmen in North, East, South, and West in realizing the aspirations of your race.'"

Amira clapped, Dawood smiled, and the scribe who handed them the paper beamed. It did not escape Dawood, however, that this letter, in addressing only one group of the Baghdadi community—Arabs—omitted all others by default. Dawood thanked the scribe and returned the paper to him.

"Now, let us be the first to celebrate a new Baghdad," said Dawood, clasping his hands together. He took Amira and Yusuf for a walk along the Tigris promenade, past the grand al-Qishla clock to the Maydan, where the scents emanating from the perfume market puffed out into the square. A group of four women hurried past them, doubling their height with towers of round crates filled with yogurt on their heads.

There were merchants and entrepreneurs of all varieties—and qualities—in the Maydan, from robed old ladies bent over boiling vats of tashrib broth who charged a half anna for bread-dipping rights, to bristly barbers who extracted teeth in the absence of orthodox patrons. In one corner a man smoking a nargilah turned sizzling kebab over a smoky clay oven. The thick charcoal smell was irresistible to all three visitors, and after a couple of minutes spent trying to resist the wafting enticement, they each emerged holding a soft bread stuffed with smoky meat chunks. Life in the Maydan stopped for no one.

Dawood spent the day showing Amira and Yusuf the scenes in Baghdad City that they had heard about their entire lives but had never seen in person. They stopped on the famous Baghdadi bridges, and watched the docked wooden bellum boats bobbing on the tawny waters. Yusuf poked his head into the Great Synagogue as he traipsed around the adjoining Hennuni market, too self-conscious to follow Dawood in for a full tour, but too curious to miss his chance for a view into Amira's life. While he waited for them to come out, he followed the irresistible aroma of fresh bread that floated through the labyrinthine caverns of the market.

He found himself in yet another bazaar, where all types of furniture were sold, from gilded chaises longues to jagged wooden stools. Yusuf realized with a quick panic how far he had walked, began retracing his steps, and found his way back to Hennuni market after two false trails. He noticed that a sweetmeat-seller had propped himself near the market entrance to the synagogue. He pulled out a scruffy pouch and pretended to count his money. He held out his only two coins to the seller, who was using the full force of his body to spread a thick batter of sugar and sesame seeds onto an enormous tray. "How much can I have for this?" he asked.

"Two pieces of simsimiya."

Yusuf hung his head, but handed the man the coins, and wrapped two pieces of brittle in his handkerchief. He allowed himself to break off a small piece from one and let it melt in his mouth. When Dawood and Amira emerged from the synagogue, he handed them the two pieces of simsimiya.

"I was too greedy to wait for you, so I ate mine," he said, turning a little pink.

Dawood took them back to the Maydan, pointing out the Thieves' Bazaar along the way, which turned out to be where Yusuf had spotted all the furniture. He thought it a bit dishonest that they would give something so boring such a thrilling name: They should have called it the Fibbers' Bazaar. When Dawood pointed out the grand red brick of the Laura Kadoorie School, Amira grabbed her father's arm.

"Wondrous," she said. She had never seen a building like it. She had never even seen a girls' school before. And this one had high windows, imposing columns, and a grand central balcony.

"I thought you might like it." Dawood smiled. "Imagine what they could do for your English and French."

"But you already have excellent English," said Yusuf. He knew he was being selfish, but the last thing he wanted was Amira in a Baghdad City boarding school, hours away from him.

"Still," said Dawood, "it's something to think about, now that the war is over."

Yusuf watched Amira staring dreamily at the building. He thought of all the things he had been denied during the war, all the lessons he had missed while school had been suspended, all the things he could be with an education from a school like that. "You should do it, Amira," he said. "You really should."

"Come," said Dawood. "Let's get a drink."

Yusuf forgot about the prospect of Amira leaving for the city when they walked into one of Baghdad's famous river cafés, where men of all walks of life came to discuss politics, play dominoes, and often—as any eavesdropper could attest—take a break from their wives. That it was the wives who prompted them to enjoy the delights of an afternoon at the café was never deemed relevant for discussion.

Yusuf sipped his tea as two men raised their voices at each other from across a table made of woven palm leaves, one accusing the other of smuggling his chess pieces from the board. They stood up, each gesturing enthusiastically with his arms, invoking the name of God to argue his case for the missing pawns. Yusuf looked around, expecting other patrons to intervene, but nobody else appeared to notice the added din above the usual hubbub of Moshi's Café; or if they did, they were unperturbed by the dramatics. Just as Yusuf thought that the accuser was sure to throw a punch, his companion stopped gesticulating, gave a gleeful smile, and lifted his fez off his head, leaving three pawns to tumble to the floor. His accuser guffawed and proclaimed his companion could steal kohl from under an eye, grabbing him by the whiskers and shaking him playfully. Yusuf was unsure whether he understood the world better or worse for having overheard the exchange.

From their riverside seats they watched children clamber onto men's shoulders in the clamor for spaces in the large Baghdadi guffa boats, and the saqaa water collectors wading waist deep into the Tigris. They saw the Kadhimiya tram pulling away on the opposite shore as delayed passengers yelled after it in the futile hope that it might slow down.

And in the afternoon, Dawood took the two teenagers to the YMCA of Baghdad. Dawood was talking to the doorman when Yusuf and Amira walked past them and found themselves in a great pillared courtyard. They had not intended to sneak in unnoticed; they just walked in, newly purchased English books under their arms, with grand notions of being welcomed as the 'Noble Arabs' from the Proclamation of Baghdad, but nobody plans for their own insignificance.

Neither had ever imagined seeing so many British soldiers—they were sprawled across the tables of the courtyard, chatting animatedly, laughing, and a few were even singing. Amira tapped Yusuf on the shoulder and pointed to a doorway. They entered the cool of an indoor space furnished with a few wooden benches and tables covered with gray cloth. Thick, towering palm trunks disappeared through holes in the roof. Apart from that, it felt surprisingly familiar to Yusuf, surrounded by local plants, low Arabic tables, and local woven rugs. A number of British soldiers were sitting on the benches, playing cards or smoking nargilah a little awkwardly. When no one spoke to them, Yusuf and Amira walked over to look at a few photographs hanging on the tree-trunks.

Yusuf had seen cameras only a handful of times before, usually in the street, or on special occasions, and once in a studio when his father had had his portrait taken. But neither he nor Amira had seen images of a mosque or a camel half smiling. He was torn between amazement at the detail of such an image, and incredulity that anyone would admire an image of the dome of Haydarkhana Mosque, when you could just step outside and look at the real thing. In his bewilderment, it took him a moment to notice the horror on Amira's face.

"What?" he said. "What's wrong?" She shook her head.

"Let's go," she said sharply.

"Tell me!" said Yusuf. Amira pursed her lips and nodded toward a table of three soldiers behind her, obscured by the huge palm tree. Yusuf poked his head around its trunk and tried to pick out some English words.

"And I said to him," said the soldier with his back to Yusuf, in a tone that Amira thought seemed almost rehearsed, "Arab Revolt? More like revolting Arabs!" He threw his head back and guffawed as his audience sniggered. Yusuf looked at Amira questioningly. She put a finger to her lips.

Yusuf wasn't sure what "revolting" meant, but he thought it must seem worse than it was. After all, the English had been very respectful toward him. As he listened to a song pick up volume in the courtyard, he told himself that the soldiers knew it was important to respect Baghdadis, even if they dressed and spoke differently from the English. They understood one another, he was sure of it.

And as though the guffawing soldier could read Yusuf's mind, he wiped the cards off the table, whisked up the graying tablecloth and put it over his head. Amira put a hand to her mouth. The man mimicked riding a camel, brandishing an arm in the air, and shouted a nonsensical jumble of thick, guttural sounds. He pulled the tablecloth across his mouth and flung out his narrow hips at his men.

"Hello, boys," he said, in a grotesque voice, which broke at the limits of his vocal range. "We Arab girls can show you a few things." He winked. "Do you like my black hair," he flicked an imaginary braid, "and my black eyes?" He fluttered his lashes. "I'm *all* black."

Yusuf wanted Amira to tell him he had misunderstood, but when he turned to speak to her and saw her face had turned a deep shade of red, he knew he had not.

"You filthy *pig*," she said, in English. She grabbed Yusuf's hand and ran out through the courtyard of soldiers just as they were singing a rhyming alphabet epic.

L is the loot which we hope we shall seize,
Wives, and wine, and bags of rupees,
When the Mayor of Baghdad hands over his keys
To the British in Mesopotamia.

Yusuf felt his hand grow sweaty against Amira's. He thought about the English soldier they had met all those months ago, about how the English were constantly proclaiming that they respected Arabs.

"Come on," hissed Amira, pulling on his hand. She led him between some clapping soldiers, through a doorway, down an empty corridor, and came to a stop beside an old oak cupboard. She released his hand, and only then did he realize he was hugging his book with his other arm.

"Lying dogs," he said. "They think we're a joke." He slumped to the floor and flipped open the book, begging God to distract him.

He turned page after page, scanning for any English words he recognized. He heard Amira say his name, but it sounded distant.

He continued scanning, and paused at the word 'Arab.' He read slowly and carefully: "An Arab would rob his own mother." He flipped more pages, scouting for that word again. *Arab.*

For the wild Kurd or Arab does not care a pin for authority, and when the impulse moves him he will satisfy his lust for blood and plunder with very little thought of consequences.

He understood enough: Wild. Arab. Blood.

"Yusuf!" said Amira. She sat on the floor beside him. "Pull yourself together!" She took the book from his hands. Yusuf was looking at Amira, but he thought of Emad, who had warned him so many times that the English did not care about Arabs or their liberation. He had never thought his brother would actually be right, and had definitely never considered that he himself might be wrong.

"We have to get out of here. What if that soldier is looking for us?" Amira said, her pitch growing higher. Yusuf became suddenly aware of her face gazing at his, her shoulder against his, her hips touching his. He thought of her leaving their river for the school in the city.

"What?" she asked, registering only panic on his face. But she realized he had forgotten all about the vulgar English when he touched her veiled hair, when he rested his face on her forehead, and when he kissed it.

33

Spring 1917
Baghdad

CARWYN FORCED A SMILE ONTO his face. He held it there in case anyone noticed him, but nobody did. They had repurposed a government building into a YMCA for the soldiers. All around him, men were singing of their victory, cheering for the fall of Baghdad from Turkish hands, making infantile jokes about the native widows they would have, singing ridiculous songs about burying the Hun. And among them his Welsh comrades. Traitors. He gritted his teeth as he walked through the mess hall, holding an awkward smirk. He wondered if this was what it was like for the sepoys, fighting for their captors. He at least had the privileges that came with his nationality. Better weapons, softer punishments, social gatherings, being treated as a human so long as he didn't step out of line. He didn't know how long he could keep that up.

He clapped when he heard other men clap, and patted strangers on the back. And when he was safely out of the courtyard, he ran out onto Rashid Street, through the North Gate and straight into his barracks. He slowed as he entered the compound. He smiled and greeted the on-duty guard with the gusto of someone celebrating a great victory.

And he paced to his bunk, jumped under his thin sheet and sobbed for all that he had lost, and all that he had become.

34

THEY WERE HEROES. THE MAJOR said it, Abdullah said it, even
the mute Abu Hamza said it once, though a little sadly. Everyone kept reminding Ahmad that he was a great liberator. All
Ahmad could think was that a true freedom fighter would
surely not need to be told he was so, would not thrash every
night at the thought of ghostly brown eyes that would never
again see, and would not be haunted by the guts of his enemies slapping the sand, twisted beyond distinction from the
intestines of horses.

He avoided thinking about the cost of liberation. As tormenting as it was to remember the sound of bullets tearing
through flesh, or the vision of life leaving a man's lips to return to
God prematurely, by his very own doing, it was easier to punch
the doubt into his stomach with the force of their triumph.

More powerful than all of this was the thought that the
victory might not have been worth it. So he didn't think it. He
told himself he didn't think it. He told himself that this was
terrible, but at least Baghdad would be free.

He spent time with their Turkish captive, Mustafa, as pen-
ance. He brought him tea, pretended to listen to his endless
babbling, and reassured him that when he was handed over
to the English a deal for his return to Ottoman lands would
soon follow.

When the day finally came to hand over Turkish pris-
oners to the authorities in Baghdad, Mustafa seemed almost

relieved. They had reached a British outpost in Baghdad and two guards emerged to escort him. Mustafa hesitated for a moment, then faced Major Downer.

"I suppose," he said awkwardly, "er, God be with you all." There was a murmur of response. He pushed past a few of them and walked toward the outpost, a guard at each shoulder. Ahmad stepped aside to make room for him to pass. Suddenly he grabbed Ahmad's arm and yanked him close. Ahmad panicked, until he heard calmness in Mustafa's voice.

He leaned in to Ahmad's ear and whispered, "Do not trust Abdullah. Every word he says is a lie."

35

Summer 1916
Basra

ABDELMAJID WITHDREW HIS FINGERS FROM Ayesha's nose and wiped them on his cloth belt. *What a stupid girl. As good as killed herself.* He surveyed her body on the ground. It was the first time he had had a good look at her. He could see her thin legs poking out from under her abaya, which was so smothered in cream, henna, and sweat that it clung tightly to her torso. He laughed as he told himself that she had the breasts of a ten-year-old boy, though it didn't stop him gawking. He thought about unbuttoning her cloak and took a step forward, but footsteps on the main path made him jump. His face throbbed, and he put a tentative finger to his face. *The whore took half my nose.* He pulled his knee high and stamped on her ankle. It gave a low crack.

He waited for the noise to grow distant and walked to the edge of the river where the feathery branches of a tree hung down and skimmed the waters. It took him eight jumps to pull down a branch. He threw it over her body and repeated the process until he thought her sufficiently covered. He pushed her cart into the river gently to avoid creating a splash. And then he ran.

He walked through the streets, pulling his ghutra across his face, and kept his head bent low. He felt his whole face begin to ache. He walked along Shatt al-Arab toward the center of Basra, past rows of shanasheel fronts before he came to his shop. He pulled out his key, stumbled in and emptied a vial of iodine onto his nose. Then he found a small ladies' mirror and examined his face.

"Oh, God," he whispered, realizing from its sudden absence just how bulbous his nose had been. "They'll know. They'll know it was me." He imagined a passerby finding a piece of nose at the girl's feet. *Or, God, in her mouth. I should have pushed her into the river too.* It was a gamble—she would either have washed ashore to be found in minutes, or float out to sea, never to be found. *Shit. I should have pushed her into the river.* He dived behind his counter, found a suitcase and filled it with any jewels, luxury spices, and high-priced perfumes he could lay his hands on. He stuffed into it his supplier ledger, the spare clothing he kept in the back, and a dagger, then shut the lid. He emptied all the money in his shop into a small leather pouch. His head was thumping. Another man might have considered death, but such thoughts were beyond Abdelmajid, who had coasted through life mistaking fortune for ability.

He unhooked a new ghutra from the shop wall, knotted it across his face, and, after locking the shop up, he raced down the street. He puffed as he lugged his suitcase, switching it between hands every few moments. He sped down an unpaved alley, weaving around corners and ducking under low-hanging laundry until he came to a stop at a battered gate. As he knocked he felt a dry coarse mound collapse under his sandal, fragments scratching the tip of his big toe.

"Shit," he whispered. The door opened.

"Well, it's a few days old, but yes." Abdelmajid looked up. He tugged at the ghutra and hooked it under his chin.

"Salam, Munir. Sorry to show up so late."

Munir waved a dismissive hand, but raised his eyebrows expectantly, glaring deliberately at the center of his face.

"I want you to have my shop, brother."

Munir's face contorted in disbelief.

"In exchange for your horse and cart."

"What's the catch?" asked Munir.

"That you don't tell anyone of our agreement."

"Why?"

"Or ask any questions like that," added Abdelmajid.

"What am I going to tell people when I open the shop in your place?"

"I don't know—say you're minding it for me while I find some new suppliers."

"In the middle of this war?" said Munir.

"Good God, do you know how much my shop and products are worth? You should be kissing my feet."

"Not after what you just stood in, thank you," said Munir. "But I'll accept your offer. Though I should warn you that, if you return and try to reclaim the shop, I won't be keeping my mouth shut about your disfigurement or hurried departure."

Abdelmajid nodded, teeth clenched, and passed him the large iron key. He pulled the suppliers' ledger from his suitcase, tore out a few pages and handed the rest to Munir.

"Don't ruin my business, for goodness' sake," said Abdelmajid.

Munir retrieved his horse and a modest but sheltered carriage from behind iron double-doors a little way up the alley. "Don't you ruin my horse."

Abdelmajid went north. In the days it took him to travel to Baghdad, his nose had scabbed over, despite the best efforts of the riverside flies. He wondered whether someone had found the other half or the girl's body. He came up with a plan. It was a terrible plan, if he was being honest, and he told himself he wouldn't have to follow through on it. Surely they were too busy fighting a war to track a woman-killer across hundreds of miles.

When he arrived in Baghdad he felt eyes on his face as soon as he dismounted the carriage. He took a room in the first cheap guesthouse he found, in a less than reputable corner of Baghdad, and headed immediately to buy supplies, enlisting the help of a boy outside the shop to help him carry them. When he got to his room, he tipped the boy generously and told him to return the next evening to pick up a new shopping order.

Abdelmajid sat on a bed of hard blankets, which sounded like it rustled if he listened too carefully. Perhaps he would have changed his mind if the stakes weren't so high, if it weren't his own life at stake. But, it turned out, the threat of being caught brought out the most courageous side of Abdelmajid.

He took the newly purchased handkerchiefs, placed them on a stool and stood in front of the cracked mirror. It had such jagged edges that it looked like a shard of a larger one. He took the dagger from his trunk and felt his heart jump, as he whispered to himself, "Don't think, just do it."

He drew the dagger below his right eye across to his left cheek, cracking the scab of his nose, and sending an ooze of red down his face. He bit on a handkerchief and yelled. He bit on his tongue, too. He shut his eyes and placed the blade on the bridge of his nose, ripping a path toward the creases under his left eye. He cried into a clean handkerchief, begging God for mercy, bargaining each of his tolerable actions as merit for relief. He stemmed the bleeding and examined his face in the mirror. *Shit*, he thought. *Not nearly enough.* He told himself that once this was over, God would absolve him of any small part he might have played in what had happened to that girl.

There was a knock at the door. Abdelmajid jumped as the room came into focus.

"Mr. Abdelmajid?" said the boy.

Abdelmajid saw for the first time the blood on the table, on the floor, on the mirror.

"Leave me alone," he called, his voice cracking. "And don't call me that again. Call me Abdullah."

Over and over, he jabbed the blood-tipped dagger into his face, tears diluting the snakes of blood that crawled across his cheeks. And when he had sliced away all traces of Abdelmajid, he fell to the floor in a puddle of blood, iodine, and piss.

Part III

36

Winter 1917
Near Ahmad and Dabriya's home,
the outskirts of Baghdad

IT IS SAID THAT ALL wounds heal with time, but those who
believe it must never have felt the ache of regret. And
although it is indelicate to compare one person's suffering
with another's, few men in Baghdad had greater cause for
remorse than Ahmad.

Even before the news from Europe reached the city, its
alleyways creaked with the weight of Ahmad's guilt. So when,
in late 1917, Ahmad sat at home and opened a newspaper
to read of the secret pact between the French and the British to divide Arab lands between them, he managed to run
only halfway to the river before the acid rose in his throat and
erupted over the earth below. They had never planned to give
Baghdad back to Baghdadis, or Basra back to Basris, they
wanted it all for themselves, and he had been foolish enough
to believe them. He thought of his rifle as he had shot that
poor boy through the window, remembering with a jolt that
he had no idea how many lives he had taken. While he had
spilled his brothers' blood in the name of freedom, the English
were drawing lines on maps across countries that were never
theirs, laughing at how easy it had been. And when there was
nothing left to retch but choked air, he knew it was because
everything he ever was had been sold to the English. They had
taken everything from him. Everything.

After Baghdad had fallen to them, Ahmad was offered a
place in the Levant rebel forces, but the request felt more like

a formality, equally to Ahmad and to the major. Both knew that there was no way he could continue to fight. Instead, Ahmad returned home to a family that had grown distant in his absence. Dabriya tried to rein in her resentment, knowing that Ahmad's regret was already heavy enough.

And, on their small patch of riverbank—where there had been hope even through war—a silent doom took root. Words were whispered only in prayer and meals were robbed of both laughter and argument. What is there to discuss when you were wrong, when you have lost?

With the Ottoman threat against Armenians gone, Mikhael returned to his home, finding a restrained peace in the return to an old way of life. He knew he should consider himself fortunate that he had escaped the fate of the thousands of Armenians in Van, of the thousands of them now in tented camps in Baquba, just a few hours' ride from Baghdad. But it didn't seem right to count himself lucky to avoid a fate he hadn't deserved, that nobody deserved.

Each person laid claim to a different quarter of the house, as though in hiding from one another. Emad was rarely home, and Yusuf took refuge behind the new flood wall in the garden, occasionally allowing Luma to join him, if she promised not to ask questions. Of course, she swore not to and, of course, it was a promise she never kept. He feigned annoyance, the way older brothers do, but mostly he was glad of any noise to break the loaded silence of defeat.

Dawood maintained his delivery of food baskets to Ahmad and, despite returning to his duties at the Jewish court, visited the family every week. Even then, they sat in silence.

"What happened to you, brother?" whispered Dawood.

Ahmad looked up. "We lost, Dawood. We lost our country."

"Are you eating well, are you sleeping?"

"Dawood, under the weight of what I have done, only a fool would sleep."

Dawood looked at his hands. "It's really not all bad, you know. You should leave the house more—see the bridges they're building, all the new jobs and streets and contraptions. If you see what they have done in just ten months, it's quite remarkable, actually."

"You should leave, Dawood. I'm poor company, and there is no way we can agree on this."

"Come now, it's not good to isolate yourself. Why don't you join me in the city tomorrow?"

"Dawood, do you know how deluded you sound? Have you any idea of the cost of those new roads? I can't think about bridges and social clubs when all I can see is blood. Everywhere. The new roads are paved with the bones of the boys I killed."

"Ahmad," said Dawood, "I can't imagine how you feel, but we have to make the best of this."

Ahmad scoffed. "So easy it must be now, for you," he said.

"What is that supposed to mean?" asked Dawood quickly.

"I think you know, brother. Who's getting all the government-appointed jobs, the new European life that they always dreamed of?"

"Think very carefully before you say any more, Ahmad," said Dawood, dangerously.

"We both know it's true," said Ahmad. "Am I supposed to be dishonest with you now, old friend?" he said, stressing the last two words.

"This is not you, Ahmad, and that is the only thing we both know." Dawood shook his head. "I'm not responsible for any of this, and you know it. We were cast as outsiders in our own home, then blamed for the role forced upon us."

"This is exactly what you wanted all along, isn't it?" said Ahmad. "From the moment you told me that the Ottomans were no good for us. You wanted me to sacrifice my soul so you could live in a colony, didn't you?"

"Are you going to make me defend myself? I don't ask you to prove your loyalties."

Ahmad knew he was being unreasonable, but he didn't care. He needed someone to share the blame for what he knew was his fault. And although it was true that the Jews of Baghdad were flourishing under British rule, he couldn't blame Dawood for continuing his life, for trying to do his best for his family. This was Dawood, who had always cared for Ahmad, even when he was on the brink of starvation. And it angered Ahmad to know this, to know that he was wrong— again. To know that he was not enough. He was always letting his friends down.

"Ahmad," said Dawood, "you're too young to be a defeated old man."

"We *were* defeated, Dawood. At least I'm living in reality. You return to your palace."

"Very well!" shouted Dawood, rising to his feet. "And you can leave me and my faith out of it," he said, as he marched toward the door. "Bloody coward." And as his only true friend that remained in the world left the room, Ahmad smiled coldly.

"Call me a fool, Dawood, but I was never a coward."

37

THE TRUTH WAS, YUSUF'S INTIMACY had scared Amira. It scared her father too. He had happened upon the two of them in the corridor of the YMCA, a little too close to one another, a little too comfortable. He didn't chastise them, or even mention the moment to Amira, but the fact remained that Yusuf had pulled away when he saw Dawood approaching. Dawood told his wife what he had seen, and Naima, far less subtle than her husband, forbade Amira to see *that boy* again.

The entire episode confused Amira, her mother's reaction, and her father's, but most of all her own. She had felt herself gravitate to Yusuf for months, catching herself looking at his rounder shoulders, now much higher than her own. She wasn't stupid. She knew what it meant that she couldn't stop thinking about his voice, or staring at his hands, imagining how it would feel to touch them. But when his head was against her own, the initial flutter in her belly was replaced by panic, and that terrified her.

Maybe if Farah had been a kindly sister, she might have told Amira that nervousness was part of the thrill and that it was natural to feel a little afraid. Maybe if Yusuf's father hadn't torn a rift between the two families, Dawood might have told his daughter that, in a few years, Baghdadi society might accept a Jewish girl marrying a Muslim boy. Maybe if the Laura Kadoorie School hadn't been so grand, or if Naima hadn't used every ounce of her persuasive power on her daughter, maybe then Amira wouldn't have run. But run she did.

Yusuf raced to the river, a rare wide grin across his face. He forgot about the daily humiliation by the English, he forgot that barely anyone in his family had said ten words to him all week, he forgot the boredom and embarrassment that had hounded him in the months since Baghdad had fallen because Amira was there to see him.

He rushed past the watermelon patch and the flood wall, around the apricot tree and through the date-palm grove. And there she was. Everything he had always wanted. Why, then, did she look so sad?

"What happened?" he asked, walking the last few paces to her. "Is someone sick?" Amira shook her head.

"What, then? Are you all right?"

"I'm going away," she said quietly, "to that school."

Yusuf's face dropped. "Oh." He paused. "When will I see you again?"

"I don't know, Yusuf," she said. And just to hear her say his name made his chest a little lighter. "I don't think I'll be seeing you for a while. Mama says it's for the best."

Yusuf pursed his lips. "Does she, now? And what exactly is your mother's problem with me?"

"This isn't about her," said Amira.

"It is, if she's sending you away."

"She isn't," said Amira, shuffling and cracking a branch underfoot. "I asked to go, I want to." She couldn't meet his eyes.

"No, you don't," said Yusuf. "I'm your best friend."

"Aren't we a little old for best friends, Yusuf?"

There she went again, saying his name. "Well, can I see you in the holidays?" he asked. "Surely you'll be back here then."

"I will, but—"

"But, what?" said Yusuf.

Amira could hear his anger and wondered what right he had to be annoyed, when he had caused all this. "Why did you have to touch me like that? Why couldn't you leave it alone?"

"I was upset, I wasn't thinking," he said. He thought about all the years they had spent by the river, all the times he had wished he could touch her face or her hand, all the times it had been the two of them against his brother or her sister. "But I don't regret it one bit."

Amira glared at him. "Well, you should regret it, because now I have to leave."

"You don't have to. You just don't want to be near me."

"And whose fault is that?" said Amira, taking a step backwards. He was infuriating. Why did he have to kiss her head like that? And why did she want him to do it again? She wished she could push the idea from her mind. And when she couldn't control her thoughts, she blamed him for that too. "You just don't understand how I feel," she said.

Yusuf laughed. "*You* don't understand how you're feeling."

Amira couldn't deny that, though she was also right: He couldn't understand how she could leave him, when she knew herself to be the only good thing in his life right now, his only friend. He wanted to tell her to stay, he wanted to say he was sorry he made her uncomfortable, but all he could think was that he'd just embarrass himself further.

And so they stood, each waiting for the other to offer a word of consolation, something that might let them part as friends or not part at all.

"Fine," said Amira. "This is how I feel. I'm leaving for the city, and I'm really excited about it." She turned on her heel. "Goodbye."

"Well," said Yusuf, "enjoy your fancy school, Amira. Always were far too good for the likes of me." And he stormed off too, hurt that it was so easy for her, hurt because he knew he would never have left her the way she left him.

He regretted it almost immediately, of course. Not running after her, not asking her to stay, not telling her she was the only thing he wanted. Thirty minutes after they had fought, when he was lying on his bed, he no longer cared how embarrassing it might be if she rejected him. He should have tried harder. He leaped off his bed and ran from his room, back toward the spot where they had spoken, half surprised when he didn't find her there. He hopped into the guffa, paddled it across the river in a few easy strokes, and ran up to Amira's house. And when he found nobody—no Dawood, no Naima, no Farah, and no Amira—he sat on the riverbank that he had shared with Amira too many times to count. When their fathers were gone, with Jemima the duck and after his watermelon rounds. He had known her every day of his whole life.

And it was the first time that he truly grasped what she meant to him. Time could run forever and there would never be another Amira. Nobody would ever know him like she did. No girl would ever share her eyebrows or her lips. And it terrified him that this was it: he had lost his only chance with the most perfect girl in the world.

He never imagined that Amira would miss him just as much as he missed her, when she awoke in her dorm, and when she had breakfast in the bustling cafeteria. She hadn't realized how noisy a roomful of teenage girls could be. She could forget about her home when she focused on French and arithmetic, but when classes ended and she lay down at night, she longed for the bright greens of the garden, for the sound of the river and its resident birds, for the evening jasmine breeze.

A fair-haired girl named Flora took it upon herself to keep Amira company, chattering away through lunch breaks and pairing off with Amira when they took their first tennis class of the school year. And Amira found that it helped. When Flora was talking about her new ribbons or her upcoming family visit, it was easier for Amira to drown the voices that told her she had made a terrible mistake. She longed to see Yusuf, to tell him she knew what she wanted now, knew how she felt. But she had been so cruel. All because of a single touch. He probably never wanted to see her again. So she went to the library to do extra reading and she played more tennis. Her arms grew stronger and her legs longer, and with the start of each new month she told herself that this time her heart would stop aching for Yusuf.

It was not so easy for Yusuf to distract himself, though. There was no noise to deaden his pain. His parents rarely talked and when they did, his mother would usually cry. Emad disappeared every afternoon to God-knows-where. Nobody spoke to Yusuf about dealing with the loss of Amira, or the loss of war, so it just hung in his heart, a shadow of what might have been.

In the beginning, he thought she might write to him. He waited on the riverbank, his ankles in the water; he waited in his room, his head buried in blankets, or in the shade of a palm tree, floating in the guffa, staring at the sky. Some days he told himself he hated Amira for forgetting him, for leaving him to this strange solitude, and on his better days he told himself he didn't care that she had forgotten him. And when he really, truly, wanted nothing more than to be with Amira, he'd sit on the riverbank with Jemima the duck, and imagine she was there with him too.

He neglected the watermelons. Nobody in the family had much energy for anything, but Emad cared for the crop and delivered the orders when nobody else did. Yusuf wondered if Emad did it to get away from them or as a kindness. He wondered if it even mattered.

The days turned from vast and biting to burned and dry, and Yusuf grew even more lonely. He longed for news of Amira's world but refused to write to her when the months of her silence left him with no doubt that she had forgotten him.

*

When Amira came home for the spring holidays of 1918, her mother told her it was time to start thinking about suitors. Amira smiled noncommittally, but inside her heart raced. She knew her mother did not mean Yusuf. In fact, she probably meant anyone in the world *but* Yusuf. But when Naima was busy cooking, and Dawood was nose-deep in a legal book, Amira slipped away to the river. She had planned to take her family guffa across to find Yusuf, and to tell him she would reject every suitor in Baghdad, if only he told her that all hope was not lost. And as she reached the edge of the bank, just as she was about to hop into the boat, she saw him. Taller, broader, but still so recognizably her Yusuf. He was pacing on the shore opposite. Her stomach sent a flutter all the way up to her throat. He had stopped pacing and looked right at her. And she knew in that moment that all would be forgotten and she smiled so broadly, her heart fuller than it ever had been, to know that all would be well between them. She raised her hand at Yusuf, and waved.

Yusuf had been on the shore for an hour, trying to wake Jemima, and coax her out of the crate he'd made into a home for her. He'd found her two weeks ago, crooning in the garden, her wing bent at an odd angle. Mikhael, who had stitched up many injured goats, and had even delivered a camel calf when it got stuck in its mother for hours, helped Yusuf to set and bandage Jemima's damaged wing. Mikhael instructed him to keep her away from water, and to release her in two weeks. Jemima, initially all screeches and flapping when Yusuf had taken her home, had grown used to his care and the crate. And he had learned to live with the painful memories she prompted. What was Jemima to him but a reminder of Amira? She made him think of all the moments he had missed, all the lessons she had learned while forgetting him. And as Jemima would murmur through the night from the

210

corner of Yusuf's room, he wondered if he would spend the rest of his life longing for Amira, on this same land, by this same river, beneath this same moon—all of it surely created just to accommodate the most wonderful girl who ever lived.

So when Yusuf finally managed to persuade Jemima to waddle toward the shore, fanning his arms toward the river, he felt a joy he hadn't known in months. He leaned against a palm tree and watched the duck, first paddling along the river, then taking flight, soaring up into the skies above Amira's house. Yusuf, who had no idea that it was the spring holiday at the Laura Kadoorie School, was too distracted to notice Amira on the other shore, waving happily right at him. He didn't see her turn and race toward her house, furious that he could still be angry with her, and furious with herself even more.

And so Amira returned to school with a new resolve. She studied harder than ever. She joined the sewing club, even though she was terrible at crafts. She chatted to Flora as they sampled the hot zengoula funnel cakes at the Maydan and browsed the trousseau and ready-to-wear clothes at Orosdi Back department store. She told herself she was glad to meet the suitors her mother brought every holiday: It was better to marry someone of her own faith. And as the terms rolled into one, she told herself proudly that she had forgotten him, just as he had forgotten her.

But one weekend in early 1919, when she visited the Tomb of Ezra with Flora, when she stepped out of the long tarada boat that dropped them off, when she saw the towering date palms and caught the whiff of jasmine, her stomach fluttered with the memory of home, with the memory of him. And she knew.

38

Winter 1919
Ahmad and Dabriya's home,
the outskirts of Baghdad

AHMAD AWOKE TO NEWS ONE day in late 1919 that the British were attempting to create a Mandate of Iraq, drawing together the three separate vilayets of Baghdad, Basra, and Mosul in a new country, ruled centrally by the British. As though statehood was as simple as drawing lines on a map, and as though slapping a title on three different peoples—who had different words, ethnicities, and customs from one another—would miraculously unite them as one and solve all of Britain's problems.

And when *Iraqis*, increasingly angered by their foreign rulers, read a conciliatory British statement, which magnanimously denounced the dastardly foreign rule that Arabs had experienced under the Turks, Ahmad was sure it must have been written in irony.

He cast aside his newspaper, already three days old, and sat back against the wall. He could not remember the last time he had laughed, or sung, or even sat with his family in silent happiness. He was sure he must walk with a hunch by now. Even Mikhael, who had returned to his home when the British had conquered Baghdad, barely visited any more, preferring the company of his animals to Ahmad's forced pleasantries.

Ahmad knew that regret was a commitment that would burden him more the longer he allowed it to fester. He wanted to be rid of it, to make room for his wife, the river games, and Ramadans of old, but how could he just wish regret away when, for two whole years, it was all the company he had known?

He knew he was feeding his remorse by pondering how it had consumed his life. He thought about it as he sowed and harvested the crops in the garden, as he walked alongside the river for so long that two prayer times had elapsed before he got home. He spent all his time thinking of a solution, even as he knew it was a problem that would not be solved by thinking.

And Dabriya saw it too, the echoes of their old lives. She longed to be able to joke with her husband, to find comfort in him, despite the suffering they had endured. So she waited for the moment when she might shatter the tension and resentment in her home.

And just when memories of shared watermelons seemed to belong to a different family—one that hadn't only survived but had done so with compassion, just when Yusuf, Emad, and Luma thought that they must have dreamed up an historic bliss, for they could surely not be the same strangers that lived together now, just before they were changed beyond all recognition——the British occupation, in its twisted, self-congratulatory way, offered itself as the unlikely remedy to a home of discomfort. It began when Emad—tired of living with strangers—asked to move away from Baghdad. Dabriya left a long pause before she replied.

"Of course son, you're free to leave Baghdad, just as soon as the English grant us independence."

Emad looked furious for a moment, but then he burst into laughter. Luma was first to join in, giggling as she looked from Emad to Dabriya. Ahmad glanced up from his paper, paused for a few seconds as all eyes were cast upon him, half terrified they had done something wrong. But he had been waiting for the moment when his children would laugh with him again, so he looked at Dabriya and said, "What do you think about getting a horse to help with the watermelon deliveries?"

Dabriya laughed harder than the remark deserved, but Ahmad felt his heart for the first time in months. And Dabriya's eyes itched with joy or sadness—she couldn't tell which—as she recognized Ahmad for the first time in more than a year. He saw her and she saw him, and that was all they needed to know that they would be all right.

"Absolutely, husband. Let's get one when we're independent," she replied with a laugh. "The English said it'll be any day now." And with that trace of their old humor, each member of the family felt weight lift from the house.

In the weeks that followed, they went out of their way to make increasingly elaborate gags about the British occupation.

When Ahmad was washing the floors of the house one morning, Dabriya rounded on him. "Look, I don't know how to say this, but I'm just not sure you're ready to be tackling those floors on your own. What experience do you have?" Ahmad's face broke into a thousand creases, a vision that had grown equally foreign to both husband and wife.

"Oh, I do apologize! I just thought that since this is my house I should clean it," he replied.

Yusuf, Emad, and Luma came running from three directions, and stood grinning as they watched their parents.

"All I'm saying is that you don't know a thing about cleaning, so how about you give me the house and I'll clean it for you, until I think you're ready to do it yourself?"

"Aha," said Ahmad, "but how will I be ready to clean it if you never give me a chance? How do you even know I'm not able to?"

"Look, my good fellow," said Dabriya, "I have a long history of washing other people's floors and I can tell by looking at you that you have no idea what cleanliness is. But I promise you, one day, you shall have a floor of your own."

Ahmad could no longer contain his laughter, stood up and swept Dabriya off her feet. Luma clapped, while Yusuf and Emad smiled at each other, before looking away awkwardly.

When Dabriya and Ahmad were chopping onions that evening, Ahmad finally spoke.

"Why did you let me leave if you would resent me so much for it?"

Dabriya sighed. "All I ever wanted was for you to find peace, even if it was at my expense."

"I would have stayed, if you'd asked," said Ahmad.

"Exactly. What kind of wife would I be to ask you to forsake our country? To pick between a home and a future?" Ahmad rested his face in his palms.

"I never asked you to choose, Ahmad, but if you want honesty, I still wish you had picked me." Ahmad's throat tightened and he nodded, too embarrassed to look at the face he knew better than any other.

"It's all right," she whispered, putting an arm around him, and pulling him to the floor beside her. "A good, honest man will always be forgiven. I will always forgive you." She wrapped her arms around his head and he wept, he wept for what he had done and he wept more for what he had not.

Although Ahmad had not lost his ghosts, the repair of his family helped him to bear the haunting. And he dared to imagine that he might have the chance to mend his city too, somehow. And although Dabriya would never forget her loneliness, and although their children had seen too much suffering to be able to act their ages, the family's shared disdain toward their British rulers drew a boundary between them and the world. And each of them in their own way discovered that darkness was a visitor that only stayed when invited. Of course the sadness would remain, in the background, surfacing when they least expected it. But the darkness that wedges itself between the hearts of loving people, that you can drive away. All you have to do is try.

And, for the first time in years, they felt like the family that had beaten the floods. Together.

39

Spring 1920
Baghdad

EMAD HAD ALWAYS KNOWN HE was different from others. As a child, he had watched from the corners as other boys acted up in return for adult applause. As he grew, he realized that other children were uncomfortable around him and, more often than not, he preferred it that way. People were foolish or stubborn or—worst of all—foolish and stubborn. He didn't care for talking unless he had something to say, and even then he didn't care for it much. Once people had a theory, they defended it to their dying breath, no matter how untrue. It didn't help that they inevitably disagreed with him. By the age of fifteen, he spent most of his time listening to other people's idle chatter, in silent disagreement and endless rehearsal of what he would say, in another world. He knew he was quiet and impulsive, but—and of this he was particularly confident—he was always right.

In his world, Emad had little need for people. He was fond of his parents, his brother, and sister, though he was never sure if they knew it. In truth he didn't really speak to anyone else, and even when guests came to the house, they did both parties a favor if they threw no more than a single greeting his way. He seldom accompanied his father to Dawood's house: The daughters were silly and giggling, and there was little in the world that was more intimidating to Emad.

So he knew it was understandable, really, that when his father was away during the war everyone's concern was for his emotional and impressionable younger brother. Emad's own concerns were there too. But as he watched Dawood arrive to take Yusuf for a trip to conquered Baghdad, he stepped out of the door and waved at his brother, waiting for an invitation that never came.

Emad knew his own flaws almost as well as he knew his strengths. He knew that, as different as he was, he was still just as stubborn as everyone else. He also knew the reason he rarely treated his little brother with the kindness he should have: Yusuf was everything that Emad was not.

But there is something about watching your only brother go from a chatty optimist to a withdrawn recluse. . . . When he spied Yusuf crying in a corner of the garden where he thought nobody would find him, a whole year after Amira had left, it was suddenly easy to stop resenting his brother for attachments that had brought him only misery. At 18, Emad, was a man now, and it was a role he would take seriously. And so he swore he would do everything he could to bring back his light-hearted little brother.

It was the spring of a new British Baghdad, and it took Emad very little effort to convince his father to take him and his brother to Abu Hanifa Mosque in the city.

Emad had never seen such an elegant mosque. It was overshadowed by so much sweeping greenery that it was as if all the trees of Baghdad had gathered to weep in pilgrimage. He must have spent ten minutes staring at it from the outside before their father tapped him softly on the shoulder. He followed Ahmad and Yusuf to remove his slippers at the entrance, where a grand archway seemed to point to Heaven, just in case they had any doubts.

And, inside, more endless mirrored arches. Emad stood beside a column and stared at the ceiling, before offering a prayer of greeting. He and Yusuf explored the mosque, pointing out their favorite patterns and intricate muqarnas, their feet rumbling across the floor faster than was respectable. And then they sat, their backs to the cold marble wall, in silent contemplation until the afternoon prayers began. Emad stood toe to toe with his father and brother, listening to the hoarse melody that rang out above him. The imam crooned about the gifts that God had bestowed on humanity: Speech for eloquence, trees for their shade, scent and fruit, and the perfect calculation of the stars and moon.

The mosque filled with the buzz that always followed the end of prayer, as people greeted friends and scrambled to the exit to retrieve their shoes.

Emad was one of the first to spot it: the imam was climbing the steps of the small minbar, the platform from which he delivered sermons.

"Brothers," called the imam, and the room fell silent almost immediately. "The English civil commissioner has released a letter to Baghdadis. I shall now read out a translation.

"'It is the duty of the mandatory Power to act the part of a wise and farseeing guardian who makes provision for the training of his charge with a view to fitting him to take his place in the world of men—'"

Indignant yells erupted from the hall, magnified by the cavernous archways.

"Please, be silent so that your brothers can hear what is being said," called the imam, and the noise petered out.

"'And as the guardian rejoices over the growth of his ward into sane and independent manhood, so will the guardian Power see with satisfaction the development of political institutions which shall be sound and free.'"

Emad felt sickness lock itself inside his gut. He had a strange light-headedness, the same kind he felt when he was fasting and stood up too quickly. This couldn't be real. His ears whooshed and he felt the sudden buzz of two hundred men, all yelling at the tops of their voices. He spotted his father's head above a sea of ghutras, grabbed Yusuf's hand, and pushed through the crowd to get to him.

"What is this?" spat Ahmad. "They're going to help us grow into sane men? Curse them. What are we now? Mindless children, who need to be taught to walk and eat, and do as they're told?"

"Worse," said Emad, softly. "We're not even people. We're savages."

"No," said Ahmad.

Emad felt a surge in his chest. Did the commissioner think that Baghdadis did not know about their conference in Italy? Did they think they didn't know this was about sharing the oil of their land among white men? Emad clenched his hands and thought he might punch a pillar. Then he saw his father throw a fist into the air.

"We aren't savages, we are people!" A wave of faces turned to face them, with a few whispers of "Abu Emad."

He lifted his fist again and repeated, "We aren't savages, we are people!" Pockets of people returned the chant. When Ahmad called out for a third time, the buzz of the mosque roared the words back, before falling silent.

"Brothers!" called Ahmad. "Let us march to our brothers at al-Kadhimiya Mosque and together our voices will be heard."

In the prayer hall a noise erupted that was halfway between a cheer and a battle cry. It boomed into the vaults, swirling up to fill the mosque's dome, giving two hundred men the voice of ten thousand. A man beside Ahmad repeated his chant, and the crowd drew a collective breath before calling back what no human should ever have to proclaim: *We are people*.

Emad, Ahmad, and Yusuf felt themselves carried away by the surge of the crowd as it spilled out of the mosque, each worshipper struggling to find his slippers before he was

coughed out into the street. Emad found himself face-to-face
with a woman who couldn't have been a day under eighty.
She brandished her forefinger and screamed, "Who's the
savage?" Her cry was taken up by a handful of women at
her flank, who joined the men out of the mosque road and
toward the riverbank.

The crowd clapped and jeered as it swelled through the
streets, bringing children out of their homes and curious eyes
from the doorways. Emad saw onlookers clapping, and others shaking their heads. A young man was hoisted above the
crowd, onto the shoulders of others, waited expectantly for
its attention, then called loudly, "Leave, leave, you thieves
and frauds!" He paused as the crowd chanted it back, then
continued, "Even *savages* can use swords!" At this there was
an outbreak of cheering. With each repetition, the chant
grew louder and angrier. Residents of the street had joined
the crowd, and smatterings of rogue chants broke out as the
crowd grew too big to hear the young man leading them.

"Baghdad for Baghdadis!"

"One Arab state!"

Emad linked his arm with Yusuf's as they stepped onto
the floating Aimmah Bridge. The crowd swayed as it filtered
onto the bridge, tethered to which were boats and buoys that
kept the pontoon bridge afloat. Emad stumbled as his toes
hit the ledge that separated the carriage lane from the pedes-
trian path. He cursed and hopped, holding the metal fencing
for support.

"Come on!" whispered Yusuf, his other arm linked firmly
with his father's. Ahmad led his children through the crowd,
acting as a breaker that gave his sons room to breathe.

"Are you sure you want to do this?" asked Ahmad, raising
his eyebrows. "It's getting a little rough."

Emad raised his eyebrows back, and Yusuf pulled at his
father's arm. "Don't even think about sending us home,"
he said.

"All right, but stay close," said Ahmad. He waited for the bulk of the crowd to pass them, then led Emad and Yusuf forward.

Ahead, the man leading the chants called back to the demonstrators. "I see it! I see the top of al-Kadhimiya Mosque!" A few boat-owners who were working on their vessels paused to watch the demonstrators approach.

"Join us!" called the chanter. One or two of the men on the shore opposite lifted a hand at the bridge.

The crowd swelled back and called in chorus, "Join us!"

The chanter raised a hand to the people behind him. "Shia, Sunni, join together, kick the colonizers out forever!" And the crowd yelled it back.

"Come on!" called Ahmad, leaning over the side of the bridge and beckoning the people on the shore. He turned the slight bend in the bridge, pulling his sons behind him.

"Why aren't they joining us?" asked Yusuf.

"Are you seeing this?" Emad asked his father. Ahmad nodded. The men had stopped working on their boats and were standing on the edge of the bank, waving both hands above their heads, crossing and uncrossing their arms.

"Why don't they want us there?" asked Yusuf. "Because we're not Shia?"

Ahmad furrowed his brow. A man on the shore was throwing his hands in their direction. Ahmad didn't understand. He kept walking. And then he noticed the man's face, and the word his mouth was forming. *Run.* "He's not trying to send us away. He's trying to help us."

"Retreat!" yelled Ahmad, moments before a column of British officers descended from the opposite side toward the bridge.

The chanter looked from Ahmad to the shoreline and called out behind him, "Soldiers! Retreat! Retreat!"

Ahmad spun on his heel, and his eyes met the familiar scarred face of his old comrade. "Abdullah!" he said, though

Abdullah looked far less shocked than Ahmad felt. "What—" he began, then remembered they were being chased. "Run," he said.

Ahmad pulled Yusuf in close on one side, Emad on the other, and ran, easily outpacing Abdullah. Already toward the back of the crowd, they passed some women, offering a hissed "Run—soldiers!"

They reached the end of the bridge only to find a smaller squadron of British troops rounding the corner. A heavy-set lieutenant with dark hair raised a hand and pointed it at Ahmad.

"This way," called Ahmad, pulling his sons down an alleyway. He heard the splash of men jumping into the water, and looked back to see some of the protestors struggling into boats. He saw the dark-haired British lieutenant instructing a young private.

"No, you stay and block the bridge. I'll catch those three at the other end." He laughed cruelly, revealing two large front teeth.

Ahmad didn't need to understand English to know they were in trouble. "Faster," he breathed.

"Wait," called a voice behind him, in a foreign accent. They continued around another corner.

"Stop! Not there," called the soldier after them. His Arabic reminded Ahmad of the major's, but it was sharper, coarser. "I'm trying to save you!" said the soldier. "One more corner and you'll run into my lieutenant."

Ahmad stopped and turned. "Don't come closer," he warned, in slow Arabic. The soldier nodded. "If you're trying to help why are you pointing that thing at my sons?" asked Ahmad. The private looked sheepish and lowered his gun.

"Emad," barked Ahmad. "Walk up to the edge of the alleyway and peek around the corner. Don't be seen."

When Emad returned, he nodded. "The lieutenant we saw at the bridge is at the other end, with two more soldiers."

"Go that way." The private pointed down a small alley-way. "It's clear." He stepped aside, and as the three walked past him, they heard a loud bang. Yusuf jumped, and the man raised his open palms.

"Not me," he said, with a nervous laugh. "Here," he stepped forward and reached into his pocket, "have a Wrigley's."

Yusuf couldn't recall how he found himself right in front of the soldier, but he felt anger rise to his head. He shoved the soldier in the chest. "I don't need your cursed Wrigley's!" he yelled, grabbing him by the collar. "God, is there an English factory where they make all Englishmen the same?"

"Hey, hey!" said the soldier.

Ahmad pulled at Yusuf's waist, trying to rip him away. "Let go!" he shouted at his son.

"I was only being friendly," said the soldier. "What's wrong with you?"

"I am a *villainous savage*," yelled Yusuf, pounding the Englishman's chest with each word.

"Yes, that's what they call me too," he replied, with surprising calm. Yusuf stood still.

"Don't be shocked," said the soldier. "You think I want to be here?" He shook his head. "And please don't call me an Englishman." He held a palm in the air, then placed it on his chest. "Nice to meet you. I'm Carwyn."

40

THOUGH AHMAD REGRETTED HIS ALLEGIANCE with the British, it had taught him a valuable lesson: that they could rule for a hundred years in Baghdad and still not understand the three principles of the land:

1. Those with power must be kind to those without it.
2. Strength is the ability to control your anger.
3. Keeping good relations between humankind is better even than keeping prayer.

Ahmad knew Baghdad had always had its troubles—that it did not always follow its own rules—but dishonesty had not been among them until the British arrived. Where once kindness and acceptance were valued, deceit and cunning now reigned. And Baghdadis did not like this, not one bit.

The Shia leader, Grand Mujtahid Mirza Shirazi, was respected and honored above all others. Even the communities he did not lead knew of his honest and trustworthy character. His reputation spread well beyond his city of Karbala, unconstrained by the new artificial borders that threatened the region. And as the country's new rulers were still dismissing the protests as tribal, the Grand Mujtahid heard news of demonstrations that blossomed not only in Baghdad but all the way down the Euphrates.

Though he knew it was the right of every Iraqi to demand their freedom, he was sure he could convince the English to concede power through negotiation and prevent the demonstrations descending into unrest. Surely, he thought, the English could not ignore diplomatic calls for them to fulfill their wartime promises. He felt compelled to remind his followers of their Islamic duty to avoid violence, to unite as one, and to show tolerance and respect toward all Iraqis. And so he wrote to his countrymen:

To my brother Iraqis,
Peace be upon you and God's mercy and blessings. Let it be known that your brothers in Baghdad, Kadhimiya, Najaf, Karbala and other parts of Iraq have agreed amongst themselves to unite and to organize peaceful demonstrations. These demonstrations have attracted mass support while also maintaining public order, demanding their rights to an Independent Iraq and, God willing, an Islamic government with one objective—that every part of Iraq sends to the capital, Baghdad, a petition for its rights and agreeing with those who are heading for Baghdad from its surrounding areas. It is the duty of all Muslims to be in agreement with your brothers and their noble principles. But take care not to disturb the peace or to hide yourselves away or to fall into disagreement with each other such that your goals would become sour and your rights, which the moment of achieving is now in your hands, would fall into ruination.
And I entrust you with the safe keeping of all the other religious communities and sects which are in your towns, with full regard for their persons, wealth and lands and never do any harm to one of them. May God give you success according to his will. Peace be upon you and God's mercy and blessings.

Mirza Muhammad Taqi al-Shirazi

With this, he ensured that the revolt would remain peaceful and objective, allowing the British the chance to implement the changes needed to fulfill their promises of an independent Arab state.

But to the British, all was well. They labeled the demonstrations transitional pockets of tribal dissatisfaction. Mosque congregations swelled in numbers but few of the British noticed the apparent surge in piety that was taking root across Iraq. They had surrounded themselves with local advisors, who, during the banquets and parties, were all too happy to tell them that the rebellion was subsiding.

In truth, dissent was mobilizing, and it came in the form of the Guardians of Independence. When the British government outlawed political gatherings, the Guardians moved their meetings to the mosques.

Ahmad, Emad, and Yusuf had spent the past month at different mosques across Baghdad and, after prayer, watched as the Guardians' leader, Jafar, took names down for petitions, consulted protestors on their demands and needs, and opened the floor to speeches and poems of freedom and unity.

And in this new world, which offered them a conspiratorial whisper of opportunity and purpose, they thrived. After morning prayer, Ahmad and his sons would ride on the backs of two donkeys for which Mikhael had traded several of his most fruitful goats, and arrived at the city by noon. They would join in afternoon prayers, whistle and cheer when men spoke words of justice, and praise God in a chorus when they felt rebellion burn in their chests. And when they had tired of uproar and plotting, they returned home to Dabriya and Luma, and told them tales of the new Baghdad. Dabriya and Luma even joined them twice, on the donkeys, in their outraged mosque gatherings. And when they did not join them, they passed their days tending their crops and Mikhael's animals, happy in the knowledge that every day would end in the company of Ahmad. No one slept much: Sleeping took away from the excitement, from the thought that maybe, this might just work.

One Friday Jafar and his closest comrade, Ali, opened the floor of Abu Hanifa Mosque to speakers and poets. Ahmad waited as, one by one, each man stood and spoke of Iraq's beauty, of freedom, of hope—and his heart pounded as he told himself not to do it. He felt his legs stand, as if he were helpless to stop them, and he walked to the gap in the congregation, willing his mouth to remain shut. His ribs barely contained his nerves as he spoke, loudly, clearly, with rage.

I am fury, I am remorse,
I am torn and fractured and burned,
But we have risen, men in force,
I am the broken man returned.

He felt his legs wobble as he stepped away, and he was swallowed into a crowd that parted for him with awe. He turned in a flash and pointed to the door, to *them*. And he yelled, "Fear the broken man returned!" And the crowd yelled it back. And he hoped that someone in the crowd understood. This was more than longing for a glorious Iraq: It was about his right to the spoils of this war.

To Ahmad, the Guardians were a glimmer of hope in a world that had betrayed him. Stepping inside the mosque, he could leave the regime outside.

For Yusuf, a sense of belonging healed the ache Amira had opened in his heart. These were his people, they were just like him, and he would help them build a Baghdad where anything was possible.

As for Emad, he had always been the boy of the rebellion, before it had even had cause to exist. In the mosques, they were free of the English, of elitism, of the weapons that had created all of humanity's problems in the first place. They were even free of the differences that divided one Muslim from another. The mosques still belonged to Baghdad. They were not defeated.

On occasion, Yusuf and Emad acted as lookouts at the mosque entrances, alerting the congregating rebels to any approaching British. Some of the older boys, who had good English, were appointed to persuade the Indian soldiers of the British Army to slip them some information. After three weeks of patrolling mosque entrances, Jafar invited them to enrol at al-Ahliya School for Boys. The British had approved its establishment as a new education center, no doubt hoping it might serve as a more savoury outlet for the wealthy patrons of Baghdad.

Before the war, Yusuf had always enjoyed school. The classes he had shared with a few of the neighborhood children had proved useful, helping him to understand some of what the British were saying. It taught him how to work out what he was owed for each watermelon—depending on its weight—and how much he owed in return. He could read God's instructions and tell you if someone pronounced Arabic with the wrong vowel. And he found it liberating to be able to find the answers to his questions without having to ask his father, or Dawood, or anyone else.

So, on his first day at al-Ahliya School, he felt a rush of competition as he wondered what a city school would be like, and how advanced the other boys would be. He thought, for a moment, of Amira, sitting in her own classroom, no more than a mile away, and he smiled sadly.

When Yusuf sat down for his first class, his stomach was churning with anticipation. He needn't have worried: Although sums and letters certainly had their place in the school, they were clearly not the main focus. The school was a convenient and harmless outlet for Baghdadi benefactors, as far as the authorities were concerned, but in reality it equipped young men with the knowledge and skills of rebellion.

A heavy-set man with a stern brow strutted in. He spun around in front of the blackboard so swiftly that his robes swirled into a vortex, before coming to a halt and leaving etched behind him the words 'Modern History,' as though it were some magical illusion. He introduced himself as Ustad Saad, clipped a map to the top of the board and took his seat.

"In the last lessons we studied the Sykes-Picot Agreement. Do you all remember?" he asked, to a sea of nodding heads. He looked pointedly at Yusuf. "What about you, er . . . ?"

"Yusuf," said Yusuf, clearly, hoping nobody heard his voice waver.

"Welcome, Yusuf," said Ustad Saad. "Now, what do you know about the agreement?"

"Well," said Yusuf, clearing his throat, "while the English were trying to rally us to fight with them, to liberate Arab lands from the Turks, they had made an agreement with the French to divide the region between them, leaving them in colonial control." He paused. "Even though they promised us independence and self-rule once the Ottomans were gone."

"A good summary," said Ustad Saad, with a smile. "Though, if we're being accurate, then they are British, not just English. Can you tell me specifically how these promises were made?"

Yusuf's clothes began to stick to his back as he rummaged frantically through his brain. "Well, they promised it directly to the fighters in the Arab Revolt," he said, "but they specifically guaranteed Arab independence to the Sharif of Mecca in 1915. It's in writing too."

"Precisely," said Ustad Saad. "Today we will discuss how the signing of the Sykes-Picot Agreement directly contradicted guarantees made to the Arab people in the Hussein-McMahon Correspondence." He stood and retrieved twenty books from his desk, and handed them out to the class.

"Page fourteen, please," he said.

Yusuf leafed through the book on the desk in front of him, and found chapters on Baghdad under Ottoman rule, the outbreak of the war and the invasion of Arab lands. Toward the back he scanned chapters on the Balfour Declaration, discrimination and prejudice in Iraq, and British rule in India and other colonies.

Jafar had warned him that the school was for the forward-thinking minds of Baghdad but, still, Yusuf was surprised by his new classes. For two hours that morning they studied English, listening to their teacher and translating his words into Arabic, practicing their dialog, then poring over the latest editions of the *Baghdad Times*.

Every morning, the boys would run the short distance around the school building, and Yusuf began to suspect it was less about the value of exercise than the necessity of fitness. For some classes, such as English, Arabic, and mathematics, the sixty-three boys of the school were split into groups of three, by age and ability, but for others, such as anthropology and biology, which few of the boys had even heard of, the entire school would congregate together.

In biology, Yusuf, Emad, and their schoolmates learned the basic components and functions of the human body, how to recognize conditions such as dehydration, heatstroke, and cholera, as well as how to dress and elevate wounds. When Yusuf attended his first anthropology class, his teachers made no attempt to conceal the true subject of study: The rights of the people for a new Arab state.

Yusuf learned the principles of the Guardians of Independence, both in the pursuit and achievement of their ideal Iraqi state. Although Iraqi nationalists had once considered permitting a certain amount of British administration, this concept was explicitly forbidden among Guardian members, when it became clear that the British had no intention of giving Iraqis any custodianship. First and foremost, the Guardians demanded complete independence. Yusuf and his classmates were guided on social matters: No grudges were permitted, no persecution of Iraqi minorities, and no looting or robbery.

"This is not about venting your anger or grievances," said the anthropology teacher, Ustad Ibrahim, to the class. "We have a tangible and achievable aim, and nothing—not sectarianism, division, or personal issues—should ever be held above this."

The school liberated Yusuf and Emad in different ways. Yusuf made friends easily, and learning about politics and the future of Iraq helped him to better understand himself: This was his home, and these were his people. Although Emad didn't make friends, he found a home in a community that inherently shared his beliefs, and put a name to a concept for which he knew he would give his life. And, to both brothers, the school gave purpose, distraction, and the possibility of a future that—just weeks ago—they thought they had lost forever.

They threw themselves into the Guardians movement. When they weren't in classes they were discussing their future state, tactics for secret meetings, or the latest arrests that the English had made. They spoke about politics as if they had years of experience in them, which, in a way, they did. Whenever they met the Guardians' leaders they hung on their every word. They would go to Moshi's or Beyruti coffee shop with boys from their school, taking with them chessboards to disguise the true focus of their meetings.

It gave them a purpose, but neither brother could deny that being part of a secret rebellion was also thrilling. After talking for hours in cafés about their vision for Iraq, they would swerve through the benches, and—if there were no British about—leave handwritten notes on the tables: "There is no honor without liberty, and no liberty without independence."

There is very little that is more important to humans than belonging. Though freedom is a natural human instinct, it is possible to survive in its absence, so long as you have somewhere to belong. So, when the British had altered Baghdad beyond recognition, Yusuf, Emad, their father, and thousands of others found a home in the hushed whispers and illegal pamphlets, and in the mosques of both sects that offered them a place where no man ruled over another.

When classes finished one afternoon, Yusuf, Emad, and three classmates sat on a shaded bench in the school grounds and composed a note, each one copying it out twelve times and scrolling each piece of parchment into their pockets, before heading to the three largest cafés of Baghdad, Moshi's, Beyruti, and Café Riche, each run by a non-Muslim family. They skirted around Café Riche, observing as a diverse group of patrons sipped treacly coffee or ruby-red tea, smoked aromatic hookah pipes, or puzzled pawns around a chessboard. The café was well known for its alliance with, and facilitation of, the rebel movement, though few knew the extent of its role. After five minutes of observation, two of the classmates crossed toward the café, tossing papers on each table, and thrusting them into the hands of anyone who would take one, before the taller of the two boys read the page aloud:

"'*To all our Christian and Jewish fellow Baghdadis,*
We are brothers. Oppression that affects one of us affects all of us. For centuries our fathers lived together in friendship, so do not consider the actions of us, the Guardians of Independence, to diminish in any way the rights that your ancestors have guaranteed you. Our single aim is to realise the promises pledged from the lips of lying Englishmen to all Iraqis.
Every Baghdadi is guaranteed protection by his fellow countrymen, no matter their beliefs. But there is no future in a Baghdad that abducts, shoots and quashes the hearts and minds of any Iraqi—Muslim, Jew or Christian.
Join us for the good of our nation.'"

A few cheers erupted, as well as the inevitable Baghdad babble of discussion. The boys slipped out quickly and returned to the rest of the group on the opposite side of the road. They headed next to Beyruti Café, which overlooked the river. They were in and out in a matter of minutes, returning to the excited claps of their classmates.

As the five boys were sneaking glances around the corner of a building opposite Moshi's Café, Emad put a hand on the arm of the tall boy. "Let us do this one?" he asked.

The tall boy shrugged. "Go ahead," he said.

Emad and Yusuf watched the open-air café for a few minutes, before crossing the road with a brisk walk. They handed out papers to all the men who looked at them, especially those who spoke Jewish Arabic. When Yusuf was down to his last paper, he stood on a chair, and read it out ceremoniously.

He was halfway through when he heard the unmistakable hubbub of approaching British soldiers. No sooner had Yusuf jumped off the chair and pocketed the flyer than a lieutenant rounded on the tables near the café entrance. "What are these?" he demanded, in English, picking up the pamphlets and waving them above the heads of a group of men who were hunched over a backgammon board. The oldest looked up at him and shook his head in disgust. Emad pulled Yusuf onto a wooden bench in the corner of the café.

"It's him," whispered Emad, not looking up. "The lieutenant who chased us on the bridge." Yusuf drew in a sharp breath, and sat lower in his seat. "He's got that white-haired soldier we met with him too."

The lieutenant walked toward the old man and shook the flyer in his face.

"Go away, boy," said the man. "Can't you see we're busy?"

"What?" said the lieutenant, who understood barely any Arabic.

"It's a piece of paper. Don't you have those in England?" called a distant voice from the café crowd. Pockets of laughter broke out.

The lieutenant spun around. "Don't we have anyone here who can communicate with the natives?" he asked.

"He can, sir," said Llyr, pushing Carwyn forward.

Carwyn jumped. "Not really, I—"

"Evans," said the lieutenant, "what did he say about England?"

"I didn't hear anything about England, sir," lied Carwyn.

The old man in front of them sniggered.

"You think this is funny?" snapped the lieutenant. "Stand up!" he said to the old man, pulling him by the collar.

The café broke out in uproar, and a handful of younger men got to their feet.

"Wait," said Carwyn. "He's just an old man, sir."

"Quiet, Evans!" said the lieutenant, still clutching the man's collar.

The café owner's son, Yaqoub, appeared. "Come, now, Lieutenant, this isn't necessary," he said, in barely accented English, with a forced smile. "This is Uncle Idris, one of my oldest and most valued customers and friends." The lieutenant looked at Uncle Idris. When he turned away, the old man pulled a face at the crowd, who tittered approvingly.

"You could let him go, sir," said Carwyn, in a hushed voice. "We don't want to start anything unnecessary."

"I'll start what I like, Evans," snapped the lieutenant. "Well, now, my old budoo," he said, in English, slapping the cheek of the old man, "what is this leaflet you've been reading?"

"I've not even seen it yet," said Uncle Idris, "but I'd be happy to read it for you. I assume you cannot read Arabic?"

The lieutenant looked at Carwyn.

"He said he hasn't read it yet, but that he could read it now and tell you what it says," said Carwyn.

"No," said the lieutenant. "You read it."

"I can't, sir," said Carwyn. "I learned my Arabic in Egypt and it's a completely different script." It was his second lie to the lieutenant but he didn't care. He wasn't going to volunteer to help the lieutenant bully the old man. And it was his own stupid fault if he couldn't tell how obvious a lie it was.

"But you can speak it," said the lieutenant.

"Well . . . yes," said Carwyn.

"Let the old man read it and you translate for me, then."

Bugger. Carwyn nodded.

"Read the letter out, please," said Carwyn to Uncle Idris.

"Why didn't you say so sooner?" Uncle Idris stroked his beard ceremoniously, held out a hand and began:

"'*Dear people of Moshi's esteemed café,*
Today we will be receiving a most honored guest, Mr. Lieutenant of England. Although I know it will be very difficult for your simple minds, please do all you can to make him feel welcome and powerful.'"

Uncle Idris paused. "Er, then there's a squiggle, squiggle, squiggle, and it finishes:

'Also, Mr. Lieutenant enjoys very much your Arab jokes. Thank you. His Majesty Mr. Wilson.'"

Titters passed around the restaurant, and the tea- and coffee-drinkers watched rapt as the best entertainment most had seen in months unraveled.

"Well, Evans?" said the lieutenant, casting a suspicious eye around him.

Carwyn paused. To outsiders he seemed deep in translational thought, but really he was trying to hold back a laugh and compose himself. He could not burst out laughing in front of the lieutenant. He'd have his head for it.

"Um," said Carwyn, "the letter is addressing the people of the café—which explains why it was distributed here." Yusuf and Emad were whispering translations of Carwyn's words back into Arabic, for the benefit of the patrons, whose snickers did not go unnoticed by the lieutenant. "It's telling them to expect a visit from you, sir, and to afford you the best possible accommodation here.'

The titters could no longer be restrained and the café erupted with cheers and laughter. The young men behind Yusuf banged their table in approval.

The lieutenant's face had turned purple. He raised a fist and Uncle Idris flinched, as the slap came down on Carwyn's face. Both of Carwyn's cheeks turned red and he glared at the lieutenant. "I translated as best I could," he said slowly.

"You're right," said the lieutenant, raising his hand again, this time over Uncle Idris' left shoulder.

Like a shot, Yusuf stood up and shouted, louder than he ever had before, "Enough!"

The lieutenant spun around and stared at Yusuf. Surely he wouldn't recognize him from that chase by the bridge, he thought. How many boys must he have chased?

"Don't," whispered Emad. But Yusuf walked toward the British men, avoiding Carwyn's eye.

"They're my flyers. I wrote them," Yusuf said, in English. The lieutenant opened his mouth and Yusuf added quickly, "I deliver watermelons," said Yusuf, pulling his voice up a few notes higher. "And in the last months we have lost many customers."

"What are you talking about, boy?"

Yusuf could feel sweat running down his back. He pointed to the paper in Uncle Idris's hand. The old man passed it to him.

Yusuf looked at it and spoke in English, trying to measure his voice as though he was reading:

"*The finest watermelons this side of the Euphrates. Grown on the rich banks of the Tigris on family land. These delicious watermelons are carefully picked at the best time that makes*

*them both sweet and large. Find us on the west side of Maude
Bridge, or to place an order, leave a note for watermelon Yusuf
at any of these places: . . .'"*

Yusuf waved a hand casually. "That's all," he said.

The lieutenant examined his face. "If this is true, why did
you not say sooner?"

Yusuf lowered his head. "Mr. Moshi forbids advertising
at his café. He beat me around the head last time he caught
me. Look." Yusuf pulled back his ghutra and showed the lieutenant a scar behind his ear, from the day when Luma had
dug her nails into his scalp for spinning her around his head
too quickly.

Yusuf looked at Yaqoub sheepishly. "I really need the
business."

Yaqoub glared at him, his eyes sparkling. "How many
times must we tell you?"

The lieutenant looked from Yaqoub to Yusuf. "And how
do I know this isn't just another cock-and-bull story?"

Yusuf looked questioningly at the lieutenant.

"A lie," the lieutenant said, impatiently.

Yusuf nodded. "Why would I admit to it if it's not true?"
he said.

"Sir," said Carwyn. Yusuf avoided his eyes.

"What is it now, Evans?"

"I bought a slice of watermelon from this boy a day or
two ago. . . . Where was it again?"

"Just on the other side of the bridge," said Yusuf, pointing.

"Yes, beside Salman the fishmonger." Carwyn looked at
the lieutenant. "His real name, would you believe!"

The lieutenant seemed to be considering his options, but
Carwyn spoke again: "I think that clarifies everything, sir."

"It would seem so," he replied.

"Shall we leave these people to enjoy their afternoon,
then?" He rubbed his slapped cheek deliberately.

The lieutenant stared suspiciously at Yusuf, but nodded. He pocketed the flyer, turned and made for the exit.

Carwyn looked at Uncle Idris and placed an apologetic hand on his chest. He smiled at Yusuf and, checking his lieutenant was out of earshot, he whispered, "That's twice I've saved your skin now, watermelon boy."

41

IN THE WEEKS THAT FOLLOWED, the ruling British forces increased their surveillance of Arab activities. Yusuf, Emad, and their classmates struggled to find a single café that was unobserved by a foreign face, poorly disguised with an awkward ghutra that surely gave its undercover wearer too much confidence.

The cafés were full of whispers of English suppression. The British mobilized an indiscreet information service, charged with discovering the political, geographical, and strategic plans of the rebellion. There were few things that unanimously brought every Baghdadi more pleasure than talking in raised voices of the false meetings to be held at fictitious locations every night. One evening Ahmad spotted a blond-eyebrowed man huddled at Beyruti Café, reading the dissident newspaper *al-Furat*. He could have looked more conspicuous only by cutting two eyeholes in the paper. Ahmad gleefully raised his voice while recounting to Emad the location of that night's meeting.

"From the Maydan, walk past Ayoub's kebab stall," he said. "Take the right turn into Widow's Lane, keep going until you pass the barber's with that thing in the window—you know the one?"

Emad snickered and nodded knowingly, winking and tapping his nose.

"Take the second left and you'll end up at the river. Knock on the biggest palm tree you find and they'll let you in."

Ahmad almost heard the scout's eyes pop through the newspaper with delight. He imagined him returning to his barracks: *I'm telling you, Lieutenant, the entrance is the tree!*

Of course, there was no tree door, no Widow's Lane, and no Ayoub selling kebabs, but the thought of a troop of soldiers knocking on every unsuspecting palm tree on the banks of the Tigris kept Ahmad amused for days.

He saw more of Abdullah too—in the cafés rebels frequented, at Friday prayers. It seemed everywhere Ahmad went, Abdullah was to be found, poking his nose into every conversation that would accept him.

Sometimes the Information Service received accurate intelligence. It did not take long for Civil Commissioner Arnold Wilson to get word that al-Ahliya School was little more than a place to educate the rebels of tomorrow, and that the Guardians of Independence were using Café Riche for more than just coffee. Week after week he ordered raids. In the basement they discovered a printing press, with freshly inked illegal materials that promoted rebellion, as well as a petition addressed to the civil commissioner himself. Anyone found in the basement was forced to sign a counter-petition, demanding that the British remain in charge of Iraq. Sami, one of the café owner's sons, was arrested, with anyone else who refused to comply during the raids.

The raiding party confiscated all the ink they could find and warned that anyone found selling ink to the café would join Sami in jail. They did not, however, think to move the press. If they had, they would have discovered the entrance to a small network of Mamluk tunnels that provided fleeing rebels with a convenient escape route, right in the center of Baghdad.

Yusuf and Emad were returning home from what they considered a hard day's rebelling—distributing flyers, hanging out with school friends, and learning rude English words by eavesdropping on soldiers' conversations. They crossed Aimmah

Bridge toward Baghdad's western bank. They passed Moshi's Café and headed south to the outskirts of the city, where they had left one of Mikhael's donkeys with an old farmer in exchange for the animal's fertile deposits. They hopped over the tracks of the Baghdad railroad, and when the buildings thinned, the wide paths became narrow lanes edged with arcades of palm trees, when the horizon turned from sand-stone to pea green, Emad stopped sharply and put a hand on Yusuf's shoulder.

"What?" said Yusuf.

"Ssh." Emad put a finger to his lips. He turned but saw only the sandy lane. "We're almost at the farmhouse. Hurry." They began jogging away from the city. Each brother pre-tended to stay calm, as though they hadn't heard the extra feet beating the ground behind them, as though they didn't know by now the sound that British shoes make on Baghdadi dirt. Yusuf threw a look over his shoulder.

"It's that lieutenant," he panted. "He has a soldier with him." Emad grabbed Yusuf's arm and pulled him into the plantation. They bolted past precisely-planted columns of date palms, putting as much distance between themselves and the dirt path as they could, until Emad pointed to a small bush. Yusuf nodded. They threw themselves under it and breathed as slowly and quietly as they could.

Yusuf felt a pair of hands grab his ankles, and he juddered along the ground as he was pulled out.

"No!" said Emad, following his brother, but he was held back by a stocky soldier on the lieutenant's orders. Emad wrig-gled but couldn't shake off the hands that grasped him. He stopped resisting when the lieutenant spoke.

"Did you really think I wouldn't find out, boy?" said the lieutenant, his lips curling. He pulled Yusuf to his feet and gripped his shoulders.

"Find out what?" said Yusuf, coolly, in English. His eyes flicked to Emad.

"That flyer. I had it translated. You lied to me," said the lieutenant. "In front of all those people."

Yusuf shrugged. "You lie to us. We lie to you."

"You're a crafty one, aren't you?" said the lieutenant. "But most of you are. Like rats," he nodded at Yusuf's dishdasha, "in dresses."

Yusuf rolled his eyes. "Tell me," he said, tilting his head.

"Don't," warned Emad.

"Tell me, Lieutenant. How do you keep your—what is the word?" He remembered—his school friend Amin had learned it at the YMCA café. "How do you keep your *balls* dry in all those clothes?" The lieutenant's eyes bulged.

"Do you carry a balls handkerchief? Or maybe—if you have to stop boys on their way home from school—maybe you don't have any balls?" Yusuf chuckled.

The lieutenant took a step toward him.

"Run," whispered Emad, in Arabic. Yusuf didn't need telling twice. He dodged beneath the lieutenant's hands, pulling his shoulders free and ran, back toward the path. He heard the lieutenant panting behind him and he laughed.

"My balls feel so light and cool in my *dress*. How are—" He felt a hand grab the back of his head and the sudden, coarse sensation of bristly bark hitting his nose. A warm wetness dripped over his lips and he was vaguely aware of his brother's shouts in the distance. He felt a sharp tug on his hair and fell back onto the ground. He coughed and spluttered, trying to empty his airways of blood. He turned his head and spat into the ground, some of the bloodied spittle spraying onto his cheek.

"Not so confident now, are you?" laughed the lieutenant.

"Such a strong man you are," said Yusuf, between gasps. "I guess we all know now that you must have really big b—" A boot landed on his stomach.

"Stop!" called Emad. "This isn't fair!" He wrestled free from his captor and chased after Yusuf.

"Not so cocky now, are you?" said the lieutenant as Emad approached.

Emad raised a hand.

"Don't," whispered Yusuf in Arabic. "You know we can't fight back." Emad hesitated. "Why do you think he's chased us down here? He has no reason to arrest us. Don't give him one." Emad dropped his arm and was clapped round the ear with the butt of the lieutenant's rifle.

"Typical budoo, scared of a fight," said the lieutenant. "Maybe it's those dresses. It's hard to fight like a man when you're dressed like a woman."

Yusuf tried to sit up. It took a lot of effort to focus his vision. He saw Emad slumped to the ground beside him. He heard the lieutenant open a pocketknife and Yusuf's heart pounded. He couldn't move. Again he was powerless against these dogs. He prepared himself. Surely this was it for him. And then he heard fabric tearing. Twice. And two more rips where Emad lay.

Yusuf forced his head off the ground and stared at his legs. His dishdasha shredded straight down the center all the way up to his thighs. Trousers.

"Come on, sir," said the soldier with him.

"Quiet, Williams. I'm teaching them gratitude." Yusuf felt the lieutenant above him, a black giant blocking the sun. His face stung and his ribs ached. And then he felt a spray of warm liquid splatter onto his stomach. It smelled sharp and ripe and he gagged. He put his hands to his face, ignoring the jolt of pain it brought him. And he held his breath as the liquid trickled between his fingers—his nostrils, his eyes, his hair smothered in the lieutenant's piss.

42

LLYR TOLD THEM EXACTLY WHERE the lieutenant had gone: He had made no effort to hide his intentions from the platoon. One of his informants, no doubt, had told him where to find the boys. Carwyn knew Lieutenant Morgan was strict, that he understood very little about the city they ruled, but surely he was not a child-beater. The man had children of his own, for God's sake. But even as he thought it, Carwyn knew that, to the lieutenant, an Arab teenager was still just an Arab.

He turned left at Moshi's and headed out of the city, onto a dry path that cut through the palm forest. He was running for so long he thought perhaps Llyr had fed him the information as a test of loyalty, or just to make him the butt of all jokes until the end of their deployment. He came to a stop on the track and examined both directions—except for the sun, they were mirror images of each other, the path and the palms diverging and disappearing into the center of the horizon.

That was when he heard the soft sobbing. He headed northward into the copse, terrified at what he would find when he reached the source of the quiet whimpering.

He saw blood on the trunk of a palm tree, and gasped as he saw the older boy dragging himself forward on his elbows. When he reached Emad he dropped to his knees.

"Let's get you out of here," he said.

"Go to the end of the path," Emad said, clutching his cheek. "Tell the farmer you're collecting the donkey for Emad and Yusuf. There's no way he can walk." He gestured at Yusuf. "Hurry," said Emad. "Please hurry."

Carwyn took one last look at the boys. The blood, the torn dishdashas, the smell. And then he ran.

"Where are they?" said Ahmad, running into Moshi's Café. "Where are my boys?"

Yaqoub grabbed his arm and brought him indoors. "This way," he said.

When Ahmad's eyes fell on Yusuf he forced himself not to speak. He was sure he would sob before he got any words out. Cartilage pierced the bridge of Yusuf's nose and his skinny torso was twisted at an odd angle. Someone had tried to clean his face but they had forgotten to wipe his neck, which told Ahmad that his son's face had been beaten so badly that the blood reached his neck. A doctor bent over Yusuf's abdomen.

Ahmad looked at the doctor and raised his eyebrows.

"Just time and care. He'll be all right, inshallah."

Emad hobbled in, one arm around Carwyn's shoulder. Ahmad looked from Emad's hand clutching his abdomen to the British soldier holding him up. His eyes narrowed and he took a step toward Carwyn.

"It wasn't him, Baba," said Emad. "He helped us."

"Who did this?" Ahmad asked, with a growl.

"There are no excuses," said Carwyn. "It was my lieutenant." Ahmad looked at him.

"He was the one who tried to corner you, that day on the bridge."

"You'll need to be more specific," said Ahmad, with a dry laugh.

"He has black hair, as black as yours. His eyes are just a little too far apart. He has two diamonds stitched onto his shoulder as he's a lieutenant."

Ahmad nodded. "The one with the rabbit teeth?"

"The very one," said Carwyn. "I'm so sorry."

Ahmad indicated to Yaqoub to send in some sweet tea. A few minutes later a waiter came in and handed round the hourglass cups. Ahmad sighed. "It is not your fault, I know this," he said, waving a hand. "You helped my sons. But how many of your people knew this lieutenant would hurt my boys? And you were the only one to help."

"That says much more about them than it does about me."

"And you? Are you not one of *them* too?"

"What do you think?" said Carwyn, a little too quickly. "Do you think I am like them?"

"A man can be two things at the same time, can he not?"

"Not me. I'm trapped, but I'm not them," said Carwyn.

Ahmad raised his eyebrows.

"Do you know what I risked to save them?" said Carwyn. "Do you have any idea what he'd do to me if he finds out?'

"I'm sure it won't be this," said Ahmad, sharply, pointing to Yusuf. "Maybe you are honorable. Maybe you don't want to be here. But haven't you shot at men who looked like me? Killed them, even?" he said, his voice a little too high. Ahmad thought of all the times he had killed for the Ottomans, killed for the English. "Don't deceive yourself, boy," he said slowly. "As long as you serve the colonizer, you are the colonizer."

43

THIRTY MINUTES AGO, CARWYN HAD been panicking. A summons from Lieutenant Morgan could mean only one thing: He was done for. Maybe Llyr had squealed on him, or perhaps Tomos had found out somehow. Regardless, the only reason the lieutenant could possibly have to call him to his office was if he had discovered that Carwyn had saved those boys. Thirty minutes ago, Carwyn had been swearing to himself, racking his brains for an excuse that might get him off the hook. He pressed his uniform and tried to rehearse what he'd say in his small shaving mirror.

But as he walked toward Lieutenant Morgan's office, he no longer felt any of that. In fact, he wondered why he had been so anxious about it. He would gladly be imprisoned instead of serving in this stupid army under a clueless lieutenant. He'd no longer have to listen to Tomos's ridiculous speeches and spend his leisure time with a bunch of traitors. He was glad. Once he was out of this place, he could look himself in the mirror again. *Do they have mirrors in prison?*

He knocked.

"Enter," said Lieutenant Morgan. Carwyn pushed the door open and stood to attention as it swung shut.

"At ease, Evans." Carwyn relaxed slightly, a little disappointed.

"I'm sure you've gathered why you're here."

"Yes, sir."

"The thing is, Evans . . ." He paused. But Carwyn was ready for his punishment. He'd save those boys all over again if he had the chance.

"I probably shouldn't have struck you, Evans, especially not in front of all those locals." Carwyn must have looked shocked, because the lieutenant continued, "Don't be so hard on yourself. You were, as you said, translating as well as you could." Carwyn stood motionless. What in God's name was happening?

"I had the flyer translated. It was extremely inflammatory, illegal, even," said the lieutenant.

"So I'm not in trouble?" asked Carwyn.

"Heavens, no, Evans. I've had far worse insubordination."

"Oh." It was hard to hide his disappointment. Just as he was on the cusp of being out of this wretched mess.

"What's the matter, Private?"

"Nothing, sir."

"I know what you're thinking," said the lieutenant, genially.

That maybe I should actually get myself arrested somehow?

"You have to understand, we can't mollycoddle the Arabs. They're rising up against what is best for them, and it's our job to stop that, for their own good."

"Right, sir."

"And when the semicivilized revolt, they don't protest peacefully like we do, they're violent and ruthless, and if we allow them the space to protest, there will be no going back. It'll be chaos, mayhem, a bloody endless mess."

"Wasn't that flyer a peaceful protest?" said Carwyn, emboldened by the apology. The lieutenant was silent. "I, er, had it translated too."

"Now, look here, Private. Our jobs depend on us being able to quash this rebellion. And you know what they're saying about us in the Colonial Office? That we're unfit and unable to control a few primitive men."

It was true. News of Britain's latest colony, and their inability to bring a peaceable rule to 'MessPot' was being lambasted in the British press and Parliament. The Mesopotamia campaign and unrest were draining money from Britain, and everyone's jobs were at risk. Lieutenant Morgan's superior had warned him that he could not afford to fail, not after he had been outmaneuvered twice already on operations he'd led based on false intelligence. He could not let the Arabs humiliate him again.

"I see, sir," said Carwyn. "You're right. That makes all the difference." *What do you want me to say?*

"I'm glad you think so. Nobody wants to be seen as the villain, but we need to bring these people to heel. Can you imagine what would happen if we let them rule?" the lieutenant laughed. "The thought of Arabs running around with weapons and in government is terrifying, isn't it?"

"Petrifying," said Carwyn, with a glassy smile.

"And, er, Private, I'd be grateful if you didn't mention the incident in the café to anyone."

"Yes, sir. Good afternoon, sir." Carwyn left the room, shut the door, and leaned against the corridor wall.

He didn't know whether to laugh at the lieutenant's ridiculous insecurity, or go back in and punch the man to get himself thrown out of the blasted British Army.

44

It was the largest Friday prayer gathering Ahmad had ever seen. The al-Kadhimiya mosque was packed so tightly that no worshipper could touch his head to the floor without coming into contact with the heels of the man in front.

This week, two sets of prayers were read, the first for the regular Shia attendees, and the second for the Sunni guests who had traveled for the most important meeting in weeks.

When both prayers had ended, the men shuffled forward to make room for each person to sit. Ahmad found a shaded spot that caught the breeze which blew across the courtyard, and pulled his sons down beside him.

Jafar and Ali, two of the leaders of the Guardians of Independence, stood on a platform in the center of the courtyard, two golden domes forming their backdrop, to address the crowd.

"Brothers," boomed Jafar, his voice echoing across the vast courtyard, "and sisters." He waved a hand to an area reserved for women. "They presume us to be uncivilized," he called out slowly, with almost effortless volume. "We have heard what they call us—'dirty, savage budoos.' We do not have to prove to them that we are not. We owe them nothing." Jafar paused to let his echo fade. "But today we will be diplomatic, and offer the uncivilized English a civilized way out of their mistakes." He looked at Ali, who spoke up.

"You will elect fourteen delegates who will meet with the commissioner to petition for an Iraqi state free from English rule. The delegates must include brothers from both mosques, and they will be led in negotiation by our respected elder and leader, Haji Suwaydi."

"Anyone may nominate himself or a fellow brother," said Jafar. "Please raise a hand if you would like to speak."

An unusual silence fell across the courtyard. An older boy Emad recognized from school put his hand up, and a wave rippled across the sea of heads.

"Yes, my son?" asked Jafar.

"Can we nominate both of you?"

The crowd bubbled approvingly, and Jafar looked uncertainly at Ali. They stared at each other until Ali shrugged.

Jafar turned to the crowd and said, "Very well."

A few young men volunteered, as well as a handful of the most dedicated Guardians, most of whom had been beaten, detained, or had made unlikely escapes during a British raid. Each nominee moved to join Jafar and Ali. Sunni and Shia elders were nominated by their communities, and even a couple of Emad's schoolmates raised their hands.

Soon enough around fifty people stood at the center of the mosque, framed on four sides by the unmistakable blue and gold minarets.

"Does anyone else wish to be considered?" said Ali, his voice reverberating through the arches.

All were silent, and then Emad raised his hand.

"Join us up here, then, yabni," said Ali.

"No, you misunderstand," said Emad. "You should send my father. There is truly nobody better."

Ahmad's head whipped around in surprise. He felt all eyes lock on him and his hands began to sweat. He stood up. "An honor, truly, but I am not the appropriate person for such a task," he said, heat rising to his cheeks. A few faces around him smiled encouragingly, the familiar ones disputing his words.

"Abu Emad, if the people wish this of you it is your duty. Please step forward, brother."

Ahmad looked from face to face, each one staring at him. He felt hands nudge him forward slowly, then felt his feet inching toward the other nominees. He didn't recall making the decision to walk—perhaps he had done so just to escape all the expectant faces gazing at him.

When Ahmad reached the center of the mosque, Jafar invited each nominee to offer a few words about what their presence would bring to the delegation. Most spoke of their dedication to independence or their experience in negotiation. Some stressed their battle experience, bravery, or speed, which resulted in cheering and confusion among the congregation, each in equal measure. Jafar said he felt honored to have been nominated, and spoke of his enthusiasm to represent the views of the city, and Ali spoke of his bureaucratic, diplomatic, and military experience under the Ottomans. The nominated elders spoke of fulfilling their duty, some with bowed heads and others throwing their arms into the air with each word. Ahmad felt his stomach drop further with each passing minute. Surely, he thought, he had never felt so nervous before a battle.

When he heard his name called, he felt sick. He stepped up beside Jafar, and opened his mouth.

"Brothers," he said, relieved that the word had come out correctly, "please elect someone from among our worthy candidates beside me." He held his hand out toward the nominees. He heard a rustle in the audience but avoided looking directly at anything. "I am not made for such a task . . ." he said, the last word trailing off as he realized what he had said.

And before he knew it, Emad was climbing up at his side.

"Forgive my father," said Emad, ignoring Ahmad's protests. He took a deep breath. "Before you stands a man with experiences few of us could ever imagine. He has suffered loss and cruelty at the hands of the English and the Ottomans." Emad glanced at his father apologetically. "Anyone who looks at my father can tell that he is a man of war and muscle, but only those who speak to him understand that, before all else, he is a man of heart."

Ahmad stared at him. He felt exposed, uncomfortable, and stunned by the words pouring out of his son's mouth. He wasn't sure whether he wanted to stroke Emad's head or give it a sturdy slap, so he ended up doing neither.

Emad raised his voice once more: "Despite all the lies, bloodshed, and defeat that he has endured, he was never broken. After separation from his family, flooding, a loss of all our crops, even the loss of his memory, he still believes that good people always prevail. Everywhere he goes, men around him recognize this. Many of those men are here today. Ask any of them, and they will tell you that the terrible things my beloved father has been a part of, in every area of his life, have made him the most humble man they ever knew. Here is a man who has made many mistakes in his life, but always for the right reasons. That is the kind of man we want to represent our city."

Perhaps the congregation admired Ahmad's humility, or believed that the only great leaders are those who do not seek leadership. Most likely, though, they simply saw that the greatest proof of an honorable man was the respect of his adult son. And that was how Ahmad, bewildered, found himself among the fifteen men of the delegation.

45

Spring 1920
Samarra

THOUGH CIVIL COMMISSIONER WILSON REMAINED unconvinced that any serious rebellion was afoot, he agreed to meet with the delegation. And, viewing the fifteen men as little more than self-appointed politicians, he invited to the meeting forty prominent Baghdadis who supported him, hoping to drown the voices of *extremist* Arabs in a sea of pro-British sentiment. Naturally, a delegation selected by his own hand held a higher legitimacy than those selected through popular election.

The languages teacher from al-Ahliya School accompanied the fifteen delegates to interpret for those who didn't understand English. They arrived in the sweltering Shia shrine city of Samarra, several hours' ride north of Baghdad. News had traveled of the meeting, and when Ahmad, Jafar, Ali, Haji Suwaydi, and the eleven others arrived at the serai where the meeting would be held, a large crowd had gathered outside, despite the extreme heat of summer and the Ramadan fast. It still felt surreal to Ahmad. He didn't hear much of what was said as he was patted on the back on his way through the grand archway of the serai building, and most of it was directed at Ali, Jafar, and Haji anyway. The atmosphere was tense and made more so by the heat, smell, and relentless shouting for freedom. There was some crude name-calling too—directed at the recently arrived civil commissioner, Ahmad presumed. He had never felt more undeserving of or ill-prepared for his role. He buried one hand in his armpit, and with the other helped an elderly blind delegate named Suleiman through the archway.

As he stepped into the enormous arch-lined courtyard, he heard a familiar voice call after them, "Don't worry, we gave them hell!"

Ahmad looked back, saw a bearded face grin at him, and laughed, a deep, face-wrinkling belly laugh. "Abu Hamza!" he almost screamed. He wanted to run back, but Suleiman pulled him forward. Ahmad waved at his friend, truly, over-whelmingly happy to see him again.

The delegates were led into a large room. The floor, walls, and ceilings were adorned with intricate tiles of leaves knotted with tulips and tesselated Ottoman geometry, col-ored deep blue and teal, rich green, and powder pink. And mounted above them were twelve enormous Union flags, which dropped from the ceiling.

Ahmad noticed the unusual layout of the hall. A long mahogany table stood at the end of the room, and facing it was a large, carpeted quadrant, clearly the designated delegate area. As soon as the men had filed into a haphazard row, nine other Arabs entered the room behind them, all well dressed and immaculately groomed. When they had first walked in, the room had felt like a cool relief from the sun, but the longer Ahmad stood, the hotter he felt. There was no draft and the walls reflected their own heat back at them.

After what Jafar termed an "appropriate power delay," the mustachioed Civil Commissioner Arnold Wilson appeared from a door behind the desk, followed by three other British men, each in freshly laundered uniforms and sola hats. They would turn out to be Colonel Balfour, the military governor of Baghdad, Edgar Bonham Carter, judi-cial secretary, and Lieutenant Colonel Howell, revenue secretary. They were followed by an Arab with a stern chin who hid his face, as, for the first time in his life, he felt more eyes on him than on his commissioner.

Commissioner Wilson sat, placing a fan of papers on the table, then cleared his throat. He indicated to his colleagues to sit, and looked for the first time at the delegates. Ahmad was sure he noted a hint of shock on the commissioner's face, but he hid it quickly.

"Good afternoon, sirs. I welcome the opportunity to explain the British government's policy in this matter. I would draw your attention to the Anglo-French Declaration, signed on the seventh of November two years previously." Ahmad looked to the translator, Kasim, who explained what the commissioner had said.

The commissioner's gaze stopped on Jafar and, to Ahmad, he appeared to frown. Beside the table, the Arab assistant was scribbling notes, his head bowed.

"These declarations represent the policy of His Majesty's Government, from which it has at no time diverged." He paused, and Jafar raised his eyebrows at Haji Suwaydi, who was sitting beside him. The Arab assistant handed the commissioner a paper, from which he proceeded to read:

"'*The goal envisaged by France and Great Britain in prosecuting in the East the War let loose by German ambition is the complete and final liberation of the peoples who have for so long been oppressed by the Turks, . . .*'"

Kasim interpreted hurriedly each time the commissioner took a breath. He did not wait for Kasim to finish before he continued to read from his paper. Ahmad shifted his weight from right leg to left and looked at his fellow delegates; he did not need Kasim to translate, because he had heard these words before. They all had. He put a hand under the right forearm of Suleiman and Ali supported his left. Jafar pursed his lips and Ahmad was sure the insult of the lecture was not lost on him either. His blood throbbed at his temples. Did the commissioner think they did not know the words of the

Anglo-French Declaration? Ahmad could have recited it to him, along with any other document the scheming Europeans had written behind his back. He took a breath and opened his mouth, but Suleiman touched the back of his hand, and whispered, "Let him finish, or he will interrupt us when it is our turn to speak." Ahmad forced his mouth shut, and, for fear of what he might do, avoided looking at the high table of pomp for the rest of the lecture.

The commissioner continued:

> "*In pursuit of those intentions, France and Great Britain agree to further and assist in the establishment of indigenous Governments and administrations in Syria and Mesopotamia which have already been liberated by the Allies, as well as in those territories which they are endeavouring to liberate, and to recognise them as soon as they are actually established.*"

Ahmad raised his eyebrows, flabbergasted. He hadn't known his country had been unestablished all this time. He focused all his efforts on studying the patterns on the walls, trying to distract himself from the assault on his ears and country. He didn't need to hear the end of the recitation. From the moment the commissioner had drawn his second breath in his speech, Ahmad had known what he would say: That neither the French nor the British wanted to impose their own ways on the region, but to allow for the fair election of a government. Somehow the irony of the current unelected government was lost on both nations.

When the commissioner finally finished reading he looked at the delegates once more and spoke of his regret that these aims had been delayed, for reasons outside British control. Ahmad bit his tongue, again, when he realized the implication that the delays were the fault of the unruly natives, disturbing borderlands and demanding the very thing that the British authorities claimed they wanted for the country.

The commissioner was aware of the measures that the Grand Mujtahid had taken to keep up diplomatic relations and discourage calls for violence and rioting. He was aware that these calls had largely been heeded, but perhaps he felt the need to rule with a strong fist. Any self-respecting Oriental secretary could tell you that Arabs only understand displays of force—and, in this vein, he reprimanded the delegates for calls to violence that had not even happened.

> "'Those who are encouraging disorder and inciting men against the existing regime are arousing forces which the present Administration can and will control. It is my duty as the temporary head of the Civil Administration to warn you that any further incitements to violence and any further appeals to prejudice will be met by vigorous action both from the Military authorities and the Civil Administration.'"

It has always been lost on the colonizer that the colonized have the capacity for diplomatic transition, and so it was lost on the commissioner that this meeting was the delegates' final attempt to avoid calling their compatriots to rebellion.

The delegates sat in a humble silence that every person present knew the commissioner did not deserve, as he described the British plans for a future independent state. He detailed his intention to appoint an Arab president and an eleven-member Council of State, both selected by the high commissioner (and "removable at his pleasure"), the majority of whom would be British. This would be the extent of the self-determined Arab state, because even "with the best will in the world, an indigenous National Government cannot be set up at once. The process must be gradual or disaster is certain."

On hearing Kasim translate this, Ahmad could not swallow his scoff, which earned him a glare from all three British officials. The commissioner thanked his audience for their patience and said he would be glad to hear any representations they wished to make.

As soon as Haji Suwaydi stepped forward, a dignified silence fell, even from the table of men who had ignored his status, and made him stand in waiting until they had finished speaking.

Haji Suwaydi pointedly reminded the British that the fifteen delegates were the only ones in the room who were elected representatives, and that they had come to negotiate three demands that the vast majority of the people and their leaders had agreed upon.

"First," began Haji, "we demand the immediate establishment of a Convention representing the Iraqi people which will lay out the route whereby the form of government and its foreign relations will be determined.

"Secondly, the granting of freedom of the press so that the people may express their desires and beliefs.

"And thirdly, the removal of all restrictions on the postal and telegraph services, both between different parts of the country and between Iraq and neighboring countries and kingdoms, to enable the people to confer with each other and to understand current world political developments."

Haji Suwaydi looked around his co-delegates, and addressed the British table. "In our capacity as delegates of the people of Baghdad and Kadhimiya, we ask that you agree to the implementation of these three demands as quickly as possible."

The civil commissioner nodded. "Thank you for expressing your opinions so precisely. However, it is with regret that I must inform you there is nothing further that can be done to expedite the process I outlined, until such time as I receive instructions from London as to how the mandate will be put into practice."

He stood abruptly. "Come along," he said, to his assistant, who was concluding his notes of the meeting.

Jafar shot up and spoke, in English: "You cannot leave, Commissioner. We have not reached an agreeable conclusion."

Ahmad stood, pacing forward behind Jafar.

"I have heard your demands and you have heard my response," said the commissioner, knocking on the table to hurry his Arab note-taker. "That is all that can be expected of this meeting."

They followed the commissioner through the halls of the serai.

"Surely you cannot mean to leave like this," Ahmad called out. For the first time in his life, he regretted not having a good grasp of English. He wanted the commissioner to understand exactly what he was saying. A cluster of eight soldiers walked toward him and put themselves between him and the commissioner.

"After all we have done for you," roared Ahmad. "Baghdadis killed for you during the war. We died for you, and all we are granted is an hour of standing in the heat and the back of your head."

He took a breath, and the rest of the delegates began shouting behind him, reiterating Ahmad's points in English. He turned and walked to the back of the group. He would find another route to the commissioner. He had not come all this way for nothing.

But what he saw at the foot of the corridor made him forget all about the commissioner. He didn't put it together at first. His friend, Abdullah, was talking to a British soldier, whose back was to Ahmad. He was about to call to him when he heard the soldier speak: "Thanks for your help today Abdelmajid, it was very useful."

Abdelmajid. Why was he calling Abdullah by that name? And he stared at Abdullah—those scars, that loose skin around his neck. *That deformed nose.*

His heart hammered in his ears. He remembered Ayesha's grandmother saying she would know the attacker when that son of a dog Abdelmajid returned and had *no nose.*

It could not be, he thought. The world is not that small or cruel. But even as he thought it, he knew it was true. He knew that his comrade Abdullah had tortured that poor girl, had choked her with henna and watched as he suffocated her out of this world. He knew that Abdullah had lost his nose to a woman determined to die fighting, and to make that man carry the memory of her on his face for the rest of his life.

And when the soldier talking to Abdullah turned to face Ahmad, he felt himself tremble uncontrollably. The two diamond patches on his shoulders. The black hair. The eyes just a little too far apart. Ahmad grew breathless.

"Lieutenant Morgan?" he called. The lieutenant looked at Ahmad and smiled. That cruel, rabbit-toothed smile.

Ahmad launched himself at the lieutenant and Abdullah. He threw his whole body into the air, and felt the arms of four men restrain him from behind.

"Abdullah! You dirty traitor!" he yelled. Abdelmajid shuffled behind the lieutenant and stared at Ahmad glassy-eyed.

"Do you know what your lieutenant did?"

"Come, Ahmad," said Abdelmajid with an uncomfortable smile.

"Say my name again!" spat Ahmad. "After everything I did for you, after everything we fought for, you turned traitor against your own people?"

"Walk away," said Abdelmajid, softly.

Ahmad spat on the floor at the man's feet. "You gave my sons to this dog," said Ahmad, nodding at the lieutenant. The lieutenant didn't need to speak Arabic to understand Ahmad's meaning. "Get this man out of here," he said, with an indifferent wave. Hands fixed around Ahmad's shoulders. He heard himself yelling vulgarities, and being restrained, but it happened extremely slowly, almost silently, and in flashes. Arms restricted his flailing fists, and when he stepped through a door, he couldn't recall how he had got to it. He knew he was outside only when he felt the punch of the sun on his face, and its rapid seepage through his clothes. Up ahead he could hear jeers and chants deriding the English and the commissioner. Jafar pulled him into the crowd and, with it, he marched through the streets of Samarra, toward the golden-domed mosque. Jafar and Ali led chants against the "lying English," which Ahmad mindlessly shouted with the rest of the crowd. He knew he should be enraged, of course, but most of all, he felt an overwhelming disbelief. He marched along, chanting, hearing noises extra loudly, and seeing faces extra sharply, his senses swamping his brain. With all the people and noise and commotion around him, it felt like an earth without air. He thought he might vomit. Perhaps it was the fasting.

They took a road that led alongside the old city wall, and Ahmad found himself ducking through an archway and running across the open desert toward the spiraled minaret of the Great Mosque of Samarra. He focused his eyes on the seashell-shaped minaret and ran. He forgot his fasting thirst and found silence in the enormous paces that made him feel—for the first time in months—his own limbs, chopping powerfully against the dead air. He felt his clothes flapping in the wind and the rhythm of his breath, and his mind was mercifully filled with nothing beyond motion and muscles stretching as far and as fast as they ever had.

Then he recalled what Abdullah had done to Ayesha. He recalled what the commissioner had said. He remembered all the boys he had shot for the sake of an enormous lie told by a nation that thought it was superior to every other. He remembered the months he had tortured his wife and children with his absence, and the words he would never get back. But most of all—more than the abstracts of what wasn't or what might have been—he remembered the blood. Forever etched to the inside of his eyelids were the unshakable images of flesh and limbless torsos crawling through filth.

Ahmad stood in an arched entrance of the ancient mosque and fixed his gaze on the helter-skelter minaret—the only thing that stood solid among crumbling ruins.

He took two steps at a time, curling his way around the twisting turret. The sharp jabs of breathlessness gave him something to focus on, something that he knew was true. He felt the earth drop lower as he propelled himself up the winding staircase. And when he stopped for a moment, just for a second to feel the wind in his clothes, or to see the earth as he had never seen it before, he was suffocated by the ache of regret. Each heartbeat taunted him with a melodic accusation.

What have-I done? What have-I done? What have-I done?

So he didn't rest. He ran and leaped further up the minaret coil until he felt as if he were higher than any man had ever been, his heart beating so violently that he imagined he must have left a trail of blood up the stairs. And when the axis had narrowed, and Ahmad found himself at the last few stairs, he hoisted himself to the flat roof of the spiraled minaret.

And when there was nowhere left to run, all the ghosts that Ahmad had outrun and left scattered up the stairway came crawling up the minaret to leap at him, like the bloody arms dragging legless torsos that played across his eyelids.

And he felt it in his shoulders, as they clung to him, and in his heart as they crushed it, and in his brain, which he knew, now, could never forgive what he had done.

Ahmad dropped to his knees and grabbed his head, and felt the two rivers of Iraq run down his cheeks, in shame at what his people were reduced to. He could almost feel the torn limbs floating down this Tigris, as they had so many times before.

Never again. Never again would he pick up a gun, he swore it. Never again would he spill a man's blood.

How could he have been so stupid as to leave his family, his home, to kill? He would drag behind him the echoes of the young men he had killed for all his days, but at last—finally—Ahmad knew that he was not a man of war.

And he roared at God in anger and for mercy, for surely no one in this land could understand what he felt. And he stood, higher than any sight he had ever seen, and threw his fists into the air, just to take him even higher into the sky, and every word ever spoken erupted from his mouth in a single howl that echoed across the scorched, stolen land below.

But the land had known howls like this before, and it would echo with many more until the end of time. Perhaps if Ahmad had known this, he might have chosen differently. Perhaps he might have thrown himself from that tower, as you will deny you wished, snapping his spine on the steps as he hurtled to the ground. But ignorance can be merciful, so instead he roared his throat raw, spitting his regret across the Samarra sands beneath him until, finally, at last, he could feel his brain. He stared at the sky above him and he swore to God and all the levels of Heaven, to the river of Paradise and the angels that might take him there, he swore: *I am not defeated.*

And he descended the stairs just as he had climbed them, with bodies at his feet and ghouls on his shoulders, but this time he welcomed their company. What drives man if not regret, if not sorrow? And he ran beyond the mosque walls, his feet beating on the desert floor, back into the city, back to the rebels, back to the shouts for justice and pumping fists. He would not let them win, not the lieutenant, not the English, not that lying bastard Abdelmajid. Ahmad was not done with them yet. He did not need to join an army to fight, to resist. He would demand his rights with the rebels. *This* would be his war. He found Jafar leading the march to Samarra railroad station. He gave Ahmad a questioning look mid-chant. Ahmad smiled at him and held up a hand. He crossed the road and pulled up a woven chair from a small café. He stood on the seat and gazed at the crowd. A Rolls-Royce armored vehicle appeared at the end of the road, positioned to control the protestors. Abu Hamza, a whole head above the crowd, was smiling straight at him.

A man crouched in the crowd, swung his arm back and lobbed a stone toward the vehicle. It struck the protective dome that hid the driver from view and fell to the road. A wave of stones followed, and Ahmad paused. He looked from the serai across from him to the crowd heaving down the street toward the armored vehicle. As soon as the throng of protestors had cleared the serai entrance, three passenger cars pulled into the street from the other end. The commissioner exited the serai and quickly disappeared into one of them. He was followed by the three other officials at the meeting.

Ahmad looked back at the crowd, searching for Abu Hamza. And a plan came to him. This was one wrong he could right.

He called his friend's name, and Abu Hamza came thundering down the street to him, separating the crowd with ease. He looked back at the serai, waiting. *Surely he would show up.*

"Hello, old friend," said Abu Hamza.

"We don't have time," said Ahmad. "Can you help me? For just a minute?"

"For as long as you like, it's not like I have anything on." Abu Hamza smiled.

"Look," Ahmad instructed, pointing to the serai. "You remember Abdullah?" Abu Hamza nodded. "He's in there and he's an informant," said Ahmad. "And his name is actually Abdelmajid. He murdered Ayesha." Ahmad hopped off the seat and scoured the floor before picking up a stone in each hand. He would make no mistake this time. The serai door opened again, and Lieutenant Morgan exited.

"I see I've missed a lot," said Abu Hamza, unperturbed.

"Quick," said Ahmad. Two of the cars pulled away as Abdelmajid emerged from the serai, and as the lieutenant got into the third car, Ahmad roared at it and threw the first stone with all his might. It flew straight through the car's small square window, hitting the lieutenant neatly on his cheekbone.

"The rebellion suits you much better than the war ever did," said Abu Hamza.

"How are you always so calm?" Ahmad said, shaking his head. He didn't know if he should laugh or scream.

"Go! Now!" yelled the lieutenant, banging his fist on the dashboard. Abdelmajid ran toward the car, his arms outstretched toward the open-top trunk at the rear but the driver put his foot to the floor.

"Wait," screamed Abdelmajid, as the car screeched away,

Ahmad drew his arm back and released the second stone at Abdelmajid's face. He yelped and ran after the car, his face in his hands. Ahmad and Abu Hamza caught up with him in moments.

"Well, well," said Ahmad. "We meet at last, Abdelmajid."

"What do you want with me?"

"That rock on the head was for my sons," said Ahmad. "But I can't have all the fun, can I?"

"Can I have a go now?" asked Abu Hamza, taunting Abdelmajid with a fist-sized rock.

Ahmad couldn't help but laugh. "Oh, I'm sure you'll get plenty of chances, if he misbehaves."

"What do you want?" asked Abdelmajid, "Money?" He pursed his lips to stop his jaw trembling.

"You're going to disappear from the English. They will never know where you went."

"Please . . ."

"You see, you and Abu Hamza," said Ahmad, removing his belt, "you're going on a journey." He nodded at Abdelmajid. "Hands," he said. Abdelmajid's eyes flicked from Ahmad to Abu Hamza. He shook his head silently.

"Please, no," said Abdelmajid.

"*Hands*," said Abu Hamza, flecks of spit hitting Abdelmajid's forehead. Abdelmajid held them out. Ahmad tied his wrists together roughly with his belt.

"Please don't kill me."

"What did you say to Ayesha when she begged you not to kill her?" asked Abu Hamza slowly.

Abdelmajid took shallow breaths. "She never asked me not to," he said quietly.

Abu Hamza smiled. "You are the most pitiful coward I ever met. I don't know if I will be able to bear his company, Abu Emad."

Ahmad laughed.

"Where are we going?" Abdelmajid gulped to try to steady his voice.

"Oh, Abu Hamza is taking you back to Basra," said Ahmad, "back to Ayesha's home, where you will wish her grandmother a happy Eid."

"How—" spluttered Abdelmajid. "Why would I—"

"I wonder what part of you she'll remove first," said Ahmad.

Abu Hamza threw back his head and laughed.

46

Spring 1920
Baghdad

MEN WHO DABBLE IN WAR and conquest seldom understand the value of identity. Is there a possession more volatile or valuable? And to steal such a thing, to maim it beyond recognition, triggers a fracture that festers in the veins of progeny for eternity. It rips souls into unnavigable pieces until the world, and time, and everything that was ever thought indestructible, crumbles, like it never was. It is a theft that can never be undone.

But in the spring of 1920, the rift was still just a crack. And time would decide whether it would split, forming a fracture for generations, or whether it would be defended, healed, reclaimed. And so, as the British mobilized to establish the Mandate of Iraq, with arbitrarily-drawn borders that joined together three independent regions, the people of Mosul and Baghdad and Basra came together to defend their futures.

With each day of fasting, the fervor of revolution grew more palpable, like static that passed inaudibly between strangers. A tingling, untouchable rebellion swelled in the air. It blew through the country with the shamal sands until almost every village in the central Euphrates was home to worshipers calling for revolt, or men who had deserted their posts in British governance, or tribal leaders withholding taxes from their new rulers. When the final day of Ramadan fell upon Iraq, it was as though the whisper of revolution was all anyone consumed.

And when the British political officer of Hillah invited a delegation of rebels to diplomatic talks, they were arrested on arrival, among them the Grand Mujtahid's son. The Grand Mujtahid warned against closing negotiations, threatening to align himself publicly with the forceful removal of the British. But it was too late. Civil Commissioner Wilson and Oriental advisor Gertrude Bell rejoiced. *We have got the wolf by the ears*, they told themselves gleefully. *The whisper of revolt is dead*. Their trusted Arab advisors reassured them, *With these leaders imprisoned, the rebellion has stopped dead*, and, of course, simple Arabs couldn't possibly be too polite to tell a man of his own unpopularity.

True to his word, the Grand Mujtahid announced: "It is the duty of the Iraqis to demand their rights. In demanding them they should maintain peace and order. But if the English prevent them obtaining their rights it is permitted to make use of defensive force."

They were the words that burst the banks of the Euphrates rebellion, flooding the country along the entire course of the river, screaming as it flowed out to the ocean and up into the Kurdish mountains, bursting both ends of the land.

It was a call of unrest that would echo for decades, from the main streets of Baghdad, or sometimes from within basements, muffled beneath the pavements and the boots that trod on them. But it was always there, the cry of Iraq, and it spoke of power—at least, it did in the beginning.

There was an air of celebration in the Maydan of Baghdad. Ramadan had ended and, whether from the success of the revolt further south, or the sense of community that the rebellion had fostered, hope filled the air. Admittedly, it was bolstered by the waft of charcoaled kebabs and syrupy sweets, but there was hope nonetheless.

Dabriya was glad to join Ahmad and her sons. She brushed away her reservations about bringing her children to the biggest square in the city during a rebellion by telling herself they needed to see it, but the truth was that she needed to see it, to know that her sacrifice had been worthwhile. And it had been safe so far, she told herself. Luma had her hair in braids for the occasion, and Dabriya had brought out her nicest abaya, with a heavy belt of embroidery at the waist. She scolded Luma for being too noisy, but everyone knew her heart wasn't in it, not on a day like today. And in the state of uncertainty, people found hope in the certainty that things would never be the same.

They walked around the various alleyways as they ate their kebabs, wiping their fingers with the last pieces of spongy flatbread. Emad burped and they all laughed. When they had finished it was almost midday. Dabriya gave Ahmad a nod and held his forearm for a second, before rushing Luma to a tailor at the other side of the square, dragging Emad and Yusuf with her, despite their protests. Once they were inside, Dabriya indicated to the owner that she wanted Luma measured and went to stand by the shop entrance.

In that square, at that moment, if you looked away, or blinked for too long, or even sneezed too ferociously, you would have missed the signal. It took just a few seconds for the eight men to catch one another's eyes and break into a chant.

Dabriya watched Ahmad draw a breath and yell, "Baghdad for?"

"Baghdadis," called seven men in reply. The second time the returning chant doubled in strength.

"Baghdadis," whispered Dabriya to herself.

And when the chant had developed a life of its own, Ahmad, Jafar, and Ali set up a platform from a wobbly wooden table. Jafar put a hand on Ahmad's shoulder for a moment, then helped him up onto it. Ahmad took a shaky breath and called, "People of Baghdad." Faces turned toward him, but the noise died only a little. This was his chance to fight not for the English, not for the Turks, but for himself, and for his city.

"People of Baghdad!" said Ahmad, louder. "Brothers and sisters, Shia and Sunni, Jew and Assyrian, Chaldean and Armenian." The only noise left in the Maydan was the sizzling of kebabs and titters of curiosity. Ahmad took a gulp of air. "It is time to reclaim your dignity." He thought of all the things from which he had run, all the wrongs he had done. Karim and Salim. The lives he had taken and the lies he had believed. His neglect of his family and of Abdullah's betrayal. But he would not let the invaders defeat him. He took a deep breath. This was it.

"From the first day that they came here, the English have lied to us. They promised us freedom and we gave our souls, our lives, and our children's lives for this dream." As soon as Ahmad felt the anger rise in his stomach, his nerves slipped away. He brandished his forefinger, too enraged to mind that everyone was watching at him. "They made us slaves to a concept we had never dared to dream of," he yelled. "And they rewarded our loyalty by beating us, imprisoning us, and murdering us." A scattered applause broke out.

"They call us savages, barbarians, dirty uncivilized budoos. Yet we are not the ones who broke our word." Ahmad saw nodding and raised fists in the crowd. He scanned the edges of the square, but saw no British guards yet, so he continued.

"We sacrificed everything, *everything*, to be released from Constantinople, only to be dragged away in English shackles. And still you ask us to thank you. You English say we are politically naive, yet you have joined north and south under one law when we have never been joined before. Well, now you can be sure that we are united in our fight against you! Basris, and Baghdadis and Mosulis, united against our colonizers.

"To the English, Arabs are not humans. A lie to an Arab is not a lie. Theft from an Arab is not theft. The murder of an Arab is not murder. And yet they laugh with one another at how dishonorable the Arabs are."

278

Ahmad stopped for a second. "The English man breaks his word more carelessly and more frequently than he breaks wind." Laughter rippled across the audience and Ahmad's heart lightened. "And I think we all know how their weak foreign stomachs tolerate the *savage* food over here," he added, pinching his nose with his fingers as the people in the Maydan laughed harder still.

"Today is the end of their integrity, it is the end of their honor, but today is the beginning of a new and just Baghdad." The crowd jumped and cheered. And he raised his fist to the sky and inhaled all the air of his beloved Baghdad, and with this one breath, he blew it across the rooftops of the city. "We are Baghdadis and Baghdad is ours!"

It was the breath that turned a spark into a blazing fire.

47

AND IT WAS A FIRE that burned so hot that not even the breath of Hell dared challenge it that summer. It fueled the thousands of feet that marched through Baghdad, through Basra, and every town between, and it drove those same feet as they ran urgently from the boots that chased them.

The rebels of Rumaytha destroyed the railroad lines that were used to send British reinforcements, fired upon trains that brought in platoons of British to stamp out the uprising. They dug trenches around the town, and within weeks the British withdrew from it and the Mid-Euphrates region.

Up and down the rivers of Iraq, the blaze spread from lips to ears, from farms to households, from mosques to schools, until the length of the Tigris glowed with the fire and blood of a land awoken and alight.

And Ahmad's family opened their doors to the blaze that it might burn the flags that dominated their land. And it swallowed them in waves of fury during the protests. And it burned in Dabriya as she raised her fists in rage like it was all she had ever known, and it burned in Yusuf as he shook the earth beneath his feet, as if he might stamp out the British claim to mastery. The blaze burned in Emad as he cried, unconcerned that Yusuf saw, and it burned in Luma, who had known no other life. As for Ahmad, he held his brow to the skies and growled at a world that dared to tell him he was less than human.

Defiance no longer came to Ahmad in the form of a gun. It came from home. Years of fighting and bloodshed had chipped away at the warrior in him, until all that remained was his instinct to protect only what he treasured above all else. Some would call it wisdom, others cowardice, but Ahmad knew better than to waste time on labels.

But all the ways that hope drew Ahmad home chased Emad away. In Emad, who had never felt another man's blood on his face, news of the rebels' success across the country sparked the urge to do something—anything—to help defend his land, his home. And as the family rode a horse-drawn tram through Baghdad, as they rode the track home on their two donkeys, Emad decided. Nothing had value in an unjust world. He didn't care about his school because dead men cannot read; he didn't care about food, beyond it keeping him alive. He couldn't believe he had ever had time to feel jealous of Yusuf. How unimportant it all was. And if his father, who had left them to fight for the English, would not do the same for his own people, Emad would do it himself. The truth was, though, that even if Ahmad had joined the rebellion, Emad would have gone anyway. He had to be a part of this.

And when he announced to his family, as they walked down the path to their home, that he would be leaving to join the Guardians' revolution, that he would pick up a gun and fight the English in the field, he expected the tears that followed.

"I'm sorry, Mama. I have to do this," said Emad.

Dabriya nodded, weeping. "I'm not sad, Emad," she said, "I'm proud."

"But you hated it when Baba left."

"I'll be very worried about you. But—"

Ahmad interrupted her. "But this time it will be different," he said. "No colonizer is ordering you to fight, or promising you something they can't deliver. You're fighting for us, for Baghdad, for the revolution."

Dabriya nodded. "And we're winning. The rebels have pushed out the English from towns across the Euphrates. You'll come back to us, Emad," she said, putting an arm around his waist. "And you'll come back a hero." She wanted to kiss his cheek, but he towered so high above her now that she planted it on his shoulder.

Emad put an arm around his mother and stroked her head. "What about you, Yusuf?" he said, with a wink. "Don't you want to come?" He felt his mother tense. "What? He's sixteen. There are boys as young as fourteen among the rebel fighters, you know."

"Don't worry, Mama," said Yusuf. "I think it is a very brave thing to do, Emad, but I had a different kind of resistance in mind."

"What do you mean?" said Emad.

"Jafar offered me a job. In the Guardians."

"Doing what?" said Ahmad.

"I'm not supposed to say." Yusuf tapped his nose gleefully.

And so Dabriya and Ahmad watched as, three days later, their two sons left for Baghdad, Emad to meet with Haji Suwaydi for further instructions, and Yusuf to the riverbank beside the YMCA.

48

Summer 1920
Hillah

COMMISSIONER WILSON COULD NO LONGER deny that, in just a few short weeks, the rebellion had conquered hearts and reconquered land. He received urgent telegrams from Westminster urging him to control the revolt by any means necessary. He put pressure on General Townshend, who put pressure on his majors, captains, and lieutenants. He was sent armored vehicles, firearms, ammunition from the neighboring colonies of Palestine and the Hejaz. In the spring, the secretary of state for war and air, Winston Churchill, had floated the idea of aerial policing. But before Commissioner Wilson was sent war planes, he was sent extra reserves of kerosene.

"So what do we actually know about these villagers?" asked Llyr, raising his eyebrows as he laid the four of spades on the pile of tattered cards.

"What is there to know?" replied Tomos, with a shrug. "We go in, we do what we always do, we leave—we don't need to know much more than that, do we?"

"It isn't 1917 any more," said Carwyn, sharply, looking up from his paper. "It's a village, not a column of soldiers—and what are we even doing in Iraq now?"

"It's still warfare, we're still soldiers and these are still our orders," replied Tomos, sharply. "Stop asking questions and do as you're told."

"Must be really easy to follow orders when you've no mind of your own," said Carwyn.

"Just because Owain is dead, don't think I'll listen to your ranting," said Tomos.

Carwyn shut his mouth quickly and his cheeks burned.

"He's right, mind you," said Llyr. "The men of these villages have been out of control, attacking our trains and killing our men. They need to be punished or it'll just keep happening."

"Keep telling yourself that, Llyr," replied Carwyn, dangerously. "You and I both know—"

"It's for the good of this country!" snapped Llyr. "I don't like it any more than you do. . . . You heard the lieutenant, all we're doing is disrupting their day-to-day lives, which we wouldn't need to do if they would just sit tight and let us install the government, th—" Llyr stopped when he saw Carwyn shaking his head.

"You know what?" said Llyr, his voice wavering, "It doesn't matter what you think. You're a soldier and this is your order."

"Really?" said Carwyn, drily. "I had no idea I was a soldier."

"Start acting like one!"

Carwyn stood. "When all this is over, and when you go home to your village and your family, will you be able to live with what you've had to do in the name of England?" he asked. "Because I won't. And now they've got us invading villages of civilians, Llyr. *Civilians*. This is not war any more."

"Iesu Grist!" yelled Tomos. "Do you ever stop? This is about creating security, political stability."

Carwyn laughed. "You still believe that shit? 'Political' is a word they use when they do something terrible and mask it as ethical."

Carwyn had always known what it was to be an outsider. Even when he was among his own, hauling coal, something had been biting at his gut, gasping to be set free through words or screams or anything that would make it feel less

286

trapped. He had been foolish to think he could leave it behind in the Rhondda Valleys. All Mesopotamia had brought his demons was company.

So he would numb himself with cheap liquor and tobacco—habits he no longer bothered to resist—and when the time came to punish insurgents for resisting the Mandate that had been forced upon them, he told himself it would be over quickly, that nobody innocent would have reason to resist. He told himself this would be one of the easy villages. And he prayed to God that He would let him forget.

They set out at night, their horses weighed down by kerosene, cloth, matches, and wood. As Carwyn rode, he stared at the desert and retreated to his old bedroom. He remembered every crack in the wall, each crooked stone. He recalled his head thudding against that wall when Robert had struck him for the first time, and when his nose had cracked against it. He had washed his own blood off it. He remembered all the times he had goaded Robert into beating him, just so that he could be left on his own. And he had told himself that if he could imagine somewhere worse than this, something worse than this, it would all be bearable. But he knew now there was nothing worse than being forced to commit the sins of powerful men.

So he took a swig of a local beer, emptied his mind and followed his platoon to the village below. They stopped a kilometer from the village outskirts, dismounted, readied the flasks, doused the cloths and lit them with matches.

"You know the drill," said Lieutenant Morgan. "March in. If they flee, our gunners will get them. If they resist, you're cleared to have some fun with them." Two cannons rang out up ahead, and they knew it was time to run through the trees into a small clearing. Carwyn saw Tomos head for the first hut he came upon, splashing it with kerosene as a man ran out, barely visible behind the arms and legs of the three children he was carrying. It was difficult to tell who was yelling louder,

Tomos or the father, but the latter got a mouthful of kerosene for his troubles. Carwyn saw them run away from the village into the vast, barren land.

Carwyn was always taken aback by how loud fire could be. Not the flames, but the noise that accompanied every blaze, of parents yelling and children crying, the *poof* of the torch lighting the kerosene. Screams in the distance and nearby, desperate chanted prayers. He could, at least, understand the noise of panic, but he would never understand why Tomos and Llyr and all the others needed to be so boisterous when they burned villages. How is anyone supposed to flee with all these men screaming at them from every direction? How was he supposed to hold a thought for long enough to know what to do?

"Get to work, Evans!" someone shouted. He switched his torch to his left hand and ran down a path that led around the village, watching as small children stuffed pots and clothes into blankets as their mothers whispered instructions. He didn't look at faces: he already knew the beast that he would find in them. When he found a small field of vegetables, he deposited as much fuel as he could, then touched his torch to the ground. It caught fire with a whip, and he ran, not waiting to see the effect. Destroying food was preferable to burning a home, but not by much.

He saw a girl of no more than thirteen standing in his path, clutching a doll to her chest. "Hey!" he yelled in Arabic. "Hide!" She stared at him, cheeks quivering. "Run, girl," said Carwyn, trying to hide his desperation. "Get away from here!" But she was frozen to the spot. A woman ran up to her and grabbed her arm, pulling her off the path just as Carwyn passed her.

He heard the woman hiss at her behind him. "What are you doing? Don't be so *stupid*, Salsabeel!"

Carwyn looked around for more small farms with which he could distract himself. He heard commands and shrieks rise above the crackling of the glowing village. He found a suitable field and set it alight, just as before, hoping that his kerosene would run out before he had to burn another. He still had almost a quarter of a flask; he rounded on a third farm, emptying his flask on the land and setting it alight. He felt a hand on the back of his arm and jumped, pulling free. His palm caught the cheek of the man who had grabbed him, but he seemed not to notice.

"Why?" cried the man at Carwyn. He wrung his hands. He had a full white beard, and deeper wrinkles than Carwyn had ever seen.

"Why?" pleaded the man, in English.

Carwyn was shaking. He opened his mouth but he knew he would not find any words to make what he had done all right. He shrugged sadly and said, "I have no choice."

The man's brief shock at Carwyn's Arabic response was quickly replaced by anger.

"You have a choice, and you chose to ruin me," said the old man, tears dribbling out of the corners of his eyes. "I survived the war to see my home of seventy years burned by a foolish boy?" He slapped Carwyn's forehead. "You are a stupid boy. Better for you to have killed me than to let me see this."

"No," whispered Carwyn. "I'm sorry." He felt his cheeks glow.

"You are not sorry," said the man, raising his voice. "You are evil."

"You don't understand," said Carwyn. "I didn't want to burn homes so I burned fields instead." He was desperate to explain. He was not a bad man, he told himself. He was not.

"Oh, thank you very much," said the man. "Thank you for burning my trees and my crops and my ducks, all because my village refused to pay your English tax." He slumped to the ground and wept.

Carwyn turned and dashed away from the flames.

It couldn't be, he told himself. They always targeted villages that had torn up railroad lines or attacked officers. The old man must have been lying.

But he knew. He could not admit it to himself then, but when he was back at the blockhouse, alone, with nothing left to burn, he would weep with the realization that they had burned that village, its land—no doubt some of its people—because its inhabitants had dared to withhold their taxes from the British Colonial Office. It didn't matter who Carwyn once was, today the old man was right.

How ashamed his father would be if he could see him now, thought Carwyn. Killing on behalf of my own father's murderer. I am my father's murderer.

49

Autumn 1920
Baghdad

BY AUTUMN, THE UPRISING HAD changed beyond recognition. The British no longer attempted to placate the rebels with promises. What the Arabs needed was not negotiation, but a firm hand. So rivers of protestors became squadrons of rebels, attacking railroads, ambushing trains of British reinforcements, and looting them of their artillery. Few British on the trains evaded death or capture, and the inhabitants of the nearest village to the attack would inevitably pay the highest price of all.

When Jafar had told Yusuf he had a job proposition for him, Yusuf expected he would be writing reports or recording meetings. But accounts of his quick thinking at Moshi's Café had reached the upper levels of the Guardians, and—after Ustad Adil of al-Ahliya School had commended Yusuf's English— Jafar told him about the very specific job he had for him.

For the past three weeks, Yusuf had been ferrying people across Baghdad in a large guffa that he had purchased with funds donated by the Guardians. He parked himself strategically on the riverbank beside the YMCA and waited for British soldiers to request a transfer across the river. Whenever any spoke to him, he responded, as instructed, "No English." Jafar had hoped that Yusuf might overhear something useful, or even gain the trust of an officer or two. But it had been disappointing work. All Yusuf had heard while standing for weeks in the blistering heat were dull stories about the soldiers' multiple lovers, and complaints about how hot and smelly Baghdad was. Once, he heard an officer complaining about the ugliness of Arab women and he had found a way to "accidentally" hit the man's head with his paddle.

Whenever Jafar asked how his mission was going, Yusuf felt ridiculous telling him about the poker being played at the YMCA and the latest ditties the English were singing.

But a few weeks into his job, an hour or two after dawn, he spotted Lieutenant Morgan walking toward his guffa, Carwyn and some men from his unit following. Yusuf bent his head low, pulling his ghutra over his face.

"You again," said Carwyn, in Arabic, holding up his fingers to mime a fare question.

"Take your lieutenant to another guffa. He might recognize me," said Yusuf.

Carwyn laughed. "No chance of that. He tries not to look locals in the face, thinks it might make him go soft."

Yusuf smiled.

"I'm serious," Carwyn said. "Besides, you all look the same to him." He paused. "No offense."

"I'll try not to be offended, then," said Yusuf, thinking it was quite insulting all the same.

"Well?" said the lieutenant to Carwyn.

"Yes, hop in," Carwyn replied.

As Yusuf steered the men across the river, he noticed that Carwyn was right: the lieutenant showed not the slightest interest in him.

"Listen," said Carwyn. "I don't know what to say."

"About?" said Yusuf, absently, pushing the water around the guffa with a heavy thrust.

"What they—we're doing to the *uprising*," he whispered the last word. "I just want you to know that I'm sorry." He swallowed. "I wish I wasn't here. I wish I wasn't ordered to burn villages."

Yusuf blinked incredulously. "You're burning villages?" he hissed. He had stopped paddling. "What's the matter with you, Carwyn?"

"Don't say my name," hissed Carwyn. "He mustn't know you know me."

Yusuf resumed paddling. How on earth could someone who had saved him be willing to *burn villages*? The shore was nearing and he couldn't say he was sorry: he wanted to be away from the lieutenant, from Carwyn, and all the rest of them. Perhaps this information about burning villages would be useful to Jafar, though.

"This is the worst thing I've ever done in my life," said Carwyn. "I've stopped sleeping."

Yusuf nodded. He looked into the boat as he brought his paddle around and spotted the lieutenant's satchel at his feet. He stared. The buckle was open.

"What is he saying, Evans?" said the lieutenant. Carwyn muttered something about the weather and the water levels.

"I had to tell you," said Carwyn.

"Right," said Yusuf. "Now you have."

"Oh," said Carwyn.

He was clearly expecting more, but Yusuf had no time to ease the guilt of a man who was killing his people. Better for him to feel it.

"Must be really hard for you," said Yusuf, his eyes still fixed on the lieutenant's bag. "All that killing and burning."

"What?" Carwyn croaked.

"Yes, I can't imagine anything worse," said Yusuf. He began slowing the boat, preparing to dock on the opposite shore.

"I know there are worse things," said Carwyn, quietly. "I know it's worse for you. But there's nobody I can tell these things to, nothing that I can do to change what I've done."

Carwyn was watching him but Yusuf was more interested in the lieutenant's satchel. He knew what he needed to do.

When the guffa bumped gently against the dock, Yusuf leaned over the edge to lash it. He spun around, dipping the handle of the paddle into the basin of the guffa, which knocked over the lieutenant's bag and sent papers across boat floor.

"Oh, sorry, very sorry," said Yusuf, in his best impression of a budoo. He bent down to pick them up.

"You imbecile!" yelled the lieutenant, hitting the back of Yusuf's head.

It sent a jolt through Yusuf and he thought he might vomit over the lieutenant's boots. Or that he might stand up and butt the lieutenant's face with his own forehead. Then he remembered Jafar, depending on him, and Emad risking his life. He could do it. What was one more humiliation?

"Sorry, mister, I get it." Yusuf stuffed a handful of papers into the lieutenant's satchel. And, hiding the basin of the boat with his body, he slipped two sheets up the underside of his dishdasha, squeezing them between his ankles. He made a spectacle of slipping around as the boat swayed, of dropping and creasing papers in the water that had collected in the bottom.

"All right, all right," said the lieutenant, grabbing Yusuf's arm. "I'll get them." Yusuf shuffled backwards and indicated for Carwyn's unit to exit the boat.

"Bloody useless race," huffed the lieutenant. A couple of soldiers bent down to help him, and Carwyn made to step onto the shore.

Yusuf grabbed his arm. "There is always something you can do," said Yusuf. "Stop complaining, and do it."

50

WHEN YUSUF UNEARTHED THE STOLEN documents from between his ankles, he expected to find reports detailing retaliatory attacks against rebels' villages, or read about the latest British losses. He did not expect to find anything that would change the course of the war. He did not expect what he read to send him into a breathless panic on the floor of his guffa.

Shit. Shit. Shit. He had to warn Jafar. *He had to warn Emad.*

Yusuf pulled off his ghutra and dunked his head in the river. *Pull yourself together.* He tucked the papers into his belt and then raced toward Abu Hanifa Mosque to leave the papers with Haji Suwaydi.

"Send word to Jafar," he instructed, "immediately." Haji Suwaydi nodded. "Do you know where my brother is?" Haji Suwaydi didn't answer. "It's not like I'm going to rush off and tell the English, am I?" Yusuf said, irritated.

Haji Suwaydi considered this. "He's a day's ride south-west of Baghdad. Follow the railroad south. He should be just north of Musayib." Yusuf thanked Haji Suwaydi, then raced to the stables on the southern shore and picked up the horse Jafar allowed him to use. He had to get home. As fast as he could.

When he rode up the path to his home, Dabriya knew something was wrong. Yusuf rarely came home during the week, and never in the morning.

"What?" she said, running out to meet him. "Is it your father?"

"What? No, where is he?"

"He's in Baghdad, I thought that's why you were—"

"No, it's Emad. I need to warn him."

"Warn him?" said Dabriya, slowly.

"I found an English report. They're sending in airplanes to bomb the rebels."

"No," said Dabriya, putting her hands to her face. "They can't."

"They already have. I saw the order myself. No more combat, no more soldiers to attack. They're just going to kill us from the sky." Dabriya had gone quiet.

"Don't worry, Mama. I'll find him, I'll tell him."

"Telling him is not enough. He needs to come home."

"What if he wants to stay anyway?" said Yusuf.

"Well, he must decide," said Dabriya, averting her eyes. "So where is he?"

"A day's ride along the railroad, somewhere north of Musayib."

"I see," she said. "Find some food for yourself, blankets, and water. I'll feed the horse."

"I should go right away," said Yusuf.

"You'll be no use hungry. And the horse needs rest too."

"Five minutes," said Yusuf, holding up his hand. He could do with a wash and some water. He went upstairs to change into a cleaner thobe, free of the mud and sweat he'd collected in the guffa.

Dabriya worked quickly. She filled two flasks with water, wrapped a watermelon in a large square of leather and tied it to the horse. She grabbed Ahmad's compass and pocketknife from the kitchen cupboard and sped outside. She checked the doorway for signs of Yusuf. Then she mounted the horse and galloped away, southwest, toward Musayib, toward her son.

51

SHE FELT BAD ABOUT MISLEADING Yusuf but, now she knew what the English were up to, she would not send both of her sons to be bombed. She wasn't even sure she could trust Yusuf to come home. He'd probably take up arms with his brother, lie in wait for the certain death of anonymous bombers. No, she couldn't lose both sons to the lying, cowardly invaders.

She kept the river on her left until she came to a bridge, with a few small boats lashed to its wooden frame. She waited for three men to pass in front of her, keeping her eyes ahead. She heard them, of course, the whispers of men who, knowing nothing about her or her situation, deemed themselves experts on her piety.

"How indecent! A grown woman riding a horse."

"No point wearing hijab if you're going to sit so provocatively."

And as convention required of such men, they lowered their voices just enough to feign decency, but not so much that the target of their judgment wouldn't hear.

On any other day the men's attempt to shame Dabriya would have angered her, but she was too anxious and desperate to spare them a thought. She pictured Emad sprawled on the ground, an unidentifiable body among scores of dead men. It was not worth dying for, not when all hope of victory was gone. What kind of fighters hide behind airplanes? She clicked her heels, rushing the horse ahead, sending weeds and dirt into the air. She left the bridge and headed south, speeding through an endless court of palm trees that towered high above her, like the arches of a mosque, the world flashing from light to darkness as she passed behind each trunk.

She raced faster still, until she gasped for every breath, until she felt she was going so fast that to fall off would mean certain death. And when she reached another bend in the snaking river, she slowed the horse. She crossed the river again, and followed it downstream, keeping it on her left until she reached a dirt crossroad. This was it. She sighed. She examined her compass for just a moment, wrapped her scarf across her mouth and nose and galloped out into the rugged southern outskirts of the Vilayet of Baghdad.

If she rode through the night, she might reach Emad by tomorrow—she might be in time. She stopped only to feed her horse water from her flask, or to navigate with her compass. She was on the strip of land that lay east of the Tigris and west of the Euphrates. She passed through farmlands and orchards, the green landscape of Baghdad diluted with swathes of sandy sepia the further she ventured from the Tigris. She carved off pieces of watermelon and ate them as she rode. As daylight faded, she found herself wishing she could afford to rest. Her throat had begun to itch, and no amount of water could soothe it. It had been hours since she had seen anything distinctive in her surroundings and the nondescript sandy tracks and indistinguishable shrubs were fading into the invisibility of night. The moment darkness fell, she felt two chills, one for the icy air, and the other at the sudden realization of how completely alone she was. How long had it been since she had felt like this? Since they had lost Baghdad? Since Ahmad had left to fight? Was this how Ahmad and Emad had felt when they had left home?

Her fingers were suddenly cold. She could feel the burn of icy sand on her toes, her thighs, her shoulders. For a second she thought she would dismount, just to rest for a while, and then she remembered Emad. She remembered his birth, when her whole abdomen had burned, like it was filled with daggers.

If she could survive that, she could do this. She would do this, even if it killed her. She had to try to save him, no matter what it cost her. At the very least, she had saved Yusuf. And she felt a surge of belief course through her. She dug her heels into the horse, and took off into the invisible dunes.

Through the night, Dabriya's eyes grew heavy on her cheeks, dust took up residence in the folds of her abaya and a thin film stuck to her skin. Her lips burned with a dry sting, and when she tried to lick them into relief, she tasted a salty grit. Her horse had slowed and she bent her head low on its neck to try to control her shivers.

When the sun broke above the horizon, it filled Dabriya's hands with glorious warmth. She uncovered her face and allowed her nose to warm too. She couldn't imagine that the sun had always felt so comforting. She stopped to give the horse some water, and took three gritty bites of watermelon from a block she hacked off, then fed the rest to the horse, which he crunched hungrily. And as she warmed her toes and knees and body out of numbness she consulted her compass, covered her face against the sand and winds again, and rode as fast as the horse would take her. When the ground grew green again, when Dabriya heard the distant trundling of a train to the west, she knew she was nearing her destination, and adjusted her route slightly eastwards: It would not do to be caught by the English now. Ahmad had told her last week that Emad's unit was tasked with sabotaging the railroad, just as his had been. As long as she didn't veer too far from the tracks, she would have to encounter Emad eventually. For the first time, she felt she could truly do it—she would find him, and bring him home. She hadn't seen or heard a single plane. There was still time. She wondered what she would say to him, what would convince a young man not to martyr himself.

But all she knew was that she would not leave without him—
so he would have to agree. He just had to.

She was shaken from her thoughts by a crack that echoed
around her, bouncing off every dune. The horse halted and
fussed, stamping his feet. Dabriya leaned forward and crooned
to him, rubbing his neck. "Don't leave me now. I need you,"
she whispered. And as the echo faded into the distance, Dabriya searched for its source. She saw a cloud of smoke to her
east, a small puff just visible on the horizon.

"Okay, okay," she said to herself, unsure what to do. She
told herself that it wasn't an airplane, though she had no idea
what they sounded like, or how low they would fly. Surely that
noise was Emad's group, blowing up the railroad? What if she
had veered too far east, and missed him as he passed? What if
that was an English attack and she was just minutes away from
being bombed too, disappearing from her family forever? She
breathed for a moment, calming herself, then patted her horse
and set off. Emad would be there, she was sure of it. She was
not sure of it at all.

It wasn't even dark by the time she spotted figures on the
horizon. She rode until it was too risky to get close on horse-
back. She dismounted and fed the horse the last of her fruit.
She gave him water, and tied him to a tree.

"I'll be back for you," she said, stroking his jaw. "Promise." She took a swig from the flask, packed Ahmad's compass
and pocketknife in her belt, and walked toward the figures
in the distance. She planned what she would do if they were
British forces, still lingering before their orders to leave all
the work to the planes. She would not let the group spot her
until she was sure they were not, but just in case, she began
weighing her options. When she got closer she dropped onto
all fours. It was tiring work and she stopped every few minutes
to catch her breath. In those moments she would talk to herself reassuringly: She had already done the most difficult part,
and her boy, her little son, now grown up, was just there, one

of those figures—maybe the one over there who was standing, leaning his weight on one leg. Or maybe the one who was sitting alone—that seemed like the kind of spot Emad would choose. And, she told herself, if these are Englishmen, I will act wild, so crazy and dirty and feral that they think I am of no interest, just some mad, diseased woman who roams the desert. Shouldn't be too hard to convince them of that.

She felt her forearms quiver under her weight and stopped to flex her arms. She crawled closer still, almost close enough to tell who the men were. She shook herself as her head grew dizzy and she felt her hearing being sucked away, as if it was disappearing into a hole in the ground. She was on her knees and elbows. She heard panting and she didn't know if it was real or imagined. *I can do it. I've done it. I'm here.* And she raised her head and saw feet, then the muzzle of a gun, and then nothing.

52

North of Musayib

"EMAD!" SHE SCREAMED. "EMAD!" SHE tried to pull herself up, then felt her wrists crack, held behind her back. She managed to sit up using her elbows. She forced her eyes open, and felt an ache in her stomach. She retched, but nothing came out.

"What are you doing out here, madam?"

Tears swarmed into her eyes when she heard the words. And then she laughed. She laughed so hard she worried they might think she *was* the feral desert woman. She threw her head back and guffawed like it was the first time in her life she had ever laughed. Arabic. The sweet, sweet sound of Arabic.

"My son," she said, composing herself. "I've come for my son."

"What's so funny?" asked the man in front of her, a flicker of amusement in his eyes.

"I thought you were an English encampment, and that I was about to be captured." She looked at her wrists pointedly. "Please tell me that Emad Ibn Ahmad is here?" A small circle had gathered curiously around her. She wondered if she should be scared, but she couldn't bring herself to feel anything except relief. She rested her eyes for a moment.

"Oh, my God," said a voice, and she heard footsteps run up behind her.

"Untie her, right now." Her arms were freed and she stood, turned and saw the face she had thought she might never see again.

"Yabni," she said, pulling herself into Emad's chest.

"Mama," said Emad. "I don't understand." He paused and examined her unruly clothes, her lopsided scarf, and her weathered face. "Mama, look at you," he said, placing a hand on the side of her head. He whispered to a man named Abu Khaled to send food and water.

"I'm fine Emad, just very tired," she said, but she took the bread and meat handed to her, and ate three bites before she instructed Emad to follow her to retrieve her horse.

The camp was well hidden. They were close enough to the Euphrates that they could hide their possessions among the wild shrubs, but far enough that they wouldn't be spotted by those traveling by boat or rail.

When Emad and Dabriya had hugged and blessed each other more times than was really necessary, Emad stared at Dabriya questioningly. "Did something happen?" he asked. "What are you doing here?"

"I'm so proud of you, Emad," she said, looking around. "To see you among these men, fighting for our freedom." Emad waited expectantly. "But I have bad news," she said.

"Is it Yusuf?" he said. "Luma?"

"No, nothing like that," said Dabriya. "Your brother intercepted an order from London. The English have given up trying to fight you in open battle, and they're sending planes. They're going to bomb all the rebels from the sky and there's no way to fight back."

Emad nodded slowly. "That is bad," he said. "Not exactly news, though. We've been hearing planes for the last two days, but they never managed to spot us."

"Don't you understand?" said Dabriya, pulling Emad's hand between her own. "This changes everything. How are you going to fight back against an invisible army?"

"Mama," said Emad, seriously, "you always knew what this might cost me. Every man here is ready to lay down his life for the future of our country, and so am I."

"And I was so proud to have a son to fight for our future, you know I was. But what's the point in giving your life when you will never win? There is no chance against these machines. You know that, don't you?"

Emad was breathing heavily.

"I know it's too soon to give up," he said. "And that sabotaging their trains is more important than ever. How do you think they are restocking their army with fuel and food?"

"They said they will crush the rebellion, bomb you from the sky—bomb us all into submission."

"And you want me to let them get away with that?"

"No, yabni," said Dabriya. "No. I want you to value your life. It is worth more than this. Perhaps we can regroup, get better weapons and machines, but to sit here, waiting for them to kill you. . . . There is no point in it."

Dabriya could feel her hands trembling. She had to make him understand. "Please. Please come home. We're losing our country and we're losing you."

"I'm sorry, Mama, but you shouldn't have come. I'm not leaving," said Emad. "What if you're wrong? What if we still have a chance to win? I have to try. But you should get to safety. Rest here tonight and begin your return tomorrow."

Dabriya shook her head. "I can't force you to come home, but you can't make me leave. I'm staying as long as you do."

"You can't! This is no place for a woman—they won't let you stay."

"I didn't see anything about no women on those flyers you were handing out. I'm staying."

And without another word, she turned and walked away.

Dabriya heard distant voices yelling and sat up. It was difficult to see anything in the desert black. She looked to her right: Emad was gone. She tried to make out any of the rebels in the moonlight, but everything her hands touched turned out to be blankets, clothes, or shrubs. She spotted distant pinpricks of light, to the west, she thought.

"Hello?" she half shouted, half whispered. Nothing.

"As if they just left me here." She walked to where her horse was tethered and kneeled down. "Time to go, boy." He stood up at once, and she climbed on, and raced after the lights.

When she had neared the rebels, she could hear the hushed voices of men both fearful and excited. "Don't shoot," she called, as she neared them, "it's Umm Emad." She could have sworn she heard a collective whine rise up from the men. The feeling was mutual. She dismounted, and felt a hand around her arm.

"You can't be here," hissed Emad. "You'll get me into trouble."

"You really expect me to stay behind?" said Dabriya.

"Mama, I have work to do. I can't sit here and guard you. You should have stayed in the camp." He pulled her with one hand, and the horse's reins with the other.

"Emad," said Dabriya, "I'm not here to be protected. I'm here to protect you."

"Just," said Emad, guiding the horse to an overgrown area, and lashing it in place, "keep down and follow me." He led his mother to a ditch in the sand, behind a raised ridge. A leader whispered a command, and all the rebels extinguished their torches.

"An English supply train will pass soon, so don't let them see you," said Emad, gesturing over the ridge with his head. Dabriya had already heard the distinct trundle of a train approaching.

"You have no idea of the position you put me in," said Emad. "Abu Khaled called a meeting last night about what to do with you." Dabriya raised her eyebrows. "You can stop looking so pleased with yourself. You have to leave," said Emad, raising his voice as the train roared past them. Dabriya shrugged stubbornly. "Mama, you're a burden on me, on all of us."

"Try to see it from my perspective," said Dabriya.

"Have you tried looking at it from mine?" said Emad. He could take no more and, sure that the train had traveled far enough, stood and walked toward the track. He came to a halt when he saw the tail end of the train and, just visible in the moonlight, a British soldier staring off the back end, who raised his hand and stabbed the air with two fingers.

"Shit," gasped Emad, dropping to his stomach. He slid back over the ridge and ran to find Abu Khaled.

"One of them saw me. I'm sorry," he whispered.

"You're not serious?" said Abu Khaled. He was tall and so thin that he seemed to arch with the wind. His face was creased into an almost permanent beam but, at that moment, his wrinkles added to his intimidation.

"I think so," said Emad. "At least, he looked right at me and did this." Emad formed a V with his two first fingers, mimicking the British soldier.

"Emad, how could you be so careless?" said Abu Khaled. "He was swearing at you, which means he definitely saw you, and if he saw you, you've ruined our ambush."

Emad felt a rush of color to his cheeks. He was glad the torches had been put out.

"First you bring your mother here, and now this. How many more mistakes can we expect?" Emad was furious that he had been so rash, furious that his mother had distracted him, and furious that he was getting the blame.

"Abu Zaynab, take your men, see if you can get ahead of the train and destroy the tracks. That'll buy us some time," instructed Abu Khaled. "The rest of you, return to camp and make sure everything is well concealed." He pointed to a group of eight men. "Stand guard around the camp, watch the skies." He turned to Emad. "And you, don't let your mother out of your sight. Keep her out of the way until she leaves tomorrow." Emad nodded and returned to Dabriya, his face flushed.

"See?" he hissed. "You're going to end up getting me killed just by being here."

"How's that?"

"That soldier on the train, he saw me because you distracted me."

Dabriya had to admit that Emad was wearing her down. Maybe it had been premature to rush after him, to take that English report at its word. What if it had been misinformation? And, if not, Emad was tasked with sabotaging their freight, not reclaiming towns by fighting the English directly. Maybe he could weaken the English, even if he couldn't defeat them.

Emad untied her horse and climbed onto its back, pulling his mother up behind him. They rode out into the darkness, following the men who had already left for the camp.

After a while, Dabriya spoke. "Emad," she said.

He turned his head. "Not n—" he began, but she had a strange look on her face. "Mama?"

"Look," she whispered, pointing to the sky with both terror and wonder. A plane.

"Go," she said, slapping Emad's shoulders, and digging her heels into her horse. They raced away, Dabriya's pulse mimicking the double-beat of the gallop. But the ground was soft and uneven, and the buzz of the plane drew closer.

"We won't make it," gasped Emad. "Mama!" And as the plane pulled down, the hairs on the back of her neck stood up. A series of thuds sent a wave of dirt into the air, a line that grew toward them. The plane lifted into the air again.

"It'll be back," he said breathlessly. He shook the reins. "We can't lead it to the camp," he said, looking around for cover.

"There!" said Dabriya, pointing to a cluster of shrubs. For once she was grateful for the excess of bushes in her country.

They were meters from the shrubs when they heard the drone of the plane returning. She imagined, one day, telling her grandchildren of their father galloping beneath the strange flying machines, improbably invincible. She would tell them how God had melded fate and circumstance and suspended all else, so that she and her son would survive the bullets of those planes. Or perhaps she would tell them how the pilot—who saw Baghdad, and the marshes, and all the villages of rebellion along the Euphrates, finally crushed under the weight of his endless attacks—thought one or two savages in the desert unworthy of his time.

It was a nice thought, but it was inaccurate, and far too sentimental. It was not God's hand, or a lazy pilot that saved Emad from a shot to the chest, but her own determination, for two people make a larger target than one. So, as the plane dipped down in a second round of target practice, it sent sixteen shots into the dirt behind them, and a single bullet through the back of Dabriya's left shoulder, spearing flesh and muscle, splitting a deep crater in her upper arm. She let out a squeak as the shot jolted her into Emad. Emad heard the bullet as it fizzed past his shoulder. He wanted to curse. He wanted to pull up the horse and whip his gun out, ready for the plane's return. But none of that would stop the warmth that was seeping down his back or the shallow breaths he felt in his ear.

"Hold on, Mama," said Emad. "Just hold on." He patted the horse's neck firmly, kicked its ribs, and sped toward the encampment.

"Medic! I need a medic!" he said, swinging himself off the horse, leaving his mother to drift forward slightly. He held his hands out to her.

"No," she said. "Don't touch my arm." She leaned forward onto the horse, swung her left leg, and slid down the side of the saddle into Emad's arms.

Emad guided her to a medical tent. He watched as the medic laid her on her back, as he tore open the arm of her abaya with a knife, as he cut away the flesh around the wound, while his mother screamed.

*

When Dabriya had been stitched up and was resting, Abu Khaled came into the tent. He put a hand on Emad's shoulder and lowered himself to the floor beside him. "Will she live?" he asked.

Emad nodded. "It just hit muscle," he said. "Could have been so much worse."

"Thank God," said Abu Khaled. He paused. "Emad . . ."

"I know," said Emad, quietly. "I know I have to leave."

Abu Khaled nodded. "Take her home," he said, "but come back to us as soon as you can."

"Really?" said Emad.

"Of course," said Abu Khaled. "We need every man we can find. You've seen what they can do."

"I thought you might not want me back."

"Take your mother home, do what you must to keep her out of our way. And then come and rejoin us."

Emad sighed gratefully. "Was anyone else hit?"

Abu Khaled shook his head. "They managed to get back to the camp in time, and you know how hard it is to spot at night."

Dabriya could hear Emad's voice, like he was on the other side of a wall, or talking from beneath a blanket. Her chest throbbed. The memory of metal in her blood and pinching at her tissue still grated inside her arm. The thought of it disgusted her, and made her furious too. She wanted those sons of bitches to pay for everything they had done to her. And although she knew the metal had long since left her flesh, although she knew that her son was coming home, she could not shake the ghost of the British bullet from her shoulder.

53

Autumn 1920
Ahmad and Dabriya's home

THE INTRODUCTION OF AERIAL POLICING to Mesopotamia had changed the face of the rebellion. Within a few short weeks, the rebels had gone from reconquering land, defending their lines, and attacking strategic military positions to being bombed and shot at from the sky by an invisible enemy. Families had retreated to their homes, with only their crops and cattle to sustain them. Entire villages were bombed for refusing to hand over their weapons, for refusing to pay British taxes, for rebelling. And those who fled their homes made good target practice.

Yes, these people now knew what real bombing meant in casualties and damage. Within forty-five minutes a full-size village could be practically wiped out and a third of its inhabitants killed or injured by four or five airplanes, which offer them no real target, no opportunity for glory as warriors, no effective means of escape.

It would not be long before Dabriya's would become one such village, notched on the stocks of guns and sewn onto the shoulders of captains.

Emad arrived home about a week after Dabriya had set off. Yusuf, Luma, and Ahmad came running out of the house as soon as they heard the horse approaching. When Ahmad saw his wife limply clutching Emad, he stopped in his tracks.

"She's all right," said Emad. "Just exhausted."

"How could you?" said Yusuf to his mother.

Ahmad put his hands around Dabriya's hips and helped her to the ground.

"I'm fine," said Dabriya. "I just need to rest."

When Emad recounted the story to his family, he didn't leave anything out; not his scolding of his mother, not his frustration that she wouldn't leave, not his fault in her injury, and not his desire to return regardless.

"We don't blame you, Emad," said Ahmad.

Yusuf bit his lip. He should never have told his mother about the English air attacks: he should have gone straight to Emad. He would have warned him of the danger, but he'd never have forced him to return. Not like this.

"I'll rest tonight and leave tomorrow," said Emad.

Ahmad looked at his son sadly. "I know you think you have to return," he said, "but there are other ways to fight the English."

"Not really," said Emad. "Not any more. They no longer meet in our cafés so we can't try to listen in on their plans. And we know what they're planning anyway. The only chance we have is to continue to sabotage their supply chain."

"Just please don't be reckless," said Ahmad. Emad nodded, but was careful to make no promises. If he was going to die, it would not be quietly, meekly, hiding away like one of those cowards in the sky.

Dabriya slept all day and through the night. She would probably have stayed in bed even longer, but British policing waits for nobody.

When they first heard a bomb fall, it was distant—but how do you know when you've never been bombed before? Luma ran, bawling, to her father, who was in the kitchen chopping onions for broth. "Are we dying? Are we dying?" she screamed.

"No, habibti," said Ahmad, shakily. "It was very far away." Luma was hopping from one foot to the other.

"Hey, hey!" said Ahmad, grabbing her hand and pulling her down beside him. "It has ended. It was far away—it just sounds close. Now breathe normally." He nodded in time to the rhythm of her breathing.

Dabriya had hobbled out of bed and into Emad's room. She found Yusuf in Emad's bed, wrapped in blankets, and Emad paused, halfway through packing a British kit-bag that Yusuf had "acquired" outside the YMCA in Baghdad.

"Come," said Dabriya, walking over to Yusuf. She touched Emad's shoulder and pulled Yusuf by the hand. "Let's all have something to eat together. Join Baba in the kitchen and we'll have dates and milk."

She refused her sons' help down the stairs, and told them, jokingly, that she would see them downstairs when she arrived in half an hour. When she entered the kitchen she found the room in hysterics.

"What's going on?" She smiled.

"We worked out what the noise was," said Yusuf, exaggerating his laughter.

"What was it?" Dabriya wondered.

"Baba told us the English get tummy aches from our food," said Luma.

"Apparently that noise wasn't a bomb," said Yusuf, grinning at Luma. "They just pushed too hard on the toilet!"

"Yusuf!" said Dabriya, turning her face to hide a smile.

"What? Baba said it, not me!"

Dabriya faced the row of grinning faces, and said, with a smirk, "Well, Baghdad is going to stink tomorrow."

Ahmad laughed and cleared some space for her. He held her right hand to help her to the floor, and he didn't let go when she sat. And he thought that maybe they would be all right, despite everything.

Yusuf leaned over to Emad. "Just one more day, please?" he whispered. Emad stared at him, exasperated. "We both know you have no intention of coming back. Please."

Yusuf always did know how to soften him. Emad shook his head.

"One more day," he agreed. Yusuf smiled. "But you could always come with me."

"I've thought about it," said Yusuf. "But someone has to stay behind and look after them." He gestured toward Luma and his parents.

"I thought you might say that."

"I'm not sure Baba has it in him to pick up a weapon again if we need defending."

"Doubt they'll come around here in person, though," said Emad, "now that they have airplanes to do their dirty work."

Yusuf wanted to feel he was a part of the rebellion still, wanted to feel he could do something about the slow grip that was closing around them. Maybe if it was just his parents, but how could he leave Luma with no brother to watch over her? Even now, when she'd grown so tall she reached his chest, she was still the little sister who needed to know that everything was all right.

The number of bombs the family could hear increased as they tuned their ears to this new noise. They could tell when a bombing was close, because it was immediately preceded or succeeded by the sound of the overhead plane that had so effortlessly wiped out a house, or a farm, or a well. Emad wondered what village had found itself the target of English intimidation. Perhaps it was home to some of the rebels, but just as likely not.

And when the air fell silent and the ground stilled, the family breathed easier for a few hours. Emad, concerned about returning to his unit in the desert, and about the welfare of Jafar's horse, enlisted Yusuf's help in bringing the terrified animal into the courtyard, where they led it into a downstairs room. It was difficult to prevent it from bolting, but it settled down once it was shut into the modest space.

All day the household remained restless, each of them waiting for the bomb that didn't fall, setting up camp in the living room. So eerie it was to feel the absence of death. But it came as suddenly as the rains. It shook the floor, it cracked the earth and it sent a wave of the Tigris crashing in all directions, extinguishing what little hope or delusion that had survived.

"I'm alive, I'm alive," whispered Luma to herself, leaping from where she was sitting and running out into the passage.

"Wait!" shouted Yusuf.

There was a roar overhead and another crack that sent bits of ceiling raining down. The air filled with dust, and Luma coughed. She put out a hand to the wall, but something hard hit her in the small of her back and she fell. A pair of hands grabbed her and Yusuf flung her over his shoulder to carry her back to the living room. Ahmad and Dabriya had collected the blankets they had laid out around the room.

"Not here," said Ahmad, his brow furrowed as he pulled Yusuf with one arm and Dabriya under the other.

"Walk along the inside wall," said Emad. "Follow me."

The five of them hurried along the interior wall of the house as the bricks melted around them, thick clouds of gray chasing them, faster, as they ran into the kitchen and flung open the door to the cool, earthy cellar, all the while trying to ignore the booms as another family, somewhere down the river, was surely gathering their children, and fleeing to safety, or perhaps not moving at all.

"Sit," instructed Ahmad, then he and Emad disappeared upstairs, returning with more blankets and some rags. Emad handed a cloth to Dabriya, and joined Yusuf and Luma down the few steep steps at the back of the cellar where a small reservoir of water was fed by the river. He dabbed a rag in the water and rubbed his sister's face clean of dust.

"I can do it myself," she said, slapping his hand away and taking the cloth. "I'm not a baby."

She washed her arms and face, rinsed the cloth and took it to her mother, who wiped herself down too. When everyone had cleared most of the grime off their faces, Ahmad threw two thick blankets on the floor.

Dabriya, Yusuf, Emad, and Luma lay down and Ahmad covered each of them with a thick cushioning of wool and leather blankets. He saw Luma's eyes peer at him through a gap in the coverings. He hadn't seen such fear since Salim. *Oh, God, Salim*, he thought, picturing sweet Luma's head as his friend's had been. "Hey," he said, smiling, "the worst is over." But Luma's eyes were unchanged.

"Cover your face, so you can't smell their toilet burps!" he joked. Nobody was fooled by his forced humor this time. Luma covered her head and Ahmad saw the mound of her tiny form quiver. "Please, God," he whispered, "do not let this be her tomb."

Ahmad sandwiched himself between his children, putting an arm over Luma, the other over Yusuf. Dabriya's face poked out from under her blankets. "This is not the day we die," she whispered, over the top of Luma's head. "I know it." And she shut her eyes, and spoke the religious verses that brought her most comfort, not even wavering when the house trembled and shuddered anew.

Emad knew that seeing his own family bombed in their home should have changed his mind about leaving them. But all he had thought as he'd raced around the house, collecting rags and blankets, was that there was only one way to stop the bombing, and it wasn't by sitting at home waiting for the next one. When tomorrow came, he would take his weapons and leave.

The tremors ended some time before sunset. Ahmad had spent the entire bombardment reassuring his family. When dust fell from the ceiling, he told them that if the plane had wanted to bomb the house the pilot would have done it in that sweep. He told them it had been ages since the last bomb, that it was over, but that they'd just wait a little longer to make sure the building was safe. He told them anything that might take away the quivers that came from where Luma lay.

A few hours after the last bomb had fallen, Ahmad disappeared to inspect the house, returning ten minutes later with a smile. When he returned, Dabriya and his children were sitting up expectantly.

"We're fine," he said.

Dabriya looked at her children, and pulled each one to her chest with her good arm in turn. "We're safe now," she said softly, as Luma sobbed.

There were several hours to go before dawn so Ahmad thought it was safe to leave the cellar. So far the British hadn't bombed them by night when it was impossible for them to spot their targets.

There was a crater, just visible from the roof, and every house in sight looked like it had been throttled. Several palm trees had collapsed and two had hit the house. And every room, every surface was coated in a chalky brown dust. Ahmad lit five candles and handed one to each member of his family. He took out some cloths and soap, then brought water from the cellar. Emad disappeared upstairs to collect his kitbag, then headed off to check on the horse.

Dabriya left her candle indoors and walked toward the river to see if any of the watermelons or peas had survived. The moon filled the river with glowing beams, lighting the film of sand that covered the garden and the clouds that mushroomed into the air as she passed by. She kneeled beside the river and filled a pot with dark brown water. She set the pot down and poured water over each pea plant, then slapped the watermelons down with the river water. It was something, at least.

When she had cleared the dirt off a small corner of their crops, she stood, a little too quickly, felt the earth move around her and a tug in her stomach. Then she saw white.

Yusuf was running faster than he ever had. He kept slipping in the sand, catching himself with one hand and thrusting himself up again. He told himself to run faster. He could barely breathe but still he ran.

"Come quickly!" he yelled, when he reached Mikhael's house. "Bring your medicine kit."

Mikhael opened the door and ran back into the house. "Tell me exactly what happened," he said, grabbing things off shelves.

"Mama was shot a few days ago in the shoulder. She passed out today."

Mikhael nodded. "You think it's infected?"

Yusuf frowned. "Maybe. I hope not."

When Yusuf and Mikhael reached the house, they found Dabriya lying down on the low supper table they had moved into the courtyard for the moonlight. She groaned.

"Someone help me up," she said.

Emad held her right arm and she sat up.

"They're overreacting," she said. "I just stood up too quickly."

Mikhael nodded to Dabriya's shoulder. "Can I?" With Emad's help she unbuttoned her abaya and pulled her arm out of the sleeve.

Mikhael asked Yusuf to fetch a candle for a little more light and unwrapped the wound. He poured yellow liquid from a glass bottle onto his hands and examined the gash. Dabriya winced, and Luma held her mother's hand.

"They cut some of your skin away?" he asked.

Dabriya nodded. "Please tell me it's not infected," she said. She couldn't go through that again.

"It doesn't look like it," he said, "but I'll put an antiseptic dressing on it just in case." He poured the yellow liquid into a bowl and dipped white gauze into it, then bandaged Dabriya's arm.

"So why did she collapse?" asked Ahmad.

"My guess?" said Mikhael. "She's doing too much. You've just been shot," he said to her, "and you need to rest."

"I wish that were an option," said Emad, throwing his hands into the air. If the English would give them a moment's peace then maybe his mother could recover. But he supposed that was the point.

"And keep that arm away from dirt and debris," said Mikhael.

"Have you seen the state of our house?" asked Dabriya.

"Then clean a room and stay in there as much as possible. I'll be back to change the dressing in a couple of days." Mikhael paused. "A word?" he said to Ahmad, as he packed his bag with bottles and unused tools.

"Thank you, brother," said Ahmad, leading Mikhael to a corner of the courtyard. "It is not lost on me what you have done for us." Mikhael waved him away.

"Won't you stay a while with us?" asked Ahmad, but Mikhael was shaking his head. Something wasn't right.

Luma hadn't taken her eyes off her mother's face, but Emad and Yusuf were standing alert, their eyes fixed on Mikhael. He knew something.

"What's wrong? Is it Dabriya?" asked Ahmad.

"No, nothing like that," replied Mikhael, but Ahmad heard uncertainty in his voice. "She is fine. It's something else."

"Well?" asked Ahmad.

Yusuf was clearly listening to them from across the courtyard, though he averted his eyes as soon as Mikhael glanced at him.

"If it's not about his mother, he can handle it. The wondering about danger is almost worse than the danger itself," said Ahmad.

Mikhael sighed. "You know they just celebrated their New Year, don't you?" he asked.

"Who?" asked Ahmad.

"Jewish Baghdadis."

Ahmad remembered Dawood and sadness cracked through the courtyard. How long it had been since he had thought of him? Yusuf headed toward Mikhael. "I'd forgotten," replied Ahmad.

"Ahmad," said Mikhael, "their New Year fell the day before the bombing began. Haven't you heard the gossip?"

"We've been too busy staying alive!"

"You're too isolated here," he muttered. "But you don't understand. You know how people feel about the English giving all business and jobs to the Jewish community?"

"Of course . . . but I don't—"

"They think they're in on it!" said Mikhael. "They heard the celebratory horn the day before the bombing began and some fool started a rumor that they were celebrating—"

"Why would they? That's preposterous!"

"Of course it is. And there's no chance they had fore-warning about the bombing but nobody trusts what they once knew any more. After all the danger and insecurity, people just assume the worst of everyone."

Ahmad held his head with one hand, rubbing his eyelids, and he felt a touch on his upper back.

"I'll go, Baba," said Yusuf, softly.

Ahmad reached for his son's hand. "No, yabni, I will. It is time. I must fix things with my oldest friend."

Emad helped Ahmad roll the guffa out of the house. He knew he had to wait, just until his father returned to protect the house.

"Watch over your mother," said Ahmad, looking back into the house sadly. He prayed he would return before the next bombing.

"With my life, Baba," said Emad. "Don't worry. I won't leave until you're home safely."

"I know," whispered Ahmad. He rested against the guffa for a moment. And then it hit him, the distant whiff of jas-mine. Like it knew what he was thinking, like it had always been there, awaiting his return. The ground cracked and rustled beneath his feet. And his cheeks were wet with tears. "What a terrible man I am."

"Baba," said Emad, softly, "what is it?"

"How could I be so wrong about so many things? How could I put politics above my brother?" He nodded at Dawood's house.

"Baba," said Emad, "none of this is your fault." Ahmad shook his head.

"I said some unforgivable things."

"Take it from someone who has rarely agreed with your choices," said Emad. "I know you always made them with the best intentions. Our rulers divided us, and maybe you believed them a little too easily, but all our problems began with them."

Ahmad bowed his head, hiding his face from his son, who put a hand on his father's shoulder until he stopped sobbing.

"Baba," said Emad. "You can still fix this."

Ahmad breathed deeply and faced Emad, putting both his palms on his son's cheeks.

"Emad, you will be a wonderful father one day."

Emad smiled. "Go with God's grace, Baba, and bring it back to us again."

Ahmad pulled Emad to his chest briefly, then turned the guffa on its side and rolled it to the river.

When he stepped out of the boat on the other side of the water, he felt around for a long reed and lashed it through a gap in the lip of the guffa, then stepped into Dawood's garden. He found himself thigh-high in thick undergrowth and jasmine. He forced his feet forward and felt sand and dust trickle off every surface, down into his sandals.

"I *can* fix this," he said, clenching his teeth. He knew what he would do. He would tell his old friend how he had missed him, how he didn't care who was right and who was wrong, how it was none of his business with whom Dawood chose to do business. All he cared about was having his friend at his side.

And he smiled as tears fell anew, splattering to the earth as he leaped toward the house. And Ahmad laughed as he felt a chill run up the back of his arms, knowing he was moments away from embracing his oldest friend. And in that instant, at last, he felt hopeful again.

"Dawood!" he called out. He leaped into the air with every step, trying to make each pace a little longer. He was halfway down the garden when he saw a figure emerge from Dawood's home. He waved a hand above his head.

"Dawood!" he called. And the figure waved back.

He bounded through the shrubs, which thinned as he neared the house. He looked at Dawood, then back to his own feet as he hurried to the house, placing one foot on a flat rock, another on a tuft of grass. He ran up the steps to the doorway where the figure stood, and raised his head to look Dawood in the face again, at last.

"Naima?" he gasped.

She was barely recognizable. Where once green eyes had set her whole face alight, two sockets of gray were barely visible beneath drooping eyelids and pallid cheeks.

"Abu Emad." She smiled weakly. "After all this time. How are you?"

"I am well, and you?" he asked, looking over her shoulder. "Please tell Dawood to come out. I must beg his forgiveness, please."

"I'm sorry, Abu Emad—"

"No," said Ahmad. "He must meet with me. I have to explain."

Naima shook her head sadly.

"Please," said Ahmad, desperately. "I said terrible things, I know—"

"Ahmad," she said, "Dawood died five months ago."

A wave of grief seemed to swell up from the river, across the undergrowth, to swallow Ahmad. A moan escaped his lips and he thumped the house wall with his fist. He wanted to run to the roof, up into the sky, anywhere. But there was nowhere to escape to, not any more, not in this Baghdad.

"You aren't safe here, Umm Farah," he said. "I came here to warn you all. Please grab whatever you can—clothes and food—and come quickly to the river. I will meet you there and explain everything."

And as he stood, waiting beside the Tigris, with another uninvited ghost hammering at his skull, he could find no reason why he deserved better than this. Maybe he would just sit here, forever, with these demons and this dirt, and this haunting, merciless river, and learn to live silently with his thundering regret.

When Naima showed up with Farah and Amira, and when the four edged to the river, Ahmad's thoughts were interrupted by a sudden visceral fear. The hairs on his neck prickled, but he couldn't tell why. He wanted to run, to hurry Dawood's family along. He offered a hand to help Amira and Farah into the guffa, then turned to Naima.

"How did it happen?"

"It was sudden. Something in his brain."

"From God we come and to Him we return." Ahmad sighed and held the boat while Naima climbed in. There it was again, an eerie static in the air.

"He always knew you never meant it," said Naima.

"What?"

"He heard that speech you made in the Maydan and tried to come after you, but you disappeared."

Ahmad bit his lip. He clambered into the guffa and untied it from the shore. "Why didn't he come to my home?"

"For the same reason it took you so long to come here, I suspect," said Naima. "He was busy, proud, and worried about what you might say."

"I should have come sooner," said Ahmad. "I wish I could have had his forgiveness before he died."

"You did, Ahmad," said Naima. "From the moment you last left our home he forgave you."

Ahmad grimaced as he pushed the boat off the shore.

Something was not right.

"Baba!" he heard Yusuf call from across the river. It was a voice that skipped across the still surface, stroking into submission every worry, every ghost, every demon.

"Yusuf," he said, "go back inside, we're coming."

"Baba!" he screamed, pointing to the sky.

How had he missed it? It was obvious now, the distant hum, the prickly air. An overhead plane.

"Go!" he shouted.

"Come!" Yusuf called back at him. "Hurry!"

"Get inside!" yelled Ahmad. "Now!" But he watched as Yusuf lowered himself into the river, beckoning them with his hands.

The sound grew louder, closer, like the plane had been waiting for Ahmad to spot it. They would be fine. Of all the homes on the river, the pilot wouldn't choose this one. Not again. As he paddled hurriedly, he thought of Dawood, of this one last thing he could do for his friend. They made it halfway across the river when they heard the drone grow louder, so unmistakably low that there was no doubt in anyone's mind. Yusuf shuffled back up to shore, crouched beside the trunk of a large tree, and rolled a large stone slab on its end to shield himself.

"Duck low," whispered Ahmad, his hand cutting through the air as he gestured. They all crouched in the guffa and Ahmad brought the paddle to rest across the lip of the boat. Ahmad watched the three women shut their eyes. Every few seconds he was sure that the plane could get no louder, but it always did. Just as he allowed himself to breathe again, a storm of bullets whizzed around him, some landing on shore, some popping the stillness of the water's surface. Ahmad held his breath and prayed. How many times had these words protected him? Maybe he had used up all he deserved of God's goodwill. He prayed that if God didn't think him worthy of saving that he would at least save the wife and daughters of the friend he had lost. They heard the bullets hiss as they flew inches from their ducked ears. The paddle shook violently as it took a hit, rattling above their heads. Ahmad grabbed it before it flipped off the edge of the guffa. Farah screamed, and Naima put a hand over her daughter's mouth. Farah nodded forcefully, tears streaming down her face and Naima removed her hand. Amira's hands were over her ears and she hadn't opened her eyes once.

The rattle of bullets had stopped, and Ahmad heard the hum of the plane's engine grow distant.

"He's probably taking a turn before coming back," said Ahmad. "Get into the water, head to shore, and when you hear the plane, stay under the surface as much as possible."

"Why are they doing this?" said Farah, through sobs. "We didn't do anything."

"I know you didn't," said Ahmad, "but you have to move now."

Farah nodded.

Naima rolled over the lip of the boat and into the river, helping Farah and Amira in behind her, each of them sucking in air as the icy waters hit them. They kicked as fast as they ever had, while Ahmad paddled the boat in the other direction. Yusuf had returned to the riverbank, whispering instructions and encouragement. The plane reappeared and rained down a hell of shots. Ahmad had almost returned to Dawood's shore when he saw Yusuf dive into the water and pull Amira by the hand. He could see splashes where the shots broke the water. A bullet whizzed past his ear, and Ahmad crouched below the boat's lip. He forced a hole through the side of the boat's mud-lined basin with the handle of the oar, and watched as his son pulled out the three women.

Ahmad popped his head out of the boat. "Run!" he screamed.

Yusuf grabbed Amira's hand, gesturing to Naima and Farah, leading them through the garden to the blessed safety of a roof.

Ahmad put his weight on the lip of the guffa and jumped into the river, flipping the boat over with him. He dove beneath the water and resurfaced in the thin capsule of air trapped beneath the upturned craft. He knew it offered no real protection, but at least it muffled the terror of the noise. He swam as deep below the surface as he could, propelling himself with his feet, as he pushed the boat above him with outstretched arms. And, faced with the prospect of imminent death, he realized how desperately he wished for company. He was a fool to ruin his friendship, a fool to believe powerful men who had promised the world but not lifted a finger themselves. And, God, how truly stupid he had been to waste years wallowing in his isolation. He thought of his three children and he thought of Dabriya, who had always cherished his tortured soul above her own.

He resurfaced under the upturned guffa to catch his breath, paused for a second to listen to the tinkling of the river against the boat, then dove again. And he kicked with the power of his thousand regrets. He was invincible. *Take your best shot, you sons of dogs.* The bullets rained down, like daggers slicing into the river. And he knew not a single one would touch him. He would not let them kill him, not tonight, not after everything he had survived, and not in his river. He resurfaced for another breath and found the world suddenly silent. He peeked through the hole he had bored in the guffa's skin and saw the familiar shore of home, just meters away. He dove one last time, and cut through the water, jumping out at the riverbank, and running through his garden, leaving a path of Tigris dripping behind him.

I am home.

54

WHEN HE HAD FIRST SEEN Amira on the other shore, Yusuf thought maybe he was dying because every moment he had spent with her began playing out before his eyes. The hundreds of times they had sat together on the shore, the games they had played with sheep's knee counters as children, the evenings they had spent in the garden with both families, the moments they had shared alone. The kiss he left on her forehead.

When he was studying in Baghdad he had told himself that, although he would never love anyone like he loved Amira, he did not love her any more. But when he saw her jump out of the guffa, struggling against the river water, when he ran in to meet her, and when he clasped her hand, he knew that no matter how many years passed, he would never stop loving her. And when she walked ashore behind him, when he turned to face her, he saw her abaya cling to a body that was taller, rounder, softer. He turned away, but he could not forget what he had seen or the quiver it sent through him.

So when he knew with absolute certainty that his feelings were unchanged, and when he saw his chance to confess it to Amira, after two years of longing and denial, he knew he had to take it.

"Someone will see!" said Amira, removing her hand from his.

Emad met the family at the door and was leading them toward the living room fire. He offered blankets to each of them. Amira's palm was throbbing where Yusuf had held it. She beckoned him down the corridor away from her mother and sister. Nobody looked at her, but she could have sworn Emad's ears were pricking, the way they always did.

"I don't care," said Yusuf, following her. "Who's going to worry about me touching your hand if we all die tomorrow?"

"We aren't dying, Yusuf." She turned to face him, checking they were far enough into the passageway of Yusuf's house that her sister and mother couldn't see them.

"Haven't you seen what is happening out there?" he asked.

"No! I was in the river to have a swim," snapped Amira.

"Amira—" whispered Yusuf.

"Yusuf, please don't." She shivered.

He was going to say it; surely, he always was. "I've loved you forever, Amira." She looked at the floor, and her face turned all the shades of a pomegranate. "Since before I even knew what love was. And as I'm a dead man, you have to let me say it."

"I'm so fond of you, Yusuf," she said softly, "but you've seen what's happening, you've seen what our city has become. They would never accept us. Our whole life would be a battle." She sighed. "Aren't you tired of war, Yusuf?"

"All I know is that there was no point in it—in any of it— if I can't be with you."

Amira shut her eyes.

"I know you remember, Amira," said Yusuf, quietly. "Us, and your sister, Baghdad, the river and Jemima the duck, and all our silences together. Don't tell me they weren't the best of days."

She bowed her head, pulling the blanket tighter around her shoulders. A tear bubbled from behind her lashes and dropped to the floor.

"I remember it all," she said softly. "And I must be an adult now; I have responsibilities that maybe you can't understand. But I promise, Yusuf, I will always remember my best friend."

She held out her left hand, still throbbing from Yusuf's touch, and lifted it to his cheek. Where once his face had been rounded and shiny, it was prickly and square. She had always wondered how it would feel under her skin. And though he was stronger, more towering than he ever had been, Amira had never seen him look more vulnerable. She brushed his lip with her thumb as she withdrew her hand, knowing this would be her only chance to know how that felt too. And before leaving him to return to her family, she spoke: "I will always remember him," she said, "always love him."

55

THE NEXT MORNING, THE HOUSEHOLD held its breath in quiet anticipation. How would the English strike next? Mikhael had returned to change Dabriya's dressing and, with Naima and her daughters, the house was filled to capacity. But when Ahmad saw a cluster of five Arab men across the river in Dawood's garden he knew he did not have the English to thank for it. Mikhael's prediction was coming true.

He shuffled his guests from across the river, each dressed in one of Dabriya's outfits, into the cellar, and sent Yusuf down with modest trays of watermelon and rice. Dabriya kept the women company with questions about Amira's time at school, and the newest lace that Naima had seen in Baghdad's markets, to distract herself from the ache at the top of her left arm. Resist as they might, they always returned to the war, the English, and the bombardment.

After scurrying food into the cellar, Yusuf stood vigil at the downstairs window where Emad had put the horse. Emad entered and jumped when he saw his brother.

"It's the best room to watch their house from," Yusuf said. "But your horse won't stand up."

"I know," said Emad. "I don't know if it's fear or hunger, but he's not taking me anywhere right now."

"So you'll stay?"

"I was thinking I'd walk, or ask Mikhael if he has a donkey I can borrow."

"It'll probably be terrified too—but you'll never make it on foot."

"I know," said Emad, but Yusuf had turned away. "But I need to get back. I have to do something other than sit here waiting for the next attack."

"Shit," said Yusuf. There was a flickering orange glow across the river and he wished to God he could blame this on the English bastards. But he knew what it meant. He raced out of the room without a word to Emad, through the back gate, down to the edge of river and held both hands in the air. "Stop!" he yelled. "What are yo—"

A hand covered his mouth before he could finish. Yusuf kicked and wriggled as he was dragged backwards behind a date palm but couldn't free himself.

"Quiet! It's me!" hissed Emad. "Don't make a sound." Yusuf nodded and Emad released him.

"What was that for?" he growled.

"Are you crazy? Do you want them to know we're hiding the entire family in our cellar?"

Yusuf bit his lip. "But we can't just let them burn Ammu Dawood's home down."

"We can and we will. Let them think they have succeeded. The house is all stone anyway. It'll survive."

"Not all their things, though."

"Look around, Yusuf," said Emad, softly. "If we get through the next few days with our lives we will be lucky. Forget possessions." Yusuf pressed his lips together to stop them trembling. Emad shook his head gently. "Come, you know I didn't mean that," he said, putting an arm around Yusuf's shoulders and leading him back into the house. "Of course we'll live. But material things aren't important. The only thing that matters is that we all survive—together. Yes?"

Yusuf nodded, too afraid to open his mouth in case he sobbed. He was too old to be sobbing, especially in front of

Emad. They heard rustling on the opposite shore, and Emad pulled Yusuf to the ground in a flash.

"Someone there?" a gruff voice called, from across the river. Emad put a finger to his lips and Yusuf nodded.

"No need to hide," the man called. "We're on your side!" Yusuf and Emad began crawling away, keeping as low as they could.

"We can hear you!" laughed a second man.

"Just walk away, we won't do anything!" the first voice shouted.

"Unless you're a traitor Jew, too?"

Yusuf felt the blood rise in his face.

But Emad was on his feet. He raised his fist and screamed, "*You* are the filthy traitor, and you have ruined our country as much as any English dog." He pulled Yusuf to his feet and they ran, away from the laughter that echoed from across the river.

When Yusuf and Emad reached the house, they found Amira, Farah, and Naima standing by the back door, weeping for a world they could never recover. Burned were their memories before the days of brutality, burned were their summers of splashing in the river and baking bread, and burned was the memory of Dawood and their home. All of it burned, forever.

Yusuf looked at the ground as he passed them. "I'm so sorry. I wish I could save it for you." He reached for Amira's hand as he passed her and, for a moment, their fingertips touched. Yusuf shuddered. It was magical and terrible all at once. He wished he could say that she was his secret, but she was the kind of girl whose sadness sent a shiver across the entire land, for surely it was sinful for anyone in Baghdad to be happy while its most wonderful daughter wept. Amira shook herself, and wiped her face awkwardly on her arm.

Naima was buried in Dabriya's chest, and Farah was hugging herself, sobbing and trembling.

Dabriya stroked Naima's head. "I am so very sorry, Naima. You will stay with us for as long as you wish. You are my sister, and our families will always be cousins." Naima nodded between sobs while Dabriya patted her back. "I know it is no comfort today, but we will never again let this happen between our communities. Never."

Emad had lost track of time. He made his way into the courtyard with the rest of the families. It was deep into the night, but he couldn't say if one hour or six remained until dawn. He'd had no chance to breathe, or to plan his return to Abu Khaled. He poked his head around the door to the makeshift stable. Jafar's horse was standing, eating. He let Emad pet him. This was his chance. He'd go upstairs, get his kitbag and some supplies, and head out before dawn broke. The English always bombed during daylight so he'd have to get far enough away before sunrise. And he felt the thrill return, pushing away the blockage he'd felt in his chest since he'd come home. But there was one last thing he needed to do.

He cornered Amira as she made her way toward a courtyard passageway. "I heard what you said to Yusuf," he said.

"This isn't the time," said Amira, turning away from him.

"It's my last chance."

"What?" she asked.

"Amira, you can't let them win."

"What do you mean?"

"All the things we lost, all the things we will lose, don't let them be for nothing. We must come out of this better than we were before or we'll always be living in our own shadows."

"I hope for that world, Emad, but I'm not foolish." It was true. She wished she could have told Yusuf that she had never stopped thinking of him in the two years since she had seen him, that she had missed him even more when her father died, when she could no longer afford to study at the Laura Kadoorie School, when all she had for company was her mother and sister. She wished she had crossed the river that day during her first spring holiday, instead of leaving in anger. She wished he would stroke her hair again, wished he would kiss it. But Baghdad was unrecognizable, split by a British rift, and she could not imagine a city that would ever accept her love for Yusuf.

"Hope is all I ask for, Amira," said Emad, "so that when Baghdad emerges from this war, alive, glorious, unified, when we and the city are older and wiser, you may marry my brother."

"In that world, Emad, one hundred times, I would."

Emad smiled and patted her arm. He heard something whiz through the air, followed by two more, and dropped to the floor, pulling Amira with him. And then nothing for a moment. Three trails of gas cans hissed over the house, one clanking to the ground five meters away from Emad and Amira. Emad pulled Amira up and pushed her into the passageway.

"Into the cellar, now," said Ahmad, and the party of nine hurried toward the entrance. Yusuf put an arm around Luma and pressed her head into his chest.

"Try not to breathe," said Mikhael. "There's something in the smoke."

The smoke was thick. It had followed them into the house, new tears mixing with old.

"It stings!" screamed Farah, scratching at her eyes. "What's happening?"

Scores of canisters flew over the house and the family stumbled about, trying to see beyond the needles stabbing their eyes.

Ahmad grabbed a pile of rags from the table in the kitchen and held one to Luma's face. "Keep that there," he said. "Go downstairs!" He pushed Luma into the cellar; she was followed by Amira, Yusuf, and Mikhael. The women joined them. Last, Emad and Ahmad stepped in, pulling the door tightly shut behind them.

Yusuf joined Ahmad in blocking the gaps in the door with rags.

Dabriya picked Luma up with her right arm and took her to a corner. Farah put an arm against the wall and dry retched, wheezing in between each gag.

"What's happening?" said Luma, holding her neck. "I can't breathe!" she screamed. "I can't see!"

56

"Gas," said Mikhael, in a low voice. "I don't know if it's poisonous, but this is bad."

"We're safe now, surely?" asked Ahmad. He was huddled in a corner with his sons and Mikhael.

"For now," replied Mikhael. "I think we've seen the last of the bombings, but don't feel too relieved. It's one thing when they torture you with bombings, day and night, leaving delayed explosions so that you're scared to go outside even when the bombing stops. But this gassing, it—it means they're planning to storm the homes."

"Why?" said Yusuf. "How do you know?"

"They want to find anyone they deem to be in defiance of the state," said Emad. "In Kafr al-Diyala they bombed for two days, poisoned their water with a cow's carcass, then gassed and stormed the place, looking for weapons. I've heard rumors of other villages in the south getting the same treatment. But never as far north as this. Sometimes they drop notes from planes, telling villages to surrender their weapons, but what sane person would do such a thing when they know they will be attacked?"

"Aren't we considered to be defying the state?" asked Yusuf.

"No," said Ahmad. "We're people, in our home, minding our own business, looking after our families and neighbors."

"Is that it, then?" asked Emad, to himself as much as to Mikhael. The gas wasn't coming from planes, which meant

English forces were here, in his village. And he knew then that he would not make it to Abu Khaled. He didn't even know if Abu Khaled was still alive. There was no way out.

"What are you saying?" said Ahmad, looking from Emad to Mikhael. "That we've lost?"

"Once your enemy drops their weapons on you from above, there's not much of a war to be fought." Mikhael sighed. "We should prepare ourselves."

Emad put a hand on his father's arm. "Let's just focus on getting through the next hours," he said.

Ahmad put his head into his hands. He imagined the hundreds of villages, just like his, quashed into obedience under the weight of bombs, until all that was left were families blown to pieces in their homes by the strange, foreign machines.

"Baba," said Emad, softly.

Ahmad looked up. "You, my children, you deserve so much more." He put a hand on Emad's cheek. "But I deserve this. Didn't I learn anything from the English?" He shook his head. "How foolish I was to believe that justice would prevail. How foolish I was to believe that they would give us a fair fight, that anything was possible. Nothing is possible when they have airplanes and bombs, and all we have is blood. All we ever have to give is our blood."

Emad put a hand on his father's back. "If not today, then tomorrow, Baba. As long as they're in our country, ruling over us, we will resist them."

Ahmad nodded, with a smile, but he didn't believe it. Never again could he believe it. Baghdad would be shackled by men who wanted the riches in her deserts. As long as there was power in Baghdad, they would never be free.

Emad stood up straight and walked toward the corner of the cellar.

"Ahmad," said Mikhael, "do you still have weapons in this house?"

"Upstairs." Ahmad wiped his face on his shoulder.

"We're not going to sit here defenseless being bombed to death," said Yusuf. "Who doesn't have a weapon? Even Mama knows her way around a rifle."

"Where do you keep them?" asked Mikhael.

"In the trunk in my bedroom. What—should we arm ourselves?" asked Ahmad. He did not want to fight again, to kill again. . . .

Emad thought back to the rifle on his bed, the dagger beside it. Did his father even know about them?

"No, no," said Mikhael, "you misunderstand me. If they find your weapons, even if they're stored and locked away . . ."

"What?" hissed Ahmad.

"They'll take you outside and execute you," said Emad. He could not return to his rebels. He would probably never know what became of Abu Khaled. But Emad knew now what he had to do.

57

"Ahmad," whispered Dabriya, from across the cellar.

"What?" said Ahmad, standing. "Is it your arm?"

"Where's Emad?" she said, her eyes shining.

"He was just here," said Amira, looking around.

"He's gone," screamed Dabriya. "No, no, no!"

Ahmad flung open the cellar door and took the stairs two at a time.

"Wait!" shouted Yusuf, running after him.

"Get back here, both of you!" shouted Dabriya. Luma began to tremble and Dabriya pulled her close. "We're safe, Luma," she said. She hesitated for a minute, then put Luma beside Amira. "Stay here," she said. "Please!" And then she ran after them.

Emad ignored the calls from his family and ran into the house. He grabbed the weapons off his bed and headed up to his parents' room, flinging open the cupboard. He found the key to the trunk on the back of the cupboard door and opened it in a matter of seconds. It was not the first time he'd checked the weapons. He grabbed the three rifles and the saber, cradling them in his arms as he turned to run downstairs. The horizon was warming in a blaze of pink, casting light on Dawood's shore. Emad saw figures moving about the charred house, which was still glowing from one room. He ducked low, peeking over the bottom edge of the window. Uniforms.

"Shit," he whispered. *English* uniforms. He ran out into the garden.

"Emad!" shouted Ahmad, grabbing at him as he ran through the garden. Emad twisted away.

"Get back inside," he hissed at his father. He nodded toward Dawood's house. "I saw them—the English."

"Hide inside," Emad said, to Dabriya and Yusuf. "I'll hide these before they can find them." Really, all he wanted to do was blast those bombing, gassing, lying bastards into oblivion. But he had seen how many of them there were. He knew what this was. He knew what would happen to Yusuf and Ahmad if he resisted, or if there was even a sniff of weapons on their hands. Bullet to the head.

"All three of you, inside, now!" hissed Dabriya. She tugged on Yusuf's shoulder as he ran after his brother. "Please!" she begged.

"Where can you hide them?" said Ahmad. "They'll search everywhere."

Emad had thought of that. The guffa. He'd tie it to a long rope and let it float midway in the river. They'd never think to look there, surely. He found himself at the edge of the garden, but the boat was still upturned and offshore from his father's escape across the river. Holding the rifles in one bent arm, he stepped into the water. He crouched slightly, grabbing the guffa from underneath and flipping it in a labored, slow movement. Yusuf and Ahmad had arrived on the shore and stopped suddenly when a voice whispered, "Hey!"

Emad jumped. He looked up and saw a soldier at Dawood's shore; Emad ducked behind the rim of the guffa, aiming his armful of weapons toward the soldier.

"No, no, it's me, remember?" said the soldier in Arabic. "From Baghdad."

A look of comprehension dawned on Yusuf's face.

"It's Carwyn, Emad. The one who helped us get away!" said Yusuf, from the shore. "What do you want?"

342

"Emad, put the guns down and come back," said Ahmad, urgently.

"Throw away your guns!" said Carwyn, nodding. "And hide."

Emad nodded and emptied the rifles into the guffa. A crack rippled across the river.

"No!" screamed Ahmad, crumpling to the ground.

Emad turned, confused. "Yusuf?" he said. His brother was inching toward him, his hands outstretched. "Yusuf, what did they do to you?"

"Get back!" barked Lieutenant Morgan from the shore opposite, pointing a gun at the family.

Dabriya emerged at the edge of the bank, and shouted, "You bastards, I'll kill you!" raising her fist at them. "I'll break your spineless necks!"

Emad looked at Yusuf. "My brother," gasped Emad, looking into Yusuf's face as tears spilled down his cheeks. "My baby brother, what did they—"

But Yusuf was shaking his head, sobbing. "Not me," he said.

Emad's mind went into shock, registering senses slowly and deliberately. And in the midst of the vague, otherworldly feelings, he thought it strange how warm the river felt. It was never this warm. He looked down and saw the murky brown waters rippled with deep pink swirls. And the hole—through his clothes, through his skin, through his chest. It was so close to his face. A slow ache began to eat at his chest, like when he ate too much or ran too fast. Like he might just swallow, and the ache and the hole and the bullet would be undone.

"My brother," said Yusuf. "Can you walk to us?"

Emad instructed his legs to move but they wouldn't listen. "I can't," he said. He looked at his family, and he knew from their faces, he knew it was time. "Please stop crying," he said.

Ahmad let out a sob. "I'm sorry, son," he said. "I've failed you. Over and over."

Emad felt his legs wobble and tried to lean on the guffa.

Ahmad stood up and made toward the river but a shot rang out in the air.

"You move again and I'll shoot another one of you," shouted Lieutenant Morgan, from the other side.

"Let them be, Sir," said Carwyn, to the lieutenant, trying to stay calm. He had to stay calm. "They might save him."

"Be quiet, Evans. This is an education for you as much as them. Do you think that family will dare to defy us now that they've seen the cost of rebellion?"

Carwyn paused. He'd never really recall what he thought of in those few seconds, whether it was his father's patience, or his stepfather's cruelty; whether it was Llwyn-ypia or Baghdad; whether he thought of Yusuf or of himself. It didn't matter much what he thought of. Not really. Not in the end.

Carwyn launched himself at Lieutenant Morgan. He punched his nose with his right hand and his stomach with the left. He got in two clean shots before the lieutenant responded, beating Carwyn back. Carwyn felt his arms restrained from behind.

"Bloody idiot, Carwyn," said Llyr, into his ear. "Do you want to be court-martialed, imprisoned, or shot at dawn?"

Carwyn laughed. "Why not? Better than this life, anyway."

The lieutenant wiped his face on his sleeve. He kept his rifle pointed at the opposite shore.

"Oh, no, no, no, Carwyn, bach," said the lieutenant. "Not getting off that easily. You're mine. For life." Lieutenant Morgan looked at Llyr. "Tie him to that tree for now. Better get used to field punishment, Evans. This is your life now."

Emad looked at his father, his brother, his mother, all three sobbing.

"Don't stop fighting them," he said, his hand slipping on the boat. He let go and dropped into the river, his neck tickled by the laps of slapping water. And the Tigris sobbed into his ears as it mourned the splashes of laughter and careless small ankles and coracles bursting with watermelons that it would never again witness in all of history.

Ahmad fell to the ground and watched his son's body float away, unable to do anything to bring him back. He heard soldiers enter his house behind him, and he didn't care. What more could they do? They would find nothing to tie him to the weapons: Emad had made sure of that. He felt Dabriya's arms close around his head as they sobbed together.

"Oh, Emad," sighed Dabriya, "how sorry I am. How wrong I was." Her head was throbbing, and she thought she must do something, say something. *Surely this is not how it feels to lose your son. Surely this is not how it feels when it was all because of you?*

"My brother, my brother," sobbed Yusuf, his breath catching between the echoes of sobbing. "How can I live when my brother is dead?"

And the family wept together on that shore as Emad's body was carried into the river, and his soul floated to a more just world. They heard the crashes and clatters of items broken by soldiers in their house, and if it were possible for them to feel greater pain, they would have. This was what they had meant, then, by the disturbance of daily life. Ahmad kneeled by the river, gasping for air. And he looked that son of a bitch in the face as he called across the ripples, a wake that echoed the greatness of his son, speaking slowly, deliberately, loudly:

> *How will I live with all that I gave*
> *For your promise we would go unchained?*
> *And now my son is just a price to be paid*
> *For being such savages, untamed.*

And he bent low over the river and beat his head with his fists. And he wailed, in the way that men believe only women do. "Oh, God, it should have been me," he cried.

There are only two ways that the name of God can escape a man's lips: as a whisper or as a cry. And today Ahmad and Carwyn both had good reason to call out to God.

Carwyn crumpled to the ground, his arms twisting behind him as Llyr pulled him up. He felt rope tighten around his wrists, and tree bark scratch his neck as his arms were placed around the tree behind him. And he sobbed. He sobbed for his father, who surely would shoot him if he could see the kind of man his son had become. He sobbed for his mother and brother, trapped with his cruel stepfather. He sobbed for Emad, whom he could not save. But, to be truly honest, mostly he sobbed for himself: for the things his hands had done, for the men he had killed and, God, for the lifetime he would spend trapped in the service of men he hated. He sobbed in the knowledge that this was all he would ever be.

Ahmad roared until his lungs dried, his voice ringing over the river, through every minaret of the land, and into every cavernous building that the British had stolen. And he begged for mercy from the ache in his chest that hurt more than blood, and for forgiveness for all of his many sins.

How glorious it sounds to demand justice at any cost, but sometimes a man must be allowed to go home and fill his cracks with remorse, with grief, and with absolution, wherever he may find it. At least, by God, do not begrudge him the chance to try.

The rebellion came too late for the man who had given everything he would ever be to dishonest men who promised a land that was not theirs to bestow. No. He would live silently as his demons clawed at what remained of his soul, forever enduring the knowledge that it had all been for nothing.

Sacrifice demands blood. It is always the young, the brilliant, the most idealistic—the ones who most deserve the world they strive for—who die in the sacrifice. And the rest are doomed to live in a circle of remorse. Never quite fulfilling their potential, never quite transcending, never quite able to achieve their liberty with the absence of these souls. Always, always on the cusp of what could have been. Oh, God, what we could have been.

History would tell of a war, fought honorably and equally by the civilized against the savage. The savage would be lucky if he were mentioned at all. It would skip the parts where the air forces shot at unarmed women and children, of entire villages burned in displays of power, or—worse still—it wouldn't skip it, and nobody would notice anyway.

Emad felt the water lapping in his ears and heard footsteps on his right.

"Wait! Wait!" screamed Luma, running alongside the river. "Where are you going?"

Emad tried to turn his head but his mouth filled with water and he coughed.

"Little Luma," he said, spluttering, a thick warmth filling his throat. "I'm going to see God now. Be good, my favorite girl." And if he could have opened his eyes, he would have seen Luma, standing at a date palm, waving at him. Too injured by a lifetime of war to understand what it meant to say goodbye.

Emad mustered his last burst of energy and lifted his right hand out of the water to face the shore opposite his home, and gestured two defiant fingers at the thieving, spineless murderers. He coughed for a moment, saw a flash of bird wings and palm leaves and tanzanite river, and left a world that was too cruel to deserve one more moment from a wise and honest soul.

Postscript

"You have to understand the Arab mind," Capt. Todd Brown, a company commander with the Fourth Infantry Division, said as he stood outside the gates of Abu Hishma. "The only thing they understand is force—force, pride and saving face."

—Dexter Filkins, "A REGION INFLAMED: STRATEGY; Tough New Tactics by U.S. Tighten Grip on Iraq Towns," *New York Times*, December 7, 2003

Author's Note

THE WATERMELON BOYS PRIMARILY SERVES to tell the story of a community that is often overlooked in chronicles of the First World War. It informs the state of Iraq as it is today, as well as the current diplomatic relationships of Arab nations with the United Kingdom.

Although *The Watermelon Boys* is a work of fiction, it is based on real events, from social aspects, such as food, dress, games and the two schools mentioned, political events, such as the duplicity of British officials, the bombing and burning of villages as collective punishment, shooting at fleeing women and children, to historical details. The description of aerial bombardment on page 311, for example, was written by a Royal Air Force (RAF) pilot. The uniting of Shia and Sunni against the British is also accurate, as are a number of smaller details of the rebellion and the war. Sheikh Andy, the exposed hand in the trench at Anzac Cove, was real, though his name is not. The civil commissioner's impression of having "the wolf by the ears" during the Arab revolt was taken from a telegram of his, now archived at the British Library, and the text that shocks Yusuf at the YMCA is from David Fraser's *The Short Cut to India*, originally published in 1909; in the same scene, the rhyme he hears in the YMCA was sung by soldiers in Mesopotamia and published in the Newton and Earlestown Guardian. Also quoted are the Proclamation of Baghdad, which Dawood comes across with Yusuf and Amira,

351

and the Anglo-French Declaration, read out by Civil Commissioner Wilson to the delegation at the serai in Samarra.

Nevertheless, a certain amount of creative license has been taken, specifically relating to time and dates and the movement of individual characters. Dawood, for example, would have been detained one year earlier. The basis for his abduction by Ottoman forces comes from the detention of Violette Shamash's father, as recounted in her memoir *Memories of Eden*. The anti-Jewish persecution that Dawood's family faces at the end of the book is based on an oral retelling by my grandfather, whose family hid Jewish neighbors in their house during a wave of persecution in 1920, an event that goes unmentioned in official historical sources, but which affected a number of families.

The inspiration for the character names Ahmad, Yusuf, and Dabriya are my paternal grandfather Yusuf, his father Ahmad, and his mother Badriya, but this story in no way reflects or rewrites theirs. Carwyn is inspired by a combination of a Welsh soldier's diary that my father found discarded, my own maternal grandfather, who served in the war (though was English, and never set foot on Mesopotamian soil), and, of course, my own childhood in Wales.

On a personal level, *The Watermelon Boys* reclaims the dominant narrative of the British Occupation of Iraq, which was largely written by the colonizer.

SELECTED HOOPOE TITLES

Sarab
by Raja Alem, translated by Leri Price

No Knives in the Kitchens of This City
by Khaled Khalifa, translated by Leri Price

The Unexpected Love Objects of Dunya Noor
by Rana Haddad

*

hoopoe is an imprint for engaged, open-minded readers hungry for outstanding fiction that challenges headlines, re-imagines histories, and celebrates original storytelling. Through elegant paperback and digital editions, **hoopoe** champions bold, contemporary writers from across the Middle East alongside some of the finest, groundbreaking authors of earlier generations.

At hoopoefiction.com, curious and adventurous readers from around the world will find new writing, interviews, and criticism from our authors, translators, and editors.